**Praise for *New York Times* bestselling author
Vicki Lewis Thompson**

"Count on Vicki Lewis Thompson for a sharp, sassy, sexy read."

—*New York Times* bestselling author
Jayne Ann Krentz

**Praise for *New York Times* bestselling author
Rhonda Nelson**

"Well plotted and wickedly sexy, this one's got it all—including a completely scrumptious hero. A keeper."

—*RT Book Reviews* on *The Ranger*

Praise for Kira Sinclair

"A satisfying balance of light kink, heart and conflict."

—*RT Book Reviews* on *Captivate Me*

Praise for Andrea Laurence

"Laurence's latest is a well-written hit from start to finish!"

—*RT Book Reviews*

Praise for Debbie Herbert

"With all the paranormal genre books out, Debbie Herbert takes one that is not as popular as vampires and werewolves are and makes it her own."

—*Fresh Fiction* on *Siren's Secret*

Because *New York Times* bestselling author **Vicki Lewis Thompson** lives in the Arizona desert, she hardly ever has a white Christmas, but she always celebrates an enchanted one. Elves and flying reindeer make perfect sense to someone who's lucky enough to write love stories all day. Vicki's writing career has gifted her with several awards and a magickal connection to readers around the world. With the life she has, how can she doubt the existence of Santa Claus? Connect with her at vickilewisthompson.com, facebook.com/vickilewisthompson and twitter.com/vickilthompson.

Vicki Lewis Thompson
Rhonda Nelson
Kira Sinclair
Andrea Laurence

JINGLE SPELLS

Debbie Herbert

SIREN'S TREASURE

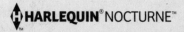

ISBN-13: 978-0-373-60979-6

Jingle Spells and Siren's Treasure

Copyright © 2014 by Harlequin Books S.A.

The publisher acknowledges the copyright holders of the individual works as follows:

Naughty or Nice?
Copyright © 2014 by Vicki Lewis Thompson

She's a Mean One
Copyright © 2014 by Rhonda Nelson

His First Noelle
Copyright © 2014 by Kira Bazzel

Silver Belle
Copyright © 2014 by Andrea Laurence

Siren's Treasure
Copyright © 2014 by Debbie Herbert

Recycling programs for this product may not exist in your area.

Printed in U.S.A.

www.Harlequin.com

CONTENTS

NAUGHTY OR NICE?   7
Vicki Lewis Thompson

SHE'S A MEAN ONE   87
Rhonda Nelson

HIS FIRST NOELLE   171
Kira Sinclair

SILVER BELLE   249
Andrea Laurence

SIREN'S TREASURE   317
Debbie Herbert

NAUGHTY OR NICE?
Vicki Lewis Thompson

To the Sisterhood of the Traveling Pens—
Andrea Laurence, Rhonda Nelson and
Kira Sinclair. We've been to Dublin, London
and Paris together, but I'm still partial to
Gingerbread, Colorado!

Chapter 1

INTERNAL MEMO: Christmas countdown, minus 20 days
FROM: Cole Evergreen, CEO, Evergreen Industries
TO: All staff
Thanks to centuries of intel monitoring, the North Pole is widely accepted as the home of Santa Claus. That misinformation has allowed the Winter Clan, under the guise of Evergreen Industries, to operate undetected in Gingerbread, Colorado, as we employ our magick in the service of Christmas.

But magick has its limits, and computer technology is more efficient for information storage and retrieval. Because of the sensitive nature of our database, specifically the "Naughty or Nice" list, our security system is constantly being updated.

However, I regret to inform you that despite our best efforts, we've been hacked. While I investigate the source of this breach, be advised that your current usernames and passwords are invalid. When you create new ones, use the strongest possible codes. Failure to maintain secrecy is not an option.

The memo, as Cole had expected it would, brought his three siblings to his office on the fifteenth floor of the Evergreen Industries building within minutes. It was the tallest structure in Gingerbread, and also the deepest. Besides having fifteen floors aboveground to house Evergreen's Christmas ornament business, it had five subterranean floors dedicated to the secret task of Christmas toy production.

Ethan, Cole's next oldest brother, arrived first with a typically optimistic attitude. There was a reason Ethan had been put in charge of Christmas cheer. Ethan was the sort of wizard who, if he found a box of horse manure under the Christmas tree, would look around for the pony.

"It was a fluke." Ethan commandeered one of the two leather swivel chairs in front of Cole's desk. "I'll bet it was a total accident and they won't be back."

"They knew exactly what they were doing. They left me a message." A message that had made his pulse leap when he realized who had been prowling through his database.

"What message?" Belle, the youngest Evergreen, walked in carrying a mug of coffee, because she had to be different. Everyone else in the company drank cocoa.

It must have been an emergency ration she'd brewed herself, because it clearly hadn't come from Cup of Cheer, her favorite coffee shop in Gingerbread. She claimed that the stress of her job as head of human (and elf) resources, especially her work with Santa, Mrs. Claus and the elves, required large quantities of caffeine, specifically double-shot peppermint lattes.

Belle grabbed the other swivel chair and glanced at her brothers, eyebrows raised. "What's the deal?"

"Whoever hacked into the database left a message," Ethan said. "Can you trace where it came from, Cole?"

"Don't have to. I know who it is." A memory of Taryn from ten years before, her slender body naked and willing beneath his, scorched a path through his brain. He ignored it.

"That's great!" Ethan looked even more encouraged. "So you can nip this in the bud, right?"

Oh, yeah. Even after ten years, Cole remembered nipping, and tasting, and... He banished that memory, too, and propped his hips on the edge of the desk. "Sort of. I'm planning to—"

"I see we're all here." Dash, two years younger than Ethan, sauntered into the office, followed closely by Noelle Frost, who'd recently come back to Gingerbread to head up company security while her father recovered from a health scare.

Dash and Noelle were exes, which made her return problematic and their working relationship tricky. Dash was in charge of elf transportation and Christmas magick, including Santa's sleigh and flying reindeer. Noelle had to make sure the sleigh was properly cloaked to avoid detection by military radar and civilian air traffic controllers. Dash and Noelle had no choice but to cooperate on sleigh duty, whether they wanted to or not.

Cole couldn't worry about their issues today. But he noted with some amusement that a love seat positioned against the wall was the only place left to sit. Noelle eventually took it and Dash chose to stand, leaning against the opposite wall, arms crossed.

Ethan turned his chair to face them. "Cole just said he knows who hacked into the database. That means we're halfway to solving the problem."

"Not exactly." Cole looked at each of his siblings in turn. Their generation was in charge now. Their parents, following a time-honored Winter Clan tradition, had turned over the operation to their adult children. The senior Evergreens were currently in Ethiopia helping create clean water sources for impoverished villages.

No one would doubt those four were Evergreens. They'd all inherited the fabled green eyes from their wizard father, and the brothers had their mother's dark, slightly wavy hair and their father's height. Belle was blonde, like their father, and petite, like their mother.

Anyone entering the room would identify Noelle, with the straight, dark hair and the clear blue eyes of the Summer Clan, as the unrelated participant. But despite not being an Evergreen, Noelle was an important component of any strategy meeting. Her experience as a CIA operative would be very helpful.

She sat forward, her gaze intent, her tablet at the ready. "So, who's the hacker, Cole?"

"An old girlfriend from college."

Dash grinned. "Ah. So it's Taryn."

"How do you know that?" Noelle was in full interrogation mode.

"Because Cole only has one old girlfriend from college who counts," Dash said. "That makes this easy, bro. Pay her a visit and find a way to offer her some of Noelle's memory-erasing cocoa. Problem solved."

"Negative on that, Dash." Noelle's tone was brisk, even a little defensive. "Our current formula isn't sophisticated enough to create selective memory loss, which is what's needed here."

Cole turned his attention to her. He hated to put her on the spot, but he needed to know his options, just in case. "How fast can you beef up the formula?"

"It shouldn't take long." She said it quickly, as if forestalling any discussion. "I'll have a more versatile batch soon."

"How soon?"

A hint of panic flashed in her expression, and was quickly replaced by a confident smile. "Not today, but very soon. I'm just saying that if you give Taryn the cocoa we have on hand, she'd forget hacking into Evergreen, but if she's trying to get a rise out of you, she'll hack in again."

"Get a rise out of him?" Dash chuckled. "Under the circumstances, you might want to rephrase that."

Noelle rolled her eyes. "Oh, grow up, Dash."

"Not planning on it, Noelle."

Their banter hit too close to home. Cole ducked his head and studied the wreath pattern in the thick green carpeting as he fought the heat climbing his cheeks. This was hell. His brothers and sister knew too much about Taryn, which was his own damned fault.

He'd left MIT in the middle of his senior year, right before Christmas break. All his fanciful dreams about Taryn had died that Christmas when he'd realized he wasn't ever going back to college. He'd abandoned her without an explanation. But what could he have said? That he was a wizard going home to help his family straighten out the "Naughty or Nice" list and make sure Christmas went off without a hitch?

Lying hadn't been an option. He'd learned early in life that his brain didn't work that way, and everything that came out of his mouth was true, no matter how embarrassing or unwise the statement. Over the years, he'd trained himself to hold his tongue in delicate situations.

But leaving Taryn so abruptly when she'd done nothing to deserve that treatment had gnawed at him. On New Year's Eve at the clan's ancestral lodge on Mistletoe Mountain, he'd mainlined champagne and spilled his guts to his brothers. Belle had found out the whole story eventually, as sisters usually do. He could feel them all waiting with bated breath for his next move.

He prayed it wasn't a stupid one. "I need to find out how she got in." He lifted his head and glanced around the room. Everyone seemed to be with him so far. "It's not surprising that she could do it. I've done some digging, and discovered she freelances as a computer security tester. Multinational corporations hire her to see if she can hack into their systems. If she can hack in, she takes care of whatever weakness she finds."

"And she's a certified genius like Cole," Ethan added helpfully. "I remember you telling us she's very smart."

Cole let out a breath. "Actually, she's smarter than I am."

"Whoa!" Dash pushed away from the wall. "They must be ice-skating in hell. Did you just admit someone was smarter than you, big brother?"

"Yep." He'd fallen in love with her brain first and her body second. He still remembered that first glance into her eyes, framed with enormous tortoiseshell glasses. The intelligence shining in those hazel depths had stolen his breath. "That's why she was able to hack in. But if I hire her to strengthen the system, then we shouldn't have to—"

"Wait a minute." Noelle glanced up from her tablet, where she'd been typing notes. "Hire her? How can you do that without creating an even bigger security risk?"

"My question, exactly." Belle polished off her coffee and set the mug on Cole's desk.

"I've given it a lot of thought," Cole said. That was the understatement of the year. He'd discovered Taryn's handiwork at midnight and hadn't slept since. "The good people of Gingerbread are convinced we operate a Christmas ornament factory in this building, and that's all Taryn has to know. I'll code her access card so she's restricted to the IT floor."

"What about the categories in the database?" Ethan asked. "Won't she wonder about those?"

Cole shrugged. "I'll say it's appropriate to our Christmas-themed business, which it is. It's not her job to worry about what's in the database, anyway. I'm hiring her to correct a flaw in our system. I'm sure she's worked with other corporations that maintain a high level of secrecy about their products."

"Yes, if you're talking about military applications and technical innovation." Noelle frowned. "But why be secretive about Christmas ornaments? It makes no sense."

"Doesn't matter." Ethan glanced up at Cole. "I see where you're going with this. The fact is we *do* make Christmas ornaments that are prized the world over. If Taryn suspects that's a cover for something else, so what? It's not her job to speculate. If she made a habit of prying into things that don't concern her, she'd be out of business in no time."

Belle swiveled her chair back and forth. "Even so, I don't like it. I can keep the elves off the IT floor while she's here, but what if she runs into Santa? He could show up anywhere, including the lobby, and he's something of a loose cannon these days."

Noelle groaned. "Tell me about it. Did you know he's started jogging?"

"Jogging? Well, *sugarplums*!" Belle let her head fall back against the chair. "No, I didn't know that." Raising her head, she looked at Noelle. "Merry told me he's acting weird and is on some crazy diet, but I hadn't heard about the jogging. I don't know how that's supposed to help matters."

"What in St. Nicholas's name are you talking about?" Cole stared at them. "And why don't I know about it?"

"I hated to bother you unless it was urgent," Belle said. "We all hoped it would blow over."

"It still could." Ethan sounded determinedly cheerful. "Okay, so Kris forgot their twenty-fifth wedding anniversary and Merry's pissed, but I'm sure after all these years together she'll come around."

"Don't count on it," Dash said. "Women are complicated creatures."

"We have to be," Noelle said, "in order to compensate for men being so—"

"That's enough of that." Cole scrubbed a hand over his face. "We need to focus. So Kris and Merry are having marital problems. What's that got to do with the diet and jogging?"

"My best guess?" Noelle glanced up from her tablet. "He's intimidated because Merry's signed up for skiing lessons with Guido, who is, admittedly, a fine specimen of Italian manhood. I think Kris is trying to recapture his inner stud so he can compete with Guido."

"His *inner stud*." Cole sighed. "But he's still on track to drive the sleigh, right?"

"As far as I know," Belle said. "If he trims down, the suit will automatically adjust, but I doubt he'll lose much weight in three weeks."

"Thanks for that hopeful thought, Belle. I want you to send a memo to Kris and Merry about Taryn's visit, though. They should avoid her if possible, but if she happens to meet Kris and notices his resemblance to Santa Claus, he can say he was hired as a mascot."

"A mascot?" Dash laughed. "Oh, he'll just love that description. Not."

"Then he needs to stay out of sight." Lack of sleep was sapping Cole's patience. "I'm leaving in a couple of hours for Seattle. I'm taking the corporate jet. I'll be back tonight with Taryn."

"Too bad you can't apparate and bring her back the magickal way," Dash said. "Speaking as your transportation coordinator, it would be faster and cheaper."

"I realize that, but I'm hoping to engineer this operation without the use of anything magickal, cocoa included. But Noelle, please get that more complex batch up and running, in case I need it for Taryn."

"I'll make it a top priority. But when you say you're

bringing her back, I hope you don't intend to take her to the lodge. There's no way I can keep security tight if you do that."

"No, not the lodge. Too much magick going on there, too many witches and wizards randomly casting spells. Even meals are…well, anyway. The lodge is out. I'll get her a reservation at the Nutcracker Inn. Dash, I'll need a car and driver for her. The less she wanders around on her own, the better."

"I suggest you be that driver," Noelle said.

"I'd rather not."

"Then who?" Noelle met his gaze. "This is our busiest time of year. Everyone's schedule is packed."

"That's for sure," Ethan said. "I'm booking talk show appearances as fast as I can to counteract the effect of Lark DeWynter's new bestseller. *The Christmas Lie* was just reviewed in the *New York Times* and it's playing havoc with Christmas cheer. I can fix that. I always do. But I have no spare time."

"Elf personnel issues tend to peak about now," Belle said. "It's the stress of the season, and with Kris potentially going off the rails, I—"

"I know." Cole hadn't considered how this part of his plan would work, but he could see the trap closing on him.

"I have to agree with Noelle," Dash said. "The driver should be someone with maximum clearance, which means it has to be one of us in this room, and we're all working on last-minute Christmas preparations. You, not so much. You're the logical candidate, big brother."

"Okay." Cole rubbed the back of his neck. "I'll take the driving duties."

"In fact, you probably should shadow her while she's here," Dash continued. "You know, keep close track of her and make sure she sticks to the program, literally."

Cole met his brother's gaze. Mischief danced in those green eyes. "She's a professional, Dash."

"If she's so professional, why did she hack into your database?"

That was an excellent question, one he'd been struggling with. "Maybe for old times' sake, to prove she could. I don't know, but I'll find that out, too. I can assure you, excessive monitoring of her activities won't be necessary."

"Maybe not." Dash winked at him. "But I'll bet it would be fun."

Cole glanced away before Dash could read his reaction. Oh, yeah. Monitoring Taryn would be more fun than he'd had in ten years. But indulging in that kind of fun would land both of them in an untenable position. He wouldn't do that to himself, and he certainly wouldn't do that to her.

Chapter 2

Taryn Harper powered down her computer, picked up her glass of red wine, and walked over to the floor-to-ceiling windows to admire the view. Her high-rise luxury apartment faced the Seattle harbor, and this time of year it sparkled with festive lights. Christmas was a big deal for a girl born on December 25, and she always made sure to party hearty.

This year she had more elaborate plans than usual, because she was about to hit the big three-oh. She was the highest wage earner among her family and friends, so she'd decided to foot the bill for a Christmas Day cruise through the San Juan Islands. Yes, it might be a tad chilly on deck, but the music and dancing and food inside would keep people warm and happy.

And she would be happy, too, damn it. So what if she didn't have a yummy guy to invite as her date on the cruise? So what if all her friends had either a serious boyfriend or a husband, and a few had kids, too? She wasn't in some relationship competition with them, and besides, being unattached allowed her to concentrate on a job that she loved, a job that allowed her to live very well.

But a girl about to turn thirty might logically take stock of her situation and look for loose ends to tie up before launching into her third decade. In Taryn's case, that meant settling the Cole Evergreen question.

She'd never found out why he had dumped her ten years before, and a lack of resolution made forgetting him near impossible. Well, that, and the memory or how perfect they'd been for each other, mentally and sexually. She needed to talk to the guy, and she knew exactly how to get his attention.

Last night she'd hacked into the Evergreen Industries database and left a clear message—*You're vulnerable. Call me. I can fix it.* If he was still the Cole she'd known and loved, she figured he would respond to that. But he hadn't called, and waiting was no fun.

Maybe he hadn't found it yet. Maybe he'd found it and was discussing it with his staff. Maybe he was discussing it with whatever woman was currently in his life. He wasn't married. She'd researched that.

But she was prepared to discover that he was involved with someone. At twenty-two he'd been so beautiful—brilliant green eyes, luxurious dark hair and an amazingly taut body for someone who didn't put much effort into keeping in shape. And he could make love like no one she'd found since. Add to that his intelligence and his adorable tendency to blurt out the truth, no matter what, and he'd been all she'd ever wanted in a man.

There was the rub. She'd compared every guy who'd come along after to Cole. No one else had stood a chance. And that was why she lived alone in this elegant apartment overlooking the harbor, and why she would be dateless for her birthday party.

Draining her glass, she turned away from the view.

Her intercom buzzed before she'd made it to the kitchen to start dinner. Setting down her wineglass, she walked to the front door and pressed the button connected to the lobby's video camera. She wasn't expecting anyone. And then she spotted the man standing in the lobby talking to Tom, the security guard, and nearly had a heart attack. Never in her wildest dreams had she thought Cole would appear in person, and unannounced, at that. She pushed the intercom button. "Hi, Tom."

"Hello, Miss Harper. You have a visitor. Shall I send him up?"

She gulped. "Yes." The elevator was fast. He'd be here in no time. Running into the bathroom, she finger-combed her short curls, but she couldn't change clothes or put on makeup, or—damn it! Her doorbell was already chiming.

Heart pounding, she made herself walk back to the front door, but she was shaking. She fumbled with the lock and finally managed to open it, but her head buzzed from a massive adrenaline rush. "Cole?"

Those emerald green eyes hadn't lost a fraction of their intensity. His gaze swept over her in typical Cole fashion, as if he were taking inventory. "Hello, Taryn. May I come in?"

"Sure." Doing her best to breathe normally, she stepped back from the door.

He strode through it confidently. His long wool coat, black as his hair, carried with it the cool tang of December in Seattle. There was another scent, too. Apparently he still wore his distinctive peppermint aftershave.

In college he'd shaved twice a day, especially if they were spending the night together. Judging from the smoothness of his square jaw, he'd used a razor sometime in the past hour. One whiff of his freshly applied aftershave rocketed her back to long winter nights spent in his bed.

Dear God, her physical reaction to him hadn't changed. He showed up and instantly her body became welcoming, yielding and decidedly moist. How inconvenient, especially because he didn't look particularly happy to see her. No smile, no warmth, only a strong sense of purpose, which she recognized from the old days.

He'd identified a problem and he'd come up with a solution. Once Cole Evergreen saw his way through an issue, he proceeded with single-minded intent. But she couldn't figure out why he had come *here* instead of contacting her by phone or even by email. That didn't seem particularly efficient.

He pulled off his black leather gloves and turned to her. "It's about the database."

"I figured." She noticed he wasn't wearing a wedding ring, confirming her intel about him not being married. The coat underscored the drama that had always lurked beneath the surface of this complicated, beautiful man. As he unbuttoned it, her quick survey confirmed that he hadn't let himself get soft in the middle. "Can I take your coat?" she asked.

"I'm not here to chat, Taryn. Obviously I need your services. Knowing your talent, the job shouldn't take long. Two or three days, at most. Can you leave tonight?"

She stared at him. "I beg your pardon?"

"I want to hire you, exactly as you suggested. You're the only person who's ever hacked into my database, so I want you to fix whatever weaknesses are there. The situation is critical. I'd like you to start tomorrow. Can you do that?"

"No, I can't do that!" She'd expected a response, a conversation, maybe even a request that she correct the problem, but not with this kind of urgency. "Look, Cole, I—" She'd thought bringing up the past would be relatively easy, and maybe it would have been on the phone. But face-to-face, her courage failed her. "Just because I did it, don't get paranoid and think you have a huge security problem. You don't. I was able to get in because I know your design habits, which made it easier for me."

"What prevents you from coming with me tonight?"

"That's none of your business."

"You hacked into my database. That makes it my business."

She wished that his forceful pursuit of a goal didn't turn her on so much. But she remembered he'd been that way in bed, too. Her pleasure had been his goal at all times, and wow, had he delivered on that promise.

He sighed and glanced away. "I'm sorry. I'm going about this all wrong."

Oh. Her heart gave a familiar lurch, as it used to do anytime he revealed the vulnerability beneath his determined exterior. With a flash of insight, she understood the motivation behind his steamrolling behavior. She'd embarrassed him by hacking into a system he'd designed.

Chances were he hadn't kept the situation to himself, either. "Who knows I hacked in?" she asked gently. "Besides you, I mean."

His attention returned to her, his expression resigned. "Everyone at the administration level of the business, which includes both my brothers, my sister and our new head of security. I had to tell them."

No, he didn't *have* to tell them, but she should have guessed that he would. His unflinching honesty and sense of responsibility would have forced him to admit that his database wasn't a hundred percent secure, no matter how painful that admission had been for him to make.

She hadn't thought of that possibility. She'd somehow imagined this would be a little game between the two of them, but instead his whole family was now involved. That was unfortunate.

"I regret pulling such a stupid stunt, then," she said. "I have no defense, really. I was curious about what you were up to, so I poked around until I found your company, and then I couldn't resist trying to crack your code."

For the first time, a spark of humor lit his eyes. "Well, that's typical."

"I know. And I have to say, it was fun figuring out how to unlock the database."

The corner of his mouth curved in something that resembled a smile. "You always did relish the idea of outsmarting me."

"I did. It gave me a challenge." She'd missed their intellectual sparring more than their sex, and that was saying something. "But I'm sorry you're on the hook because of my prank."

"Then get me off the hook, Taryn. Come to Colorado and strengthen my security so even you can't get in."

It was a gold-plated opportunity to have her personal question answered. But if she was still attracted to him, and he was over her, spending a few days working together could be hard on her ego.

He cleared his throat. "You do realize I'll compensate you for your time, right?"

"Well, yeah. You said in the beginning you wanted to hire me, so that usually involves money." She wished she could figure out what was going on in that excellent brain of his. "Unless you had some other type of compensation in mind?"

Heat flared in his eyes for just a moment. "No."

Interesting. That bit of heat had indicated he wasn't totally immune to her. But he might not be available. "Forgive me if that was inappropriate. You probably have a steady girlfriend. Maybe even a fiancée." She could at least satisfy her curiosity on that score.

"I don't."

"Really?"

"Really."

She waited to see if he'd ask about her love life. He did not. So if she'd cherished a tiny hope that he had something besides business on his mind, she should kill that hope right now. Once she'd thought he was in love with her, but then he'd abandoned her without a word. She'd been hurt and confused, but she hadn't been able to convince herself that his feelings had been bogus.

Perhaps she should finally face the possibility that he'd grown tired of her and hadn't wanted to say so. Honest as he was, he would have blurted the truth if she'd asked him. She wanted to ask now, but she hesitated. Sad to say, he still had the power to hurt her.

He focused his green eyes with laser precision. "Are you in the middle of a project you can't leave for a few days? Is that the stumbling block?"

"As it happens, no. I only take small local jobs in December, so I have time to celebrate Christmas and my birthday." It was the truth, but she didn't mind that it also served as a little dig. Ten years ago she'd invited him home for Christmas and her birthday, and he'd accepted. Then he'd bailed without an explanation.

"Right. Your birthday." His expression once again became difficult to decipher. "I promise you'll be back here long before then. I remember how much you looked forward to Christmas."

"I do."

He glanced at her tree. "But if it's Christmas cheer you're after, you'll find plenty of it in Gingerbread. It's Christmas year-round there, but winter snow adds a lot to the ambiance."

"I saw the pictures online when I was looking up Evergreen Industries. Cute little town." The landscape had reminded her of the long walks in the snow at MIT when she and Cole had been lovers. They'd often debated the merits of some new computer technology, and whenever they'd disagreed on some obscure point, the argument usually had turned into a snowball fight, which led to kissing, which led to racing back to his apartment to have sex.

"I've booked you a room at the Nutcracker Inn."

His comment detoured her trip down memory lane. "You've already booked me a room?"

"It seemed like a good idea. They're extra busy in December. The place is loaded with Old World charm. All the rooms have feather beds, and yours is one of the few with a woodburning fireplace."

"I admit that's tempting."

"There's more. The proprietor, Mrs. Gustafson, bakes apple strudel every morning. She brings a tray to your door with warm strudel, fresh-squeezed orange juice and hot coffee."

"Sounds pretty cozy." Too bad when she pictured staying at the Nutcracker Inn, she automatically put Cole in the picture, too. He wouldn't be there, and she needed to remember that.

"It is cozy. Or so I'm told by anyone who's stayed there."

"You mentioned hot coffee as if that's a selling point. Don't tell me you're a coffee drinker at last."

"Nope."

"Wuss." She used to tease him about that all the time.

He smiled. "Addict." His gaze held hers, and his voice softened. "Whatever happened to those big glasses you used to wear?"

"Got contacts." As she looked into his eyes, she remembered another very important thing. Before they'd been lovers, they'd been good friends. Sex had been an enhancement of that friendship, at least in her mind. But sex had raised the stakes, too. At the time he'd left, they'd been so deeply enmeshed that they couldn't have dialed back the relationship to a friendship level.

After ten years, though, they ought to be able to do that.

She'd like to stay in touch. Not many people communicated on the intellectual level that she and Cole had.

"Okay," she said. "I'll take the job."

His shoulders sagged with relief. "Thank you. That means a lot to me."

"I'm doing it as a friend, though. I'll be insulted if you try to pay me."

"That's not right. You should be paid your going rate. In fact, because I'm hauling you away during the holidays, you should get more than your going rate."

She folded her arms. "Then you're willing to insult me?"

"No! But let me pay you. Please."

"Nope. Either I do it because I'm your friend or I don't do it at all."

He opened his mouth as if to offer another objection. Then he closed it again. "All right. I'll take you any way I can get you."

Her traitorous pulse leaped at that comment, damn it. She'd have to ride herd on her emotions and not allow them to get the best of her. Agreeing to this might have been a mistake, after all.

Chapter 3

Cole had what he'd come for, and now he wondered how in hell he'd survive the next few days in close contact with Taryn without doing something stupid. Like kissing her. She'd been dynamite at twenty. At almost thirty, her sexuality had gone nuclear. The men in Seattle must have been blind. They should have been lined up outside her door.

She was still tall, still slender, but her curves had a lushness that hadn't been there before. How he longed to pull her into his arms and explore those curves. She moved with more grace and assurance than she had when they'd been in college. He knew, just *knew* that she'd be an even better lover now, and she'd been terrific back then.

They had to get out of her apartment and on that plane, where they'd be properly chaperoned. He glanced around her living space. Her computer was turned off and he didn't smell dinner cooking. "How soon can you be ready to leave?"

"What time is the flight?"

"Whenever I tell them."

She blinked. "Oh. You came in your own plane. I didn't realize that. Is it tiny?"

"It's the Evergreen corporate jet, which is a decent size."

"Evergreen has a corporate jet? The Christmas ornament business must be booming."

"We do okay. Can you be packed in about fifteen minutes?"

"Uh, I guess so. But aren't you hungry? It's dinnertime, and I could make us something."

That wasn't going to happen. Even if he didn't have the jet waiting at SeaTac, he wouldn't dare sit through an intimate dinner in this apartment. He'd noticed the wineglass she'd left on an end table. Wine, a little candlelight, the glow from the Christmas tree, and he'd be done for. They'd be stretched out on her pricey rug in no time.

The thought of that scene had a predictable effect. He walked toward the window and pretended to take in the view so she wouldn't notice the state of his crotch. He had a spell for controlling an inconvenient arousal, but it involved muttering an incantation, which would make him sound crazy as a loon.

He was feeling sort of crazy, but he didn't want her to know that. "The galley's stocked and we can eat on the way," he said. "It's getting late. By the time we fly into Denver and make the drive to Gingerbread, it'll be after midnight. We should get going."

"I suppose you're right." She turned and started down a hallway. "Give me ten minutes to throw some things into a suitcase," she said over her shoulder.

He watched her walk away and swallowed a moan of frustration. A pair of old jeans and a faded sweatshirt shouldn't be the sexiest outfit in the world, but on Taryn, it was. Her cap of milk-chocolate curls made her look sassy and down-to-earth.

You could mess around with a woman like Taryn, because she wasn't coifed and tailored. He'd always loved that about her. She could roll in the snow, run home to have sex, and never give a thought to how she looked. In those days, all he'd had to worry about had been her precious glasses.

Once she'd left the room, he called the car service he'd employed and told them to be waiting in front of the apartment building in fifteen minutes. Then he prowled around the living room and recorded impressions of who Taryn was, now. The fireplace mantle was crowded with framed pictures. These would be the family and friends he'd been destined to meet during that Christmas vacation when he'd abandoned her.

Knowing she was surrounded by loving people cheered him. Knowing she hadn't found the right guy gave him an unholy amount of satisfaction. That was wrong of him, and he knew it. He should want her to find Mr. Wonderful, settle down with him and be blissfully happy.

For years he'd assumed that had happened, but after finding her cheeky message on his database, he'd investigated to the full extent of the internet's capabilities. The evidence had been conclusive. Taryn didn't have a man in her life.

Although she didn't realize it, she currently had a wizard in her life. And if that wizard really cared for her, he'd keep his hands to himself and deliver her back to this apartment without ever once giving in to the urges that plagued him whenever they were together. Even if she wanted him to. And he could tell that she did.

After replacing each picture frame exactly as he'd found it, he wandered over to her Christmas tree. And there, nestled in the branches, was an Evergreen Industries ornament. He'd forgotten that he'd given her one right after Thanksgiving ten years ago, when they'd reunited after the long weekend.

He'd chosen it with care out of the hundreds manufactured that year. The round ball was green, but through a trick of the light and a sprinkling of wizard magick, it seemed to glow from within, as if it held sunlight inside. That theme was echoed in a gold filigree border circling the sphere with repeating sun symbols.

Cole loved the green ornaments most of all, because they symbolized the Evergreen family name, which in turn harkened back to the trees that stayed green all winter. The sun represented light, both physical and intellectual. He thought of Taryn as the embodiment of light, and he'd told her so when he'd presented her with the ornament.

"Yes, I still have it."

He turned to find her standing in the living room wearing a tan parka with the hood thrown back, a khaki messenger bag over her shoulder. A small black suitcase sat upright beside her.

"I wouldn't have blamed you if you'd gotten rid of it," he said. He didn't want to talk about their breakup, but he wasn't sure how to avoid talking about it.

"I considered giving the ornament away, but quite honestly, it's the prettiest one I have, and I couldn't part with it. I don't know how your company manages to make something glow like that when there's no solar chip involved. Is the entire covering solar? Is that how it works?"

"Can't tell you. Company secret."

She cocked her head. "Do other ornament companies try to steal those secrets? I wouldn't expect that, because it's so contrary to the spirit of Christmas, but I suppose anything's possible."

"I doubt they could steal that particular secret." The incantation involved was known only to the Winter Clan, and no other wizard would be able to make it work right. In the wizard world, this incantation had the equivalent of a fail-safe component attached to it.

"But maybe they'd try, and that's why you're so intent on shoring up your security system."

"Something like that. Ready?"

She nodded. "Just need to put out the cat."

"The *cat*?"

"Gotcha! There's no cat, and even if there were, I couldn't very well put out a cat on the eighteenth floor, now could I?"

"Guess not." He'd forgotten how much she enjoyed teasing him. It was easy to do, because he didn't expect anyone to say things that weren't true.

"I'd love to have a cat, preferably a black one, but that wouldn't be fair. I travel too much."

"I didn't know you liked cats." Cole thought of the lodge on Mistletoe Mountain, which was chockablock with cats, especially black ones.

"In our life at MIT, it didn't come up. Both of us lived in places that didn't allow pets."

"Guess so." He was impressed with how she referred to that time so casually, as if the memories didn't affect her at all. Maybe they didn't. He might be the only one who had vivid color images of those days rolling through his brain. And right now that video was playing in a continuous loop.

He gestured to the tree. "What about the lights?"

"They're on a timer. The apartment is as maintenance-free as I can make it. I'm gone so much." She reached for the handle of her rolling bag.

He started toward her. "Let me get that."

"Why? It's my suitcase." She released the handle, though, as if sensing he wouldn't take no for an answer.

"But you're my guest." He came up beside her and grasped the handle.

"Your guest?" Her eyebrows lifted. "I thought I was your independent contractor."

"You would have been if you'd allowed me to pay you." Instead of kissing her, which was what he wanted to do, he rolled the suitcase across the thick carpeting to the door.

"But now that you've insisted on doing the job for free, that makes you my guest."

She followed him to the door. "I think you're bossier than you used to be, Cole."

"No, I'm not. I've always been this bossy." Or so he'd been told by his siblings.

"Maybe you're right." Once they were out the door, she locked up and dropped the keys in her messenger bag. "I might not have noticed it because we spent so much time in bed, and I kind of like a man to be bossy in bed."

His sharp intake of breath was pure reflex. He couldn't have stopped himself from doing it if someone had put a gun to his head.

"Whoops. Did I say that out loud?"

He turned to her, his heart racing. "Yes, ma'am, you did." He couldn't tell from her expression if she'd truly slipped up or if the comment had been deliberate, like her line about the cat. She seemed unapologetic as she met his gaze, so he suspected the latter.

She quickly confirmed his suspicions. "I'm trying to figure you out, Cole, and I'm having a very tough time doing it. Sometimes, when you look at me, it's like the old days, as if you're ready to gobble me up. But then you turn all logical and businesslike, and claim that the only thing you care about is shoring up the database. Which is the real you?"

He gave the only answer he could come up with. "Both."

"What the heck does that mean?"

"It's complicated."

"Apparently. And you seem really stressed about it."

"That's because I am." How he hated to admit that.

She took a deep breath. "Okay. Can you explain what the issues are? Because I didn't get that explanation ten years ago, and I'd appreciate hearing it now, before we hop on that plane."

He wondered how he'd ever expected to get involved with her on a business level and keep it from morphing into something more personal. Of course it would. They'd been together less than an hour and it already had.

Facing her, he realized he'd missed a blindingly obvious fact. "That's why you hacked in, isn't it? To get that explanation."

"Yes, it is. So if you'll tell me, then I'll go fix your computer system. All will be well."

If only it were that easy. "Do you trust me?"

"In some things, yes. In other things, no."

"Fair enough. I deserve that. Let me put it this way. Do you trust me to want the best for you?"

Her answer was a long time coming, but at last she nodded. "Of course you want the best for me. You're a nice guy. But the problem with that is you can't always know what's best for me. I'm a far better judge of that than you are."

"I'm sure that's true in general. But in this particular situation I'm confident I know what's best. You and I aren't meant to be together." Even though he knew that with a white-hot certainty, saying it cut like a knife.

She didn't seem to like hearing it, either. "Why not?"

"I can't tell you that. You have to trust me to know what I'm talking about."

"Okay, look, before we walk down the hallway and get on the elevator, I need to know at least this much. Are you involved in criminal activity?"

That made him smile.

"It's not funny! I care about you, but I'm not willing to be an accomplice!"

"You care about me?" The words warmed him more than he could say.

"Of course I do." Her voice softened. "I'll never forget our time together. Which is why, now that I'm about to turn thirty, I wanted closure on that relationship. I hacked in to get your attention and an explanation. You probably wish I hadn't."

"I'm not sorry you hacked in." That popped out before he'd known he was going to say it, but once he had, he knew it to be true. This episode promised to be a challenge, but having a chance to see her again and talk with her was worth any inconvenience. He never tired of looking into her hazel eyes and imagining the wheels turning in that amazing brain.

"I'm glad you're not sorry. Neither am I." Without warning, she stepped forward and pressed her lips to his.

He'd been hanging tough until that moment, but as her velvet mouth made that achingly familiar connection, he came unglued. Her suitcase toppled to the floor when he let go of the handle, but the resulting clatter barely registered because he had Taryn in his arms again. A herd of reindeer could have stampeded through the hallway and he wouldn't have noticed.

With a groan, he pulled her close, enveloping the whole package, including her bulky parka and her messenger bag. She could have been wearing a space suit for all he cared, as long as he had access to her sweet lips. This kiss, this Taryn kiss, had been ten years in the making, and he was desperate for it.

As he reveled in the remembered pleasures of her mouth, his world clicked into focus for the first time in ages. He hadn't realized how blurred his view had been, but holding her made one thing crystal clear. She was the only woman he'd ever loved.

He was still cruising in the land of infinite joy when she grasped the back of his head in both hands.

Holding on tight, she drew back, depriving him of that amazing connection. "Open your eyes."

He obeyed. In his current state of mind, he would have

jumped from the eighteenth floor if she'd commanded him to.

"Tell me the truth, Cole. Are you a crook?"

He had to clear his throat before he could talk. "No."

"Then what's the problem?"

With his arms around her and his mouth inches from hers, he couldn't think straight. She was the only person he'd ever known who could short-circuit his brain. "I can't tell you."

She tightened her grip on his scalp. "Yes, you *can*. You just *won't*. I've thought of every possibility. I know you're not gay, not by the way you kiss me. And you said there's no other woman in your life. Are you dying?"

"No. Well, technically we're all dying, but—"

"Don't give me some existential bull. Are you terminally ill?"

"No. Taryn, don't quiz me, okay? It's getting us nowhere."

"It could get me somewhere, because if I guess the right thing, you won't be able to lie about it. I know that about you."

"You won't guess it."

"That's what you think." The light of battle gleamed in her eyes. "I've solved tougher puzzles than this, buster."

"Then I'm asking you, for both our sakes, to stop trying. Please let it go."

"But that means I have to let *you* go."

"And vice versa."

"And that's what you want?"

"No." His brain continued to fizz with sexual frustration. "Well, yes, for your sake."

"Damn, you're stubborn."

"Says the pot to the kettle."

She looked into his eyes for a moment longer. Then she sighed. "Okay, then, let's head to Colorado and get this over with." She loosened her grip on his head and backed out of his arms.

"Right." He leaned down and picked up the handle of her suitcase. He couldn't remember feeling more lost and alone.

They walked in silence to the elevator. As the doors opened and she stepped inside, she glanced at him. "Nice kiss, by the way."

"Thanks." He was afraid his longing was being reflected in his eyes, but he couldn't summon a poker face right now. "You, too."

She leaned against the brass railing as the elevator started its descent. "So let me get this straight. You want me, and I want you, but we can never be together for reasons you can't tell me, and it's all for my own good. Is that what you're saying?"

"Yes." He stayed on the opposite side of the elevator.

"But, because I hacked into your database, you need me to correct the weaknesses in your system, which means we'll be in the same general area for a few days."

"True. In fact, I'll be the one driving you back and forth from the inn to the office."

"Hmm." Speculation shone in her hazel eyes.

He'd always enjoyed watching her think about technical issues, but now she was thinking about *him,* and he wasn't entirely comfortable with that. "I'm the logical one to do it."

"Makes sense. You hired me, and we already know each other. I also assume you want to know about what I find, so we'll have to work together during the day."

"Some."

"Won't that be…frustrating?"

He couldn't pretend to misunderstand. "Probably."

"Won't you want to kiss me again?"

"Yes."

"And take me to bed?"

He swallowed. "Yes, but—"

"Then why not enjoy each other before we go our separate ways?"

His heart hammered. Earlier today he'd been very clear in his mind about why that was a bad idea. But he wasn't the one who'd suggested it, which made all the difference. "You'd be okay with that?"

She smiled. "I'll take you any way I can get you."

Chapter 4

Taryn loved having the last word, and handing Cole's earlier comment back to him had been a triumphant moment. The elevator opened immediately after she delivered that line, which worked out well, because they were no longer alone, and wouldn't be for some time. He'd have hours to contemplate her suggestion with absolutely no way of acting on it.

At the end of that time, he should be a testosterone-driven, heat-seeking missile. That was the Cole Evergreen she wanted in her feather bed at the Nutcracker Inn tonight. And tonight would be only the beginning of her two-pronged attack.

Now that she knew he wanted her, she wasn't about to let him get away, at least not easily. He might refuse to tell her what the barriers were between them, but she was heading into his territory, and the answer was there. She just knew it.

By day, she'd take every opportunity to snoop around. By night, she'd drive Cole insane in bed. If she hadn't made him hers by the time she left Colorado, then maybe it was an impossible task. But she wasn't giving up without a fight.

The Evergreen corporate jet proved to be a luxurious way to travel. Increasingly, she had trouble believing that Christmas ornaments, beautiful though they might be, were financing this kind of perk. If nothing illegal was going on, and she trusted Cole's answer on that, then what explained the company's success?

If she found the answer to that, she might discover the big secret that Cole wouldn't reveal—the one that kept them from living happily ever after. She hoped it wasn't a dangerous secret, the kind that a person had to be killed for once they knew it. That was highly unlikely. Cole would never put her in danger. She knew that as surely as she knew he loved her.

She'd figured that out two seconds into their kiss. As a college student she might have confused love with lust. She wouldn't make that mistake now. He lusted after her, all right, but the passion of his kiss included a large measure of tenderness. Then she'd made him look at her, just to be absolutely sure.

He was in love and always had been. Ditto for her. If she'd ever doubted it, that doubt was gone. For some reason, he hadn't been able to figure out a way around the issue that divided them, whatever it was. She brought a fresh perspective, and—if she allowed herself to be honest—a tiny bit more analytical ability than Cole had.

Once she understood what she was dealing with, she'd find a way to make everything work out. They deserved each other, and they'd already missed out on ten years of happiness because she hadn't been proactive. She didn't intend to let them miss out on any more.

Throughout the first half of the flight, Cole kept glancing at her, as if still wrestling with the ethics of her suggestion. They couldn't talk about it, of course, because the flight attendant never strayed far. She served the meal and refilled their wine glasses. Then she cleared the main course and brought out dessert.

Taryn made small talk about changes in the tech industry since they'd been in school together. Cole participated in the discussion, but his mind wasn't on it. She could always tell those things. He was thinking about whether he was capable of a fling.

Poor man. He wasn't the kind who had sex with a woman for the hell of it. Even in college, they hadn't taken that step until they'd established a solid friendship. The thought of a short-lived affair would stick in his craw.

She didn't intend for it to be the least bit short. If all went according to plan, this affair would last for the rest of their lives. But she couldn't tell him that and tip her hand. She had to mislead him, which was heartbreakingly easy to do.

After she'd accomplished her goal, she would never lie to him again. She'd been touched by his willingness tonight to believe what she told him, even when it had been something as illogical as putting out the cat eighteen stories up. His trusting nature would serve her well in the days ahead, but in the long run, a man like Cole should never be lied to. That was taking unfair advantage of an endearing trait.

Toward the end of the meal, he smothered a yawn.

She glanced over at him. "You're tired, aren't you?"

"A little."

"Then take a nap."

His dark eyebrows rose. "Now who's the bossy one?"

"Just don't think you have to entertain me. If you're sleepy, recline your seat and rest up." She fought the urge not to smile. Little did he know she had ulterior motives for wanting him well-rested when they arrived in Gingerbread.

"Nah, I'm fine."

"If you say so. But I'm going to read for a while." She dug in her messenger bag and pulled out her tablet. Moments later, she glanced up from the screen. He was out. For all she knew, he'd been up all night worrying about her invasion of his database.

She couldn't help feeling remorseful about what she'd put him through, but apparently it had been for a worthy cause. He'd been pining for her as much as she'd been pining for him. She returned to the screen, but it wasn't nearly as interesting as the man beside her. Turning off the tablet, she leaned her head against her seatback and watched him sleep.

She used to do that all the time in college. Maybe his habits had changed, but at that time he'd required eight to ten hours a night, while she could get by on five. When she'd wake up in his bed and he'd still be dead to the world, she'd lie there and study his features—the high cheekbones, the elegant nose, the square jaw.

Sometimes she'd sketch that face. Tucking her tablet back in her bag, she took out the small sketchbook she carried with her, along with her favorite pencil. Although she'd never taken an art class and had no desire to study the subject, she sketched because it relaxed her.

After Cole had left MIT so abruptly, she'd ripped up every sketch she'd made of him. Then she'd regretted destroying them, because they'd captured him in a way photographs never had. Now she could create some more.

She became so lost in her work that she was surprised when the pilot announced they were landing. The flight attendant sat down and buckled up, which put her out of earshot.

Cole blinked and lifted his head. Then he glanced at the sketchbook in her lap. His gaze met hers. "You're still drawing?"

"Yep."

"You used to have a whole bunch like that. Well, I looked younger in them. In this version I notice a few extra lines here and there."

"Gives you character."

"Sure, it does." He chuckled. "Whatever happened to the other ones?"

"I tore them up."

He flinched. "Don't blame you." He lowered his voice. "That was a bonehead way to leave, but I had no choice."

"So I gather."

Regret darkened his green eyes. "That idea you had? It won't work."

She wasn't about to let him wiggle out of her trap. "I was twenty when I ripped up those sketches. I'm not that same girl. I've toughened up."

He smiled. "Maybe I haven't."

"Well, I can't speak for you. But personally, I think it would be a crime to waste the opportunity." She tapped the eraser end of her pencil against her lower lip, hoping to draw his attention there.

It worked. He watched as she caressed her lip with the eraser. "I'm worried…" He stopped to clear his throat. "I'm worried about fallout."

"Are you?" She nibbled on the eraser. "We never had that problem before. Everything stayed where it was supposed to."

He launched into such a violent coughing fit that the flight attendant called back to ask if he needed water. "I'm fine," he said in a strangled voice. "No worries."

"Here." Taryn took out the complimentary bottle of water she'd been offered during the limo ride to the airport and thrust it into his hand. "Drink."

He nodded and gulped some water. Then he sank back against his seat. "You need to warn me before you say something like that."

"That would take all the fun out of it."

He handed her the bottle with a grin. "Honest to God, Taryn. There's no one quite like you."

"I am somewhat of a special snowflake."

His eyes probed hers. "Can you promise me you won't melt?"

"Absolutely."

His voice dropped even lower. "Because you tempt me more than I can say."

"Back atcha. Oh, and I've been told that someone booked me into a room with a feather bed and a wood-burning fireplace."

"Is that right?" His tone was casual but his expression was not. "How thoughtful."

"So what happens after we land?"

"I left my car at the airport, so I'll drive us to Ginger-bread and…drop you off at the inn."

She didn't think it would go that way. "Will I need to check in?"

"Not tonight. I didn't want to disturb Mrs. Gustafson at this late hour, so I asked her for the front door key and your room key. You'll sign the register in the morning. You're on the second floor. You can go straight to bed."

She lowered her lashes. "That sounds lovely."

"Doesn't it, though?"

"I'll need some help with my bag."

"I bet you will. I suppose you'd like me to bring it up for you?"

She lifted her lashes. "Oh, yes, please. All the way up."

"Good Lord." He sucked in a breath. "What have I gotten myself into?"

"Nothing, yet. But I'm hoping before too long, you'll remedy that."

"*Taryn.*"

"If you keep feeding me these great lines, how can I resist?"

"The bigger question is, how can *I* resist?"

"You can't, and you know it." She smiled at him. "Surrender to the inevitable, Cole Evergreen."

Cole was going to do exactly that. He'd been a sucker for her smart mouth back at MIT, and nothing had changed. She still delighted in taunting him, and he wanted her more with every saucy word that passed her sweet lips. Luckily he found a twenty-four-hour drugstore on the way back to Gingerbread.

Because he had to concentrate on his driving instead of thinking about sex, especially on snowy roads, he resorted to a trick he and Taryn had come up with at MIT. Switching on the car radio, he found a station that played eighties tunes—the same music they'd memorized as kids. Then the two of them belted out the lyrics along with Duran Duran, a-ha and The Police all the way to Gingerbread.

Somewhere on that journey, as they laughed and sang together, he became twenty-two again, complete with reckless thoughts and powerful sex drive. When he'd first heedlessly plunged into a relationship with Taryn, she was the hottest, smartest female he'd ever met.

She was everything he'd wanted, with one tiny exception. She wasn't a witch, let alone a witch from the Winter Clan. He'd glossed over that detail, certain that he'd find a way around her inconvenient status as a non-magickal being. But then, he'd been called away on a family emergency and he'd never gotten the chance to return to college and figure out a way to address the problem.

Someday he might bitterly regret falling in with her plan. But that was someday, and this was now. A now filled with the kind of heart-pounding excitement he hadn't felt in a very long time.

After parking the sleek black sedan in a lot adjacent to the inn, he hauled her suitcase out of the trunk and they hurried, still laughing from their sing-along, to the inn's front porch.

She stood next to him, shivering a little, as he located the keys in his coat pocket. "I feel like a kid out after curfew."

"It's the music. We stepped in a time warp." He opened the front door and gestured for her to go inside.

"Exactly." She spoke in hushed tones. "It's just like that first time we spent the night together. Remember that?"

"I'll never forget it." He breathed in the scent of lemon oil and apple strudel. The main floor was dark except for a small light on the antique desk by the front door. Wall sconces glowed at intervals along the stairway leading to the second floor.

"I was so nervous." Taryn walked on tiptoe to the bottom of the steps. "I was afraid you'd think I was too skinny."

He followed her up the stairs, careful not to let the suitcase bump against the railing. "I was afraid I'd come too fast."

"Which you did." She giggled softly.

"Yeah, but I made up for it later."

"Yes, that's true."

"Saved my rep." That first time, he'd been so incredibly turned on by her he'd lasted about thirty seconds. But at twenty-two, his recovery time had been phenomenal. During the next go-round, he'd given her two orgasms.

"That was my first orgasm with a guy."

"It was? Wish you'd told me. We could have celebrated."

"I was too shy to admit it. I figured you'd think I was a dork. I wanted you to think of me as cool and sophisticated."

"I did."

"Really?"

"You were the coolest girl I'd ever met. You understood string theory." He paused. "Your room's at the end of the hall, on the right."

She headed down the hallway, her footsteps muffled on the patterned carpet runner. "I didn't want to be cool because I was smart. I wanted to be cool because I was sexy."

"You were sexy, too."

"You're just saying that."

"Nope." He followed her down the narrow hallway. Soon. Very soon. "Smart is sexy, at least to me, it is. Besides, you had a killer body."

"*Had?*"

"*Have.*" He thought it was cute she was worried about that, especially when she had nothing to worry about. "Still. Even more so."

"Yeah, right. You're supposed to say stuff like that when you're about to see me naked for the first time in years. I'm nervous just thinking about it."

"You think you're nervous? I figure I'm destined to repeat that first night."

She reached the end of the hallway and turned back to face him. "That's fine with me." She smiled as she looked him up and down. "As long as you repeat every bit of that first night."

His cock jerked in response to that seductive smile, and his heart hammered at the prospect of being inside that room alone with Taryn and a big feather bed. "I will, but I'm not twenty-two anymore. The second time might not happen as fast."

"I'm in no rush." She held his gaze. "We have all night."

Lust slammed into him with such force he stood there trembling.

"Do you have the key?"

"Yeah." He dug into his coat pocket and handed it to her. "You'd better open it."

Her eyes widened. "Are you shaking?"

"Yes." He clenched his jaw against the primitive urges rolling through him. "And if you don't open the door and go inside *immediately*, I'm going to take you right here in the hallway. Better move it, Harper, before we give Mrs. Gustafson the scare of her life."

Chapter 5

And *that*, Taryn thought as she quickly opened the door and walked into the dimly lit room, was why she'd never forgotten Cole Evergreen. No other man had ever wanted her so intensely, as if he might spontaneously combust if he couldn't have her in the next ten seconds.

Ten seconds was about all she had to drop her messenger bag to the floor, shrug out of her parka, and glance at the unlit fireplace and the giant four-poster bed that dominated the room. Then the door clicked shut, the lock shot into place, and Cole was there, spinning her around to face him. He made a sound low in his throat, something between a growl and a groan, and then he claimed her mouth.

If he'd kissed her this way in the hall outside her apartment, she might not have been so certain that he loved her. This kiss didn't have a lot to do with love, but it had everything to do with lust. That worked for her, because she was just as desperate for him.

They wrenched at each other's clothing, and didn't succeed in getting much of it off before he shoved her down on the feather bed. She still wore one leg of her jeans, and although his coat was on the floor and his shirt was unbuttoned, that was all he'd accomplished. With a soft oath he unzipped his fly and tore open a condom packet.

He no longer trembled. Instead he moved rapidly and deliberately to sheath himself. She sprawled across the bed, and he grabbed the damp crotch of her panties. With one swift tug, the seams gave way.

The thrilling sound of him ripping her panties from her body nearly made her climax. He'd never been like this. She moaned, needing him, aching for him…and then he was there, surging into her with a powerful thrust that made her gasp.

His mouth hovered inches from hers. "I have you, now, my precious."

She would have laughed, because *Lord of the Rings* quotes had been inside jokes of theirs during college. But his wild assault had left her breathless, and *hot*. She'd never been so turned on.

He seemed to have achieved total immersion, but somehow he rocked his hips forward and settled himself deeper yet. "There. Right *there*."

The jolt of his penis set off her first tremor. "*Cole*."

His laugh was low and rich with satisfaction. "Ready for me, you are."

Hysterics and passion bubbled equally inside of her. "Not Yoda, too!" She gasped. "You're killing me here!"

"I'm distracting myself. Turns out I don't want a repeat of that first night, after all." He eased back slowly, setting off little explosions across her skin. Then he drove in again, filling her as only Cole could.

Her blood pounded through her veins as another spasm hit, and another.

"Ah, Taryn, you're going to come first." And he stroked her again, and again, and again.

Cupping his face, she pulled him down, needing his mouth on hers, because she was about to come, and if she yelled, she'd wake Mrs. Gustafson. He made love to her mouth with his tongue, mimicking the same steady rhythm of his hips. He required an embarrassingly short time to achieve his goal. As he swallowed her soft cries, she arched upward in a powerful climax. If he hadn't had her pinned to the bed, she believed she might have flown.

As her world spun and she quivered in his arms, his rhythm changed. Now his hips rocked with more speed and less care. Lifting his mouth from hers, he began to pant. "Yes…yes…now…Taryn…*now.*" With one final thrust, he drove home, his body shuddering with the aftershocks of his orgasm.

Sliding both hands under his shirt, she caressed his sweaty back. Her hands remembered the texture of his skin and the ripple of his muscles. He liked to be caressed after sex. She'd forgotten that. Each memory that surfaced was a treasure she'd kept locked away, but now she could uncover them all. Cole was back in her arms at last.

Cole's technique had lacked eloquence, but he was pleased with the end result. Brushing a kiss over her full lips, he eased away from her and gave her a Schwarzenegger "*I'll be back.*"

"You'd better be," she murmured. "And next time I want it long and slow."

"Me, too." He headed for the little bathroom with its white antique fixtures. He'd never stayed here, but he'd toured the place. Whenever they had non-magickal folks visit Evergreen Industries, he put them up at the Nutcracker Inn. Everyone raved about it.

Good thing he wouldn't ever stay here, because now the place would be loaded with memories of Taryn. A sharp pain in the vicinity of his heart reminded him of the risk he was taking by falling in with her plan. These few days could turn him into an emotional cripple, but he was willing to pay that price.

Now that he realized no one else would do but Taryn, and Taryn was forbidden to him, he'd stay single forever. That might have sounded harsh to someone else, but to Cole, it made perfect sense. Marrying someone he loved less than Taryn would be unkind to them, and to himself.

Taking off his shirt, he walked back into the room and paused. She'd always been speedy at undressing, but she must have set a world record this time. Gloriously naked, she crouched beside the fireplace with a lit match in her hand.

The small flame illuminated her delicate features, and another pain sliced through his heart. So beautiful. She tossed the match into the fireplace and swore when it fell uselessly through the grate. Opening the box of matches, she struck another one.

Silly as it was, he wanted her to succeed, but he didn't give her method much chance. Focusing on the logs arranged in the fireplace, he timed his muttered incantation to her match-tossing. The logs caught.

"Yes!" She turned to him, her smile bright. "You were standing there thinking I wouldn't get it started, weren't you?"

"Actually, I thought you would." He'd simply increased her odds.

"Let's make love here in front of the fire."

"Why not?" He was touched that she'd ask, and that she'd used the phrase *make love* instead of *have sex*. They used to make love in front of the fire. His duplex had been a real find—a rental with a woodburning fireplace. He'd used magick to keep the blaze going while they were otherwise occupied.

An unmagickal fire required constant tending, which meant having sex by the fire was romantic in theory but inconvenient in practice. She'd never questioned the consistency of their fires. He hoped that was because she'd been too busy enjoying herself.

He wondered if she'd ever tried having hearthside sex with anyone else. If so, she would have discovered it didn't work quite the way it had with him. Selfishly, he liked knowing that their experience would stand out in her mind.

She rose from the hearth with an unselfconsciousness that showed she hadn't really been worried about revealing her body. He couldn't stop looking at her. She was the same, yet different.

The tiny mole positioned over her heart was still there, waiting for his kiss. But her breasts were more voluptuous now, and her hips flared a bit more, emphasizing her narrow waist. His gaze traveled the length of her slender legs. He had fond memories of those legs wrapped around his hips. She knew how to lock him in tight while giving him room to move. He didn't need much, just enough to create the right kind of friction....

She said something, but he was so lost in memories he missed it.

"Earth to Cole."

"Hmm?"

"Your clothes, Evergreen. Lose 'em. I'll fix us a bed by the fire."

He grinned at her and snapped a quick salute. "Aye, aye, cap'n."

"Smart-ass."

"Sweet-ass." How quickly they'd become comfortable with each other again. Ten years had vanished, replaced with the easy relationship he remembered so well. Taryn got him. Well, not completely, because she didn't know about the magick. That should have been a huge omission, but somehow, when they were together, it didn't seem to matter. They made their own magick.

By the time he'd shucked the rest of his clothes and located another condom, she'd spread a quilt on the floor and tossed a couple of pillows there, too. He walked toward her, his cock already standing at attention. "You made your bed. Now lie in it."

"I thought I would." Dropping to her knees, she stretched out on the fluffy quilt with the lithe movements of a cat. Then she glanced up at him. "Come on down."

"I will, but I just realized what's different. You're not squinting."

"No, I'm not. Want to see my bedroom eyes?"

"Absolutely."

"Watch this." She lowered her lids to half mast and her eyes took on a smoky quality.

His balls tightened. "That's good." He swallowed. "Very good." He started to kneel.

"Wait. I'm not done." Her gaze dropped to his feet. Then it traveled slowly up his calves to his knees, and beyond his knees to his thighs, until finally coming to rest on his pride and joy. At that point, she ran her tongue over her lips.

"Now you're done." He sank to his knees before she figured out he was shaking again.

"No, I'm not." She beckoned to him with a crook of her forefinger. "C'mere."

A stronger wizard would have refused the temptation she offered. He'd intended this session to be all about her. Apparently he wasn't as strong as he'd like to think he was. He stretched out on the quilt and allowed her to have her way with him, and it was so good the fire roared in the hearth.

She drew back, startled. "Why did that happen?"

His breathing wasn't very steady, but he gulped in air and managed a quick explanation. "Pine knots. They flare up."

"Oh." She wrapped her fingers around his bad boy and leaned toward him. "Sorry for the interruption."

"No, it's a good thing." He cupped her cheek, stopping her descent. "I was about to get carried away."

She glanced up at him with a seductive smile. "That's the idea."

"Not this time. I have a few plans of my own. Be fair. Take turns."

She hesitated.

"You used to really like some of the things I did."

Her eyes darkened and her breath hitched. "Yeah."

"Let me do those things again." He stroked his thumb over her cheek. "You know you want me to."

"Okay." She flopped back onto the quilt like a ragdoll. "You convinced me, Evergreen. Do me."

"You bet." And he proceeded to. Revisiting all his favorite Taryn places felt like coming home, and she rolled out the welcome mat for him. In seconds she'd abandoned herself to the process of being seduced.

By the time he put on a condom and slid into her, she was on the brink of climax. One firm stroke on his part, and she came. He muffled her cries with the flat of his hand and kept pumping into her.

"Again," he murmured.

She pulled his hand away, gasping. "I can't breathe."

"Then, here." Bracing himself on one arm, he cupped the back of her head and lifted her so she could press her mouth to his shoulder. When she came the second time, she bit him.

He didn't care. In fact, it made him happy to know she'd marked him. Eventually the mark would fade, but until it did, he'd have a physical reminder of loving Taryn.

Slowly she relaxed in his arms and he eased her head back onto the pillow.

She looked up at him, firelight dancing in her eyes as she massaged his back. "Amazing. Stupendous."

"Mmm." His own climax hovered, but he'd managed to keep the urge from overwhelming him. Holding her gaze, he eased in and out. "We've still got it."

She nodded.

"There's no one like you, Taryn."

"I'm a special snowflake," she murmured.

"Uh-huh. Very special."

"So are you, Cole."

And there was that pain, burrowing into his heart. He might carry that ache forever, but that was okay, too. The pain would remind him that, for a little while, he'd had Taryn to love again.

She grasped his hips. "Your turn."

"Not yet." He hated for this moment to end.

"We can do this again tomorrow night."

"I hope so." But he had no guarantee of that. His intuition was excellent, and it told him he'd better treasure this moment and not count on any more.

Her grip tightened. "I think I can come again. Let's do it together."

"All right." He'd mastered that little trick before. The secret was watching her eyes and timing his response to what he saw there.

He bore down and increased the pace. Yes, she was right with him. Her pupils widened. He slowly slipped the leash on his own response and his heart began to pound.

The glow in her eyes was impossible to misunderstand. She loved him. His eyes surely reflected the same emotion, because he loved her, too. And because he did, he had to let her go.

But in this moment, as they surged toward a shared climax, he was hers and she was his. He held nothing back as he drove in one more time. She arched against him and he pulsed within her, each of them silencing their cries and their words of love. Yet their eyes said all their voices could not. And the fire roared.

Chapter 6

Cole left long before anyone in the inn was awake, and Taryn understood why he'd done that. Whatever mysterious element was keeping them in limbo would naturally figure into his reluctance to let anyone here know they were lovers. She wouldn't give him away, either. She'd act strictly professional today at Evergreen Industries.

She hated that he couldn't stay to share the breakfast tray that had arrived outside her door, though. Cole had a sweet tooth—he preferred cocoa to coffee. She'd bet Mrs. Gustafson would have made him cocoa to go with the apple strudel and fresh orange juice.

Placing the tray on a small desk by the side window, she drew back the lacy curtains and peeked outside for the first time. Cole hadn't been kidding about the charm of Gingerbread. Judging from the slice of town she could see, it was a full-size version of the Christmas villages in Seattle shop windows this time of year. The architecture reminded her of Europe, with a fairy-tale element thrown in.

Old-fashioned lampposts each sported a wreath and a red bow. Every shop featured garlands in the window, and larger garlands hung at intervals across the snowy street.

The late-model cars that drove by seemed out of place. Horse-drawn carriages would have fit in better. Then she saw one of those, with laughing people bundled up in blankets in the back, enjoying an open-air ride.

One lone high-rise building was visible above the peaked rooftops covered with snow. Evergreen Industries, no doubt. Beyond that, where the land sloped upward and the pine forest closed in, a snow-capped mountain pierced the blue sky. Although other mountains were visible in the distance, this one was quite distinctive. She decided it must be Mistletoe Mountain, which had been mentioned during her internet search.

Until now, she hadn't thought about what would happen if and when her plan worked and she eliminated whatever problem was keeping her from a happily ever after with Cole. Her business didn't require her to live in a certain place, which meant logically she'd be the one to move.

She let that idea percolate to see how she felt about it. Turned out she was perfectly okay with leaving Seattle if it meant being with Cole. The decision wouldn't even be that difficult. As much as she traveled, she could see her friends and family when she was between jobs.

But her home would be here in Gingerbread with Cole, wherever he lived. Come to think of it, she had no idea what his place was like, which seemed odd to her, considering they'd been naked together so recently. She'd ask him about it when he came to pick her up later that morning.

Remembering that she had to be ready soon, she tucked into her protein-free but delicious breakfast, took a quick shower in the claw-foot tub with its old-fashioned circular shower rod, and dressed in a clean pair of jeans and one of her nicer sweaters. Until she understood the corporate culture at Evergreen, she'd go with something a bit less casual than her usual techie outfit of old jeans, a faded T-shirt and a hoodie.

She was in the lobby chatting with Mrs. Gustafson about things to do in town when Cole walked in. Taryn might have been prejudiced, but the guy knew how to make an entrance. He swept in wearing that long black coat, a green wool scarf, and no hat. His tousled dark hair gave him a rakish look she'd never been able to resist.

"Ah, Cole!" Mrs. Gustafson, plump and graying, clasped her hands together. "Your guest is a delight. She's already in love with our little town. I hope you're planning to give her a tour."

Cole's bemused smile indicated he hadn't planned anything of the sort. "Uh, sure. Why not? But first we have some business to take care of at Evergreen."

Mrs. Gustafson waved a hand at him. "Well, I know *that.* The guests you bring here always have business at Evergreen. But Taryn has taken a real interest in Gingerbread, haven't you, dear?"

"I have." Taryn had to work hard not to laugh at Cole's uneasiness. "And I'd love a tour if we have the time."

Cole's green eyes flashed with amusement. "I'll see to it. Shall we go?"

"I'm ready when you are."

"Have fun, you two!" Mrs. Gustafson called after them as they left the cozy lobby.

"We will!" Taryn called back.

"Chatting up the landlady?" Cole said once they were on the front porch.

"Is that a problem?"

"No, I just…do you really want a tour of Gingerbread?"

"I wouldn't mind." She took a deep breath of the crisp air as they started down the sidewalk toward the parking area. "I like it here."

"Well, good…that's good."

She glanced at him, and his cheeks were ruddy. It could

have been from the cold, but she suspected he was agitated. "You'd prefer I never come back here, right?"

"I can't stop you from doing that if you want to."

"But it makes you nervous."

"Yes."

"You're the one who raved about the Christmas cheer in Gingerbread. And sure enough, the place is charming. I have friends who would love to vacation here."

He sighed. "Then they should."

"I think so, too." She longed to assure him everything would be okay, because she was going to figure this out, but saying anything like that would alert him to her covert plans. For now, he couldn't know what was in her mind and her heart. Soon enough, he would.

Getting into his sleek black sedan reminded her of their songfest the night before, but she doubted he wanted to repeat that. He was tense this morning, and she had a hunch as to why. He was second-guessing his course of action. Pulling out of the inn's parking lot, he drove slowly down the street. As they rolled along, Taryn checked out the shops.

Cup of Cheer bustled with morning activity. "Cute coffee shop," she said. "I suppose you never go there."

"No, but my sister Belle does."

"She still lives in Gingerbread?" Back in college, he'd mentioned two brothers and a sister, but she hadn't thought to ask where they lived now.

"We all work for Evergreen."

"Oh. That's nice." Or it could have been, except that if everyone had to keep the same damned secret, what kind of life did they have here? "Will I be meeting them?"

"We'll see. Depends on everybody's schedule."

"You don't want me getting chummy with your siblings, do you?"

He glanced over at her. "The thing is, they know you were my college girlfriend."

"Aha!" That pleased her immensely. "Then I'd be surprised if they didn't want to get a look at me. I would, if I were in their shoes."

"They probably do want to." He sounded resigned.

"Great. Then I will meet them." She settled back in her seat with a smile.

Cole, however, was not smiling. In fact, his profile resembled an ice sculpture.

She'd have loved to thaw him out. "You know, I realized this morning I have no idea where you live."

His throat moved as he swallowed. "It, um, doesn't really matter, does it?"

"It does to me. I'm not in the habit of taking my clothes off for a man when I have no idea where he lives or what his place looks like. Until this morning, I hadn't thought about that discrepancy. You do live in Gingerbread, I assume?"

"Outside of it, but yes, in a sense. It's the closest town."

"Will you let me see your place?"

"That's not a good idea."

"Why not?"

"Taryn, don't push."

"I hardly think it's pushing to want to see your home. Back at MIT we went back and forth between my apartment and your duplex all the time. I knew what was in your refrigerator and you knew what was in mine. Having no idea about your living space feels weird, Cole."

He sighed. "We're not at MIT. And I can't show you where I live."

She heard the note of finality in his voice and tucked that information away. Wherever he lived, the secret lived, too. If that weren't so, he'd have agreed to take her there.

Although she had a million more questions, she didn't

ask them. He was already on edge. But she was about to enter a place filled with other sources of information.

As they approached the tall building she'd identified from her bedroom window, a portly man in a red jogging suit lumbered past on the snowy sidewalk. He had on a knit cap instead of a fur-trimmed one, but his white beard was very Santa Claus-like.

She'd decided not to make any more comments, but seeing the jogging Santa look-alike was a safe enough topic. "That guy we just passed looks exactly like Santa Claus."

A muscle in Cole's jaw twitched. "I know."

"Is he some local character?"

"Something like that."

"It's kind of cute, don't you think? A middle-aged guy lives in Gingerbread and decides to take on the persona of Santa Claus. It's like the role players in old Western towns like Tombstone."

"Guess so."

"You don't seem to appreciate the charm of it, my friend."

Cole took a deep breath and looked over at her. "I'd forgotten that your brain is always analyzing, always evaluating, sifting and cataloging."

"Of course. So's yours."

He flicked on a turn signal and pulled up to a wrought iron gate with scrollwork incorporating an elaborate E. "I'm going to ask you to focus all that brainpower on the Evergreen database. Pretend you have blinders on and ignore everything else."

"Sounds like censorship, Cole."

He touched a button on the dash and the gates swung open. "That's because it is."

"For the love of God, what's going on in this building?"

Pulling into a parking space labeled with his name, he shut off the engine and turned to her. "I promise you that what goes on in this building is benign. There are no criminals here, no terrorists and no drug dealers. Nothing bad happens here, Taryn. Can you accept that and just do your job?"

"If it's nothing bad, why can't you tell me?"

"I can't tell you because…" He looked into her eyes and his throat moved. When he spoke, his voice was husky with emotion. "I can't tell you, not ever, and I really wish I could, because…"

"Because why?"

"Because I love you."

She gasped, shocked that he'd said it, but thrilled, too. "But I love you, too! And people who love each other share things they wouldn't tell anyone else."

"Not in this case." His gaze searched hers. "I need you to analyze the database. You're the person for the job— maybe the only person who can do what I need done. Will you do that for me?"

"Yes, I will." He hadn't asked her to promise she'd wear those blinders. Maybe he secretly wanted her to find out what was going on.

Whether he wanted her to find out or not, she intended to. This was ridiculous. They belonged together, and she wouldn't let him throw their future away, at least not until she knew why he was so intent on doing it.

The lobby was decorated for Christmas, which she would have expected. A blue spruce that had to be thirty feet tall stood in the center of the two-story vaulted ceiling. Evergreen ornaments hung from every branch. Many of them gave off that mysterious glow she'd noticed in hers.

Display cases filled with ornaments lined the walls, and each ornament was labeled with the year in which it was manufactured. Taryn didn't have much time to look, but she'd swear at least one of them dated back to the 1600s. "Cole, some of those ornaments are really old."

"The company's been around a long time."

"Did it originate in Europe?"

"Yes, it did, in fact. Let's get you signed in." He guided her toward an ornate desk that looked as if it might have been imported from Versailles. Behind it sat a sweet-faced woman who could have been anywhere from fifty to seventy. She wore a red velvet dress, and the nameplate on her desk identified her as Jolie S. Garland.

Taryn wanted to ask her, with a wink, if that was her real name. But something about the woman's calm gaze kept her from doing that. Taryn suspected it was her real name, and she'd be insulted if anyone suggested otherwise. Whether she'd found her perfect job or the job had found her, she'd discovered the right spot for a person with that particular name.

Smiling, she handed Taryn a gold pen. "Sign here, Miss Harper, and I'll give you an access card."

Jolie reached into a drawer and came up with a sparkling gold card with Taryn's name embossed on the front and a magnetic strip on the back. "This will allow you to board the elevator, which will take you to the IT center on the twelfth floor. If you need anything, please come back to the lobby and I'll assist you."

"Thank you, Jolie." Taryn returned the woman's genial smile, but she had the distinct impression she'd been given a ticket to the IT floor and nothing else. Once she and Cole were inside the shiny gold elevator, she confirmed it with him.

"That's all you were hired to do." He unbuttoned his coat and loosened his scarf, but he stood on the opposite side of the elevator.

She found that significant—depressingly so. "I thought you might give me a tour of the building while I'm here." She hadn't really thought that, but it was worth a shot.

A ghost of a smile touched his lips. "Would you settle for a tour of the IT department? It's my favorite floor."

"I'm sure it is. But your parking space said you were the CEO. Who's in charge of IT?"

"I am, for now. I haven't found anybody I'd turn it over to, so I'm doing double-duty."

"That can't be easy. This looks like a huge operation. How can you handle the IT department when you're supposed to be the head honcho of Evergreen?"

"Obviously I'm not doing a very good job of it. You hacked in."

"You shouldn't let that bother you. As I said before, I know your MO. The average hacker wouldn't have nearly such an easy time of it."

"Nevertheless, you exposed my vulnerabilities. I want those protected."

That, too, was a telling statement. She was the woman who knew too much. He'd hired her to barricade him against future invasions, both business-related and emotional, and then leave.

The elevator came to a smooth stop on the twelfth floor. It hadn't stopped once since they'd left the lobby. Other people had to be working in this large building, and yet she'd never know it. Jolie S. Garland was the only employee she'd met. That was spooky.

"I gave the rest of the IT staff the day off to go Christmas shopping," he said. "I wanted you to be able to work undisturbed."

That meant he didn't want her talking to anyone. He'd done his best to isolate her from the rest of the workers at Evergreen. After they'd gotten so close at MIT, he should have realized the more he tried to deny her access to information, the more determined she'd become. If she hadn't believed her investigative plan was for his own good, she'd feel disloyal. But he'd refused to give her all the facts, and without those facts, she couldn't make an informed decision. Maybe, once she knew what the issues were, she'd agree with him that they had no future.

She seriously doubted that, though. Every problem had a solution. He'd been conditioned to believe this particular problem couldn't be solved. That wasn't a failing. Everyone had blind spots. Because she loved him, she would help him to overcome his.

After they left the elevator, he led her past several offices, but the hallway was ghost-town silent.

At the end of the hall, Cole opened a door into a larger office. An L-shaped dark walnut desk held multiple monitors, a top-of-the-line keyboard and a mouse pad in the shape of a round Christmas ornament. A Santa mug sat to the right of the keyboard, but that was it. No framed pictures, no flowering plant, no cluttered in-basket.

She glanced around. "Is this your office?"

"Used to be. I still work down here when I need to."

"Where's your regular office?"

"Fifteenth floor." He seemed reluctant to share that information. "Let me take your coat so you can have a seat and get started."

"Fine." She put her messenger bag on his desk and instantly the work space looked more welcoming. As she started to shrug out of her parka, her hands bumped his. He was helping her take off her coat. She froze. "I can do it."

"Right." He backed away. "Sorry. Habit."

Slipping off her coat, she turned to him. He looked positively miserable. "You can leave," she said. "I know how to turn on a computer." She smiled. "And I already know your password."

He laughed at that, although it wasn't a happy laugh. "So you do. Then maybe I will leave you to work for a while and I'll check on you later. I…uh…didn't realize that giving the IT staff the day off would have an unintended consequence."

"That we're all alone up here?"

His green gaze burned with frustration. "Exactly."

"Then go, before one of your siblings shows up and catches us in a compromising position."

Heat flared in his eyes. "I'll come back and check on you. Is there anything you need?"

"Besides the obvious?"

"Stop."

"Okay. I would love a good cup of coffee sometime in the middle of the morning. Is that possible?"

"I'll make it happen."

"Thanks. See ya." She made a shooing motion with both hands. She hoped his siblings did pop in to see her. She'd figure out a way to make that work to her advantage.

Chapter 7

Cole barreled down the hall and waited impatiently for the elevator. When it came, he was glad it was empty. He used his card and punched the number for the fifteenth floor. How could this have become so complicated? He hadn't factored in the possibility that she'd be as hot for him now—hotter, in fact—as she'd been before. And still in love with him, as he was with her. What a disaster!

Ethan got on the elevator as Cole got off. "Is Taryn in the building?" Ethan asked.

"Yes, and I hope you'll leave her alone to work."

Ethan laughed. "I will, for now. I have to deliver some ornaments to the Denver Chamber of Commerce. Their president read Lark's damned book, and the cheer level of their Christmas display is way down. But if Taryn's here when I get back, I'll stop in and introduce myself."

"Don't hurry home."

"I love you, too, big brother." The elevator door closed, obscuring Ethan's grin.

Cole blew out a breath and started down the hall. Then he remembered Taryn's coffee request and stopped at Belle's office.

She glanced up from her computer. "Is Taryn here?"

"Yes, and she's a coffee drinker."

"Cool! I like her already."

"She asked for a good cup of coffee mid-morning, and I thought, since you always go to Cup of Cheer around ten, you could bring back something for her."

"Uh, sure." Belle's gaze flickered. "I have some errands to run in town, though, and they could take a while."

Something was going on with her and these errands, but this time of year, Cole knew better than to quiz his family when they acted mysterious. For all he knew, she had been planning to buy his present that morning.

"How about this?" Her expression brightened. "She can walk down there with me. I'll buy her coffee, and then I'll send her back here while I run my errands. That way she can see what they have and get the flavor she likes. Will that work?"

"Guess so." Cole wasn't crazy about the thought of Taryn on the loose in Gingerbread. But he also wasn't ready to be alone with her again.

"Then we'll do it that way. I look forward to meeting her."

"You'll watch what you say, though, right?"

Belle's green eyes widened innocently. "You don't want me to tell her how destroyed you were when you had to break up with her ten years ago?"

He scowled.

"Don't worry, big brother. Your secrets are safe with me."

"Thanks." He remembered he wanted to mention seeing Kris. "Our wayward Santa was out jogging when we drove past. Taryn decided he's some guy who's into role-playing."

"That's good. Excellent. And I've been meaning to tell you that Louie, one of our elves, has designed Spit-Up

Baby Susie. He thinks it's more realistic and should go into production ASAP."

"Have him send the prototype to me."

"You're not thinking of approving it, I hope!"

"No, but I'm curious to see how it works." Any distraction, including a vomiting baby doll, would be a good thing.

Taryn needed caffeine. Mrs. Gustafson's brew had worn off, and while Cole's whimsical database with its dopey categories like *"Lots of Toys for Girls and Boys"* was entertaining, Taryn needed hot coffee, and she needed it now.

When a green-eyed blonde wearing a trench coat tapped on the open door, Taryn hoped her visitor was there on a mission of mercy for the caffeine-deprived.

"Taryn, I'm Belle." Smiling, she hooked her purse more securely over her shoulder. "Cole said you drink coffee."

"I do. Is there a pot brewing somewhere in the building?" She wondered if Belle might give her access to a different floor. That would be exciting.

"Not really. Get your coat and I'll walk you down to Cup of Cheer. They make the best java in Gingerbread."

"I'm all over that." Taryn saved her work and powered down the computer. "I was about to send out an SOS."

"Trust me, I understand. Don't bother bringing your bag, though. This is my treat. Just make sure you have your access card."

"It's in my coat pocket." Taryn took her parka from the coat-tree in the corner. "Sounds like the Evergreen coffee room isn't up to your standards."

"There is no coffee room. Just a cocoa room."

"You're joking." Taryn followed her out the door. "Who doesn't have a coffee room?"

"Evergreen Industries." Belle headed briskly down the hall. She could walk fast for a short person.

Taryn had trouble believing the building had no coffee available. "Don't the employees complain?"

"Just me. Everyone else is fine with the cocoa. So I make the trek to Cup of Cheer every morning." She swiped her access card through the reader and the elevator opened.

"Thanks for inviting me along." Taryn noticed Belle's access card was the same as hers and Cole's. The only difference was in the coding and the name embossed on the back. What Taryn wouldn't give to have possession of that card for thirty minutes.

"I'm glad to do it. I'd walk back with you, but I have some things that require my attention in town. I'm sure you'll find your way back okay."

Taryn laughed. "I can't imagine anyone getting lost in Gingerbread. Hiking around Mistletoe Mountain could be a different story, but I don't plan on doing that."

"That's good." They reached the lobby and Belle waved at Jolie S. Garland, who was still on duty. "That's a treacherous mountain. I'd stay away from it if I were you."

"I didn't bring my hiking boots, anyway." Taryn zipped up her parka as they started down the sidewalk that led to the heart of town. "What's your job at Evergreen?"

"I'm in HR."

"So you're in charge of the elves."

Belle's head whipped around. "What?"

"I figured you knew, but maybe not."

"Knew what?"

Taryn thought it was strange that Belle actually seemed upset. Maybe she was the sort of person who didn't like being the last to find out what was going on in the company. "Cole's put all sorts of goofy names in the database. It fits because you're a Christmas ornament manufacturer, but I had to laugh. HR is titled '*Elves*,' and customers are listed under '*Naughty or Nice*.' Like I said, goofy."

"Oh." Belle let out a breath. "I guess I did hear something about that system. Leave it to my geeky brother."

"He's one of a kind, all right."

"He is. Gotta love him."

Taryn thought it wise not to respond to that comment.

Belle switched the topic, which was probably a good idea. "You're from Seattle, right?"

"I am." For the rest of the walk, Taryn answered questions about her native city, one Belle had never visited. Cole's name didn't come up again.

The coffee shop seemed even busier than it had when Taryn and Cole had driven by first thing that morning. She and Belle had to stand in line, and Taryn took that opportunity to scan the extensive coffee menu. Belle kept looking around the shop, almost as if she were expecting to see someone. She seemed agitated.

The line moved slowly, and Belle continued to glance over each time the door opened. "Do you know what you want?" she asked as she continued to survey the crowd.

"I'm getting an extra-large eggnog espresso. That should do the trick."

"It should." She looked away again. "Aha. I just saw someone I need to talk with." She fished in her purse. "Here's my wallet. Order me a large double-shot peppermint latte, and I'll be right back."

"Okay." Taryn's heart began to pound as she realized the opportunity she had. What she was about to do was wrong. When she was caught, and she would be, she'd have no excuse other than the fact that she was doing it for love. But if she didn't overcome her scruples immediately, she'd lose her chance.

Opening Belle's wallet, she took out the golden access card and replaced it with her own. Then she tucked Belle's card in her pocket. Her heart was racing so fast she felt light-headed. Belle hadn't returned by the time she'd ordered and paid for both drinks. She walked over to the window where the orders were coming out, and she waited. The crowd was so dense and Belle was so short that Taryn couldn't see her.

Taryn's coffee came up first, and right after it did, Belle appeared, her cheeks bright red. "All set?"

"I have mine." Taryn handed her the wallet, which by now felt like a ticking time bomb. "Thank you."

"You're welcome. Listen, you don't have to stay. I have to go in the opposite direction, anyway."

"If you're sure." Taryn could hardly wait to get out of there.

"I'm sure. Nice meeting you, and I'll see you later."

"Same here, Belle." With what she hoped was a smile and not a grimace, Taryn left the shop. Instantly she began drinking as fast as possible without scalding her tongue. The caffeine would give her the courage she'd need for what she was about to do.

Once she was out of sight of the coffee shop, she chugged the last of her coffee and tossed the cup in a nearby trash can. Then she picked up the pace, but she couldn't run. That would attract attention.

She slowed down again twenty yards from the Evergreen building. She couldn't pant when she called out a greeting to Jolie S. Garland. She would have trouble acting normal as it was.

Jolie smiled at her. "Did you get your coffee, dear?"

"Sure did. Drank it already. Back to work!" She kept moving. Her hand trembled and she had to swipe Belle's card twice before the elevator doors opened. Luck was with her. It was empty. And lo and behold, all the numbers were lit.

Her finger hovered over the button for fifteen, but pressing it would have been stupid. No doubt she'd run smack into Cole the minute she stepped off the elevator.

Wait a minute. Besides the fifteen floors above ground, there were five below. She hadn't been able to see those with her original access card. And everyone knew secrets were always hidden in the basement. She punched B5.

The car started its slow glide down, and her stomach began to churn. She reminded herself Cole had promised nothing bad was going on in this building, and Cole was incapable of telling a lie. Unlike her. She was both a thief and a liar. She prayed Cole loved her enough to forgive her.

The elevator slid to a stop and the doors rumbled open to reveal…a paint and body shop? She wasn't tremendously familiar with them, but she recognized the giant paint sprayers. Positioned in the middle of the area, its new coat of red gleaming in the overhead lights, was a giant sleigh. The curved metal runners had been taped, as had all the metal fittings. A workbench along one wall was lined with various sized brushes and a large can of paint.

No one was in the shop, so she crept forward and looked at the white label on top of the can. *Sleigh, Gold Pinstriping, Formula 896* had been typed on the adhesive label. Could this be a prop for an advertising campaign?

If so, she couldn't imagine why she wouldn't be allowed to see it. No wiser than before, she returned to the elevator and rode to the next floor. This time, as the doors began to open, she was greeted by quite a racket. Staccato tapping filled the space, as if dozens of tiny hammers were being wielded by…elves.

Stepping through the open doors, she stared at tiny people wearing pointy caps, green tunics and leggings, and shoes that curved up at the toe and were each decorated with a bell. They didn't notice her. Of course they wouldn't. Christmas Eve was drawing near and they were *making toys for girls and boys.*

She blinked, but the scene didn't change. Conveyor belts snaked through the two-story work area carrying finished toys to a wrapping machine. The toys emerged covered with bright paper and festive bows. Then they disappeared into a tunnel.

Slowly she backed into the elevator. This couldn't be real, and yet she was wide awake. She pinched herself to make sure. The secret, the one Cole had refused to tell her, was incredible, but she couldn't deny it now. Evergreen Industries, through some process she didn't understand but Cole obviously knew inside out, was responsible for making Christmas happen.

Cole glanced at the clock. Taryn would have her coffee by now, and he should probably contact her to see how she was getting along with the database. Texting her seemed like the best option. He'd begun composing one when his phone chimed. Noelle's name popped up on the screen.

He abandoned his text message and answered the call. "What's up?"

"You'd better get down here."

He'd never heard Noelle use that tone, which was part command and part freak-out. "Be right there."

Moments later he was in her office staring at the pictures coming from her surveillance cameras and swearing softly under his breath. "How did she get in there? Her access card was only coded for the IT floor!"

"Don't ask me, but we officially have a major security threat."

Cole's chest tightened. Deep down, he'd known this would happen. He should never have brought her here. "Do you have the cocoa ready?"

Noelle hesitated. "Yes."

"Will it work?" He was worried about Noelle's slight hesitation.

"It should."

"It will erase all memory of me and of this place, but nothing else, right?"

"Uh, yes."

He didn't like the faint tremor in her voice, which told him she wasn't all that confident about the cocoa. But even if the effects only lasted for a while, it would buy him some time, and it was better than nothing. "Get me some and bring it to my office. I'll go find her."

"I'll meet you there."

At this point, he didn't have to hide his powers anymore. Closing his eyes, he willed himself to B4, where Taryn was wandering through displays featuring the historical origin of the Christmas tree. He materialized next to her while she gazed up at a Scotch pine with candles attached to its branches.

"Having fun?"

She jumped and turned toward him, wide-eyed. "Where did you come from?"

He looked into her eyes. "I'm a wizard." In some ways, it was a relief to finally say it. "I can travel simply by wishing it."

"You're a…" She stared at him, her face drained of all color.

"A wizard. From the Winter Clan. As you've just discovered, we're in charge of Christmas."

"But you can't be. What about the North Pole? How does that figure in?"

"It's a decoy. The North Pole would be way too much trouble—no decent facilities at all up there. Colorado is much more convenient for our purposes."

"So this is what you couldn't tell me."

"That's right. And because you've breached our security, I have to take care of that. How did you, by the way?"

"I stole Belle's access card while we were in the coffee shop. Don't blame her. It's not her fault."

"I don't. If anybody's to blame, it's me for bringing you to Gingerbread in the first place. But I'll fix that." He held out his hand. "Hold on."

"Why?"

"We need to go to my office, and this is the quickest way." He gazed at her. "Trust me, please."

"All right." And she put her hand in his.

That simple act broke his heart. But he had a job to do, so he closed his eyes and willed them to his fifteenth-floor office. When the swirling stopped, he kept holding her hand. Anyone new to apparating needed some time to adjust.

She took a shaky breath. "Wow. How many Gs do you think we pulled?"

"Don't know. I've never tried to measure that."

"Next time you should. It would be fun to know."

"*Fun*? This isn't about fun, Taryn."

"Of course it is! This is a *blast.* I just found out the man I love is a *wizard.* How cool is that?"

"I don't think you quite understand."

"No, but I want to. Where do you live? Can you tell me now?"

He shrugged. "I suppose it can't hurt. The Winter Clan has a lodge up on Mistletoe Mountain."

"I knew it! That's why Belle warned me not to go hiking up there."

"You wouldn't have found it even if you had. We have it cloaked."

"Cloaked! I love it! What about the elves? Where do they live?"

"Their village is just below the lodge. They travel to and from the workshop through underground passageways." He looked into her shining eyes and frowned. "At this point any normal person should be hyperventilating and questioning her own sanity. Why aren't you?"

"You're kidding, right? This is me you're talking to, the woman who has read *Lord of the Rings* at least four times and has watched the movie more times than that. Cole, you're a *wizard.* Like Gandalf, only way sexier! I'm geeking out!"

"Knock, knock." Noelle appeared in the doorway holding an ornate silver mug on a silver tray. "I have the cocoa."

"Thanks, Noelle. You can set it on my desk."

She did. Then she walked over to Taryn and held out her hand. "I'm Noelle Frost, temporary head of security. I don't know how you breached our system, but I'm impressed. I wish I could get to know you better."

"Maybe you can," Taryn said.

"I don't think so." Noelle glanced at the cocoa and then at Cole. "It should be fine."

"What?" Taryn whirled around to face him. "What's with the cocoa?"

Cole stepped forward and grasped her shoulders. "It's a special batch. I can't allow you to remember all you've seen, so the cocoa will erase those memories. Then you can return to your life, your family and your job as if this never happened."

"No, I can't."

Noelle cleared her throat. "I'll just head on back to my office. Call if you need me."

"I will," Cole said. Then he returned his attention to Taryn. "Yes, you can. It's the way things need to be."

"I didn't finish my work in IT."

"That's okay. I can do it."

"What if I hack back in?"

He shook his head. "You won't. I've asked Noelle to brew this batch so your memories of me will be selectively removed." He hoped Noelle had managed that.

"First of all, you may be a wizard and all, but that doesn't sound doable. I don't think it's possible to untangle my memories of you without screwing up all my memories from MIT."

"I believe it can be done."

"You mean you *want* to believe, but I can tell you're not a hundred percent sure."

"Taryn, listen to me. We have to try so you can live a normal life. I saw the pictures on your mantel. The burden of keeping a secret like this from those you love would be *huge*."

She gazed at him for several seconds. "Now I get it. The burden would be huge for you, because being open with those you love is so important. It's important to me, too, but if I have to keep a secret from my friends and family so I can be with you—it's no contest."

"Taryn, I—"

She cupped his face in both hands. "You are the best thing that ever happened to me. And now, on top of your brains, your sexy body and your intense love for me, you're a wizard. Do you think for one minute I'm going to dutifully swallow some iffy potion that might make me forget you? I intend to remember you for the rest of my life."

A tiny kernel of hope took root in him and began to grow. "You need to think this through very carefully. Snap decisions are never a good idea."

"I've been thinking it through for ten years, buster. And when I hacked into your site, I promised myself if I ever got my hands on you again, I would never let go."

He couldn't stop the smile from spreading over his face. "Really?"

"Really." She wiggled out of his grip and walked over to the desk. "Is this one of those fancy offices with a bathroom attached?"

"Yes. Do you need to use the facilities?"

"I do. Where are they?"

"Through that door." He was a little perplexed, but when a woman had to go, she had to go.

"Good." Taryn picked up the mug of cocoa and marched through the door he'd indicated.

"What are you doing?" He heard the toilet flush.

She came back bearing the mug and set it on the tray. "No more cocoa. You're stuck with me, Cole Evergreen. And you really need me, too, because you can't run this corporation and the IT department. I'll take that on."

Heart full, he gathered her in his arms. "I just plain need you. But I was so afraid I'd ruin your life."

She gazed up at him. "Then you don't know me as well as you think you do. Can we do that apparating thing again?"

"Why? Where do you want to go?"

"Your bedroom in the Winter Clan lodge. It's time I saw where you live."

He drew her closer. "It's the middle of a business day."

"Yes, but you're the CEO. Besides, I want to see your magic wand. You do have one, don't you?"

"Is that a loaded question?"

"What do you think?"

"I think it is. And that's what I love about you, Taryn Harper." Closing his eyes, he carried them both off to begin a life more magickal than he ever could have imagined. And he had one hell of an imagination.

* * * * *

New York Times bestselling author, two-time RITA® Award nominee, RT Reviewers' Choice Award nominee and National Readers' Choice Award winner **Rhonda Nelson** writes hot romantic comedy. You can find her at readrhondanelson.com, follow @RhondaRNelson on Twitter and like her on Facebook.

SHE'S A MEAN ONE
Rhonda Nelson

For my fellow novella-mates,
Vicki, Andrea and Kira. I believe this book
represents what makes us work as dear friends
and plotting partners—sheer magic.

Love y'all bunches!

Prologue

December 24th, 1996

Seven-year-old Lark DeWynter sucked in a startled breath, and then shut her eyes tightly. "He's not there. He's not there. He's not there," she repeatedly whispered. "And I am *not* crazy," she added, defiantly lifting her chin, a bit of a growl entering her voice.

The scent of sugar cookies and hot cocoa suddenly wafted around her and a low chuckle sounded from directly in front of her. "Of course you're not crazy, child," a merry voice said. "Whoever told you such nonsense?"

Lark's eyes popped open. And there he was.

Santa.

Just like he was every year. Red suit, black belt, snowy white beard tumbling from a rosy-cheeked face and the kindest, twinkling eyes Lark had ever seen. Just looking at him made bubbles of happiness burst in her chest.

Lark choked back a sob and flung herself at him, knocking a surprised grunting laugh from his big belly. She clung to him, profoundly relieved that he was real, that she wasn't crazy, but more than anything, that everyone else was *wrong*. "Oh, Santa!" she cried. "They don't believe me! They don't believe that you're real, but I know that you're real. I *know* that you are!"

"Whoa, there," he said. "What's all this about?" he asked, drawing her away so he could look down into her face. Concern clouded his gaze. "You're not supposed to cry on Christmas Eve. You're supposed to be tucked away in bed, dreaming of toys and surprises."

Lark scrubbed a tear off her cheek and peered up at him. "But I never do that. I always wait for you."

His eyes softened and his especially pink lips curled into a warm smile. "That you do," he said fondly. "You're one of the very, very special few who do that, Lark. Did you know that?"

Her? Special? Really? "But they don't believe me."

He inclined his head, a grave expression on his face, though she sensed that he was merely pretending. "Ah," he said, as though giving it some thought. "Well, that's hardly surprising. Adults have a hard time believing in magic," he said. "Isn't that sad?" He cast a significant glance around the living room. "They can see the tinsel and the lights and the stockings, but the actual *magic* of Christmas?" He gave his head a tragic shake and tsked. "It eludes them, the poor dears."

She'd never thought about it that way before and for a moment felt pity for her parents and for sad Dr. Nancy, who had lots of wrinkles and smelled like mothballs. How terrible that they couldn't see Santa, that they didn't notice the occasional wink of a toy soldier, the flash of a smile from a nutcracker, the flutter of angel wings from the topper on their tree, the extra shimmer on many of the other ornaments.

There was one, in particular, that seemed to shine with an internal glow.

The snowman.

It was pearly white, like moonlight on ice, and seemed to change a bit from year to year. This time he had ivy sprigs on his top hat instead of holly berries, reindeer on the scarf around his neck in place of the snowflakes that were there the year before—even his expression changed. Some years he looked happier than others, when his eyes beamed with a mischievous twinkle. There were years, too, when he looked almost bored. It was odd, but in a strange sort of way it was comforting.

Naturally, that ornament was her favorite, and every year when it came time to dismantle the tree, she fought to keep him out. She had even gone so far as to hide him in her room. It seemed a tragedy to put away all of the decorations, but even more so when it came to her special snowman. He wasn't merely a "Frosty," Lark had decided, and had renamed him Mr. Cool.

She glanced at him now, where he hung front and center on the tree, nestled between a handprint reindeer and a green glass ball, and grinned when his raisin smile widened, his button eyes gleaming with encouragement.

An upside-down head suddenly emerged from the chimney. "Oy, what's the hold up? We're on a schedule here, Big Red," the little man hissed impatiently, the point of his cap dangling dangerously close to the flames. He cast a glance around the living room, stopping short when he spotted the pair of them.

"Oh. It's you." He rolled his eyes—which looked especially odd since he was upside down—and heaved a put upon sigh. "I should have known."

Lark smiled at the elf, despite his surly greeting. "Hello, Edgar."

"Edgar," Santa admonished with a significant arch of his brow. "What did I tell you?"

Edgar's guilty gaze slid away and his mouth flattened. "Christmas is for children," he said glumly.

"And what is Lark?"

He released a long breath and looked everywhere but at Santa. "She's a child."

"And what does that mean?" he prodded.

"She's more important than the schedule," he said, a hint of resentment creeping into his voice. Edgar reminded her of her older brother, John, who at thirteen was a champion door-slammer and could communicate his displeasure with a scowling huff of breath that never failed to make their mother grit her teeth.

Santa beamed at him all the same. "Excellent! You're learning."

Considering that they had the same argument every year, Lark thought Santa's optimism was impressive.

"Nevertheless," the older man said with a regretful grin as he returned his attention to her. "I'm afraid Edgar is right, my dear. Lots of houses left to visit before the dawn."

She nodded. This, too, was a familiar conversation.

He patted her on the head, turned and made his way over to the chimney, then withdrew a handful of glittery purple powder from his pocket and tossed it onto the flames, which instantly died down. Pausing before stepping into the fireplace, he shot her a look over his shoulder. "And, Lark, always remember this—believing is believing."

She frowned. Believing is believing? Didn't he mean *seeing* is believing? "But—"

He chuckled at her expression. "Anybody can see and believe," he told her, anticipating her next question. "But not just anyone can believe without proof. Those people are special, and you're one of them."

She smiled, pleased. "All right, then," she said. "See you next year, Santa."

"See you next year, Lark." He winked, then stepped into the fireplace and disappeared...permanently, it would turn out, from her childhood.

Chapter 1

Ethan Evergreen stared across the news desk at his nemesis, his archenemy, the perpetual thorn in his side, and couldn't decide if he wanted to strangle her or kiss her. Perhaps both, but in which order remained to be seen, he thought darkly.

"...and that is why it is *imperative* that children know there is no Santa Claus, that he's simply not real," Lark DeWynter insisted passionately, her pale violet eyes glowing with conviction. "Lying to them to perpetuate an increasingly commercialized tradition isn't just reckless, it's detrimental." She nodded once. "It devalues truth."

Yes, but whose? Ethan wanted to argue. It was the same tired old debate every year and had been for the past five. Santa wasn't real, children needed more honesty from their "moral instructors," imagination based on lies was unhealthy.

Blah, blah, blah.

He heaved an internal sigh. No doubt had anyone but Lark been making the claim he'd have gotten exceedingly bored by now.

But it wasn't just anyone. It was *her*.

Her, with her pale pansy-colored eyes—not quite blue, not quite purple, but an intriguing shade in between that put him in mind of a rare arctic flower of a similar hue. They were a little wide-set, almost kittenish, and fringed with dark, sooty lashes. She had a wide forehead—*undoubtedly to house that diabolical little brain,* Ethan thought uncharitably—and delicate cheekbones, which narrowed into an adorably sharp chin. And the mouth that sat above that chin? Of its own volition, his broody gaze dropped there and lingered, sending an unwelcome strike of heat directly into his groin.

Positively carnal, that mouth.

Ripe, naturally rosy and full, with a perpetual upturn in the left corner that suggested she was always savoring a secret joke, one he often imagined was at his expense.

She shifted and cleared her throat, which had grown slightly pink.

Ethan's gaze bumped up and collided with hers, and he resisted the immediate urge to recoil at the strength of emotion that slammed into him as a result of that seemingly innocuous non-contact—happened every time he looked at her, damn her. He had caught the faintest flash of longing in those startled eyes before she had disguised it with sardonic contempt.

He arched a pointed brow, one that told her he knew better, and had the pleasure of watching her lovely jaw harden. *Close, but no cigar,* he thought. He knew he hadn't really rattled her until she ground her teeth.

In a strange twist of what could be only considered wicked, vengeful irony, they were wildly—unhappily, miserably, potentially lethally—attracted to one another.

"Any rebuttal to Ms. DeWynter's argument, Ethan?" the toothy talk show host, Mavis, asked. She'd propositioned him earlier, letting him know exactly what she'd like under her tree this Christmas. As if he'd never heard that one before.

Meh. Not interested.

He never was this time of year; he routinely went through a three-month dry spell. It wasn't just because of the stress of being the official face of Evergreen Industries, or because he was busy designing and bewitching ornaments to help add Christmas cheer. But this year held even more pressure. This year he was running Grinch Control, making sure that said Christmas cheer stayed at a high enough level to maintain the magic because her *damned* book—*The Christmas Lie*—had zoomed to the top of every equally *damned* bestseller list. Add in the fact that Santa and Mrs. Claus were in the throes of a marital crisis and his job had never been more challenging. *Leave it to Kris to forget their twenty-fifth wedding anniversary,* Ethan thought with an inward sigh. *Bad form, Bearded Wonder. Bad form.*

No, much as it irritated and galled him to admit it…the sexual hiatus was because of her.

Because, after being around her, every other woman simply failed to capture his interest. For reasons that escaped him—penance for some unknown sin, possibly—Lark DeWynter utterly fascinated him. She was fire and ice, passionate but cool, with a razor-sharp wit and a mind so quick and fiendish he was often torn between being impressed, turned on and mildly terrified.

The rest of the time, he wasn't torn—he just felt all three simultaneously.

It was enough to drive any man insane.

Even more insane? He looked forward to it, looked forward to seeing her every year across the table.

And, of course, he'd offer a rebuttal. That's what he was here for, after all. Damage control. He smiled at Lark and assumed an expression indulgent enough to make her unusual eyes flash with irritation, then launched into his spiel. "Naturally, no one at Evergreen Industries is promoting dishonesty—"

She snorted.

Ethan upped the wattage on his grin. "Instead, we're in favor of indulging the imagination of children, of perpetuating a fantasy that feeds their creativity and builds family memories to last a lifetime." He leaned forward in earnest. "Listen, the way we look at it, kids are going to have the rest of their lives to learn about truths—some of them less palatable than others—and, knowing that, I don't think that it's fair to rob children of what's ultimately a very small window of opportunity to—" he lifted his shoulders and smiled helplessly "—believe the unbelievable."

"Aw, Ethan," Mavis said, pressing a hand against her chest, seemingly overcome by emotion. "That's just beautiful. What a lovely sentiment."

He heard it then, the faint grinding of enamel against enamel, and watched Lark's expression darken with fury. He grinned widely.

"Sentiment over truth?" Lark asked, her voice climbing, her eyes widening in outrage. "Really?"

Mavis purposely ignored Lark and looked at the camera. "I'm afraid that's all we've got time for today, folks. Stay tuned for *Cooking with Constance*. She's whipping up several tried-and-true holiday desserts over in the kitchen."

Ethan waited for the all clear from the producer, then carefully plucked the microphone from his shirt and placed it on the desk. He could hear Lark grumbling under her breath.

"Despicable sentimental bullshit. 'Believe the unbelievable,'" she mimicked scathingly, her sleek black brows winging up her forehead. "Sounds like a damned campaign slogan, not a valid argument."

Mavis laid a bejeweled hand upon his arm and leaned in

to better display her cleavage. "Brilliant as always, Ethan," she said. "I'd love to hear more about those new ornaments you've designed for this holiday season." She arched a hopeful brow. "Got time for a drink?"

From the corner of his eye he caught Lark's smirk, right before she turned on her heel and headed off. Ebony curls tumbled over her slim shoulders and the ruffled hem of her hooker red skirt fluttered with each seemingly exaggerated swing of her lush hips.

"Um, no, sorry," he said, unreasonably annoyed by her hasty departure. They always had a second go at one another after these little on-camera feuds. "I've got to get back to Colorado."

Before Mavis could respond, he pivoted and made his way unhurriedly across the studio to the double doors that opened into the hall. From there he bolted, eager to catch up with Lark.

"Thought you were going for a drink," she drawled as he came up behind her.

"Look at that," he said, hurrying forward to get the next door for her. God, she was gorgeous. Just stunning. "You're so sensitive to my presence you knew it was me before you could even see me. I must ping the hell out of your sonar."

She snorted indelicately and shot him a look. "Don't flatter yourself. It's your cologne, fool. It's quite—" she wrinkled her nose distastefully "—distinctive."

"I'm not wearing any cologne," he lied. It was new, dammit, and he'd bought it with her in mind. He'd overheard her tell a makeup artist last year that she loved the smell of sandalwood.

That plump mouth curved into a provocative smile. "Right," she said. "Just like you aren't wearing pants."

He fell into step beside her. Why? Who the hell knew? "I am wearing pants," he replied. "It's underwear that I'm not wearing," he added, just to needle her.

She made a small choking sound and her gaze dropped to his crotch before darting back up again. "Why are you following me?"

"Who said I was following you? I'm leaving, same as you are."

She stopped short and pointed to the ladies' room door. "I'm not leaving. I'm going to the bathroom." She directed a red-tipped nail toward the other end of the hall. "If you'd wanted to leave, you should have gone in the other direction." She frowned, feigning concern. "Do you need me to draw you a map?"

Bullshit. He didn't need a map any more than she'd been going to the ladies' room. He shook his head. "Not necessary," he told her, then leaned casually against the wall. He pulled out his cell and began to idly scroll through his email. "I'll just wait for you and follow you out."

"Surely you have better things to do."

He looked up and smiled benignly. "I don't, actually."

"Has it occurred to you that I might?" she asked tightly.

"Of course. But I hardly see how me following you outside is going to hold you up." He'd work that bit out later. For now, it was just enough to be this close to her, to annoy the hell out of her, to make her feel half as irritated and out-of-control as he felt right now.

Or any other time he was around her, for that matter.

Clearly he'd lost his mind. And instinct, however misguided, told him she was the key to finding it.

Chapter 2

Lark DeWynter braced her hands on either side of the sink, leaned forward and peered at her forehead. She was relieved to find that "Moron" wasn't written across it. She growled low in her throat, willed her rapidly beating heart to slow into some semblance of a normal rhythm.

"He's just a man," she told herself as she stared into the mirror. "Just a man. There is absolutely nothing special about him. He's got the same parts as any other man." She looked at herself, released a breath and whimpered, "Except that his parts are way more beautiful and compelling and hot and sexy than those of any other man I've met."

The stall directly behind her opened, startling her, and her gaze met a pair of twinkling dark brown eyes set in an equally dark brown face. "Mmm-hmm." The woman grunted knowingly. "That's the way of it, all right. The Curse of the Sparkly Penis."

Lark choked. The curse of the *what*? "I'm sorry."

The woman sidled forward and pumped the soap dispenser, then lathered her hands. "The Curse of the Sparkly Penis. Girl, you know what I'm talking about. There's always one, sometimes two or even three, if you're lucky," she mused, her expression turning thoughtful. "And when a man has the sparkly penis, there's nothing a girl can do. She's powerless. Everything about him just shines a little bit more. Because he's got the Sparkly Penis, see?"

Though Lark had never seen Ethan's penis to know whether it was sparkly or not—she snickered at the thought—her imagination nonetheless conjured up images of his undoubtedly impressive penis bedazzled with rhinestones and jewels, a little Christmas wreath proudly hanging from the root.

A bark of laughter bubbled up in her throat, making the woman next to her join in until they were both nearly bent double, tears streaming down their faces.

"There you go," the woman said, nodding approvingly, her gaze wise. "Next time that man's got you tied up in knots you just imagine him with a few rhinestones on his junk and you'll be right as rain, you hear me?" She mmm-hmm'ed. "Ain't nothing a few sparkles can't fix."

Lark giggled again. "Indeed."

A tentative knock sounded at the door. "Lark?"

Lark gasped and her new friend's eyes widened. "Is that him?" she hissed.

"Lark, is everything all right in there?" Ethan asked, anxiety tingeing his silky baritone. Heaven help her, the man had the *best* voice. Low and smooth with a soft rasp at the finish that put her in mind of tangled sheets and bare limbs, of candlelight and a whole hallelujah chorus of orgasms.

Oh, who the hell was she kidding? *He* did that to her. *Just him. Only him. Ever.*

It was hardly fair to blame it solely on his voice, when everything about him made her want to forget that he was her biggest adversary. She knew that she was supposed to hate him, that she was a champion for all the confused children in the U.S., the ones like her who had suffered heartache and insecurity and been the target of countless jokes and ridicule for clinging firmly to Santa Claus delusions. But it was hard—so hard—because Ethan Evergreen did the one thing that no other man had ever been able to successfully do for any length of time.

He made her remember that she was a woman.

He made her belly ache with longing, her lips tingle with the anticipation of an imagined kiss. Her palms itched to touch his bare skin, to thread her fingers through that glorious dark chestnut hair, to run the pad of her thumb over the full, unbelievably sensual curve of his bottom lip. She wanted to lick, taste and suckle every beautifully proportioned inch of his body, but more importantly, she wanted him to do those same things to her.

On a rug. In front of a fire. In some remote cabin in the woods with no television, internet or cell phone reception.

Indefinitely.

"We're fine in here," the woman called out to him.

After a long pause, he returned with, "Lark?"

Though secretly touched at his concern, Lark heaved a put-upon sigh, marched over to the door and pulled it open a crack. A beautiful, startlingly green eye stared at her.

"Ethan, for pity's sake, I'm in the ladies' room." She arched an imperious brow. "How about a little privacy?"

The green eye narrowed suspiciously and tried to peer around her. "It sounds like you're having a party in there."

Lark purposely shifted, obstructing his view. "So what if we are," she said. She flicked her fingers at him impatiently. "Shoo."

"Shoo? Really?"

"*Go away.*" She shut the door once more, and leaned against it, pressing a palm to her forehead.

"Mercy, he sounds pretty."

A wan smile curled her lips and she hung her head and laughed softly. "That's because he is."

"Then what's the problem?"

Another weak laugh. "*The* problem implies that there's only one."

"Chemistry is chemistry," she said. "Problems have a way of sorting themselves out when we stop thinking with our heads and start listening to our bodies."

That sounded awfully new age and open-minded, Lark thought. It also sounded like excellent advice...if it were in relation to anything other than Ethan Evergreen.

But him? Er, no. Her mind was constantly at war with her body when it came to him. Inside of her, self-preservation went toe-to-toe in a bare-knuckled brawl with lust—right now, self-preservation was holding its own, but it flagged every time she was around him. That's why she'd bolted the instant the interview had been over. Ordinarily she would have lingered and they would have exchanged a few more barbs, then gone for a drink where they would have continued to flirt under the guise of a heated debate—one that inevitably would have been punctuated by a little laughter and a lot of longing—and then she'd come to her senses and leave in a huff, and he'd smile because he'd realize she was just running scared. That was the trouble, in a nutshell, Lark thought. He knew too much about her. Instinctively. Sometimes when he looked at her she was utterly convinced he'd just opened up her head and taken a peek inside. It was unnerving. And slightly comforting, which she'd no doubt need to ask her therapist about, she thought with a frown. Why in the hell would she find that comforting? That sort of invasion of her mind? Her very thoughts?

Possibly because, in an odd sort of way, she thought he *got* her.

Singular, that. No one had ever gotten her, not even her parents. She'd been *that* child, the fragile one with the delusions of Santa Claus, with the hyper imagination that had animated ordinary Christmas decorations. Even now, almost twenty years later, a doctorate degree under her belt, she still fought the delusions.

Hell, just that morning she'd caught a glimpse of a wink from a nutcracker in a store window.

And then there was her snowman, Mr. Cool, who she'd snuck outside and rescued from the garbage bin all those years ago when her parents had purged all the ornaments and decorations from the house. For reasons that escaped her, she'd hung on to him, unable to let him go. A sentimental weakness, she supposed. She'd tried several times to toss him into the trash or put him in a donation box, but she could never make herself do it. He presently hung from an artificial ficus tree, a lone reminder of her past, both the good and the bad.

"Lark?" Ethan persisted.

She groaned and massaged the bridge of her nose.

Her new friend finished applying a fresh coat of lipstick. "He's persistent, isn't he?"

Yes, dammit. "Like a dog with a bone."

She shot her a knowing look. "Then clip a leash on him, honey, and bring him to heel."

Ha! As if. She'd have about as much luck clipping a leash onto Ethan Evergreen as she would onto a rabid wolverine. And that's exactly what he would turn into if she landed that coveted slot on the *Ophelia Winslow Show*.

He'd *flip*.

Naturally, that thrilled her to her little toes. And sent the teensiest dart of panic into her chest. Ethan's family, steeped in Christmas tradition, had founded Gingerbread, Colorado—"Where Christmas is always in season!"— more than two hundred years before. His entire family worked for Evergreen Industries, as did many of the residents of Gingerbread. It wasn't merely a livelihood, it was a way of life. And she was threatening it.

The success of the book had brought plenty of media opportunities, but nothing as grand or potentially far-reaching as the *Ophelia Winslow Show.* The ultimate feather in her cap, it would be a game-changer. It would give her the opportunity to share her message with millions of dedicated viewers who considered Ophelia to be a virtual oracle on all things, from the best pair of women's pantyhose to the best facial cream on the market. Lark would learn this afternoon whether or not the show was a go and, with every second that ticked by, her anticipation and anxiety increased.

She shot a helpless look at the door and imagined the man on the other side of it—tall and gorgeous, with those unusually bright green eyes—and a snake of heat coiled in her middle, making her nipples tighten behind her bra, her muscles melt with desire. She closed her eyes tightly and beat back the urge to howl in frustration.

He was not helping matters.

To hell with it, Lark thought. She needed a drink.

She thanked her new friend for the advice, then squared her shoulders and exited the bathroom without sparing Ethan a single glance—the view from the corner of her eye was enough to make her pulse trip—and started down the hall.

"It's about time," he said, naturally falling into step beside her. God, he smelled good. Lickable. "I was on the verge of sending in a search party."

"You could have left."

He chuckled. "And miss the pleasure of your company?" he drawled, the smart-ass. "Never."

"Just out of curiosity, how long do you plan on following me?"

"Why?" he asked suspiciously, shooting her a sidelong glance. "Thinking of getting a restraining order?"

Lark felt her lips twitch. "No, but a Taser might be an option."

He feigned a gasp and tsked under his breath. "Bodily injury? Really? You wound me."

A laugh tickled the back of her throat and she rolled her eyes. "Please," she said. "Only if your Arrogance Shield has failed."

He pushed through the double doors, which led out into a small alley behind the studio. The smell of diesel fuel and garbage hung in the air—Eau de New York, she'd dubbed it, missing the scent of woodsmoke and cedar in her north Georgia home.

"Arrogance Shield? You've given me a superpower? Like a superhero?" He looked positively delighted, damn him, with that endearingly boyish grin. A deep dimple emerged in his right cheek, one that only made an appearance when he smiled with his whole face.

That dimple was downright dangerous, because it made her forget that he was the enemy, that she wasn't supposed to like him, much less want to tie him to her bed with tinsel and eat him up like a Christmas cookie.

"It was an insult," she reminded him pointedly.

His grin widened. "Only if I take offense. And I don't. How about a drink, Chickadee? Got time for one more argument before you fly south?"

Chickadee? That was a new one. He'd called her everything from Sparrow to Crow over the years, good-naturedly needling her because of her "bird" name. He wasn't the only one—she'd been getting ribbed since grade school—so she was used to it.

"Might as well," she said with a sigh. "I need to make sure my Bullshit Detector is up and running. Keep talking, would you?" She smiled sweetly. "You're my best diagnostic tool."

He gave her a small bow. "I am ever at your service."

Lark grinned up at him, charmed despite herself. "Yep. It's definitely working."

She inwardly girded her loins, thinking only a magical chastity belt would provide the kind of superpower she'd need.

Heaven help her...

Chapter 3

Looking more like he was leading her to the gallows than into a local pub, Ethan smothered a smile and held the door open for Lark, then waited for her to pass through before following her inside. He caught a whiff of something spicy and sweet, like cinnamon and vanilla, and felt his groin tighten. Honestly, *only* she could smell like a damned pastry and he'd find it a turn-on.

She picked her way through the lunch crowd and found a spot at a bar in the back, then slid her lush rear end onto a stool. A bit of the tension eased out of her spine, but it still hovered around her shoulders like a shadow she couldn't shake.

He empathized.

Odd that the source of his tension was the remedy, as well.

Just being around her wound him up, but it offered a bizarre sort of release, like he could suddenly let go of breath he didn't know he'd been holding.

He settled onto the stool beside her and signaled for the bartender, then ordered a shot of Jameson.

"Hitting the Irish this early?" she asked, a faint twinkle in her lovely blue eyes.

He shrugged. "Your sincerely misguided book hit the *New York Times* best-sellers list," he drawled. "We're celebrating. What are you having?"

She shot him a slightly exasperated look, one that somehow managed to be both sexy and endearing. "'Sincerely misguided,'" she repeated. "So I'm wrong, but since I believe it, you're willing to forgive me for my opinion?" She chuckled darkly and glanced at the bartender. "Give me a Jameson as well, but make it a double. I think I'm going to need it for this particular conversation," she added, a grim undertone shading her voice.

"Are you sure you want to do that? You know you can't hold your liquor."

She lifted her adorable chin. "I can hold it just fine, thank you."

He winced significantly. "Sincerely misguided," he repeated. "It's a theme with you, isn't it? Remember that I warned you when you start coming on to me."

She snorted. "Sure. Right."

"Last year, Minneapolis," he reminded her, bringing the tumbler to his lips.

She sucked in a small gasp and glared at him. "That was a combination of new medication and alcohol," she hissed. "And I wasn't coming on to you, dammit. I was a little unsteady on my feet."

"Yes, you were," he remarked, his lips twitching. "You were all over me." *Her soft breast against his side, her head on his shoulder, her arm around his waist as he'd helped her walk back from the hotel bar to her room.*

It had been an excruciating exercise in restraint, and they both knew he could have very easily taken advantage of her. He hadn't, of course, because when the time finally came for him and Ms. Anti-Claus to share skin on a mattress, he wanted her to be fully aware of what they were doing. He wanted her to want him, to make the *deliberate* choice, not one compromised by a new migraine medication and tequila.

She peered at him, squinting thoughtfully as though she were perplexed. "How do you do it?" she asked.

"Do what?"

"Carry around that *massive* ego. It's a miracle the weight of it doesn't cripple you."

He smiled. "Lift with your knees," he said, winking at her. "That's the trick."

She chuckled softly and rolled her eyes, slid a slim finger down the side of her glass. "I knew there had to be one."

"So how have you been?" he asked. "I'm assuming writing and promoting the book has taken up a great deal of your time."

"It has," she admitted. She took a sip of her whiskey and rolled it around on her tongue, savoring the flavor. "But in a good way, you know? I've logged less hours at the clinic this year, but I'm okay with that."

Because her message was more important. Because she believed what she said. It wasn't merely a talking point for her. She was genuinely passionate about protecting children, about preventing the heartache and pain she'd hinted at in her book.

Yes, he'd read it.

Theoretically so that he'd be able to refute it. But it had actually been out of blatant curiosity and the desire to know more about her. He wondered if she knew the insights she'd provided, if she was even aware of how much of herself she'd inadvertently left on the page. Probably not.

"What about you?" she wanted to know. "How's your year been?"

"Most recently, quite hellish," he told her with a pointed smirk.

"What?" she asked innocently. "But I thought all PR was good PR…"

"Not when you're the one handling it, I assure you."

"Come on," she teased, pushing her hair away from her face in the process. "It would ruin your Christmas if you didn't have me to argue with."

Yes, it would, damn her. "You mean fight with."

"That, too," she conceded.

"Ah, but the best part of fighting is making up, and we never seem to get to that point, do we, Chickadee?"

He watched a pretty blush bloom beneath her creamy skin and her pupils dilate. She took a bigger pull from her drink. "I saw the new ornaments for this season," she said, obviously deciding a subject change was in order. "They're quite lovely."

"Thank you. I've been pleased with them." That was an understatement. Other than his debut "Frosty" series, he'd been happier with this set than he had any other, and he'd been designing ornaments for the Evergreen Collection since he'd turned thirteen. Typically ornament design fell to the women in the family, but Ethan had inadvertently shown he'd had a knack for it when his little sister, Belle, had failed spectacularly at it. He'd come to her rescue and the rest, as they say, was history. He took a little needling from his brothers, of course—boys will be boys— but when his designs had started outselling all the others and had increased the company's overall bottom line, the ribbing had stopped.

Besides, it was his outlet. He could plead "artistic solitude," go to his studio and lock himself away from the rest of the world for hours. Being the smiling, perpetually upbeat and happy face of the company wasn't exactly an easy job, but it was expected and he was good at it. He didn't complain because he was certain that each and every member of his family felt the same way about their own roles.

But it was for the greater good of the Evergreen family, so...

"The inspiration?"

"*The Night Before Christmas*, the 1949 edition illustrated by Leonard Weisgard." Ethan loved Weisgard's work. He'd written and illustrated many books throughout his career that showed incredible technical expertise, but the sense of movement and the confident use of vivid colors were especially impressive. The style was less Victorian and more contemporary, particularly for the late 1940s.

A small line appeared between her brows. "I can't say that I recognize that edition, but if the colors are as bold as your ornaments, I'm sure I'd like it."

He was sure she would, as well. "I have an extra copy," he said. "I'd be happy to mail it to you."

She looked intrigued for half a second, then practicality prevailed. "No, thanks."

Ethan smiled and leaned over, purposely crowding her personal space. Naturally, she didn't budge. "It's just a book, Lark," he confided. "Not propaganda."

"It wouldn't matter if it were," she said, deliberately lifting her drink to her lips. "*I'm* not drinking your Christmas Kool-Aid."

"Me neither," he said with a grimace. "Our wine is *so* much better."

Her mouth dropped open. "You're in the wine business now, too? Seriously?"

Ethan chuckled at her slack-jawed expression and shook his head. "No, but that's a thought. I'd never considered marketing it before. My father makes it just for the family."

An odd expression suddenly crossed her face. Seemingly embarrassed, she looked away.

"What?" Ethan asked, intrigued.

"What, what?" She adjusted the salt and pepper shakers so they were perfectly aligned. She liked order, he'd noticed. And right angles.

"That look."

She blinked innocently. "What look?"

"Cut it out, Lark," he said, smiling. "You know exactly what I mean. What was that look for?"

A slow grin teased her lips, consenting defeat. She let go of a small sigh. "Oh, all right. Since you refuse to drop it… It was the comment about your father."

He frowned. "My father? What about him?"

She shifted uncomfortably. "I'd, uh, never thought about you having one before."

Ethan blinked and a bark of startled laughter broke from his throat. "Never thought about me having one before?" he repeated incredulously. "A father? Really?" he teased. "Did you think I'd sprung fully grown from Santa's bag of presents?"

"Or the loins of Satan," she quipped, chuckling softly, her eyes twinkling.

"Satan?" He shook his head, chewed the inside of his cheek. "*Wow*."

"I'm only teasing," she said, still laughing.

"It might surprise you to know I have a mother, too," he said. "And a couple of brothers, and a sister and grandparents and great-grandparents, aunts, uncles and cousins. A whole family tree that is quite large, multi-forked and healthy."

She was wheezing because she was chuckling so hard now. Her eyes had watered and, most significantly, the tension he'd noticed in her shoulders had melted away. She looked happy and relaxed and…gorgeous.

Her brow briefly folded in confusion. "Multi-forked?"

Ethan tossed back the rest of his whiskey and signaled

for another. "Well, you know what they say about family trees that don't fork…"

Understanding lit her gaze and she inclined her head. "Ah, right. Well, I never said I thought your parents were closely related," she pointed out.

"No, only that you thought I didn't have any, and that, if I had a father at all, it was the Prince of Darkness."

She grinned at him, not the least bit repentant. "He's royalty, isn't he? Glass half-full, remember?"

The bartender slid him a new drink and he lifted it up to send a toast in her direction. "I prefer my glass completely full."

Her cell suddenly vibrated against the tabletop, drawing her attention. An instant smile bloomed over her lips and her eyes lit with excitement. "If this call means what I think it means, you're going to need a lot more *full* glasses."

Oh, hell. That didn't sound good. Inexplicable dread suddenly swelled in his gut.

"Well?" she asked by way of greeting. "Please tell me you've got good news."

Lark gasped delightedly and, impossibly, her smile widened. When she aimed it at him, it had a distinctly cat-in-the-cream-pot element that he found more than a little disturbing.

"This Friday? Wow. That was quicker than I'd imagined, but you know I'm ready."

He'd just bet she was. And whatever it was she was ready for was undoubtedly going to make his life hell and put him in full-blown defense mode.

Like there wasn't enough going on as it was.

He'd gotten a text message from his brother that featured a new picture of Santa and had the caption "WTE?" (What the Elf?) In addition to the twenty pounds he'd lost recently, he'd dyed his hair shoe-polish black and shaved his beard. Evidently trying to look more like Guido, the thirty-something ski instructor Mrs. Claus had recently started taking lessons from. Lord… Merry was on Cougar Patrol and Kris, the very epitome of Christmas, was rocking the "old Elvis" look.

Not good. *So* not good.

"Yes, yes, I know. I'm actually looking forward to seeing his face as well. As it happens, I'll get to do that in just a second." She was staring at him, the she-devil, looking absolutely triumphant.

The dread intensified.

"Oh, yes. We're having a drink. Yes, right here with me. Oh, yeah. I'm going to get to gloat in person."

Ethan feigned dispassion and tried to appear indulgent rather than curious, though admittedly she'd set the hook and was simply toying with him until she could scoop him into the net.

But that didn't mean he had to make it easy for her.

He glanced at his watch, deliberately noted the time with an exaggerated wince, then finished his drink. He was in the process of throwing cash on the bar and sliding off his stool before she realized what he was doing.

She started. "Sorry, Lisa. Gotta run. Will get back to you later this afternoon." She ended the call and arched an accusatory brow. "Where are you going? I thought we were having a drink."

"I've had several," he said, making sure he'd added a decent tip. "I've got to get to the airport."

"Please," she scoffed. "You have a private plane. You don't have to leave right now." She shot him a calculating look. "You're running scared. Hmm. That's disappointing. Never pegged you as a coward."

Ethan chuckled. "What am I supposed to be afraid of, Chickadee? You?" he goaded, purposely baiting her.

Predictably, those pretty violet eyes sparked with irritation. "Yes, actually, but I can see how you'd underestimate me." She tapped a thoughtful finger against her chin. "I wonder if you'll still feel that way after my special guest spot on *Ophelia* airs this Friday."

Ethan stilled and the dread that had been collecting in his middle hardened into a sickening lump. *Ophelia?*

The cat-in-the-cream-pot smile again. "Ah," she breathed. "Scared now, aren't you?"

Yes, actually, his mind whirling with the potentially catastrophic implications of her little bombshell revelation. With a platform like the *Ophelia Winslow Show*, she could quite literally *ruin* Christmas. She could squash the Christmas spirit to the point that the magic wouldn't work and the millions of children around the world who anxiously waited for Santa to arrive with their presents would be so disappointed that it could take *years* to overcome. A hit like that...

It could be the end of Christmas.

The end of life as he knew it, as his entire family knew it.

And it was Ethan's job to keep that from happening.

His gaze slid to her once more, his frantic mind flipping through the various ways he could thwart her plan. Ultimately, he settled on the most drastic solution. He sent a text to his driver, summoning his car.

The only way he would be able to keep her off that show would be to make it *physically impossible* for her to be there.

All righty then, Ethan thought, resolvedly. He'd just have to kidnap her.

Chapter 4

A prick of unwelcome sympathy pinched Lark's heart at the expression on Ethan's face. She'd never seen that look before—it was an almost panicked sort of dread—and the idea that she'd put it there didn't make her want to gloat at all. In fact, she had the irrational urge to comfort him, to tell him not to worry. For the briefest of seconds he'd looked impossibly alone, the weight of the world on his shoulders.

Which was ridiculous. He wasn't alone. He had his entire family—even the parents she'd never imagined him having—at his disposal, not to mention a cache of wealthy socialites waiting in the wings. (Yes, she occasionally Googled him. No, she wasn't proud, particularly when it came to her reaction to seeing him with any of the said socialites. Like she wanted to yank out their perfectly coiffed hair and break their fake fingernails.)

"Congratulations," Ethan told her, not a hint of the previous concern visible. He was his cool, unflappable self, the quintessential beautiful businessman. "I know you've been angling for an invitation there for years."

Yes, she had. She'd expected him to cry foul, to immediately launch a counterattack. His graciousness unnerved her. She shot him a suspicious look. "You know you won't be able to offer a rebuttal, right? I'm going solo on this one."

"Of course you are. The Powerful O doesn't do rebuttals, at least not during the same show."

"Ah. So that's your angle. You're going to try to weasel your way in after me, aren't you?"

"I don't know that 'weasel' is the right word," he drawled, shooting her a sidelong look. "Shall I walk you out?"

Still confused over his behavior, it took Lark a minute to catch his meaning. "Oh. You're really leaving?"

He glanced at her, his direct gaze tangling with hers. "Yes. I'd mentioned the airport, remember?"

Right. Yes, he had. She nodded, annoyed with herself. "You did."

He lifted a brow. "When's your flight? Can I give you a lift? LaGuardia, right?"

She nodded, torn. Her plane didn't leave for another three hours, but by the time she cabbed it over and made her way through security no doubt it would nearly be time to board. But there was no point in hiring a cab when he was headed to the same place, anyway. "Yes, you can, actually. If you're sure you don't mind."

He smiled at her, just the merest arch of his lips, and she felt it all the way down to her little toes. "Not at all."

"Excellent." Lark snagged her purse, then proceeded toward the exit, Ethan strolling along behind her. She could feel the weight of his gaze slide down the back of her neck and over her shoulders, and then linger on her ass. Another sparkler of need ignited in her belly, making her bite the inside of her cheek.

On second thought, being cooped up in the back of his limousine with him probably wasn't a good idea.

Ethan reached past her shoulder and pushed open the door with a mouthwateringly large hand. He was close enough that she could smell his cologne—something musky with a whiff of sandalwood—and could feel the heat of him behind her.

Yep. Definitely not a good idea.

"You know, I think maybe I should just—"

A soft, knowing chuckle slipped past his lips, as though he'd predicted this outcome. "Who's the coward now?"

Lark didn't know what she liked less—being predictable or being called a coward—but since she was determined not to be either of those things, she smiled as the limo driver accommodatingly opened her door. She climbed into the back of the car, Ethan close behind her. Though he could have easily sat on the opposite side, he moved in right next to her, his powerful thigh brushing hers.

He was doing it on purpose. She knew it.

Maybe that was his game, she thought. Maybe he planned to drive her so crazy with desire that she'd ultimately snap and not be able to do the *Ophelia Show.* Instead she'd be locked up in a little padded room with no windows or sharp objects, a blubbering mess in need of a bath and a brush.

Was she overreacting? Yes, of course she was, but it was better than the alternative, which was letting him get into her head more than he already had—or, more importantly, getting into her body.

She scooted over.

He laughed again. *Bastard.*

"So what's next on your agenda?" he asked her. "Got anything lined up between now and the show?"

Lark didn't know why, but an alarm sounded inside of her. It was an innocent enough question, one that often came up when they were making the talk show and radio rounds, so she didn't know why the inquiry seemed off this time…but it did.

He turned to look at her when she didn't readily answer and a shocked brow arched over his right eye. "Really? You relish the opportunity to tell me about Ophelia, knowing there's absolutely nothing I can do about it, but now your other engagements are off-limits as well?" A bark of laughter erupted from his throat and he shook his head. "Wow. Talk about good sportsmanship. I guess the gloves are really off, aren't they, Chickadee?"

How was it possible for him to sound so confident and irritating one minute, then disappointed and vulnerable the next? More importantly, why did either of those things affect her so much?

Ultimately it was the disappointment she couldn't stand. Anybody who didn't welcome the opportunity to debate their position didn't hold a firm enough one, in her opinion. Ethan might have been a pain in the ass, but he'd never been one she resented or minded.

"Lisa is rescheduling everything until after Friday," she said. "It was part of the agreement with the producers."

He turned to look at her, his gaze even. "That makes sense. She's going to want a break in your message if she's going to launch it from her show. Think she's on your team?"

She smiled. "My team?"

He returned her grin. "You know what I mean."

She did. "Honestly, I'm not sure. I know she's read the book, but… Guess I'll find out on Friday, won't I?"

"I guess you will," he said. His gaze sharpened, making his green eyes appear impossibly brighter. "Tell you what. If you're free until Friday, why don't you come back to Gingerbread with me? I'll give you the official tour. Give you a tour of my design studio, show you how the ornaments are made. I can take you to Cup of Cheer for peppermint cocoa, and we can go snowmobiling on Mistletoe Mountain." He essayed another grin. "Even introduce you to my parents, if for no other reason than to prove I've got them."

If there was anything more shocking than his invitation—where the hell had *that* come from?—it was her actually wanting to accept it. The picture he painted struck a whimsical chord, sparked a yearning so strong in her breast it nearly stole her breath. It was crazy and wrong on so many levels that she didn't know where to start, but...

Lark shook her head. "I can't."

Another flash of something unreadable—disappointment? "Can't or won't?"

"Doesn't matter. The outcome is the same." She paused. "Why?"

"Why what?"

"Why did you ask?"

He looked away. "Selfish reasons," he said. "I figured if you were going to destroy my family and my town, then you should at least see it first."

Her chest squeezed. "That's not fair."

He lifted a shoulder. "I don't think it's fair that I'm not going to get a rebuttal, either, but that's the way it is. Put the shoe on the other foot, Lark, and tell me you wouldn't feel the same way."

"That's beside the point."

"Whose point?" he scoffed. "Yours?"

They were on the expressway headed to LaGuardia now, she realized, noting the signage. "I'm flying Bluebird," she mentioned. "Would you let your driver know?"

Yes, of course she would feel the same way, but that didn't change the fact that she'd landed the slot and he hadn't, and she'd worked too hard to get her message out there to miss an opportunity like this.

She couldn't afford to squander it on things like fairness and sentimentality.

Ethan leaned forward and muttered something to the driver. But when they reached the airport, to Lark's chagrin, he drove right past the terminal for Bluebird.

"He missed it," she said, wondering if the man needed his eyesight checked. "Just have him pull over. I'll walk back."

"I can't let you do that."

"What? Walk? Why the hell not? I'm not an invalid." She leaned forward. "Here is fine," she said. "Just let me out here."

"He's not going to do it," Ethan told her.

"Not going to do it," she repeated, getting as annoyed as she was confused. "What do you mean? He's going to circle again? He doesn't have to do that. I am perfectly capable of walking back to the correct terminal. Tell him to stop."

"Just remember that I asked you nicely, okay?"

She blinked. Asked her nicely? "What?"

"Not that it'll matter, but…"

Lark caught a blur—a flick of Ethan's wrist, a little burst of light—and then suddenly darkness pulled at her. She felt her cheek land against his chest, his arm come around her shoulder, and thought she heard a faint "Ho, Ho, Ho" before the world went black.

Chapter 5

Ethan hadn't expected the whole damned family to be home when he arrived with an unconscious Lark in tow, but had anything recently gone according to his expectations?

Six pairs of startled eyes turned from the grand dining room as he made his way past, stopping him in his tracks. He blinked, not entirely sure how he planned to explain himself.

He'd *acted*. That was his job after all. Damage control.

Naturally, it was Belle who spoke first, her trusty iPad in hand. Her lips quirked with sardonic humor. "Well, this is a change, brother. Ordinarily you don't have to knock them unconscious to bring them home."

"What are you talking about?" Cole asked her. "He never brings them home. He uses the lounge attached to his studio to *entertain*," he remarked, innuendo dripping from the last word. Taryn shot her new husband a scolding look and elbowed him in the ribs, which resulted in a startled grunt of pain and a wounded frown.

She turned to look at Ethan. "Is that who I think it is?"

"Probably." Though they were both geniuses, clearly in this instance Taryn was the smarter one.

"Who do you think it is?" Dash wanted to know, ever curious, a burn hole in his shirt from his latest glassblowing project. "Should we know who it is?"

Taryn ignored him. "Cocoa?"

Ethan nodded, relieved that someone seemed to recognize the gravity of the situation. "Yes, please."

To the Evergreens, cocoa wasn't just a hot chocolate beverage—it was a magical cure-all that could do everything from eradicate the common cold to wipe out memories, which was naturally its most important purpose.

"Protect the secret" had become synonymous with "Drink the cocoa." And since the secret had to be protected at all costs...

"Son?" his mother queried cautiously, clearly wanting an explanation.

"Ethan?" his father seconded.

"I'll explain later," he promised, then headed for the stairs to take her up to his apartment. The entire Evergreen family lived in the massive Art Deco–themed lodge, each member with a set of rooms to furnish and decorate as he or she pleased, and to escape into when too much togetherness threatened to drive one insane.

Togetherness was something the Evergreens lived, ate and breathed.

Ordinarily it was a comfort—nothing ever felt quite right when he was away from his family for any extended period of time—and, of course, like most magical families, theirs was stronger when they were together.

Right now, however, as the *entire damned family* trouped along upstairs behind him, peppering him with questions he didn't know the answers to, *"comfort"* was not the word that sprang immediately to mind.

He wished everyone but Taryn would go away. His

new sister-in-law was *helping*—the rest of them were just being nosy.

"Shouldn't you be working on that new software program?" he shot at Cole. "Wrangling the reindeer?" he slung at Dash. "Feeding your caffeine habit at the Cup of Cheer?" he aimed at Belle, who blushed before a mutinous expression settled over her face.

"My work is in hand, big brother." Trekking along beside him, she dropped her pointed gaze to the unconscious woman in his arms. "Yours, however, seems to be in question."

"Oh, I'd say he's got it in hand," Taryn quipped. "Or *her*, rather."

"Her?" Dash repeated as they rounded the corner.

Belle suddenly inhaled sharply. "You don't mean… No. Surely not…"

Taryn hurried around him and opened his door. "Thanks," he muttered. He continued through his sitting room into his bedroom. He actually had a spare bedroom as well, but for reasons that were all too obvious, he preferred to deposit her onto his own mattress.

A tiny frown appeared between Lark's brows as she settled against his duvet and mewled lowly, stretched and then relaxed like a sleepy kitten into the pillows. Dark lashes painted half-moon shadows beneath her eyes and her skin seemed particularly creamy against his royal-blue bedding. Her hair tumbled in long curls away from her face save a lone curl that hugged the underside of her jaw. He ached to sweep that hair back and put his lips there, feel her pulse beneath his mouth. Taste it.

"Do you need a moment?" Dash asked, laughter in his voice.

"*Explain*." The single word came from his father and was delivered with calm but powerful authority, effectively silencing the rest of the room.

Ethan straightened and looked up, hoping his expression didn't reveal just how spun-out he felt. "This is Lark DeWynter," he said. "Author of—"

"*The Christmas Lie*," his mother finished, her gaze sweeping back over Lark's sleeping form. Her lips curled. "I didn't recognize her with her mouth closed."

A titter of laughter sounded through the room and Taryn turned her head to hide her smile.

"Ah," his father said, as though that were reason enough. "So you have the situation under control. Excellent."

Belle's eyes widened and she turned to her father. "You think this is under control?" she asked, her voice climbing. "He's brought our most vocal enemy *here*. Into our *home*." Her gaze swung back to Ethan. "Have you lost your mind? Inhaled too many paint fumes in your studio?"

Ethan resisted the urge to slap a Mute charm on his sister, but that would undoubtedly result in a magick war— and they'd certainly had their share of those, some of them especially epic—which might give him momentary satisfaction, but which would not solve the issue at hand.

"Why did you bring her here?" Cole wanted to know. Unlike Belle, his older brother wasn't questioning his judgment, but was merely looking to gather facts.

"Because she's got a slot on the *Ophelia Winslow Show* on Friday and I had to stop her."

A beat of shocked silence sucked the air out of the room before Cole gave his head a small shake. "No, no, that's not what I meant. Logic demanded that you'd have proper motivation for such drastic action—and the *Ophelia Winslow Show* is certainly that," he added grimly. "I mean why did you bring her *here*? To the house? Instead of putting her up at the Nutcracker Inn, or arranging for one of the Sugarplum cottages on Holly Lake? Belle's right," he said, glancing at their sister, who nodded triumphantly. "Bringing her here increases our risk of exposure."

"It was ignorant," Dash chimed in, blunt as always. Why use five words when three would do?

"I can't afford to let her out of my sight," Ethan improvised, thankful that his reasoning sounded believable.

The truth was it had never occurred to him to bring her anywhere but here. It had never entered his head to arrange for a suite at the Inn, or one of the gingerbread house replica cottages on the lake. The image of her like this—spread out on his bed, that gorgeous hair spilling over one of his pillows—had haunted him for so long that he hadn't considered an alternative at all.

Which in retrospect was—as Dash had so succinctly put it—ignorant.

Cocoa or not, it was a risk he shouldn't have taken. He could have just as easily taken a room alongside her at the Inn—the cottage scenario would have been more difficult—or assigned an elf to follow her. His gaze slid to Lark, who'd snuggled deeper into his mattress, and something shifted in his suddenly too-tight chest.

"Of course he couldn't have taken her anywhere but here," his mother said briskly, shooting Dash a scolding look. "And I don't appreciate any of you questioning his judgment on this matter. You should be ashamed of yourselves. While I'm sure the rest of us have things we don't like about our roles within the company—"

"Here, here," Dash grunted, shoving his hair out of his face. "Nothing sexy about shoveling reindeer shit."

"If I have to deal with one more disgruntled elf, I'm moving to Holland," Belle announced with grim determination.

"The eyestrain I deal with on a day-to-day basis is hardly a cakewalk," Cole muttered.

Taryn glanced at Belle and lifted an intrigued brow. "Why Holland?"

Belle smiled. "Because that's where the tallest people in the world live."

Taryn returned her grin.

"Be all of that as it may," their mother went on determinedly. "Do any of you want to trade positions with Ethan? Be the official always-smiling-even-when-he-doesn't-want-to face of the company? Make sure the Christmas cheer stays high enough to maintain the magick? Without it Christmas isn't the only thing that disappears, you know. So does our way of life. Our very purpose. Can you imagine the responsibility? The pressure he's under *every year* to make sure our family doesn't fail?"

Belle's expression had turned thoughtful and Dash's easy grin had flatlined, leaving him unnaturally somber. Both Taryn and Cole were looking at him as though seeing him for the first time, as if he were some sort of science project under a microscope.

His father merely smiled, indicating this was a conversation he and Ethan's mother had had before.

"And this year, in particular," his mother went on with a significant eye roll. "Merry and Kris are in the throes of a marital crisis. Have you seen her lately?" she asked Ethan's father as an aside. "She's wearing hot pink lipstick and enough eyeliner to make a drag queen jealous. It's unseemly."

"That's nothing," Cole interjected. "Kris has dyed his hair black and shaved his beard."

"And bought a new Harley," Dash added. "I saw him on Yuletide Drive this morning. No helmet, by the way."

His mother inhaled sharply. "*Santa is breaking the law?*" She shook her head. "This is much worse than I thought," she said. She glanced at her husband. "You're going to have to talk to him."

His father shrugged helplessly. "I've tried."

"You'll have to try again. We can't have a...a *rogue* Santa," she finished.

Cole stroked his jaw. "Strictly speaking, it's Belle's job, correct?"

Belle glared at him. "Way to throw me under the bus, big brother. Appreciate it."

"Back to the issue at hand," his mother continued doggedly, her patience clearly wearing thin. "Ethan has this under control. I am confident in his ability and his judgment in this matter." She leveled a look at his brothers and sister. "Be grateful that the weight of this responsibility is on his shoulders and not your own and offer assistance as needed." She swept forward and kissed him on the cheek. "If I can do anything to help, just let me know."

"Me, too, son," his father added, and then the pair of them exited the room.

"You've always been her favorite," Belle grumbled. She looked up. "But she's right. I wouldn't want your job. Give me an unhappy elf any day over the continuing survival of Christmas and our legacy."

Dash grinned. "I'll keep my shovel, thanks. Least I can bitch and moan when the mood strikes."

Cole slung an arm over Taryn's shoulder and shrugged. "I like my job. We're here if you need us."

He knew, but he appreciated the sentiment. "Thanks."

"Me, too," Dash said. "Not sure what I could do, but if you need to keep her occupied, then a tour of the farm would probably be nice. Tourists love it, and Rudolph has really been putting on a show." He frowned thoughtfully. "Getting a bit of an ego, actually. I think having a fan club might have gone to his head." He slapped Ethan on the shoulder, and then with one last look at Lark, he shook his head and walked away, leaving just Belle.

"So...what's your plan?" she asked. "Aside from cocoa?

I mean, I'm assuming since you hit her with a Sleeping Beauty charm she's not here of her own volition."

"No, she's not."

Belle frowned. "Eek."

"In my defense I asked her to visit first, but she said no. Had she been cooperative I wouldn't have had to..." He struggled to find the right word.

"Abduct her," Belle supplied.

"*Contain* her," Ethan improvised. "I can't let her go on that show, Belle. I can't do a rebuttal and with the success of the book, I'm already working twice as hard as I did last year. If Ophelia takes up her cause..." He shrugged. "I don't know that I can do enough damage control to save Christmas."

She nudged him admonishingly. "Why didn't you say something?"

"It's my job."

"You make it look easy."

He chuckled darkly and passed a hand over his face. "It's not."

Belle's gaze slid to Lark. "And it's her fault? This book she's written?"

"It's called *The Christmas Lie*, and she believes it, Belle. She's not a nut or a fanatic. Other than her penchant for trying to ruin Christmas and by default my life, she's actually quite nice."

His sister's gaze sharpened and then lit with an uncomfortable amount of understanding. "Oh, she is, is she?"

"Save it," he told her, annoyed with himself. "I've been arguing with her for years and I've done my homework here." He explained her history, her insistence as a child that Santa was real, that she could see ornaments move. He added that she'd even met an elf, that her family had placed her in therapy and stripped the house of any reminders of Christmas.

Belle swallowed. "Wow."

"I know."

"Yes, but how do you know? Did she tell you?"

Ethan hesitated. "Not exactly, but she alluded to enough of it in interviews and in her book that I was able to put the pieces together. I slipped her former therapist a little cocoa and reviewed her case history."

His sister was thoughtful for a moment. "Do you think she was telling the truth as a child? That she could really see the magick? I mean, lots of children can see Santa, but *elves*? *Animation*? *Like us*?"

"It's rare, but it happens," he told her. "I've got to do some more research."

"What do you hope to accomplish by bringing her here?"

The question startled him. "I want to keep her off the *Ophelia Show*, obviously."

His sister merely smiled, stared at him for a long moment. "That's your objective, E, but it's not your end goal."

Ethan's heart had inexplicably started to pound and his mouth had gone bone-dry. "I don't know what you're talking about."

"Oh, I don't doubt that," she said with an infuriating little smile. "But I'm sure it will come to you." She leaned up and kissed him on the cheek. "And, oh, to be a fly on the wall when it does. I'll have Cook bring up some cocoa," she said as she turned to leave. "And Ethan?"

Still unaccountably shaken by his sister's cryptic little comment, he started. "Yes?"

"Did you bring her any clothes? Toiletries? Even a toothbrush?"

He blinked, and then he swore.

Belle grinned and shook her head. "Don't worry. I'll take care of it. I'll call Baubles and have him put some things together for her. You'll need to tell her that they're hers and pack it into some luggage."

He nodded. "Right. Yes. I'll do that."

"How long before the charm wears off?"

He winced as he thought about it. "Two, maybe three hours."

She smiled. "Then you'd better get busy."

Yes, he'd better, Ethan thought. He had to get his story straight—and the props to go along with it—if he was going to pull this off. Because cocoa or no, convincing Lark DeWynter that she was there by choice was going to be a hard sell.

And he had a lot riding on her buying it.

Chapter 6

Like a flower blossoming in the morning light, Lark awoke slowly, a feeling of contentment, of warmth and happiness, clinging to the instant smile that shaped her lips. The taste of chocolate haunted her tongue as she stretched and blinked sleepily awake...

...in a bed that wasn't hers, in a room she didn't recognize.

The carved mahogany canopied bed, draped in heavy royal-blue velvet, was something straight out of a fairy tale, and the room was equally opulent. A barreled ceiling gave way to watered silk, and heavy wooden paneling covered the walls. An enormous oriental rug—probably Aubusson—lay spread invitingly over the floor. Candlelight danced in sconces and firelight flickered from the massive marble fireplace against the opposite wall. The room was furnished with lots of beautiful antiques and comfortable, squashy chairs. It was gorgeous and masculine, and it had a lived-in feel. There were books and reading glasses on the table next to the window, a green silk tie slung over the arm of a chair. Wait a minute. She recognized that tie. It belonged to a man with eyes of the same color, and...

Lark sucked in a breath as she scrambled into a sitting position.

"Ah, you're awake," a familiar voice drawled.

Her gaze swung to the foot of the canopied bed. Ethan sat in one of the chairs flanking the massive carved fireplace—how in the hell had she missed him?—his feet propped up on a footstool, a cut-crystal tumbler of golden liquid in his hand. He wore a pair of jeans, a dark gray cable-knit sweater and an equally thick pair of gray socks on his feet. There was something about seeing him without shoes—or hell, even in jeans—that made her feel acutely off-balance.

He was formidable enough in a Tom Ford suit, but in casual wear? In what was obviously *his* room, in *his* house— which meant this had to be *his* bed—he was positively lethal.

And if this was indeed all of those things—his room, his house, his bed—then that meant she was in Colorado… and she had absolutely no recollection of getting there.

Lark frowned and gave her head a little shake. She had so many questions she didn't know which one to ask first. Her memory was muddled and fuzzy, and what should have been obvious answers hovered just out of reach.

"Um… How did I get here?"

Ethan grinned. "We flew," he said. "Honestly, Lark, I knew you'd had a little too much to drink, but I didn't think you'd had enough to forget a cross-country flight." He lifted a brow. "Do you want to shower before dinner? We've got reservations at eight."

Too much to drink? At the bar? But she remembered leaving the bar and heading to the airport. And after? She wracked her brain as she struggled to remember.

He stood and made his way over to her, lifted a pretty silver cup from the bedside table and handed it to her.

"Here," he said. "My mother is a firm believer in cocoa and says there's nothing a little of it can't fix."

Lark unthinkingly accepted the drink and took a sip, still desperately trying to make sense of things. Oddly enough, she wasn't afraid or even terribly alarmed, but she felt like she should have been. It was weird…and, *oh sweet heavens*, this was the *best* cocoa she'd ever had in her life. It was creamy and rich—positively decadent. An immediate warmth spread through her limbs when it hit her belly.

"Mmm," she said. "This is good."

"I'm so glad you agreed to come out here with me," Ethan told her. "It was the honorable thing to do, all things considered."

She opened her mouth to argue, but the words instantly died in her throat. Truthfully, she didn't remember agreeing to come out here with him, but since she was here and she never did anything she didn't want to do, it only stood to reason that she had. Right? Right.

"Honorable?" She took another sip of cocoa.

"You know. Since I'm not going to get a rebuttal on the *Ophelia Winslow Show*, you thought it would be good for you to at least see my world and my town before launching your agenda from a platform that doesn't offer a quid pro quo." He smiled sincerely. "That was very fair of you. I appreciate it."

Once again the instinct to argue arose, but it died a swift death and she nodded. It *was* good of her. And it *was* fair. But…it didn't exactly feel right and, more importantly, it didn't explain how she'd gotten into his bed.

"Erm…"

Seemingly anticipating her question, he smiled again, this time a little sheepishly. "You passed out," he said. "I've never seen you drink that much. You were 'celebrating,'" he added with a significant look. "I had to carry you from the plane to the car, and then carry you into the house. I suppose I could have gone a few extra steps into the next room—" he jerked his head toward a door across the room "—but it was just easier to put you here."

Lark's cheeks burned. He'd had to *carry* her? *Really?* Rather than being alarmed that she'd ingested enough alcohol to incapacitate and give her memory loss, irrationally, she was more irritated over not being able to remember *that* part. Being carried. By him. In those mouthwateringly powerful arms. Her mouth close to his neck.

Need licked through her veins, making her aware of the mattress beneath her and Ethan's exceedingly close proximity.

His eyes suddenly darkened and dropped to her mouth. "Unless you intend to stay in here, you need to stop looking at me like that, Chickadee."

She blinked, feeling her face warm even more. With effort, she swung her legs over the side of the bed and stood, forcing him to retreat a step. "My room is through there, you say?" she asked, pointing toward the closed door.

"It is. Because it was a spur-of-the-moment trip, my sister, Belle, arranged to have some clothes and toiletries delivered. If there's anything else you need, or if something doesn't fit correctly, let me know and I'll take care of it."

She blinked again, startled that she'd done something so out of character, something that had required someone else to think of her clothes and toiletries. Lark was an obsessive planner. She lived by her calendar. In fact, she'd gotten pretty anal about it, actually keeping track of her time to the point last year that she could graph it out and look at exactly how much time she'd spent working, sleeping, socializing—the woefully smallest sliver of the pie chart—and everything that fell in between. She couldn't decide if that was efficient or pathetic. Probably both.

"Thank you," she said, feeling even more at sea. "And thank your sister for me, too."

Another grin dimpled his cheek. "Oh, you'll be able to tell her yourself. I'm sure you'll see her around."

"Around where?"

"Here," he said, as though it should be obvious. "She lives here. Like I do. Like my whole family does."

Surprise rippled through her. "You live with your family?"

"Yes. We've each got our own set of rooms, of course—" he gestured to his "—but we're a tight-knit family, and the house is big enough to accommodate us all, so…" He shrugged. "It's nice."

Wow. She never saw her family. Her older brother had been resentful of her for ruining Christmas, and her parents had decided to homestead in Alaska right after she left for college. So much for going home for the summer. Though she'd occasionally gone to visit them over the years, they seemed entirely too nervous with her around for her to ever feel at ease. It saddened her to think about it, and she envied Ethan his close-knit family.

"You should wear the dress," he said, startling her.

"What?"

"To dinner. We're going to the Crystal Snowflake. It's nice. I think you'll like it."

She was sure she would, but she'd pick out her own clothes out of the clothes she hadn't picked out, thank you. She lifted her chin. "I think I know how to dress myself, Ethan."

His smile widened and those gorgeous bright green eyes twinkled with humor. "I'm sure you do."

Lark nodded and took another sip of her cocoa. She was strangely at peace, completely unconcerned about everything, including the fact that she'd journeyed to Colorado to stay with Ethan out of the goodness of her heart and in fairness to her upcoming visit on the *Ophelia Winslow Show.*

And though, deep down, it felt a bit out of character, Lark was certain it wasn't. And anyway, the cocoa was divine…

Though Ethan knew he was doing the right thing for his family and for everyone who enjoyed the magic of Christmas, he couldn't shake the guilt. Watching the cocoa work its magic and override that stubborn, bull-headed, opinionated woman's natural objections and tendencies had been as comical as it was…wrong.

But he didn't know what else to do. He absolutely *couldn't* let her go on that show.

The greater good, he reminded himself. Eyes on the prize.

Lark chose that moment to walk through the door and that last thought took on a whole new meaning.

Mercy.

"You decided to wear the dress."

Her lips curved. "How could I not? It's incredible. Your sister has excellent taste."

That she did. A deep purple, the dress was scoop-necked, with long sheer sleeves accented with crystal-studded cuffs. It hugged her curvy frame like a second skin, molding to the luscious swell of her breasts and clinging to her womanly hips. The hem stopped just above the knee—it was long enough to be appropriate, but short enough to reveal a serious amount of leg. She had paired it with black pumps and a matching bag, and with her hair hanging loose around her shoulders and her make-up a little more dramatic than usual, she looked…stunning.

Prior to her arrival, Ethan had been practically starving, but a hunger of another sort suddenly took hold of him. Longing coiled through his body, settling hotly in his groin, and his mouth actually ached for the taste of her. He wanted to slide his nose along the creamy column of her throat, slip his tongue over the swell of her breasts, sample the valley in between them. It took a supreme amount of effort to pull himself together and say something that sounded somewhat normal.

"You look beautiful," he said, his voice oddly rusty.

Those unusual violet eyes warmed and shifted away, almost shyly. Her? Shy? Had she gotten into more cocoa?

"Thank you." She nodded at him. "You look nice as well."

He chuckled. "This old thing?"

She rolled her eyes. "Old, my rear end," she scoffed. "The only thing that seems the least bit old around here is the furnishing, and in that case, it's a good thing."

"I like antiques," he said. "They've got character."

She nodded. "And better craftsmanship. I've got a few as well."

He'd just bet she did. He hummed thoughtfully under his breath and considered her. "I've often wondered about your lair," he said musingly.

Lark laughed, her eyes widening briefly. "My lair? You make me sound like a comic book villain."

"Well, I've never pictured you in a bat cave, if that helps," he said, chuckling. "More of a secret tree house, with a hidden elevator in the trunk."

She chewed the inside of her cheek. "Like a nest."

Ethan felt his grin spread. "Exactly like a nest."

She released a little breath. "I wish my parents had named me something simple, like Jane or Sarah," she said, giving her head a rueful shake.

"No, you don't," he told her. "You're neither of those. The bird name suits you. I like it." A thought struck him. "What's your middle name?"

"Lark is my middle name," she said a little too quickly. "Shouldn't we be going? You said our reservation was at eight." She checked her watch. "It's a quarter til now.

How long does it take to get to the Crystal Snowflake?" she asked rapidly as she headed out the door, despite the fact that she had no idea how to locate the car, or the restaurant, or hell, even the front door.

Intrigued by her cat-on-a-hot-tin-roof response, Ethan followed her into the hall, where she drew up short. "Oh."

One direction must have looked the same as the other to her. Ethan smiled and guided her forward with a touch to the small of her back. "It's not nearly as daunting as it looks. This way," he said.

"It's…massive."

"I told you that my entire family lives here. There are too many of us to have any smaller of a place. We'd drive each other crazy. Still do sometimes," he added with a grim smile, remembering how they'd followed him upstairs earlier. "But the central staircase is just up and to the right. See?" he told her as they rounded the corner.

He heard her delighted gasp and felt a dart of pleasure land in his chest. It was his home, but it was impressive.

Particularly the central staircase.

Carpeted in thick jewel-toned colors with the Evergreen coat of arms cameoed throughout, bounded by rails and spindles intricately carved with garlands, pine cones and bows, the staircase was a testament to fine elfish craftsmanship. Creamy marble inlaid with subtle wreaths of holly leaves and berries blanketed the foyer floor and the enormous arched double doors matched the exquisite carving on the staircase.

"Wow," she said, running a reverent finger along the banister as they descended the stairs. "This is incredible."

Just wait until you see Mistletoe Mountain and Gingerbread proper, Ethan thought. Rather than use one of the elf tunnels that led directly to different parts of the town—their own magical subway system—as he normally did, Ethan had called for his car. To get the full effect of his little piece of earth, one needed to be aboveground. He was looking forward to seeing Lark's reaction to it.

"Thank you," he murmured. "So what's your first name then?"

She snatched her hand away as though she'd been burned. "I'd rather not say."

Ethan smiled. "I'd rather you did. Your reluctance is intriguing. It must be something ghastly if you're this determined not to share it." He paused. "Is it another bird name, I wonder? Like Falcon?"

She shot him a you've-lost-your-mind look. "Falcon Lark? Really? That's your best guess?"

"Not my best guess, just my first," he told her as he opened the front door. "And I've got the rest of the week to keep trying."

It was ridiculous how happy that made him, the excitement that tripped through his blood. He had a sense that something fantastic was near, but was still hovering just shy of his grasp.

It was the challenge, Ethan told himself. Nothing more. It was his determination to succeed.

And if he made a Christmas convert of her and finally managed to take her to bed and get her out of his system, all the better. He smiled.

Two Larks with one stone.

Chapter 7

With the "rest of the week" comment echoing in her ears and the faint hum of an alarm bell ringing along with it, Lark stepped through the huge double doors. If she'd been impressed by the house, then "blown away" was a more accurate description for the view that greeted her outside.

It looked like a scene straight from a greeting card.

Moonlight glittered with a luminous, almost other-worldly blue glow over rolling hills blanketed with snow. Enormous spruce trees, equally covered, their branches sagging beneath the weight, cast dark shadows in the night. Swans glided across a large lake, its center illuminated by a tall carved-ice fountain shaped like an angel tree topper, and twinkling lights from what had to be Gingerbread shimmered in the valley below like diamonds on a jeweler's cloth. She smiled, charmed despite herself.

"That's incredible," she said, giving her head a disbelieving shake.

"What? Hortense?"

"The fountain."

"Yes, Hortense. My brother Dash named her this year."

They descended the steps to what she presumed was his

car, a sleek black Jaguar that suited him, and she waited while he opened her door. "So it's a tradition, then?"

"Yes."

She missed traditions. She'd established her own, of course—she always worked at the local soup kitchen on Christmas Day—but it wasn't the same as having one with a family. Though she'd tried to forget, she remembered that much about their early Christmases. Decorating the tree, making cookies for Santa the night before, eating a big pancake breakfast after opening presents. A needle of pain pricked her heart at the memory. She hadn't allowed herself to think about that in years.

"I named her last year," Ethan announced as he slid behind the wheel and turned the ignition, and then slipped the gear shift into drive.

"Oh?" she asked, thankful for the distraction.

"Yes."

"So who was she last year?" Lark asked. "Trixie? Tiffany? Celeste?" she drawled, immediately wishing she could pull the words back into her mouth.

He turned briefly to look at her, his expression a combination of surprise and delight. "None of the above, though I think it's sweet that you've been paying enough attention to my social life to read about the dates I take to charity events."

Crap. She feigned shock. "Those are the names of the women you've dated? Really? Wow. I had no idea."

He merely smiled. "Right. I'm sure you didn't."

"So what was her name then? The fountain angel?" she asked, eager to move past *that* particular topic.

He negotiated a bend in the road, one that left an unobstructed view of the little town as they grew closer. The lights were brighter and the colors more vibrant, and she found herself inexplicably leaning forward, eager to see more.

"Flossie."

A startled chuckle broke up in her throat and she turned to look at him. "Flossie?"

"Yes, Flossie," he said with a nod. "What's wrong with Flossie?"

"Not a thing." Lark looked ahead once more, surprised to see that they were just coming into town. Wide side-walks lit by candy cane–like gas lamp posts lined a street called Yuletide Drive, and live evergreen garlands fes-tooned with big bows and curling ribbon were draped from posts, storefronts and even the grills of local cars. Christmas lights spun around trees, dripped from eaves and sparkled in windows. Life-sized nutcrackers marched along the streets, small people dressed as elves darted to and fro, looking busy and important and Christmas orna-ments dangled from…*everything*.

An overwhelming wave of joy suddenly swept through her, followed by a delight so profound she could feel it ex-panding in her chest. It was the strangest sensation, a com-bination of relief and odder still…homecoming? There was a familiar shimmer to the ornaments, a certain glow and, as they passed a pair of tall wooden toy soldiers stationed outside a store called Baubles, she could have sworn that one of them actually smiled at her.

But it couldn't have. Because it wasn't a real person. *Logic, Lark,* she reminded herself, struggling not to panic. *Use your brain.* What was she doing here again? Why had she agreed to come here with him? It didn't make any sense. "Is something wrong?" Ethan asked, his voice heavy with concern.

She started. "No, no. I'm fine. Just hungry," she im-provised.

She could feel his gaze on her, the weight of it as he studied her, but thankfully he didn't push it. "Well, we've come to the right place, then," he said as he pulled the car into a space. "You're going to love the Crystal Snowflake. It's got the *best* cocoa in Gingerbread."

Lark chuckled. Unless it was laced with something alcoholic, she didn't think plain old cocoa was going to take the edge off. Between Ethan's perpetual sexiness pinging her sonar, the conflicting emotions about being here in Christmas Land and the niggling sense of something being not quite right, she was going to need something much stronger.

Ethan's fingers suddenly landed against her chin, turning her toward him, and his mouth met hers for the briefest of seconds, sending shockwaves of heat through her body. Her blood instantly boiled up beneath her skin, her breath caught in her throat and pleasure bloomed through her, petals of sensation so intensely hot and sweet she didn't know whether to kiss him again or weep. Probably both.

Lord, she was a mess—an absolute mess—and it was all *his* fault.

Seeming every bit as startled as she felt, he drew back to look at her, those singularly gorgeous green eyes lacking their usual irreverence and bravado. "I'd say I was sorry, but it would be a lie," he told her, his voice low and husky. "I've wanted to do that for years."

And she'd wanted him to do that for years. Lark knew that under ordinary circumstances she'd offer some sort of flippant remark, one that would be witty and slightly cutting, but for reasons that escaped her, the comment wouldn't come.

She swallowed, her gaze drifting of its own volition to his mouth. Her belly gave a little drop and longing ballooned inside of her. "Years, you say? Really?"

He nodded.

She hummed a regretful breath. "Seems like you'd have given it a little more effort, then. Maybe lingered a little—"

The smile that suddenly curled his lips did the same

thing to her toes, and he leaned in, a mere hairbreadth from her mouth. "Critiquing me, Chickadee?" he asked, his strong fingers slipping into her hair. "You telling me there's room for improvement?"

A thrill whipped through her. "I'm not sure yet. It didn't last long enough for me to make a proper assessment."

"Hmm. I understand. I'll give it another go and you let me know how I do, okay?"

The next instant that supremely beautiful mouth molded to hers, slipped across her lips with expert skill—soft but firm and oh so hot—and his tongue dipped into her mouth and tangled around hers. The rest of the world just fell away, shrinking until there was nothing left but the two of them and a fog of desire so thick she could barely catch her breath.

A few moments later, hands trembling, Ethan drew back and rested his forehead against hers. "Well?" he asked, his voice slightly strangled. "How did I do?"

How'd he do? He'd practically set her underwear on fire and turned her into a melted puddle of goo. Parts of her were aching that she didn't know could ache, bits of her body were shaking that had never shaken before. And he had the presence of mind to ask for marks on his performance when she could barely string a coherent thought together?

Considering all of that, *she* was probably the one who had room for improvement.

Lark pulled in a breath and pretended to mull it over. "Better," she said. "Definitely better."

Ethan chuckled. "Hardly the ringing endorsement I'd hoped for," he said. "But I'm eager to improve and you know what they say about practice."

Yes, she did. And, heaven help her, she looked forward to working on his technique.

Chapter 8

"So you're giving her the guided tour this morning, eh, son? What's first on the agenda?" his father wanted to know.

"You should take her to the Cup of Cheer," Belle said, slathering jam on her biscuit. "They have the *best* peppermint cocoa," she confided with a look at Lark.

"You can get good cocoa anywhere in Gingerbread," Dash argued good-naturedly. He loaded a stack of bacon on his plate before passing the platter to Cole. "Don't waste your time there. Bring her out to the reindeer farm. They're beautiful animals. Very sweet. Most of the time," he added grimly. "That Rudolf..."

"Still having trouble with him?" their mother wanted to know. "I warned you about that fan club, but did you listen?" She shook her head.

Having paid attention to the Evergreen family chatter for the past few minutes, Lark's eyes widened. "Rudolf has a fan club?"

"He does," his mother confirmed, adding sugar to her cocoa. "And it's gone straight to his head. You wouldn't think fame could go to an animal's head, but it has." She tsked under her breath. "I don't know what you're going to do with him. But the deer is out of the barn now. It's too late to close the door."

"I've got it under control," Dash assured her.

"You should bring her to the offices," Cole suggested. "Show her Evergreen Central."

"Or," Taryn interjected with a secret smile, "you could actually *ask* her what she'd like to do and let her make the choice."

Every pair of eyes at the table swung to Lark and waited expectantly. Her cocoa cup halfway to her mouth, her hand stalled. "Er…"

Ethan decided to save her. "She's my guest," he reminded them. "I have every intention of making sure that she stays entertained."

And if kissing her counted as entertaining her—and since this was his rodeo and he was making up the rules, it did—then he was already ahead by leaps and bounds. It had taken every iota of willpower he possessed to actually let her go through to her own room last night. And honestly, even now he couldn't explain why he'd done it. Why, when she was *right there* and for all intents and purposes, his for the taking…he'd let the evening end with a kiss.

He'd never thought of himself as particularly old-fashioned or chivalrous, but that was the only explanation his mind could produce that made any sort of sense. Watching her as they'd driven into town last night—seeing her expression go from awestruck wonder and delight to abject fear and despair, seemingly in a heartbeat… He couldn't imagine what she'd witnessed that could have put that haunting look on her face, but it had done something to him, seeing her that way. She was scrappy, a fighter. The Lark DeWynter he knew didn't back down, didn't run, but she would have last night if it hadn't been for the cocoa.

He was sure of it.

And that was ultimately the problem. He'd tricked her into coming here. For good reasons, he knew, but…

He couldn't trick her into his bed.

That was a different kind of betrayal, one he suspected would again put that terrible look he'd noticed on her beautiful face last night. He wouldn't be able to handle it, knowing he'd hurt her like that.

So he wouldn't. And that would be his penance. Not having her, when everything inside of him yearned with a need so powerful and magnetic that he literally *ached* with it. His gaze slid to her, over the lovely slope of her cheek, the upturned corner of her ripe mouth, and his groin tightened painfully, his chest squeezing with some peculiar emotion.

Fair enough, Ethan decided. Fair enough.

Having been to the Cup of Cheer for the peppermint cocoa—Belle had been right, it was divine—and out to tour the reindeer farm (where she thought she'd seen Rudolf's nose blink a few times, and yes, the animal had definitely developed a bit of an ego) Lark was presently strolling around Ethan's studio, which was housed on the very top floor of Evergreen enterprises.

It was not at all what she'd expected.

In the first place, it was a tall, sleek metal-and-glass building. One would assume it would be outfitted with commercial-grade carpet, serviceable paint, efficient work stations and low-tiled ceilings.

But, no.

Much like the rest of the village, the interior was more in keeping with a Swiss village motif. Lots of rich paneling, oriental rugs, framed portraits of Santa and Christmas scenes and, though she was trying to avoid stereotyping, there were lots of little people, some of them dressed in business casual, some of them dressed more like elves.

Everyone wore interesting badges with their clearance level—Ethan's was gold, which indicated he had executive clearance—and everyone seemed extraordinarily busy and happy.

She stopped at a few sketches of birds—chickadees, doves, red and blue birds—and turned to look at him. "Is this what you're thinking about for next year?"

In the process of inspecting a new batch of ornaments—quality control, he'd explained—he looked up and smiled. "Ah, yes," he told her. "Do you like them?"

She hesitated. "I do."

He stilled. "You do, but?" he prodded. "I know there's a but. I heard it in your voice."

Of course he had. He heard everything, whether she said it or not. It was unnerving. Less so than normal, which she somehow knew but couldn't explain. Sitting beside him at breakfast this morning, sharing the first meal of the day with all of them and listening to them good-naturedly rib each other, talk about their plans for the day...

Something about it had made him *more* than the Ethan she knew. She was familiar with the rich, sexy executive, the one who argued with her, goaded and teased her, enflamed her. But he was so much more than that. He was part of something huge, a centuries-old heritage.

And he *did* have parents, she thought with an inward chuckle, and brothers and a sister, and they were all part of a team, one that was at odds with her own pitiful team of one. Somehow being here made her feel not necessarily less committed to her cause, but almost petty for clinging so tightly to it.

Though she was exceedingly reluctant to admit it, he'd been right about her visiting his little town, meeting his family, seeing just exactly what it was they all stood to lose when she went on the *Ophelia Winslow Show* on Friday. She was glad she'd done the right thing by coming here.

She couldn't say that it had changed her position—though seeing that toy soldier wink at her had certainly rattled her last night, and there'd been a couple of instances already this morning that had made her question her eyesight—but it had certainly given her a more well-rounded perspective.

Kissing him, she told herself, had absolutely nothing to do with it. *Nothing,* she thought more forcefully, remembered heat snaking through her limbs. Nothing, nothing, nothing. She wasn't that shallow. She couldn't be. She wouldn't let herself be.

Not that he seemed inclined to do anything more than kiss her anyway, which had been both surprising and disappointing. He'd been flirting with her for years, priming her for what she could only imagine would be the best sex of her life and last night, when he could have pressed his advantage—hell, his bed had been *right* there—he hadn't. And after that kiss…

It had been quite…irritating.

Granted she wasn't exactly an expert on all things sexual, but she could generally discern when a man was attracted to her and that magnificent bulge against her belly last night when he'd given her a final farewell kiss, well… It had been pretty telling. She didn't know why he hadn't—

"Lark?" he prodded. "You all right?"

She blinked, momentarily startled. "Yes, just gathering my thoughts."

He rested a hip against the table. "Are you going to tell me what it is that you don't like about the birds?"

"Oh, they're beautiful," she said. "And it's not that I don't like them—I do." She struggled to find the words for what she was feeling. "It's just…I don't know. There's something different about them. They don't have that whimsical feel that all of your other designs have." She went to the case where all of his designs were displayed. "For instance, look at this teddy bear—there's a sparkle in his eye. And this nutcracker? There's something about his smile. He looks like he's in on a joke I'm not aware of." She moved farther down the case. "And this—" She stopped short.

Ethan frowned and followed her gaze. "Oh, that's Frosty," he said, smiling, as he moved to stand beside her. "He was my first ornament."

She reached out almost reverently and slid a finger over him. "I called him Mr. Cool," she said softly.

She'd called him—but— Ethan's heart skipped a beat. There'd only been a few hundred produced, nothing compared to his designs now, and she'd had one? "You had my Frosty?"

Her lips faltered with a smile. "Have him," she corrected. "I rescued him from the garbage bin after my parents purged our house the last year we celebrated Christmas." She turned to look at him. "I've never told you that, have I? I mean, you know enough about my past to put things together—you're clever, after all—but that's what happened. I really *believed*, Ethan. My delusions were so detailed, so real, that I believed I talked to Santa, and his elf Edgar," she added with a rueful laugh. "I believed so deeply that my Mr. Cool even changed his clothes—his scarf would have holly berries one minute and snowflakes the next. I'd see toy soldiers wink, nutcrackers smile, angel wings flutter."

So he'd been right, Ethan thought, her confession tearing at him. She *could* see the magic.

And no one had believed *her*.

She lifted her shoulders in a fatalistic shrug. "I don't blame my parents," she said. "It's no wonder they thought I was crazy. Hell, there are still times when I'll catch a glimpse of something and think I'm crazy."

A *glimpse*, Ethan thought, his brain seizing on the word.

That's what she was. A glimpse. One of those rare, rare children who could see the Christmas magick.

And, more importantly, could *still* see it.

That's what was missing from the birds. They were merely drawings at this stage, hadn't been enchanted with the magick. And that's no doubt what had happened last night. She'd caught sight of something and had immediately panicked, thinking she was experiencing a delusion.

His heart ached for her and he instinctively put an arm around her, pulling her close. How terrible it must have been to be so sure of your own mind, your own eyes, only to have the world convince you otherwise. Even your own parents. No wonder she'd fought as hard as she had. No wonder she was so passionate about her cause.

She relaxed into him, seemingly grateful for the support. "I'm so sorry, Lark," he said. "I—"

Her cell suddenly went off and she shifted away, almost guiltily, and pulled it from her purse. "It's Lisa," she said, reading the display.

Lisa? Oh, hell.

"Hey, Leese," she said. "What's up?"

Ethan turned and discreetly muttered a few choice words under his breath.

Lark suddenly frowned. "Lisa? I can't hear you. We've got a bad connection. Must be the building. I'll give you a call back in a few minutes."

Oh no, you won't, Ethan thought. "Come on," he said. "We'll go downstairs and grab some cocoa and a cinnamon roll, and have a mini picnic by the lake."

She smiled. "Thanks, Ethan. That would be great."

He nodded and returned her grin. He had turned to leave when she stilled him with a touch of her hand. "And thanks for listening a few minutes ago," she said sheepishly. "And for not making fun. I appreciate it."

"Anytime," he said, his throat suddenly getting tight.

He'd been on the verge of telling her the truth—that she hadn't been crazy or delusional, that she'd been right. A cardinal sin among their kind.

Protect the secret.

And yet, for the first time in his life, he deeply resented that edict. She deserved to know the truth—to know that she was special, not damaged. And yet he couldn't tell her.

Because what if she didn't believe him? What if she decided he was the one who was delusional and it only reinforced her own position in her own mind? There were too many what-ifs, too many things that could spell disaster for his family.

And while he could argue that he could tell her now, give her that peace of mind for however brief a moment and then hand her the cocoa, wouldn't that be crueler? To fully open her eyes to the magick and then take it back? Ethan swallowed.

He'd be no better than everyone else who hadn't believed her.

He couldn't do it.

And honestly, at this point, he didn't have a frigging clue what he was going to do, other than spend as much time with her as possible, show her his world…and keep his hands to himself.

Chapter 9

"That was *amazing*," Lark said, feeling the rush of excitement and the burn of adrenaline tripping through her veins as she climbed off the back of the snowmobile. "Absolutely incredible."

In the process of dusting the snow off the front of his pants, he looked up and shot her a smile. "I'm glad you liked it. I told you you would."

"Yes, you did. You were right," she said. "Feel better?"

He nodded, the wretch. "Yes, I do, actually. You'll have to come back soon and I'll teach you how to drive."

A bubble of sadness burst inside her at the thought of leaving the next morning. The past few days had been so unbelievably bizarre. She'd spent practically every minute with Ethan, which had been a combination of fantastic and torturous. Or as she liked to call it…

Her own personal hell.

She'd known deep down that there'd always been something special about him—aside from the off-the-charts attractiveness—but seeing him in his element, watching him in his studio and at his family home… He was a genuinely great guy. He had a wonderful sense of humor; he was an excellent conversationalist; he was witty and clever and, as she'd learned recently, he had more willpower than anyone she'd ever met.

She knew he wanted her—*she c*ould feel it when he looked at her, when those startlingly green eyes raked over her body. She could feel his longing in her damned bones. But despite the fact that she'd all but crawled into bed with him, he'd very politely—and regretfully—kissed her good night at her bedroom door.

And that had been all.

For the life of her she couldn't understand it. It didn't make the least bit of sense. They were both adults, both consenting and, after tomorrow when her *Ophelia Winslow Show* aired live, it was entirely possible they'd no longer be friends. Or even frenemies, as they'd been up to that point.

Which, of course, depended on what she said when she actually went on the *Ophelia Winslow Show,* and the truth was…she was no longer sure what that was going to be. Everyone's perception was their own reality. And the Evergreens? Christmas tradition, Christmas spirit…it was their way of life. It was the only way they knew. And the town, with Baubles and Cup of Cheer and the Toy Shop and all the beautiful decorations? It was more than charming—it was *special*. She could feel that, too. The air here was different, and it seemed to shimmer and glow a little more brightly.

Oddly enough, she'd felt more at home here in the last few days than she had in Georgia, where she'd lived her whole life. And, sad as it was to admit it, she liked Ethan's family more than she did her own.

"I thought we'd eat upstairs tonight," Ethan said, opening the back door for her. A blanket of heat from the house wrapped around her and she smiled as Cook pressed a cup of cocoa into her cold hands.

"Mustn't get chilled, dear," she said.

Lark murmured her thanks, wrapped her fingers around the pretty little cup and took a sip. The rich flavor spread over her tongue and into her limbs and she sighed with pleasure. Man, she was going to miss this stuff.

"Is that okay with you?" he asked. "Dinner upstairs?"

Lark nodded. As much as she enjoyed the meals with his family, tonight she'd just as soon be alone with him. "That sounds good to me," she said.

"Great," he said, smiling at her. "Why don't we both have a shower, thaw out a little bit, and then we'll open a bottle of wine and have dinner?"

An image of his naked and body, water sluicing over supple muscle and masculine hair, suddenly materialized in her mind's eye, rendering her momentarily mute.

"Chickadee?" he prodded with a smile, as though he knew exactly what she was thinking.

Lark lifted her chin and nodded stiffly. "Sounds great." Having learned her way around the house at this point, she set off toward the door that would lead her to the central staircase.

"I'll be along in a few minutes," he called after her. "I need to talk to Belle."

All too aware of how little time she actually had left with Ethan and the Evergreens, Lark hurried upstairs and quickly showered. She took a little more time with her makeup and hair than she normally would have, and she donned a long nightgown and robe instead of actual clothes. She'd expected to find Ethan in the sitting room when she entered, but he wasn't there. Puzzled, she crossed the room and carefully nudged his door open.

"Ethan?"

Peering inside, she saw him sprawled in one of the chairs in front of the fire, his hair damp from a shower, his chest and legs bare, a mere towel fastened loosely around his waist.

And it was sagging.

He was asleep, she discovered, and something about seeing all that beautiful masculinity in vulnerable repose, gilded by firelight, made a wave of longing swell deep inside of her. Her mouth and eyes watered simultaneously, and her heart thundered in her ears.

She crept closer, unable to help herself, her feet moving quietly along the carpet.

Mercy, he is beautiful, Lark thought. High cheekbones, lashes long and obscenely curly for a man—why hadn't she ever noticed that? His dark locks were uncombed, looking as though he'd merely toweled them dry. A teensy bit of golden stubble shaded his jaw.

But ultimately, it was his mouth that did her in.

A little too full for a man, but incredibly beautiful, it was sin incarnate, wicked and carnal. Suddenly it wasn't enough to just look at it—she *needed* to taste it.

She bent low, carefully touching her mouth to his, and she knew the exact instant he awoke, because that wonderful mouth moved beneath hers, coaxing her closer, and one hand crept up and cupped her neck while the other grasped her hip and pulled her into his lap.

A shivery thrill eddied through her as she landed against him, deepening the kiss. Like butter over a hot bun, she melted over him, her soft to his hard...and mercy was he *hard.* She could feel the long, stiff length of him against her bottom and her feminine muscles clenched in response, sending a rush of dewy warmth over her folds.

Ethan suddenly drew back and pressed his forehead against hers, his expression agonized and futile. "Chickadee..." he breathed. "You're killing me."

"Yeah," she said, smiling. "But you like it."

He chuckled and kissed her. "Yes, I do."

"You know where you'd like it better?" she murmured, threading her fingers through his hair.

"Where?"

She gestured across the room, where his giant bed loomed invitingly. "On a mattress."

He chuckled again lowly, and then his eyes darkened with desire, flashed with purpose. He wrapped her up in his arms and headed for the bed. "I believe you're right."

Excitement and anticipation bubbled through her, pushing a laugh out of her throat. "I'm sorry, I didn't catch that. What did you say?" she queried lightly as her back landed against velvet and his warm body landed against hers.

"I said I believe you're ri—" He stopped, smiled darkly and drew back to look at her. "Trust you to home in on that little comment," he told her. "You like being right, don't you?"

She rocked her hips against him and arched her back, her sensitized nipples straining against her gown. "Beats the hell out of being wrong."

Ethan pressed his hot mouth against her neck, sucking the air from her lungs, and she squirmed against him, desire and desperation winding through her, making her impatient. She'd been waiting for this for *years*, had been thinking about it for *years*… She loved the feel of him beneath her hands, sleek muscle, smooth and warm and oh so wonderful. She tugged at the loose towel, tossed it aside and then palmed his length.

Ethan sucked in a startled hiss and parlayed with a long suck of her pouting nipple. He flexed against her, his slippery skin working against her palm.

"I've got a clean bill of health," he said, as he pulled the robe and gown impatiently off her body, baring her to him. "You?"

Lark bent forward and licked a path up his throat, curved around his jaw and then nipped at his earlobe. "Clean. Protected. *Now*," she said, opening herself to him.

Ethan threaded his fingers through hers, pinned her

hands over her head, and then entered her in one long, beautiful thrust.

The breath vanished from her lungs, her feminine muscles clamping tightly around him while the rest of her body went strangely limp, and every cell in her being sang with joy, with impossible recognition.

Her startled gaze met his equally shaken one and for the briefest of seconds she saw something there that made her want to weep—something so pure, so sweet and so genuine there wasn't a name for it. Affection? Yes. Love? Maybe. But it was more, too. Bigger.

And then he drew back and pushed into her again, and again and again, harder and faster, angling deep, the engorged head of his penis hitting that one elusive spot that elevated a garden-variety orgasm to something akin to a religious experience. Like a storm gathering force in the distance she could feel it swelling within her, and she welcomed the feeling.

Like a crack of lightening, she came, her entire body feeling gloriously illuminated and electrified. She sucked in a breath and couldn't let it go. Every muscle atrophied with pleasure and then let go with a soundless scream, and as the hot, sweet rain of release washed over her she knew without a doubt that she'd never be the same…

Lark DeWynter was unquestionably gorgeous.

Lark DeWynter naked beneath him, her hot, tight little body squeezing around him in a violent orgasm?

Indescribable. Beyond words.

Dark hair fanned out over his pillow, pale, creamy skin, rosy-tipped breasts absorbing the force of his thrusts, the tiny, almost heart-shaped mole beneath her jaw…

He'd been so proud of himself for resisting her the past few days, of being able to stop at a kiss when what he really wanted to do was kiss her all over, lay her out on the rug in front of the fireplace and learn every curve of her body. Every indention, every freckle, every taste.

And had she not kissed him awake—before he could put his defenses in place—and not sat in his lap, putting that delectable part of herself so close to the part of him that wanted her the most? He might have been able to keep it together.

Might being the operative word.

But she hadn't. She'd tasted like cocoa and desire, familiar yet exotic, and he'd wanted her, just wanted her. And now, as her greedy hands slid over his body, her muscles contracting around him to create a delicious draw and drag between their bodies, Ethan knew he'd *always* want her—there would be no getting her out of his system.

He'd been an idiot to think he could resist her.

She was part of him, as important as any vital organ, and the idea of her leaving in the morning, of not telling her the truth, of allowing her to continue to believe that she was delusional...

He couldn't let any of that happen. He just couldn't.

He didn't know how he was going to fix it, how he was going to make everything work out, but there had to be a way to be honest with her *and* protect his family.

But one thing was for damned sure, Ethan thought as his balls tightened and every hair on his body stood on end—a prelude to what he instinctively knew would be the best orgasm he'd ever had in his life—there was no way in hell he was going to make her drink any more magick cocoa.

Every decision she faced going forward would be made with her own mind, one that he hoped she checked with her heart first.

the effect on Ethan and his family—who she'd come to adore—and the little town of Gingerbread would be jeopardized…and she just didn't think she could do that.

In fact, she didn't just think it—she knew it.

It suddenly seemed imperative that she tell him that to put his mind at ease. She'd noted the worry in his face over the last few days, and it had tugged at her then, knowing that she was responsible for it.

Determined to find him, Lark rolled out of bed, donned her robe and made for the door to the sitting room. She'd just put her hand on the knob when she heard the low, heated murmur of voices and something made her pause and listen.

"I'm not going to do it, Belle. I can't. I just wanted to give you fair warning," Ethan said.

"Fair warning?" Belle echoed, sounding incredulous. "You call letting me know a few hours in advance that you're going to let her leave here and go and destroy our family *fair warning*? Really?" She exhaled a pent up breath. "Look, brother, I know you're in love with her— we all do—but that doesn't change the fact that you have a job and part of that job is protecting the secret. And to protect the secret, she's *got* to drink the cocoa."

Drink the cocoa? What the hell? Lark thought, her heart beginning to pound.

"Listen, I adore her," Belle went on. "I think she's great and I think any woman who can go toe-to-toe with you deserves your respect and your heart. But…she's got to drink the cocoa."

"No more," Ethan insisted. "It's been terrible watching her struggle with what she knows and what the cocoa makes her believe. I can't do it to her," he insisted. "She thinks she's crazy, Belle. *Crazy*," he emphasized. "Because she can see the magick. She's a *glimpse*," he told her. "I confirmed it with Edgar—Kris was too busy try-

Chapter 10

Pleasantly warm, with a feeling of contentment deep in her bones, Lark smiled sleepily and stretched a hand toward Ethan's side of the bed...only to find it empty. They'd skipped dinner and reached for each other repeatedly during the night, talking, dozing, and then making love again.

Goodness...

He *definitely* had the Sparkly Penis, and if this was her curse, she'd count herself lucky. He was a phenomenally attentive lover, paying particular attention to parts of her she'd never realized were sensitive. The crease of her upper thigh, the bend of her knee, hell, even the spot just above her elbow.

Though they'd avoided the subject of her leaving and her impending spot on the *Ophelia Winslow Show,* she knew they'd turned a corner, come to some sort of unspoken agreement. While she hadn't necessarily changed her opinion on lying to children about Santa Claus, Lark had to admit she'd gotten swept back up in the Christmas spirit by being in Gingerbread. But more importantly... she'd gotten swept up in Ethan Evergreen.

If Ophelia came round to her way of thinking, then

ing to decide on his tattoo to listen to me," he said, sounding exasperated. "But Edgar remembers her. Do you have any idea how hard it's been for me to know the truth and not tell her?" he asked, his voice climbing with frustration. "I can't do it to her, Belle. I won't. I'm not going to let her continue to believe she's delusional when *I* know the truth. I know she's *special*."

A glimpse? Special? See the magick? Surely she'd misunderstood. Surely she—

"Edgar remembers her?" Belle asked.

"He does," he confirmed. "But even if he hadn't, I still would have known. You should have heard her when we were in my studio. She systematically pointed out the magick in each ornament. She even knew there was something wrong with next year's collection because she *couldn't* see it. She knew." He let go of a breath. "And that's good enough for me."

"Say you tell her the truth and let her leave without altering her memory, and she thinks *you're* delusional and goes on the show. Then what? You'd risk everything? For her?"

Ethan was quiet for a moment and she could sense his anxiety, his determination, his agony. "I trust her," he said simply, bringing tears to Lark's eyes. "And I'm going to believe in her, because no one else ever has, Belle. And she belongs here. With me."

Yes, she does, Lark thought. And she was going to prove it once and for all.

It took Ethan less than ten minutes to confirm that Lark had snuck into her room from the hall, collected her things, and asked Cook to arrange for a ride into town because she wanted one last peppermint cocoa before she left. From the Cup of Cheer she'd rented a car and driven herself to the nearest airport, where she'd promptly switched her ticket out for an earlier flight and left.

Ethan was so stunned he was numb.

He couldn't imagine what would have made her sneak away like that without saying goodbye…unless she couldn't bear the thought of telling him that she was still planning to go forward with her platform on the *Ophelia Winslow Show.*

Much as he wanted to be angry at her, he couldn't, not when his own intentions—however well-motivated—were in question.

But that still didn't change his job, which was to protect his family. He wasn't going to lie to her, but at the very least he wanted to plead their case. With that thought in mind, he readied the jet and two hours later found himself in Atlanta, at the studio, where the show had already gone live.

His gaze locked with Lark's just as Ophelia finished her introduction.

"I have to tell you, Ms. DeWynter, I absolutely love Christmas. I love the presents and the food and the joy and camaraderie. I love making cookies with my kids and decorating the tree, and doing crafts. I love the scent of pine and cinnamon, the excitement that hovers in the air. The *humina humina* from a little time under the mistletoe," she added, drawing a tittering laugh from the audience. She paused dramatically. "But I have to say there are aspects of your argument that particularly resonated with me."

Oh, no, Ethan thought, his heart jumping into his throat. He wracked his brain for a solution. A mute charm? A quick power outage? A—

Lark smiled reassuringly at him, and there was something in that grin that made him pause. "There are certainly aspects of my book that I find valuable, too, Ophelia— in particular, honesty—but I have come to appreciate the value of a child's imagination, the innate certainty they have of their own minds and their own realities. Rather than squashing the innocence of that early creativity, I think we should indulge it."

Ophelia blinked, clearly taken aback by Lark's very obvious change of heart. "But in the book you say—"

Lark grinned, picked the book off the table and held it up. "I know what I say, and when I wrote the book I was sincere—" her gaze locked with Ethan's "—but I was *sincerely wrong.* Let me tell you a story," she said. "Once upon a time there was a little girl who believed in Santa Claus— believed so thoroughly that she could talk to him and see his elves and see toy soldiers smile and nutcrackers wink and angel wings flutter. She had a great imagination, but one that frightened her parents, so her parents took away Christmas and set up regular appointments with a therapist. The girl grew up believing Christmas was bad because it had caused her so much grief, and she believed that it was the Christmas lie, in particular, that was so harmful." She paused, swallowed, her eyes shining with tears. She lifted her shoulders in a tiny shrug. "But what was the harm, really? How long would the little girl have continued to believe the unbelievable? Another year, maybe two?"

With tears in her eyes as well, Ophelia handed Lark a tissue.

She took a bracing breath. "It's my professional opinion now that it would have done less damage for the little girl to have a harmless fantasy than for her to believe there was something wrong with her, that she was defective in some way. And her family would have been stronger as result of having Christmas tradition. Because what is Christmas if not a tradition?" she asked. "The things you mentioned, Ophelia—the making cookies and the wrapping presents, the special dinners, the mistletoe. Those are traditions, and traditions are built to bond a family. They make them stronger."

Ophelia wholeheartedly agreed, as did the rest of the audience. Ethan's phone lit up with text messages and the app his brother had designed to measure Christmas spirit glowed brighter than it ever had.

All because of her.

"You know we have Mr. Christmas himself in the audience, right, Ophelia?" Lark asked her.

Ophelia's brows lifted and she scanned the crowd until she found Ethan. "Ethan Evergreen," she said, smiling. "Why don't you come up here and join us?"

He was glad she'd asked because he was ready to rush her stage and wasn't eager to get thrown out. He mounted the steps, his gaze on Lark, and then reached out to shake Ophelia's hand. "Thank you for having me," he said.

"Pleasure." She grinned. "So this is quite a turn-around. Ms. DeWynter is typically your biggest adversary, wouldn't you say?"

Ethan reached over and took her hand, threaded her fingers through his. "Yes, she was. But you know what they say about your enemies," he said leadingly.

Ophelia noted their hands with an "mmm-hmm" and arched a knowing brow. "Keep your friends close, and your enemies closer."

"That's a good one, but it wasn't the one I was thinking of," Ethan told her.

"Oh?"

"Yes. The best way to get rid of an enemy is to make them your friend." He squeezed Lark's hand. "But I've got an even better solution."

Lark's eyes widened as Ethan suddenly slid to one knee in front of her and the audience went absolutely wild.

Ophelia was smiling so widely she could barely talk. "And what's that?"

Ethan looked at Lark, his gaze searching hers. "Make her your wife." He essayed a grin. "What do you say, Chickadee? Will you marry me?"

"I believe I will," she said with a watery smile. She bent forward and kissed him, and then she drew back. "And you won't even have to make me drink the cocoa to do it. I heard you this morning," she whispered. "Thank you for believing me," she said, a tear slipping down her cheek. "You can't know what it means."

Ethan returned her smile, gesturing significantly at the audience. "Oh, I think I've got a pretty good idea."

"Ho, ho, ho," she murmured with a chuckle, and kissed him again.

* * * * *

Double winner of the National Readers' Choice Award, **Kira Sinclair** writes passionate contemporary romances. Her first foray into writing fiction was for a high school English assignment. She lives out her own happily-ever-after with her husband, their two daughters and a menagerie of animals. You can visit her at kirasinclair.com.

HIS FIRST NOELLE
Kira Sinclair

I'd like to dedicate this book to an amazing group of women—Andrea Laurence, Rhonda Nelson and Vicki Lewis Thompson. Working together on this project has been one of the highlights of my career...well, you know, except for the tooth fairy and bloody teeth.

Love you guys!

Chapter 1

"We have a problem," Noelle Frost said, not bothering to knock before barging into the one room she'd been avoiding since returning to Gingerbread, Colorado.

Dash Evergreen's sharp green eyes swiveled to pierce straight through her. Noelle felt his loaded gaze catalogue everything about her body in mere seconds. From the severe cut of her black business suit down to the compact body that she considered her greatest weapon and spent hours honing. This man knew all of her weaknesses and strengths. Her knife-edged longings and pulse-pounding fears. Dash Evergreen absorbed it all and then dismissed her. Found her wanting.

Although that was nothing new.

Born of two rival clans, she'd never been completely accepted by either. She might have been raised in Gingerbread, Colorado, as a member of the Winter clan, but her Summer-blue eyes were a visually dynamic reminder to anyone who cared to look that there was a part of her—however small—that was different.

And not even the fact that her father was head of security for Evergreen Industries and a highly trusted member of the clan had stopped people from holding her at arm's length. Or the other kids from teasing her.

There had been a time in her life when she'd thought Dash was different. That he saw beyond all the conflict and accepted her for who she really was.

But then, there'd been a time when she was young and naive, too.

Noelle ground her teeth together and tried not to let his dismissal hurt. But even after eight years, her ex-husband still had the ability to wound her with nothing more than a simple glance. But she'd be damned if she'd let him know that.

Her years of CIA training had prepared her for deep-cover operations. She could kill with her bare hands, slip into some of the most secure facilities undetected and rub elbows with the elegant and elite.

Apparently that training was also useful when trying to protect herself from the man who'd broken her heart.

She'd been back in Gingerbread for several months, utilizing those skills to fill in for her father while he was recovering from a heart attack and emergency open-heart surgery. So far, she and Dash had managed to avoid each other. Mostly.

Unfortunately, thanks to this latest snag, it was going to be difficult to continue to do so.

Noelle knew just how much Dash hated to be disturbed when he was in his hot shop, and frankly, if she'd had any other choice she would have waited until he was through.

Dash all hot and sweaty, his muscles all slick and gleaming, had always been her weakness.

Pushing farther into the room, Noelle glanced around. Nothing much had changed. She could see the orange-red glow the fire emitted through the square opening in the furnace. Huge metal implements that looked more like they belonged in a medieval torture chamber rather than

Dash's private lair had been placed on the tables scattered around the room.

He didn't glance at her as she moved closer to get a better look. One wide palm rolled the hollow metal rod back and forth across the raised platform of the workbench. A glowing ball of molten glass twirled in front of him as he worked it, poking, prodding and coaxing it into the shape he wanted.

Color had already been added, a breathtaking swirl of blues that reminded her of a cloudless summer sky. With quick movements, he pulled a long finger of glass from the spinning globe. A flick of his wrist here, a quick snip there. The ornament would be gorgeous—as every piece Dash produced was. For the briefest moment, Noelle fought the desire to have the ball hanging on her own Christmas tree.

But it wasn't for her.

With practiced movements, he separated the piece from the pipe and stored it in the annealer, which allowed the glass to gradually cool without cracking.

While she'd never used any of the equipment in the room, she was intimately familiar with every piece. Dash had spent hours explaining to her just what they were used for. He didn't let many people into this space—not even his brothers or sister. At the time that access had made her feel…special.

Apparently all he'd really wanted was inside her panties. Noelle couldn't fight down the twist of a sickly smile as it crossed her face. She might have been impressed with his talent and turned on by the heat of his sweat-slicked skin, but her parents had raised her right. She'd still held out until he'd asked her to marry him.

If she'd known the high price of agreeing to that hand-fasting she probably would have saved herself the trouble and just let him have her here. Maybe then it would have just been hot sex instead of a soul-crushing disaster.

Dash stalked back across the room toward her, a soft, worn T-shirt clinging to his impressive chest. Damp patches arrowed down leading straight to the valley where she knew a six-pack was hidden. Tattered jeans clung to narrow hips, the thighs so threadbare she could see through to the bare skin underneath.

Most women would probably swoon at seeing Dash Evergreen in a perfectly tailored three-piece suit. And he definitely knew how to rock that look. But this, *this,* was what she dreamed about. Not the perfectly polished businessman or the responsible member of the Winter clan ruling family.

Nope, her fantasies were filled with the man—his dark hair disheveled and slightly damp and his green eyes snapping from an internal fire he worked hard to bank around most people. But she'd seen it. Knew the dangerous edge, the prowling restlessness and the burning passion.

Noelle's muscles began to quiver, a fine tremble that she seriously hoped he wouldn't notice. Dammit! What was it about this man that cut through every single shred of self-preservation she possessed?

As if she hadn't learned her lesson.

Her head might have, but apparently her body still craved more sweet punishment.

He stopped in front of her, arms crossed over his wide chest. The hard line of his jaw tensed. A single muscle ticked rhythmically just below his left ear. The only sign that he was thoroughly pissed that she'd interrupted him.

Tough.

"We have a problem," she said again, modulating her voice to something crisp and professional even as awareness and need crackled across the surface of her skin.

"So what's new? All we seem to have lately are problems. Let Cole or Ethan handle whatever it is. My plate's already full preparing the sleigh and overseeing the packaging."

She didn't want to hear the thin line of weariness buried deep inside his words, but Noelle couldn't help it. Fine lines of strain flared out from the corners of his eyes, and the faint smudge of exhaustion bruised just below them. What was the idiotic man doing in the hot shop when he should obviously be in bed catching up on some much-needed sleep?

Exasperation flickered through her, and she almost stepped closer, intent on running her hand down the slope of his shoulders and convincing him to get some rest. But somehow she managed to stop herself. It wasn't her job to care about him anymore. Hadn't been for a very long time.

Unfortunately, what she was about to say was going to add to the strain. But there was nothing she could do about that.

With a deep breath she said, "Kris has decided not to take the sleigh this year."

The dark slash of his eyebrows winged up in confusion. Noelle completely understood. That had been her initial reaction, as well.

"What are you talking about? Of course he's taking the sleigh. How the hell else is he going to get around the world in twenty-four hours?"

At her sides, Noelle clenched her hands into fists. He wasn't going to like this any more than she had.

"He wants to take the Corvette."

The moment the words left her mouth, Noelle cringed, preparing for the inevitable explosion. But it didn't come. Instead, Dash blinked at her and waited…possibly for a punch line that would never come.

Silence stretched between them. Noelle's gaze darted across his face looking for any clue to his reaction, but there really wasn't one. His face was thoroughly blank.

Just as she thought the tension building between them might actually crack like one of his pieces of glass, he said, "The damn thing is yellow. Yellow."

His voice dipped down, the smooth, even cadence going slippery with horror and temper.

"How the hell are we supposed to hide a yellow convertible flying across the sky?"

Dash had really hoped she'd been kidding. He should have known she wasn't. Just the fact that she'd entered his domain after months of avoiding him should have been clue enough.

Noelle Frost certainly wouldn't have come all the way down to the lower levels of the lodge just for some sick joke. That wasn't her style. Actually, he couldn't remember the last time he'd seen her crack a smile, let alone laugh.

It made him sad, but there was nothing he could do to change it. She wanted nothing to do with him, and that was probably for the best.

There'd been a time when he'd known every nuance of Noelle—her body, her mind, her soul. She'd shared pieces of herself with him she'd held in check from everyone else. And he'd done the same.

But eight years was a long time, and she wasn't the quiet, passionate girl he remembered.

Nope, now she had a hard edge to her that made him want to tear into whatever had put the wary caution in her soft blue eyes. She insisted on keeping her beautiful dark hair pulled ruthlessly into a knot at the nape of her neck. And the holster resting beneath the cut of her suit coat… the first time she'd popped it open and he'd gotten a look at it he'd wanted to rush her to the nearest room, lock her inside and make sure there was never a reason for her to need the damn thing.

When she'd walked into his hot shop just now, he'd first

thought she was a figment of his imagination. Breathed to life from the thoughts whirling around inside his overly tired brain. He needed sleep. The weeks leading up to Christmas were always his busiest. But no matter how exhausted, the moment his head hit the pillow and his eyes closed images of Noelle were burned into the backs of his eyelids.

And if he did manage to drift off, those images would change from still photographs to flickering images with movements that left him panting and frustrated with a raging hard-on he couldn't do anything with.

So, to exorcise his demons, he'd come down to the one place he always found peace. But she'd even invaded there. He hadn't realized the ornament he was working on was the exact color of her eyes until it was too late.

And then she'd been standing there, her mouth tight and her eyes burning as she watched him work. Did she remember the feel of his hands on her body as he'd tried to teach her how to work the glass? Did her body ache with memories and unfulfilled needs?

There was no way to know by looking at her. The CIA had worked her over well. Her expression was always perfectly, pleasantly blank. Initially, he'd thought it was him. But then he'd realized that was her new default position. Or it had been when she'd first returned. After a few months some of the severe reserve had begun to fade. He'd seen her let her guard down, a little, with Belle, Taryn, Lark and his brothers.

The mask was still firmly in place with him.

Although he wasn't really surprised. Their history didn't exactly breed open friendliness. The passion that crackled between them had always been too explosive for that kind of easy camaraderie. They burned hot, just like the furnace at his back.

But now wasn't the time to think about any of this. Not if what she was saying was true.

"Surely to God someone can talk some sense into the man. A Corvette? The damn thing is barely bigger than a Tinkertoy. How does he expect to get all the deliveries packed inside?"

Noelle's eyebrow swooped up into a silent version of "did you really just ask me that?"

"Yeah, yeah. Magick. But we both know there are limits to what I can do. Especially less than two weeks before Christmas. Maybe if I'd had a year to prepare…the cloaking spell alone is going to be almost impossible."

She sighed, the heavy weight of it lifting her shoulders and breasts tight against the dark cut of her jacket. "I know. But…I've already spoken to Cole, Ethan and Belle. With all the other 'issues' going on, we're agreed that it's probably in everyone's best interest to accommodate this request."

Irritation rolled through Dash's chest. "The man is having a midlife crisis and the rest of us have to pay the price?"

The mountain was already buzzing with the muted whispers of gossip mingled with suppressed panic. He had no idea what they were going to do with a Santa who'd taken up jogging and refused to eat cookies. In a few weeks millions of children would be leaving him enough to counteract twenty years' worth of exercise.

And he didn't even want to think about the snowy white beard the man had shaved off. At least that could be fixed with some strategically glued stage makeup.

Making a damn car fly was going to be the last straw.

Even if Dash was a little miffed at being left out of the family discussion—probably because they already knew what his answer would be—he grudgingly recognized their point. Everyone was walking on eggshells around Kris. Personally, Dash thought it was useless. The guy's wife was going to leave him. Everyone could see it. The sooner he accepted the reality and moved on the better it would be for everyone.

Dash's wife had walked away from him without even bothering to tell him she was leaving. He'd managed to survive. Somehow. So would Kris. Just not in a Corvette flying across the sky.

If this crisis had struck at any other time during the year, Dash would have dug his heels in and refused. He would have forced everyone—Kris, Cole, Belle, Merry— to deal with the reality of what was happening.

But it was two weeks before Christmas, and the last thing they needed was for Kris to go comatose with heart- ache. Hell, he could barely remember the first few weeks after Noelle had left. They were a whiskey- and fire-fueled haze. And he had the scars to prove alcohol and molten glass were a lethal mix.

Noelle watched him, patiently waiting for his reaction. It was one of the things he'd always loved about her, the way she'd instinctively known when he needed space for the wheels to spin and had always given it to him. Unlike his brothers and sister, she didn't push.

Which was good, because if she had he probably would have balked on principle alone.

Picking up the nearest handy object, a pair of metal tongs he used to shape the glass, he threw them across the room. The metallic rattle as they hit first the wall and then the floor was less than cathartic.

Noelle didn't even blink at his outburst, which only made him regret the less than helpful gesture.

Her smoky voice, the sound of it making him think of flickering fires and her lithe body spread out across the soft surface of a white rug, swirled across his skin. "Feel better?"

"Not particularly."

A smile, all the more enticing because of its rarity, teased at the corners of her lips. "Yeah, me either. Although I do feel guilty for leaving a dent in the wall of my father's office."

"Your office."

Noelle's startled gaze collided with his. Her mouth went slack with surprise before she snapped it shut again.

"My father's. I'm only here temporarily."

"Yeah, that's what you keep saying."

Was it wrong that he wanted her to stay? Had always wanted her to stay. But she hadn't. She had a life outside Gingerbread, one that she was pretty damn good at apparently. One that he knew nothing about.

The spike of sadness surprised him. Reaching up, he rubbed at the ache of it in the center of his chest.

"Fine. Let's go figure out how to make a damn car fly."

Chapter 2

Noelle tried not to pay attention to the way his body moved, but it was difficult not to notice. Especially when she had to quicken her strides, forcing out two for every one of his, just to keep up with Dash. Even in her four-inch designer heels the top of her head hit just even with his chin. Unfortunately, it gave her a great view of the dimple there.

Jerking her gaze away from him, Noelle forced herself to pay attention to what they were doing.

"Sir, Kris had the car delivered to the barn fifteen minutes ago."

From the expression in the elf's eyes it was clear the general consensus was that this was an idiotic idea. Noelle didn't disagree...they just didn't have many other options.

With a nod, Dash followed the tiny man around the back of the lodge to the huge structure waiting there. *Barn* was a misnomer. It might have looked like one on the outside, but it resembled a warehouse on the inside.

On one end were large bay doors that would be rolled up so the sleigh could be brought out and loaded. Noelle's gaze swept across the ancient vehicle. It had been used for centuries. The wooden boards and gold-leaf paint seemed laced with magick. The runners gleamed beneath the fluorescent light. She used to creep inside the sleigh, curl up on the soft velvet seat and pretend she really did belong here.

She hadn't seen it in years…and until that moment hadn't realized how much she'd missed the outward sign of her heritage. A little prick of longing shifted inside her, but before she could do anything about it, Dash was striding off across the cavernous space.

The Corvette stuck out like a sore thumb. Not because they didn't have modern conveniences. The clan kept a huge fleet of vehicles available for use by anyone.

A crowd stood around staring at the huge yellow monstrosity. Their heads barely reached the top of the low-slung car. Several of them whispered back and forth to each other. Off to her left, Noelle heard a bleating sound that seemed to echo the consternation swirling around. Apparently the reindeer weren't oblivious to the fact they'd just been replaced.

The crowd split, clearing a space for them to pass.

Dash frowned. "This is a bad idea," he mumbled beneath his breath. If the elves loitering around weren't blessed with preternatural hearing, she would have been the only one to hear his words. Big pointy ears had their advantages.

"Maybe, but we're doing it anyway," Noelle countered in a loud voice filled with as much certainty as she could muster.

Shaking his head, Dash ordered the staff to clear the area. Everyone fell back, although they didn't completely disappear. Small faces filled the large bay opening.

"Why don't you try the cloaking spell first? Let's make sure we can hide this monstrosity before I try to make it fly."

Logically, she knew he had a point. But that didn't stop

the infinitesimal tremor she felt. Her magick had been... finicky. For months she'd been working hard to cover up her issues. She'd been lucky. But it looked like that good fortune was about to run out.

She felt sick with nerves. The sensation wasn't completely unfamiliar. There had been plenty of times she'd felt the same churning mix of anxious apprehension, usually moments before she plunged into a deep-cover assignment. Those jitters never lasted for long because she knew she had the skills to handle the situation.

She didn't think she had what she needed to pull this off. Growing up, she'd struggled to keep up with the rest of her classmates. The spells and casts they could do in their sleep she'd had to fight for. She'd spent hours practicing, determined that she would not let herself be different from the rest of the kids. But she was. And everyone knew it.

This was it. The moment everyone realized she'd been lying from the day she'd come back. They were about to get firsthand evidence she didn't belong with the Winter clan. The Evergreens would decide she couldn't fulfill her position and kick her out. Her father wasn't strong enough to resume his duties yet. He'd lose his job, and while the Evergreens wouldn't boot him to the curb, he needed his job. He needed something to fight for in order to get better.

Well, it had been a good ride. She'd actually lasted longer than she'd expected.

Here went nothing. Closing her eyes, Noelle pulled out her wand and concentrated on the car in front of her. In her mind's eye she recalled every detail so the memory was as complete as possible. The glaring color. The glint of light on the chrome. The squeak of brand-new tires against the coated concrete floor.

Whispering words in an ancient language only a few remembered, she started at the hood and moved backward, imagining the entire thing disappearing beneath a blanket of nothing.

She breathed evenly, drawing on the surge of light that kindled deep in her belly and radiated out.

A murmur started behind her, the sound of it growing to the point of annoyance. Didn't they realize she needed to focus?

Beside her, Dash shifted. His arm brushed against her. And she reacted. That single moment shattered her concentration as everything inside her centered on the man next to her. The picture in her mind was no longer of the car, but of Dash as he'd worked the ball of blue glass with expert precision. The bunch and pull of his muscles. The glowing heat on his skin.

A strangled sound erupted from Dash. Smothered laughter. Noelle's eyes popped open and she stared blindly at the car. A very blue Corvette.

"Well, it's definitely an improvement, but not quite what we were hoping for."

Dash tried desperately to smother the laughter, but he wasn't succeeding very well.

"At least we don't have to worry about flying lemons anymore." His foot connected idly with the tire. "Blue would work well…if Kris was traveling through the sky on a warm summer afternoon."

A choked gurgle erupted from Noelle. Dash jerked his gaze away from the car and back to her. She stared at him, horror and hurt filling her eyes for the briefest moment before that damn mask slammed back over her expression.

But he'd seen it.

"Jesus. Elle." His voice was low, full of the regret rolling through him. He took a single step toward her, planning to wrap her in his arms and soothe away the damage he'd unintentionally caused. But she stumbled backward, shaking her head.

Dammit! He knew how touchy she was about her powers. Knew how much she'd struggled growing up. But it had been easy to forget those old insecurities and assume they were long gone. From the moment she'd come back, Noelle had been nothing but competent, confident and efficient.

But that didn't excuse what he'd just done. He'd hurt her, and that was the last thing he'd ever wanted to do.

"You know that's not what I meant. My mouth gets me in trouble."

Her eyes flared. Her gaze dragged down to his mouth. A hot blast of need shot through him. Part of him wanted to follow through on the unwitting invitation. He'd wanted to kiss her from the moment he'd walked into the Evergreen boardroom and seen her sitting in one of the dark leather chairs.

He could make her forget, soothe the emotional wound he'd just inflicted. Coax her to forgive him with his tongue instead of words. But that tactic hadn't exactly worked well for them in the past. Anytime she'd gotten upset about something, his solution had always been to distract her with sex. To remind her just how compatible and perfect they were together.

Instead, he rolled his head, stretching tight neck muscles, and tried to find the core of control that was slowly slipping through his fingers.

"Don't beat yourself up over this, Elle."

"Don't."

He wasn't sure whether she was talking about the nickname or his pacifying words.

"It's a difficult spell. Even the most powerful from the clan would struggle. Besides, you almost had it right until the last moment."

Her gaze collided with his. "What…what do you mean?"

He shrugged. "Half of the car had disappeared and then it…was back. And blue."

Eyes wide, her beautiful mouth fell open. It only made him want to kiss her more.

Slowly, a brilliant smile melted across her face. It was like watching the best sunrise, the ache of it difficult to take. It lit up her eyes, making them shimmer just like his glass.

God, she was gorgeous. And he loved to see her happy. There was a time when his whole existence was tied up in drawing out that smile. Even then she'd been so serious and intent.

"I did it?" she whispered.

This time when he moved closer she didn't pull back.

"Yep. What happened?"

Her teeth clicked together. Her gaze jerked away. And a soft burst of color seeped across her skin. "Something distracted me."

Reaching for her, Dash ran his hands down the curves of her arms. Why did she have to be wearing that jacket? He wanted to feel her skin.

"Okay. Then why don't we try again?"

Turning her back to face the car, he flicked a glance over his shoulder and found Montreal, his head elf, in the crowd. Dash silently flashed his right-hand man the order to have the area cleared and knew it would be followed.

Wrapping an arm around Noelle's waist, Dash let his palm settle across the taut expanse of her tummy.

"What are you doing?" she asked, her voice low and husky. The sound of it burned across every nerve ending in his body, but he ignored the reaction. That was not what she needed right now. Or wanted.

"Helping you."

"I don't need your help."

"Probably not, but you're going to get it anyway. Relax."

A harsh sound that was a combination of disbelief and jagged humor escaped her.

She shifted, probably completely oblivious to the fact that the tiny movement rubbed her rear straight across his groin. If she kept it up she was going to get irrefutable evidence of just how much he still wanted her.

Dash tightened his hand, holding her still. Her spine stiffened, and then she slowly began to melt against him. Her head dropped to his shoulder and she let him take her weight.

Her arms hung limply at her sides, her fingers still wrapped tightly around her wand.

Bending, he brushed his lips against the delicate shell of her ear and whispered, "Close your eyes."

She did, the softest sigh slipping through her parted lips.

Dash bit back a groan.

He touched her throat, unable to stop himself from running the pads of his fingers down the slope of her exposed neck. But he forced himself to continue, over her shoulder, down her arm to the hand holding her wand.

Twining his own fingers with hers, he raised her hand and pointed the slender blade of wood at the car.

"Start again."

She shook her head, the round point of it rubbing against his chest.

"I've got you, Elle," he promised. "It's only you and me here."

Her ribs expanded under a deep breath. She held it in before slowly blowing it out again on a steadying stream.

This close to her, he could feel the moment her powers surged to the surface. The glow of it was intoxicating. He'd never understood how she couldn't get it.

Her entire life she'd struggled against being different. She'd tried desperately to fit in. The problem was she couldn't. She *was* different. That was what he'd loved about her.

Unlike everyone else, her power was fueled not just by the cold core of Winter, but also by the bright sunlight of Summer. Together, the best of both worlds entwined inside her. Her skin glowed with the force of what she held deep inside.

She was one of the most powerful witches he'd ever met. She just didn't trust herself…or accept what was there. She fought to close off the piece of her that she didn't think belonged, which only drained her energy instead of feeding it.

So he'd help her tap into that potential. At least for today.

"Do you feel that?" he whispered. "The ball of energy churning deep inside you?" His hand flexed where it rested over her belly. "You must. I can feel it, and I'm only holding you."

Slowly, his fingers spread wide, slipping farther out across her body. "Let it go."

A small sound of refusal squeaked out of her.

"Yes," he argued. "All of it."

He could feel her struggle, not just in the tensed muscles pressed hard against him, but in the twisting center of her power. She was trying to cut it in half, to cordon off what she thought wouldn't help her.

"No. Don't fight it. Don't try to force that warmth down. I want to feel it, Elle." His mouth grazed her skin and his breath slipped across the sensitive spot just behind her ear. "Let me," he growled.

The burst of it nearly knocked his hands away from her body, but his muscles instinctively tightened and held on. Heat rippled down his body. Wherever they touched burned, but it didn't hurt. In fact, it felt heavenly. Like the warm cocoon of his hot shop.

He was so preoccupied with the revelation of just how powerful she really was now that the lock holding her Summer magick captive had burst open that he hadn't been paying attention to the car.

It was gone. Or, rather, it appeared gone. If he reached out, his hands would still brush across metal.

Unlike before, when the car had disappeared an inch at a time, one burst of energy and it had vanished.

"Elle," he murmured. "Open your eyes."

She did, her eyelids dragging slowly up as if weighted with sleep. He remembered that sated, drowsy, satisfied expression and wanted it again. More than his next breath.

Her gasp of surprise had him chuckling.

She whirled in his arms. One moment she was completely pliant and the next she was shoving at him like he'd suddenly turned into a serial killer.

Shocked, Dash let his arms drop from around her body and stumbled back a step.

The accusation that filled her expression slammed against him.

"What the hell do you think you're doing, Dash Evergreen? I really don't appreciate you playing with me. Aren't you a little old to be pulling that kind of shit? Grow up."

He opened his mouth to argue with her, but he had no idea what to say. How could he? What the hell was she talking about?

Spinning on her heel, the hard click of her stilettos hitting the concrete floor blasted around him like gunshots. His own temper flared. Before he could think through the implications of his actions, he was striding after her. Grasping her arm, he whirled her back to face him.

She glared, the sharp cut of her beautiful eyes slipping straight between his ribs. "What the hell are you talking about?"

Her teeth ground together as if she didn't want to dignify his question with an answer. Too bad. He shook her shoulder, not hard enough to rattle anything, just to make her realize he had no intention of letting her go until she explained what she meant.

"That stunt back there. I have enough bullshit to deal with right now. I don't need one of your pranks piled on top of everything else."

"Prank? What prank?"

"All that husky whispering and those touchy-feely hands." She dropped her voice down into a growling register. "'I've got you, Elle. Let it go.'"

A sharp breath pulled in through her teeth. For the briefest moment he thought he saw the glitter of tears in her eyes, but she blinked and they were gone.

"What the hell did you hope to get? Me falling back into your arms?"

He did not appreciate her harsh laughter.

"Why let me think I was doing all of that?" Her hand swung to encompass the car, still perfectly invisible. "If you were just going to do it your damn self."

She thought he'd cloaked the car. The realization did nothing to bank the anger flickering through him. It increased it. Why did she constantly underestimate herself?

His voice was silky and dangerous when he said, "That was all you, Elle."

She scoffed, the harsh sound scraping across his eardrums. "Yeah, right."

Jesus, he wanted to shake some sense into the woman. And then he wanted to strip her completely bare and revel in her heat and fiery passion.

"I. Did. Nothing," he bit out.

"I felt it." She flung the words at him like an accusation. "The burst of energy. I felt it." Her voice wobbled. Her chin quivered. Her throat worked overtime, trying to swallow.

And the anger just…evaporated.

He didn't mean to, but somehow his fingers tangled into her hair. His palm cupped the nape of her neck. Closing the space between them, he tipped her face and made her look at him.

The slick sheen of tears covering her eyes nearly sent him to his knees.

"God, I hope so," he rumbled. "That was you, Elle. The piece of yourself you've kept locked down for as long as I've known you. That was you finally letting all of your power free."

His control stretched to the breaking point, Dash couldn't hold back. No longer remembered why he should even try.

His mouth slammed down over hers. He wanted to be gentle, knew he should hold back and coax her. But couldn't find the willpower to do it. Not when he'd struggled to keep his hands off her for months. Not when it had been so long since he'd tasted her.

He might regret the moment, but not now.

Her squeak of surprise quickly morphed into a groan. Her mouth opened beneath the probing force of his. She let him in. More than that, met him measure for measure.

Her tongue tangled with his, taking just as much as she was giving. Hands tugged at his hair, coaxing him closer. She went up on tiptoes, pressing her body flush against his.

The past and the present melded together. The taste of her was just the same, peppermint and sunshine.

But the moment his hands brushed against the cold leather of the holster tucked between her shoulder blades cold reality came crashing down around him.

They both jerked back. Panting, they stared at each other. Dash didn't know what to do or say. His body wanted her, so much that he throbbed with the pain of it.

But this wasn't the girl he remembered. The one he'd fallen in love with so long ago.

This was the woman who carried a gun everywhere she went. The one who'd left him.

Chapter 3

God, she shouldn't have kissed him, Noelle thought later that evening. Rubbing her hands down her face, she tried desperately to wipe the memory from her brain. Yeah, like that was going to work.

Even hours after walking away from him, she couldn't seem to think of anything else. Her body still buzzed with energy and ached in all the right places. It would have been so easy to get swept up in the moment and give in to what they both obviously wanted.

And if she'd shared that kind of unbelievably over-whelming kiss with anyone else, she probably wouldn't be pacing restlessly inside her room, but instead stretching languidly next to a warm male body.

Dash had been the one to make her body light up like a damn Christmas tree. He'd always been the one to do that. The only one. She'd dated and even taken lovers since she'd left him. But none of them had made her feel as raw and alive as Dash always had.

With a growl of frustration, Noelle yanked open her bedroom door and stalked out into the silent hallway. It was almost dawn. No doubt she'd need copious amounts of Diet

Coke to keep her eyes open today, but for now, whenever she put her head down on the pillow all she could think about was rolling across the bed tangled in Dash's arms.

Maybe a walk would clear her head and exhaust her body enough that she could at least get a few hours of sleep.

Like the barn, from the outside the lodge resembled a quaint ski cabin. But the place was big enough to house the entire Winter clan. The elves had their own village close by, protected by magick just as the lodge was.

Everyone had their own apartments but shared common spaces—the dining room, a game room, a movie theater, and a huge living area with soaring ceilings and a man-size fireplace. The lower floors housed the communications and security hub and Dash's hot shop.

At this hour the hallways were quiet and deserted, or at least she thought so, until she rounded a corner and ran smack into someone. Belle's high-pitched *oomph* and rounded green eyes greeted her.

"Noelle," Belle said, her voice filled with anxious surprise.

"What are you doing wandering around in the middle of the night?"

Belle's gaze jerked sideways, refusing to meet hers. Noelle had enough interrogation experience to know when someone was hiding something.

Her sharp gaze catalogued Belle's attire, the same outfit she'd worn earlier but a little more rumpled. She clenched her fist around the familiar Cup of Cheer mug as if it was a lifeline. The shop had been closed for hours.

Noelle's eyebrows quirked up and a smile threatened the corners of her lips. If she was reading the signs correctly, Belle Evergreen had just returned from a midnight tryst. For weeks she'd wondered just what the youngest Evergreen had been up to. *Coffee breaks, my ass.*

"I won't tell your brothers," Noelle promised.

Belle's startled gaze flew to hers. "What are you talking about?"

"As long as you're not spilling company secrets, I don't care who you're sleeping with, Belle. And neither should your brothers, although we both know they're likely to go all caveman the moment they find out. So, I won't be the one to tell them."

Her entire body sagging with relief, Belle flashed Noelle a brilliant smile. "I appreciate it."

With a shrug, Noelle left Belle standing in the hallway. It was none of her business, and women had to stick together.

The encounter with Belle gave her something else to think about as she wandered around. Eventually she hit the ground floor. She told herself it was simply to check in with her nighttime team. But she never quite made it that far.

For some reason her feet stopped outside the closed door to Dash's workroom. Light shone through the crack at the floor. He was inside. Of course he was. This was where Dash came whenever something was bothering him.

Toward the end of their marriage it had upset her that more and more he'd sought out the hot shop instead of her. She'd woken up countless mornings to an empty bed, her heart a little crushed. Maybe if it had been another woman, she could have fought, but it wasn't.

She had felt him slipping through her fingers and hadn't known how to stop it. The more he'd hurt her, the more she'd withdrawn. The more she'd withdrawn, the more he'd disappeared. Looking back, she could see the vicious cycle their marriage had dissolved into. Maybe if they'd been older...

But they hadn't been. Leaving Gingerbread and taking the position with the CIA had been what she'd needed. The chance to challenge herself in ways that didn't require the use of magick. Considering she'd spent all of her youth struggling to become as adept at using it, it seemed like a good idea to try living without it. She'd had to learn how to rely on just her intelligence and physical strength.

And she'd been damn good at her job.

What surprised her was that so far she wasn't missing her work with the CIA. The long hours, isolation and cloak-and-dagger existence had been starting to wear on her. And she hadn't even realized it until she wasn't part of it anymore.

She'd left the lodge certain it could never be home. But the moment she'd walked back inside it had felt…right. Where had those misfit feelings fled to?

And then what had happened this afternoon with the car?

Noelle wasn't entirely certain what to make of that. Had it really just been *her?* Part of her wanted Dash to have given her a little boost, but looking into his deep, honest eyes, she hadn't been able to believe he was lying to her.

But what did that really mean?

She had no idea.

Thinking about that burst of heat that had spread through her like she'd mainlined hot cocoa brought her full circle to the man who'd been holding her. The spread of his hand low across her belly. The way his fingers had rested right beneath the curve of her breast. His fingers entwined with hers. The unavoidable buzz of need.

God, even now she wanted him. Her body was begging her to open that door, forget everything that was between them and give in to the need.

Her hand rested on the knob, indecision freezing her muscles.

No. She couldn't do this. This man had destroyed her. Broken her heart and let her walk out of his life without even a single word asking her to stay.

Her hand dropped uselessly to her side. But before she could turn away, the door jerked open. Dash was framed there, blinking at her like she was a mirage he was trying to clear away from his brain.

"Elle?" he asked, his voice low and fluid.

His hand wrapped around her arm, holding her in place when everything inside her urged her to run.

"What are you doing up?"

She could have told him she was just checking in with her team. Or that she hadn't been able to sleep and was wandering. But she didn't. She didn't say anything. She couldn't. Her throat refused to work. All she could do was stare up into his eyes, the hum in her body steadily increasing as if someone was ruthlessly turning up the volume on her desire.

His skin glowed with heat. Several damp strands of hair clung to his forehead. He needed a haircut, but what else was new? His dark hair was always just this side of too long. It had been a running joke. Slowly, she reached up to push the mess away from his face. She wanted to see him.

The moment she touched him she knew it was over. All the struggle to pretend she didn't still want him. Dash Evergreen had always been her weakness.

"Elle?" His fingers tightened around her arm, biting into her.

She knew what he was asking, but she didn't really have an answer. Shaking her head, she swiped her tongue across her suddenly parched lips.

The groan that rocketed up from his chest made her tingle in the strangest places. Before she could blink, they were both back inside his shop. The door slammed shut behind them and her back hit the hard surface.

Caught between the thick slab of wood and the towering height of Dash's body, she couldn't think. Didn't want to.

His mouth devoured her, touching everywhere. The

hard press of his lips trailed across her exposed collar-bone. For the first time she questioned the intelligence of prowling the halls in the tiny shorts and tank top she liked to sleep in. Until the tip of his tongue slipped beneath the low edge of her shirt to find the tight tip of her breast.

"Oh, God," she breathed, her fingers clenching his hair to hold him close.

Her body was on fire, as surely as the banked furnace pumping heat into the room.

She didn't protest when he grasped the hem of her shirt and pulled it straight over her head. She played tit for tat and made his own damp shirt disappear.

God, the man had a body. He was rock-solid, hard muscles beneath her questing fingers. Bulging biceps from all the glass work. Abs that made her want to lick him everywhere.

Her own mouth grasped for any patch of skin she could reach, greedy for the taste of him after so long. His skin was salty-sweet. She'd always loved him best when he'd come straight from the shop. It had taken her a long time to convince him she didn't want him to shower after he'd been down here.

The familiar smoky scent of the fire clung to his skin. She breathed it in, filling her lungs and holding him close.

Grasping her hips, Dash boosted her into the air. Her legs wrapped around his waist, bunching tight as she clung to him. She reveled in the feel of him sliding against her.

The hard ridge of his erection settled exactly where she wanted. Her own hips ground against him, pulling a ragged sound from between his lips. The brush of heated breath whispered across her skin.

Throwing her head back, she delighted in the feel of him.

"Jesus, Elle," he groaned against her belly, her own muscles tightening beneath the caress.

But his mouth moved away, and suddenly there was nothing but cool air touching her skin. His hands bracketed her face, scraping hair off her forehead. He stared up at her, the intense glitter of his green eyes nearly her undoing.

"Do you have any idea how much I want you? I can't get you out of my head. Haven't been able to since the moment I caught you sneaking out of your bedroom window when we were eighteen. The tempting swell of your ass in that tight little skirt as you shimmied down the drainpipe. Your tart mouth when I came out of the shadows to order you back inside."

Strangled laughter burst from her chest. "The way you tailed me to the Gingerbread party and interfered with every guy I tried to hook up with."

"None of them were good enough for you."

"Oh, and you were?"

The words were out before she thought about the consequences. With regret, she watched the manic heat fade slowly from his eyes.

"Hell no."

He tried to set her down, but Noelle just shook her head and tightened her thighs. "Oh, no you don't, Dash Evergreen. You are not going to light my body up like the Fourth of July and then send me back to my room unsatisfied. I've been fighting this since the moment I walked back into Evergreen Industries, and I'm tired. I don't want to do it anymore. I want you."

To prove her point, she arched her back, letting the door take all of her weight as her body went off center. His hands scrambled to hold her, but she wasn't worried. Dash would never hurt her, at least not physically. She trusted him with her body and always had. It was her heart he'd screwed with. But as long as she could keep that piece of herself out of this...

Her legs flexed, driving her body higher, before she

relaxed and brought them even tighter together. The soft cotton of her shorts rubbed perfectly against his denim-encased length. The combination of rough and soft nearly made her whimper.

It had been so long. She was close enough that if she rubbed in the right place she might just go off. But that wasn't what she wanted. If she'd wanted quick and easy she could have done that for herself.

Noelle wanted Dash deep inside her, filling her up and rubbing in all the right places.

"I tried to do the right thing, Elle," he ground out. "But no matter what, I just can't seem to succeed. Not where you're concerned. You trump every one of my good intentions."

"I don't remember asking you for good intentions, Dash."

With a snarling growl of surrender, Dash wrapped his arms around her back and spun. Swiping his arm across one of the metal tables in the middle of the room, she heard the clatter as tools hit the floor.

She hissed when her naked back hit the cold steel. He didn't wait, but followed her down, keeping their bodies locked tight together.

He ripped her shorts from her body, literally tearing them straight down the seam. Some small part of her wanted to protest, but she didn't. How could she when the gloriously naked heat of him descended on her?

He played with her, teasing fingers slipping through the evidence of her desire. A strangled cry erupted from her lips when he finally plunged inside. Her entire body bowed off the table, searching for more and delighting in the pleasure.

He drove her to the brink, leaving her gasping and whimpering, but he wouldn't let her go over. The moment she got close he'd back off, pressing featherlight kisses across her belly, down her thighs and over her eyelids.

Good thing she didn't need to see to feel him. He wasn't the only one who could dish out a little torture. Her fist wrapped around his hard length, remembering just what would drive him insane. She dragged several gasps and guttural groans from him.

They were both delirious, completely consumed with each other. If he'd asked her to walk across hot coals at that moment she would have done it. Done anything. If he'd just give her what she wanted.

"Please, Dash. Please. I need you. Now."

He panted, his ribs expanding and contracting erratically beneath her hands. "I know. God, baby, I know."

Grasping his hips, Noelle widened the cradle of her thighs and settled him right at the entrance to her body. A snarling sound of relief slipped through his parted lips just as he flexed and thrust deep.

The sound that ripped from her throat was part ecstasy and part torture. They fit together perfectly, just as she'd remembered.

It was overwhelming—more than she'd expected. Her chest tightened even as her body began to completely unravel. Both of them were too close to the edge to be gentle or deliberate. Instead, they came together in a flashing pump of hips, the glorious friction of bodies and brutal slice of long-denied passion finally finding a delicious outlet.

Her throat constricted just as her body spasmed. The dark spiral of release tried to suck her into oblivion, but she wasn't ready to let it have her. She waited for him, holding out so that she could feel the swell and pulse of his release deep inside her. And when she had it, she finally gave in. Wave after wave of pleasure washed over her. It was too much. It wasn't enough.

Dash sank down beside her, their arms and legs tangled in a knot she didn't have the energy yet to unravel.

Noelle lay there—the cold press of metal at her back and the heat of him draped over her like the warmest blanket on the harshest winter night. Her chest heaved, and every cell in her body seemed to quiver, energized and newly alive.

She didn't realize she was crying until Dash lifted himself onto an elbow. The smile of satisfaction that stretched his face faded.

Swiping a thumb across her cheek, he said, "Hey, hey. What's this?" and held up a single glistening tear.

Chapter 4

Dash hated to see her cry.

Hated to be the reason for Noelle's tears.

And he'd been responsible for quite a few of them in their relationship.

Gathering her in his arms, he rolled around until his back was against the table and Elle was pressed tight to his chest.

She tried to bury her face in his shoulder, but he wasn't having any of that. Part of the reason they'd crashed and burned was because they hadn't taken the time to communicate. He wasn't making that mistake again.

Because now that she was back in his arms, he wasn't sure he could let her go. It had nearly crushed him the first time.

Tipping her chin up, he forced her to look at him.

"What's wrong?" he asked, trying to make the words as gentle as possible.

"Nothing."

Her tears might have stopped, but he could still see the tracks where they'd been. Swiping his thumb through the ghost of them, his mouth tightened. "That isn't nothing, Elle. Talk to me. What did I do?"

Her gloriously blue eyes went wide with surprise. "Nothing, Dash. You didn't do anything. Well, at least nothing wrong. It's just been…a long time since I've felt that…connected to another person." She pulled against his hold, trying to duck and cover her face. "I was a little overwhelmed."

The tight ache centered in his chest began to ease.

"That was pretty intense."

She laughed, the sound of it rolling across him. Her body relaxed, going pliant. Folding her arms across his chest, she cradled her chin on her hands and looked at him through the cover of her lashes.

"It was always intense. You and I. The bedroom was never our problem."

A low chuckle curled up from his belly. "No. Definitely not. Maybe I should have handcuffed you to the bed. Kept you there, naked and waiting for me."

She frowned, but he still saw the brief flash of interest before she extinguished it.

"Oh, absolutely. Because forcing me to do what you wanted would have solved all our issues. Why *not* handcuff me to the bed? You wanted me to give up all my dreams for yours anyway."

"What?" he asked, his voice incredulous. "I never asked you to give up your dreams, Noelle."

"Please. You wanted me to be the perfect Winter wife. Bake cookies, serve cocoa, never complain and wait patiently for you to decide to come home."

His fingers tightened around the curve of her hip. She winced, telling him he was holding on too tight, but he couldn't make his hands uncurl.

"What do you mean wait for me to come home? You make it sound like I was screwing around on you."

How could she possibly think that? Hell, even at twenty he'd barely had the energy to keep up with her. Not when he was struggling to handle the responsibilities and pressures of his new position with the clan as well as a new wife.

"No. I actually think I would have preferred it if you were. Do you know how much it hurt to wake up alone in an empty bed and know you'd rather be here instead of with me?"

He'd had no idea. Stunned, his mouth opened and closed without anything coming out.

"You shut me out, Dash."

The shock was quickly devoured by long-repressed outrage. "And your solution was to leave? I was working all the time, Elle, trying not to drown beneath my stressful and exhausting job. My wife, a woman I loved desperately, seemed more and more unhappy the longer we were together. I couldn't figure out how it had all gone to shit so quickly. Or how to fix it."

His jaw flexed. He could feel the tension whipping through every muscle in his body but couldn't force himself to relax. The tears were back in her eyes, glistening across the bright blue surface. He should let it go, but he couldn't make himself shut up.

"You didn't even say goodbye. I came back to the lodge and you were just…gone. Not even a note, just an empty closet and a missing suitcase. It was weeks before I realized you weren't taking a break. You were never coming back."

Unable to stay this close to her while the memory of that pain ripped through him all over again, he wrapped his hands around her hips and lifted her off.

Grabbing his jeans, he slipped the worn denim over his hips. Turning to search for his shirt, he was in the middle of buttoning the fly when he caught a glimpse of her from the corner of his eye.

His hands stilled. She stood there, completely naked and utterly vulnerable. A contradictory mixture of the girl he'd fallen in love with and the woman she'd become. She might not have on the suits she liked to use as armor, but her body was still perfectly straight. Her shoulders were tight and her chin was tipped upward in a challenging show of confidence. But deep inside her eyes he could see the shadow of her insecurity and doubt. And something else—the slice of pain that he recognized because he wore the same damn scar.

"I heard you," she whispered, so low he almost didn't pick up the words.

Taking a single step closer, he said, "What?"

"I heard you. That night. Talking with Cole about our handfasting. *You* were the one to insist on the ancient practice, wanting to honor the custom of our ancestors. But the year and a day was coming up, and you weren't talking about making the union permanent. You were going to leave me."

"What?" he asked again, his heart suddenly lurching painfully inside his chest. A scathing protest was hot on his lips, but the words died before he could speak them. The look of utter devastation crumpling her face was difficult to argue with.

She truly believed what she was saying.

"I barely saw you. When you weren't working you were here." She flung her hands around his workroom. The bitterness in her voice cut straight through him.

He wanted to protest that he hadn't been hiding away inside his shop, but he knew the words would be lies. He had come here to avoid the fact that his marriage was crumbling and he had had no clue how to stop it. At the time he'd convinced himself he was giving her space.

But the reality was he'd had no idea how to handle what was going on between them, and he'd used the hot shop to pretend everything was okay when it clearly wasn't.

"When you did actually come home we inevitably ended up fighting."

Or channeling that pent-up frustration and passion into ripping each other's clothes off, but he didn't mention that. He didn't think that reminder would be helpful just now.

"I was so afraid I was losing you. I couldn't be what you wanted. I didn't fit in with the other women. I burned every batch of cookies I tried. I even managed to screw up cocoa." She threw her hands up into the air, letting them fall back around her in frustration. "It takes a whole lot of talent to screw up hot cocoa, Dash. It's milk, chocolate and a tiny bit of power. But I couldn't even manage that.

"You didn't want to spend time with me, and frankly, I didn't blame you. I hated myself. The harder I tried, the more I just managed to screw up and push you away.

"When I heard you talking with Cole about what your options were at the end of the year and a day, I knew you were planning on leaving. Hell, I would have left me, too. Rather than put us both through that humiliating ordeal, *I* left. It was easier that way."

Dash let his eyes slide closed. He breathed in through his nose and out through his mouth, using the warm weight of it to ground him. It was either that or give in to the pounding need to scream at the universe.

When he thought his emotions were back under control, Dash opened his eyes and stared straight into Elle's churning gaze. "I had no intention of ending our marriage, sweetheart. But I thought you might. Especially after you screamed that our handfasting was a mistake."

He tried to keep the ache of her words from his voice, but didn't quite succeed.

She gasped. "I didn't…" Her words trailed to nothing. He could see the memories as they flashed back across her mind. The moment she remembered saying the words to him in a blinding fit of angry tears.

"I didn't—" she tried again, but the statement didn't come out any clearer the second time around.

Her throat worked hard as she tried to swallow. Soft hair whipped around her face as her head jerked back and forth in denial.

The third time went better. "I didn't mean it."

With a sad smile tugging at his lips, Dash closed the space between them. She stared up at him, her eyes filled with a jumble of emotions so tangled up together he couldn't pull one from another. He knew exactly how that felt, to be so tied up in knots that you didn't know what the hell you felt.

Running the pad of his finger down her cheek, he whispered, "Apparently you did."

Noelle stared at the computer screen on her desk. There were words and numbers. Information she was supposed to be absorbing and managing. She didn't see any of it.

The only thing she could see was the expression on Dash's face right before he'd walked away from her last night. As if she'd ripped out his heart and fed it to a reindeer.

Her own chest still ached with the realization that she'd hurt him.

And right now, she had no idea what to do with that knowledge. What did it mean? What did last night mean?

Could they go back and start again? Was that even a possibility? Would he forgive her for leaving, and could they work out the issues that had driven a wedge between them in the first place?

What about the life she had back in D.C.? And while everyone else seemed to accept her presence here, there was still a part of her that didn't feel like she belonged. Not when she was struggling with the simplest requirements of her job.

She could direct her personnel, devise security protocol and implement diversionary tactics with no problem. But that wasn't all the Winter clan needed from their head of security.

Eventually they were going to figure out she wasn't qualified for the job.

And then what?

"Baby girl." A loud booming voice echoed outside her office door. Well, actually, it was his office door.

"Daddy," she said, a smile lighting her up inside. The sight of him always made her happy. Especially after the scare of almost losing him.

He was the only parent she had left. The only family, really, since she wasn't close with any of her Summer relatives.

Pushing up from her desk, Noelle allowed herself to be wrapped inside the warmth of a crushing hug. Her father was tall and broad-shouldered. Silver was finally starting to thread the dark, burnt-toast-brown of his hair.

He was her rock and always had been. Bigger than life and indestructible. Getting the phone call that he'd collapsed had nearly sent her to her knees.

Although he was definitely looking better these days.

She almost offered him the chair she'd been sitting in, but before she could he dropped onto the hard chair across from her. He settled back, the plastic creaking ominously beneath the bulk of his body.

"How's my gorgeous girl today?" he asked.

"Good. Fine. How are you?" she asked, trying not to put unnecessary emphasis on the words but failing miserably.

The doctors kept telling her that he was going to make a full recovery. Sure, he'd have to make some lifestyle adjustments, but that was typical after suffering a massive heart attack that required emergency open-heart surgery. At least his skin no longer had a sallow look.

He gave her a weak smile. "Good. Just came back from physical therapy in the village. Those are some sadistic bastards. I thought I was going to puke right there on that damn treadmill."

Shaking her head, Noelle said, "They're trying to make your heart stronger, Daddy. Do what they say."

Frowning, he grumbled something beneath his breath, but she couldn't hear it. Maybe it was better that way.

Pushing up from the chair, he leaned across her desk and touched his warm lips to her forehead. "Just wanted to check on my girl since I was walking through. I'm going back to the lodge to take a nap."

Flipping her hand in goodbye, Noelle watched her father disappear back out the door.

She wasn't happy. Not once did he ask her about work. And he hadn't since the day she'd agreed to take over for him. At first she'd thought it was simply because he didn't have the strength to think about it. Now she wasn't so sure.

Growing up, work had been his life. It bothered her that he didn't seem to care about it at all anymore.

But she wasn't quite ready to push him on the issue.

Shaking her head, she turned back to the spreadsheet open on her screen. At least his visit had accomplished one thing—she'd stopped thinking about Dash and last night.

Although the reprieve was short-lived. A couple hours after her father's visit, the walking distraction himself breezed into her office.

Noelle looked up, startled. She'd been back for months, and Dash hadn't come into her office in all that time.

She wanted to berate him for interrupting her concentration, but the words died in her suddenly dry throat. Gone were the work clothes he'd had on yesterday, replaced by the kind of brilliantly tailored clothes the citizens of Gingerbread expected from the VP of Evergreen Enterprises.

The man could fill out a suit. Maybe it was knowing

just how hot and sweaty he could get beneath the veneer of civility the expensive material provided, but Noelle felt like she was about to start drooling.

It didn't help when he reached behind him and closed her door. He leaned heavily against the wood, his intense gaze running across her from tip to toe. Her body responded, going all liquid and needy.

After he'd walked away from her last night, she'd expected him to go back to pretending she didn't exist. Apparently, that wasn't the plan anymore.

"What are you doing?" she asked, her voice much more breathy than she'd meant it to be.

"Look, we could throw accusations at each other all day. The reality is there's plenty of blame to spread between both of us. We were young. We made mistakes. But last night proved there's still something there."

She'd be lying if she said the heat that flared inside his eyes didn't kindle something deep in her own body. Those blazing green eyes sent a flood of tingles ripping across her skin. He could make her a puddle of mush with nothing but a glance. Had always been able to get to her like that.

At one time she'd seen her response to him as a weakness. Another power that tied her irrevocably to him and made her vulnerable.

Now she recognized it for what it was. The kind of physical connection that was rare in the real world.

"I don't know about you, but I'm not willing to ignore it."

Pushing away from the door, he stalked across her office. Spinning her chair, he planted his hands high on the arms, caging her in.

"I can't keep my hands off you, Elle. And I'm tired of trying."

Tipping her chair backward, he let the springs take her

off center. Her feet left the floor, and the world felt like it was falling out from beneath her.

The hard length of his thighs bracketed her own. She stared up at him, unable to do anything else. Her heart thudded desperately against her ribs.

Licking her tongue across her lips, she watched as Dash groaned. His eyelids slid closed. A pained expression crossed his face, and his entire body shuddered as if he'd been punched in the gut.

When his eyes opened again she was the one gasping. Heat and savage need filled her, spilling over her in a shower of sparks. No man had ever looked at her that way—not even Dash when they'd been together before. Now he looked as if his world might end if he wasn't buried deep inside her within the next sixty seconds.

All the doubts she'd been harboring fled, at least for the moment. How could she think about anything else?

Never in her life had she felt so beautiful and perfect and…necessary.

Fisting her hand in his crisp white shirt, she wrapped her legs around his hips and used her leverage against him. She jerked and had him tumbling against her body. The chair creaked in protest, but she didn't care. Not when his hot mouth found her and seared a path up her throat.

He was crushing her, but she still wanted him closer. She couldn't breathe and felt a little light-headed.

They tore at each other's clothing. She shoved his half-opened shirt away from his chest and leaned up to sink her teeth into his shoulder. He grunted and then groaned when she licked the tiny dents she'd left behind.

"Wicked little hellcat," he breathed, retaliating with a nip at her earlobe.

She laughed, the effervescent sensation bubbling up through her chest.

His hand was slipping up her thigh, pushing it relentlessly toward her waist. She was panting. Desperate. Her body raw and aching.

The door burst open behind them.

"Holy shit," someone said.

Instincts and training kicked in before Noelle's brain could pause long enough to consider what was happening. With a heave of her body, she shoved Dash away from her. Her hand was at her side and the gun from her holster pointed at a wide-eyed Cole before she could blink.

"Holy shit," he said again, holding up his hands in the universal sign of surrender. His eyes were wide, but mirth glittered dangerously inside them anyway. For the briefest moment, Noelle contemplated the merits of shooting him. Not to hurt, just to wipe the knowing smirk off his face.

However, she was intelligent enough to realize firing on her boss wasn't smart, not even if he was her pain-in-the-ass ex-brother-in-law.

She watched his eyes travel from the dark barrel of her gun down to the man lying at her feet.

Dash's bemused expression would have been comical if it wasn't also accompanied by an edge of irritation. She wasn't sure whether it was directed at her or at his brother. Probably both.

Holstering her weapon, she held out a hand to help him off the floor. She realized her mistake about five seconds too late.

Instead of bringing them palm to palm, his hand slipped higher, wrapping tight around her wrist. And it was his turn to tug. She probably could have stopped it, although not without possibly hurting him.

She sprawled against him, sending them both collapsing to the floor. His hard body cushioned hers, absorbing the shock and giving her a safe place to land.

One hand tangled in her hair while the other clamped around her hips, holding her hard against his still aroused body.

"What do you want, Cole?" he growled without taking his eyes off her.

"Uh…" Cole shifted behind them. She couldn't see him, but could hear the scrape of his feet against the deep green carpet.

"You have about sixty seconds before you're going to get an eyeful you probably don't want," Dash warned.

"Never mind," Cole finally said.

"Smart man." How could eyes smolder and twinkle at the same time? Noelle had no idea, but somehow Dash managed to pull it off.

Before the door to her office could close, Dash said, "By the way, your head of security is taking the rest of the afternoon off. And so am I."

There was a pause. Noelle felt it more than heard it, could practically taste the tension wafting off Cole.

"Whatever, man. I hope you know what the hell you're doing."

She tried not to let the disapproving edge in his voice bother her. But it did. Cole didn't approve of what was going on between them. But then, what was new?

While none of the Evergreen family had ever said anything, there were plenty in the Winter clan willing to voice their dissatisfaction with the match. Dash was an Evergreen and could have any girl he chose.

No one wanted him with a half-Summer witch.

She tried again to scramble away, but his hold hadn't loosened. Cole was long gone when Dash leaned forward and whispered against her cheek, "I know exactly what I'm doing."

Chapter 5

Dash had spoken some big words. Now he just hoped he could back them up. He'd stormed away from Noelle and his hot shop last night, furious and hurt all over again. It had been a defense mechanism easily deployed. But the moment his temper boiled away only misery was left.

He couldn't do it. For months he'd been walking around this place trying to pretend it wasn't killing him to see her, talk to her, smell her damn perfume whenever he walked down the hallways. It was a lie, and it wasn't getting him anywhere.

It certainly wasn't saving him the agony.

And touching her, tasting her, losing himself deep inside her again only made it worse.

Somewhere in the early morning hours he'd realized he had no intention of making this easy on her. She wanted him, responded to him, just as fiercely. He was going to use every weapon in his arsenal to convince her she belonged with him, with her clan.

And he wasn't above engaging in a few dirty tactics, namely of the physical variety. He hadn't been completely kidding when he'd threatened to handcuff her to his bed naked. If he wasn't half-convinced she'd know how to escape…

His body was still humming from the frantic release they'd found together on the floor of her office. It hadn't been nearly enough. The next time they were together it would involve a bed and uninterrupted hours that he'd use to explore all of her.

However, when he'd whispered that plan in her ear she'd gone from pliant to ramrod-straight in his arms. The afterglow hadn't lasted long before she was shoving him away again and ordering him out of her office. She had too much to do to leave right now.

He'd wrung a compromise out of her. They'd have dinner alone together in his apartments.

Which meant he had hours to fill until then. Striding through the enchanted tunnels that led from the lower levels of Evergreen Industries up the mountain to the lodge and elf village, Dash turned a corner and came up short.

Gabriel Frost was hunched over, his wide shoulders practically bowed halfway to the floor.

Dash's first instinct was to rush forward and help the man. The last thing he wanted was to tell Noelle her father had suffered another heart attack. But his brain quickly dismissed the fear as his eyes registered just what he was seeing.

Three elves huddled close to the man. Dash recognized them immediately. They were part of Gabriel's trusted team. No, they were part of Noelle's trusted team. What the hell were they doing powwowing with her father in the tunnels?

Sensing something was off, Dash slowed his steps and hid in the shadows.

"There are no problems?"

"You mean aside from Kris's midlife crisis, Merry's

snit, Cole's hacker discovering our secret and Ethan going toe-to-toe with Lark DeWynter on television?"

Gabriel sighed, his shoulders lifting as he pinched the bridge of his nose. "But those issues have all been handled. Well, all except Kris and Merry, but that will run its course eventually."

One of the elves grunted. "Kris is demanding he take the Corvette instead of the sleigh."

The three glanced at each other, exchanging the kind of look that carried the weight of shared agreement.

"When are you coming back, sir? Noelle is struggling. She's had trouble with several of her spells, although so far she's been able to hide it. But that can't last forever. And when the Evergreens learn she isn't capable of performing the job..." The tiny voice trailed off ominously.

"Not yet," Gabriel growled. "She isn't ready to admit this is where she belongs. Until she is, she'll leave again the minute I return to my duties. I won't let her do that."

Dash gasped, the full extent of what was going on finally hitting him.

All four heads jerked around, the shadows not strong enough to hide him from their direct gazes.

The three elves shrunk backward, dropping their eyes to the ground.

Straightening from his slump, Dash moved into the light. Grasping for the mantle of authority laid across his shoulders at a young age, he strode forward.

Sweeping the three with a heavy stare, he said, "What kind of trouble is she having?"

One of them stubbed his toe into the packed ground, his mouth tightening in the kind of sealed line that indicated he wasn't saying a damn thing. Dash appreciated the man's loyalty to Noelle, although it wasn't helpful at this precise moment.

The other two exchanged a glance. Through silent

agreement, one stepped forward. "They're minor issues. We thought at first it was simply because she'd been away from us for so long and needed to get reacquainted with her power. But it's been several months, and she's still having issues."

Frowning, Dash murmured, "The cocoa."

The elf nodded.

"Thank you for telling me." Thinking back over the way she'd cloaked the car yesterday, that ball of energy and light erupting from her core, maybe what had been holding her back would no longer be an issue. But just in case…

"I saw her cloak an entire car yesterday. Whatever happened before, I don't believe there'll be any more problems. Since that's the case, I'm going to keep this information quiet."

Dash didn't miss how their shoulders slumped with relief.

"However, if there are any issues, I want your promise you'll come to me immediately."

"Yes, sir," they said in unison.

"Excellent. You may return to your duties."

Without even a nod, the three disappeared.

Alone, Dash swung his gaze over to Gabriel's. He half expected to find Noelle's father cringing just as the elves had been. He should have known better. Gabriel hadn't risen to head of security by cowering. He'd been a trusted friend and colleague of Dash's own father and often an adviser to the Evergreen children as they'd stepped in to take the reins when their parents had retired.

However, the man would find intimidation tactics that had worked on Dash as a teenager no longer carried any weight.

"What do you think you're doing, Gabriel?" he finally asked.

The older man's mouth firmed with determination.

"Whatever I need to to keep her here. If you'd taken better care of her eight years ago she never would have left."

The blow was meant to hurt, and it definitely hit the mark. Especially after Dash's conversation with Noelle last night and realizing she'd been scared and upset and bruised. By him.

Gabriel visually braced for an argument, but Dash had no intentions of giving it to him. "You're right."

The other man's mouth opened, but before words could tumble out he snapped it shut again.

His ex-father-in-law studied him for several moments before jerking his head up in silent agreement. "So, what are you going to do?"

"Let me just make sure I understand what's going on first. I'm going to assume you're medically cleared to come back to work?"

Gabriel nodded again, his jaw going rigid beneath the white fuzz of his beard.

"When?"

Gritting his teeth together, he said, "Six weeks ago."

Something twisted deep inside Dash's belly. If Gabriel had told Noelle he was fine six weeks ago, none of the past few days would have happened. It made him physically ill to think he might have missed his second chance with her because he was being a blind, stubborn ass.

Blowing a calming stream of air out between his parted lips, he had to let go of the what-ifs and focus on what was in front of him.

Gabriel must have taken his shaky silence as a bad sign, because he blurted out, "Don't tell her. Don't cost me my little girl again."

He could tell Gabriel hated himself a little for the pleading, watery tone in his voice, but Dash didn't really blame him. If their roles were reversed, he'd most likely be the one begging.

He had two choices. March back up to her office, tell her and possibly watch her walk away again. Or let Gabriel continue to deceive her. Just for a little while. Until he had enough time to convince her this was where she belonged. With him.

It had already been six weeks. What could a few more days hurt?

As much as the weight of it settled over him like a tiny burr beneath a reindeer saddle, there was really no question what his decision would be.

Licking his lips, Dash said, "I don't want to lose her either, Gabriel. I still love her."

He brought his own eyes up to meet his ex-father-in-law's steady, understanding gaze.

"I know you do, son," Gabriel said.

"We're having dinner tonight. With a few more days I might be able to convince her to stay no matter what."

"So we won't tell her."

It had been three days since the afternoon in her office. She and Dash had spent more time together in those three days than the last three weeks of their marriage. Even when she was working he was constantly finding reasons to find her.

And she was doing the same thing. Popping over to the barn pretending to do a security check. Her favorite place to catch him was still the hot shop. There was just something mesmerizing about watching the man work. It was the only time he was completely…himself.

She knew he enjoyed his job with Evergreen Industries and took his responsibilities for the Winter clan seriously, but those things weren't his passion.

As much as she tried to just let things unfold the way they should, Noelle couldn't quite shake the tension that was steadily building deep inside her.

She was falling for him all over again. Which wasn't exactly true. It implied that she'd let him go at some point, which was far from the truth. There was a piece of her that had always—and would always—love Dash.

It was too soon to worry about what would happen tomorrow or next week or three months from now. But the permanent knot lodged in her tummy didn't quite agree with the carefree attitude she was trying to adopt.

She was worried about her father, but for the first time since she'd gotten the phone call that he was ill, she was happy his recovery was taking longer than expected.

If he told her he was ready to come back to work then she'd be forced to make a decision. And she wasn't sure which one she'd make.

"Ms. Frost! Ms. Frost!" The low voice filled with panic hit long before the tiny man burst through her open office door.

Agitation turned sourly through her stomach, but Noelle pushed it away. No sense getting freaked out before she even knew what the problem was. And whatever it was, she'd handle it. She'd managed every other shit-storm so far.

The man doubled over, gasping for breath as he pressed his hands to his knees. Sucking in oxygen, he panted, "We…have…a problem."

"I already figured that out, Roscoe. Take a deep breath and tell me what's going on."

Shaking his head, he didn't wait for that. Grasping her hand, he began tugging. Noelle tried to resist, but the elf was damn strong. And she was wearing four-inch heels and a tight pencil skirt. She really didn't want to end up sprawled across the green carpet with her ass in the air.

So she followed, patting her side just to make sure her gun was still tucked next to her ribs.

The moment she tumbled out the main doors of Evergreen Industries it became patently obvious a gun wasn't going to help.

She wasn't the only person standing outside gaping up at the bright blue afternoon sky. And the obscenely yellow car streaking above the town like a banana.

"What the hell?" she screeched out.

Beside her, Belle muttered beneath her breath, "Fruitcake. Just…fruitcake."

Behind her, Cole burst through the doors, Ethan and Dash hot on his heels. Dash's gaze rounded with shock before narrowing into a roiling temper. His skin flushed a dangerous shade of red, the kind of color that reminded her of the glow of his furnace. She really hoped he wasn't angry with her, although he had every right to be.

Ethan stared up into the sky and then burst out laughing. Cole shot him a cutting glare. Ethan tried to smother his reaction, but didn't quite succeed.

Cole's eyes blazed, the only sign his temper was close to exploding. Slowly, his gaze scraped across the street in front of them, which was crowded with the citizens of Gingerbread.

With a growl, he swept a cutting glare across his brothers, sister and her. Noelle felt the cold prickle of it slide down her spine like ice. "In my office. Now."

Accepting the fact that they'd follow his order, he turned to the phalanx of elves scattered around them. "Get a communication link up to them and tell them to get their asses back down here before I shoot them out of the sky."

No one believed he'd actually do it. That would create a bigger mess than they already had. But he was definitely pissed, and if Kris and Merry were smart, they wouldn't push him.

Everyone piled into Cole's office.

Today, instead of crossing his arms over his chest and leaning against the far wall, Dash sank down beside her on the love seat. He didn't look at her, but the hand he dropped onto her knee steadied her in a way she hadn't expected. Or known she'd needed.

Squeezing, he gave her a jolt of comfort and support before pulling his hand away. Noelle drew in a deep breath, using it and the heat radiating off him to soothe her jangled nerves.

"This is a clusterfuck," Cole muttered, leaning his head back and scraping his hands through his hair. Ever the worrier.

"It isn't that bad," Ethan, the eternal optimist, countered.

"You're kidding, right?" Belle asked, her own voice going up into the squeaky range. "This is bad. Very bad."

"I didn't say it wasn't bad, just not a mortal wound."

"Weeks before Christmas," Belle groaned. "Seriously, someone needs to knock some sense into those two. Whatever the ho, ho, holy crap is going on with them needs to stop. Now. Before they ruin Christmas completely."

Cole rubbed his hand over his face, jumbling up his words, although not enough that she couldn't understand. "Agreed. But first problems first. What are we going to do about the entire town seeing a damn flying car?"

Ethan shrugged. "That's easy. I'll arrange a free Evergreen Industries event for the town. Hot cocoa and cookies for everyone. Holiday outreach to the citizens who support us. We can hold a toy drive. It'll be great PR."

Only Ethan could spin a huge cover-up into something positive. And as much as the idea made Noelle want to vomit, it was a good plan. A great plan, actually. If only she wasn't the one required to supply all the cocoa. She'd struggled to make a batch strong enough to wipe Taryn's memories…how was she going to manage to produce enough to wipe the entire damn town?

Before she could open her mouth to come up with a protest, Cole's hand dropped from his face, and he stared at Ethan, hope flickering deep in his eyes. It caught and grew.

"You are brilliant, Ethan," Belle said.

"I know," Ethan said, spreading around his charming, egotistical smile.

Oh, shit. She was in serious trouble.

Her hands trembled. To hide the weakness, she clasped them together and dropped them into her lap. Dash silently reached over and covered them with one of his own. He might have meant to help with his gesture, but it didn't. In fact, the tremors increased, moving up her arms and engulfing her entire body.

She had to stop this. She had to speak up and tell them she couldn't do it.

Her mouth opened, but before the words could fall from her lips, the door to Cole's office burst open.

Kris walked in, his normally jolly expression thunderous and cheeks red for a completely different reason than Christmas cheer. Merry, quiet as always, slipped in behind him, her eyes cast down to the dark green carpet.

"What were you thinking, Kris? How could you take the car out like that? What did you think would happen when the entire town saw you?"

Kris bellowed. Behind him, Merry cringed, placing her hand on his arm in an attempt to cool the temper that was clearly about to erupt.

Somewhere in the back of her mind, Noelle registered the utter violation of Santa lore as she watched him completely lose his shit. Although, without his beard, paunch and snow-white hair, it was a little less weird.

"What did I think? What did I think?" he asked, stalking toward Cole and slamming his hands down onto the desk. "I was thinking that I should take the car for a test drive before I attempted to fly it around the world on the most important night of the year. I was thinking a quick trip up and down wouldn't hurt. I was *thinking* that the cloaking spell would hold."

Noelle gasped. Her eyes squeezed shut and her head dropped back against the curved edge of the love seat.

"What are you talking about?" Cole asked, his voice steady as he ignored Kris's burst of emotion and focused instead on his words.

"Everything was fine until I got above Gingerbread. The car shuddered and then it was…there. Nothing I could do about it at that point. I headed back as quickly as I could, but…"

"There's no hiding a flying car the color of a school bus," Ethan muttered.

Kris nodded sharply.

For the first time since they'd sat down, Cole's gaze swept over to her and Dash. "What the heck is he talking about?"

For the second time, Noelle prepared to spill her guts and tell the Evergreen clan just how unqualified she was to hold the position they'd given her. This problem was too big for her to continue pretending. But before she could, Dash's hard voice blasted into the room.

"The cloaking spell wasn't ready." His eyes glowed with banked heat. "If you'd bothered to tell us what you were planning, Kris, we could have told you that. The spells cast over the sleigh and reindeer have been in place for hundreds of years. They require only small infusions of power each year as a kind of booster for the magick that lingers inside each item."

Everyone else in the room might have been buying the line of bullshit he was selling, but Noelle knew better.

This was all her fault.

Chapter 6

The moment they were alone in her office, Noelle spun on him. "What were you thinking?" she cried, slapping her hands onto his chest and pushing him backward with the force of her words and her displeasure.

"I can't do it, Dash. I could barely pull off the cocoa for Taryn. There's no way I can make a batch big enough for the whole damn town. By tonight."

Horror and dismay edged her expression. In that moment, Dash's only concern was to calm her down. They weren't going to get anywhere with her spun up into a panic.

Grasping her arms, he pulled her tight against his body and covered her mouth with his. She fought him, struggling to yank her lips away. Capturing her chin, he held her in place. Slowly, her body overruled her brain, and she began to melt. The gradual transition was entirely erotic and threatened to pull him down into the moment right along with her. The soft sigh that brushed across his lips was almost his undoing, but somehow he found the strength not to succumb. Elle needed him right now. The passion building between them would have to wait.

When he was certain she wasn't going to revert the moment he let her go, Dash pulled back.

She blinked up at him, her eyes glazed with passion and her lips slick and temptingly swollen.

Sliding his hand around to the nape of her neck, he locked her in place. Slowly, reason returned. He hated to watch it seep back into her expression. Her breathing evened out, but the frenetic terror didn't return.

"You weren't surprised when I told you I struggled with the cocoa for Taryn." It wasn't a question. He hadn't realized the error of what he'd said until that moment. He tried not to flinch, but couldn't keep the reaction from flowing through him.

"No."

"Why not?"

"Because one of your elves told me."

He waited for the eruption, but it never came.

"How long have you known?"

"A few days."

"Why didn't you say anything?"

"Because I didn't think it was a problem anymore."

A harsh sound scraped through her throat. "Yeah, right."

Shaking his head, Dash pulled her across the office to the chair positioned behind her desk. Dropping into it, he pulled her down into his lap. He had fond memories of this chair. Was this where those moments would end?

He hoped not.

"Elle, you've got to stop suppressing your Summer half. As long as you won't access all of your power, you're going to struggle."

"What are you talking about? I'm not suppressing anything."

Running his hand up and down her back, he enjoyed the feel of her against his palm. "You are. Do you remember that burst of energy and light when you cloaked the car? The one you thought I was responsible for?"

She tentatively nodded. "I'm still not sure you weren't."

"I promise I had nothing to do with it. Well, nothing aside from relaxing you enough that you couldn't hold it back anymore. I distracted you."

Her beautiful mouth twisted into a grimace. "You mean you blinded me with lust."

His own lips quirked up into a half smile. He couldn't stop himself from leaning forward to brush his mouth down the exposed column of her throat. "Yeah. That. It worked, though, didn't it?"

Her body went liquid in his arms. Her head dropped backward, arching her neck so he could access more of her. A sound of agreement vibrated against his lips.

"You can do whatever you want, Noelle. You just have to trust yourself. And your power." He pressed the words against her skin. "You might be part-Summer, but that's what makes you unique. I love your blue eyes and the way you smell like fresh-cut flowers. The inherent glow to your skin, a light that radiates from deep inside you."

He watched her struggle to accept the words he was saying. The fear and hope and remembered hurt.

"I don't..."

She looked at him helplessly. Noelle was a powerhouse. A whirlwind of competence and bravado. But he saw the insecurity beneath it all. And loved her more for it.

"You can do this, Noelle. I'll be there to help you. We all will."

She swallowed and reluctantly nodded her head. He expected her to jump up and get right to work. They had a lot to accomplish in a few short hours. Instead, she curled against him, tucking her head beneath his chin. Her fingers tangled into his messy hair and held on.

For the first time he could ever remember, she needed

something from him. And was letting him give it to her. He'd watched her eyes darken with desire. Had lost himself deep inside her body as she'd surrendered her own to him. They'd been as close as two beings could possibly get.

And somehow, this moment felt more. More important. More profound. More terrifying.

He'd been upset when she'd left the first time. After this, he wasn't sure he'd survive if she disappeared again.

Whispering against her soft hair, he said, "You're the only one who ever thought you didn't belong here, Noelle."

Noelle had done it. It had been a rough start, but listening to Dash's soft voice, she'd managed to unlock the piece of herself she'd kept hidden for so long.

Until that moment, she hadn't completely believed what he was telling her. But now that she'd felt it again…he was right.

How could she not have known? How could she have been oblivious to the fact that she was closing off part of herself? Maybe she'd been doing it for so long it was subconscious.

But the feeling of euphoria and elation that rippled through her body along with the full heat of her power was addictive. She wasn't sure she'd be able to lock it away again, not now that she knew it was there.

But maybe that was a good thing.

She managed to keep her professional facade in place while they finished the cocoa and prepped it for transportation to the festival Ethan had thrown together at the last minute. Belle, who apparently knew the owner of A Cup of Cheer, had arranged to use their facilities.

Although the moment the details were all handled, Noelle couldn't hold back anymore. Launching herself at Dash, she trusted him to catch her even as her arms circled his neck. She rained kisses down across his cheeks, nose and chin.

"I did it," she said breathlessly.

"I never had any doubts."

"I know." She grinned at him like an idiot, finally beginning to understand just how much this man believed in her and supported her. And always had.

As much as she wanted to drag him back to her office and show him just how much she appreciated his help, neither of them had the luxury of time for that. She had to settle for a single, deep kiss.

Pulling away, she headed out to check on her elves. Dash followed behind her, his hands stuffed into the pockets of his dress slacks. She knew he'd be more comfortable in a pair of his ratty, worn jeans. But as Evergreen executives, they were all putting in face time at the event, so he was dressed accordingly.

Stopping to check with several of her team, she continued to the shipping bay, where the vat of cocoa was waiting to be loaded onto the delivery van.

She was beside the driver's door when two voices rumbled deeply from the other side.

"We can't load it yet. Zarla volunteered to test it. If it doesn't work on her, we'll just switch her batch with the one Gabriel made."

Noelle gasped. She thought it was under her breath, but the sound of it must have been louder because a scrambling clatter sounded from the other side. Two faces peeked around the edge of the van, shock, terror and apology written over every tiny, wrinkled inch.

"What do you mean the batch Gabriel made? When did my father make cocoa? I thought everything he'd made had been used or thrown out as unstable." After a few weeks, the magick had begun to weaken and become dangerously erratic, which was why they produced the concoction on an as-needed basis.

One of the elves cleared his throat nervously. The other's gaze flickered to the floor.

Pulling out her best "boss" voice, she demanded, "Tell me what you meant. Now."

Dash wrapped a hand around her arm and spun her to face him. But Noelle wasn't finished with the elves. She glared at him, but he wasn't even looking at her. His gaze was focused completely on the men behind her.

"Why don't you both go fetch Zarla?"

Before she could pull in enough breath to order them not to leave, they were scurrying away like roaches from the light.

The hurt blooming inside her chest was quickly being overrun with anger, and Dash was making himself the perfect target.

Pushing into her personal space, he forced her backward. Her spine collided with the hard panel of the van. Lodged between her open legs, the hard press of his thigh rubbed against her. A thrill of need whipped through her, but she bit down on it and forced it away. Now was not the time.

She ground out, "What are you doing?"

"Talking some sense into you before you do something you'll regret." His hard voice softened. "Elle, he did it because he didn't want you to leave. He loves you and missed you and wanted you to stay."

Unexpected tears stung her eyes. She tried to blink them away, but it didn't help. "He didn't believe I could handle it, Dash. My own father thought I was going to fail."

His mouth turned down into a frown and his beautiful green eyes flooded with sympathy and softness. Part of her wanted it. She wanted to let him wash over her like a balm, soothing away the pinch of pain lodged in the center of her chest.

But that wasn't the kind of girl she was. At least not anymore.

"He didn't understand, Elle. How could he? You've locked everyone out, including him. He was trying to protect you. Help you."

"By lying to me? How in heaven's name is that supposed to help, Dash? 'Let's let the poor thing think she's good enough to handle this while we secretly clean up all her messes?' That's no way to live."

Letting go of his hold on her arms, he slid his finger over the ridge of her cheekbone and smoothed her hair away from her face. "I know, sweetheart. I'm not saying I agree with his methods, just that his actions came from a good place. You have every right to be angry with him, but just take a deep breath and think before you figure out what to do about it. Don't let your emotions force you into a decision you'll regret later."

Slowly, she nodded. His chest rose and fell on a deep sigh. He let his head drop, bringing them forehead to forehead. "I'm sorry, Elle."

Warmth slipped into her veins. Not the familiar blast of explosive need, but something gentler and more comforting.

Maybe if the churning heat had been there, her brain never would have started spinning, but it did. That lull left enough time for a single, irrevocable thought to slam into her.

Shoving his shoulders, she forced Dash backward.

Confusion, sadness and comfort all mixed together inside those damn mesmerizing eyes. Maybe they were enchanted, because they definitely had the ability to blind her.

"You knew what he was doing."

Dash started to shake his head, but stopped just shy of actually making the denial. Dismay and guilt swirled across his expression before he managed to slam a blank wall down.

"I knew he was hiding that he was well enough to return to work, but not what he planned to do with the cocoa."

"Oh, because that makes it better?" Her voice rang with accusation. "He lied to me. You lied to me."

He started to reach for her again, but Noelle flinched away from him. Dropping his hands to his sides, he let them curl into tight fists.

"What would you have done if he told you he was ready to return to work, Elle?" The hard edge in his voice cut across her skin.

"Gone back to my life and my job."

Something bright and painful flashed through his eyes before he gave one hard nod. "Exactly. Elle, you don't belong in D.C. or with the CIA. You belong here, with your clan. With your father." His voice dropped low, a shattering whisper that made her heart ache even as the rest of her body lit up with need. "With me."

She shook her head. Fear and hope and hurt tightened like a band across her chest, stealing her ability to breathe.

Jerking her gaze away from his, Noelle stared up the slope of the mountain she'd once called home. The sharp stab of longing surprised her, but it didn't change anything. Not really. "I don't belong here, Dash. I never have."

Strong hands wrapped around the curve of her shoulders. He moved in front of her, filling her gaze and forcing her to look at him. "You do, Elle. There are people here who love you. Accept you for who you are—everything you are."

Did he mean himself? Did he love her? And if he did, did it matter? Could she give up everything for him? Try again and risk getting her heart ripped into shreds again?

Fear made her entire body tremble. She wanted to. The urge was so strong she almost collapsed into his arms in a sobbing mess. But she couldn't. Noelle Frost was stronger than that. She'd worked hard to figure out who she was and where she belonged.

"Stay, Elle. I want you to stay. I *need* you to stay."

He didn't say he loved her. Or that he wanted to get married again and make this permanent. He'd lied to her. Manipulated her.

She couldn't think when he was this close. She needed logic and space.

Pushing him away again, she stared up into his deep green eyes and said, "Then you shouldn't have lied to me."

She walked away. And once again, he let her go.

Chapter 7

Almost the entire clan was in Gingerbread, making merry and serving mind-wiping cocoa to the entire population, Noelle thought as she looked around her room. Dark wood glowed with a warmth so inherent to the place that it seeped into every nook and cranny.

She was going to miss it. The realization startled her, although she wasn't entirely certain why. Whenever she'd thought back on her life at the lodge, it had been difficult to remember anything other than the painful memories.

Today all the good ones flooded in instead. The few memories she had of her mother, a soft, lilting voice that trickled over her like the melody of a babbling brook. Comforting arms and shocking blue eyes that matched her own.

Moments with her father, his gruff exterior hiding the heart of a teddy bear. She was still angry with him, but Dash had been right. What he'd done had been out of love, even if he'd gone about it the wrong way. But, now that her anger had burned off a little, she could admit some of it was her fault. She could count on one hand the number of times she'd seen him in the past eight years. Whatever had happened between her and Dash, her father hadn't deserved to be punished for it.

And whatever happened now, she made a vow it wouldn't continue that way.

Turning her back on the life she once had, Noelle wheeled her suitcase out into the empty hallway and headed downstairs.

Her chest ached with the force of holding back the tears that wanted to slip free. There was a sense of déjà vu. The memory of leaving eight years ago melded with now. The difference was that today hurt more.

Why did it hurt more?

It was difficult to see through the sheen of unshed tears. And she was so lost in her own misery that she wasn't paying attention.

Her body slammed into something soft and solid. A high-pitched squeak blasted into the air. Noelle wasn't sure if she'd made the sound or if the person she'd nearly bowled over had.

Automatically, her body shifted to compensate for the change in her center of gravity. Reaching out, she steadied the woman, finally realizing she'd run into Merry.

The older woman blinked up at her with wide, unfocused eyes.

"Noelle, dear, what are you doing here? I thought everyone was in town."

Noelle shook her head, and for some reason the kindly eyes moving softly over her from head to toe were her undoing. Everything she'd been holding back spewed out in a choking sob. Huge, fat teardrops flowed down her face.

Without thought, the other woman reached for her, wrapping Noelle tight against her short, plump body.

"Oh, sweetie. Everything's going to be fine."

Noelle couldn't force words past the gurgling, shrill cacophony of her breakdown, so she just shook her head.

Merry's arms tightened around her. Her hands slipped comfortingly up and down Noelle's spine. She rocked them back and forth as if Noelle was a child and hummed a soothing melody beneath her breath.

Noelle had no idea how long they stood there, but eventually her sobs began to fade. The heavy weight of her grief and fear eased from her chest, leaving nothing but a hitching hiccup.

When the crying jag was finally over, Merry held her at arm's length. She looked deep into Noelle's eyes and smiled. "Better?"

Noelle nodded, not sure what else to do or say. She'd known Merry her entire life and liked the woman immensely. Who wouldn't? She was sweet and kind and Mrs. Claus, for heaven's sake. But they'd never been overly close. Until today. For some strange reason, Noelle wanted to spill her guts to the woman who reminded her of the grandmother she'd always wanted and had never had.

Merry's gaze dropped to the suitcase at her feet. "Going somewhere?"

"I'm leaving," Noelle croaked out.

"That's a shame. Everyone's going to miss you, Noelle. Especially Dash and Gabriel."

She shook her head, an echo of her earlier anger slipping back. "My father lied to me. He's been well enough to resume his job for weeks. Dash knew and didn't say anything."

A sad smile flitted across Merry's lips. "Sometimes we do hurtful things to the ones we love, Noelle." Plump fingers slipped across her cheek. "Lying to you was wrong, but maybe they had good reason. And at the end of the day, you have to decide what's more important. Are you going to let one mistake destroy everything? Are you going to let your own fears and insecurities come between years of history and love?"

For some reason, Noelle thought maybe Merry was talking about more than her relationship with Dash and her father, but she didn't understand enough to untangle the undercurrents flowing beneath the words.

"Do you love Dash? Do you want a life with him?"

Noelle swallowed and nodded.

"Then what are you doing standing in the hallway with your suitcase? You're a strong woman, Noelle Frost. You've forged and fought. You stand toe-to-toe with anyone who gets in your way. Why are you walking away from what you want without a fight? Again?"

Goose bumps spread across Noelle's skin. Merry was right. She'd looked some of the most dangerous criminals in the eye—murderers, terrorists and spies—without flinching. Why did the thought of opening herself up to Dash make her want to run and hide?

Not anymore.

The smile hardened across Dash's face. He'd been wearing the expression for what felt like days, but was probably only a couple hours. The lie hurt. When would this torture end?

He desperately wanted to get to his hot shop. Not so he could bury his misery in something creative, but so he could smash anything he could get his hands on into tiny, irrevocable shards of glittering glass.

But he had a job to do first. Beside him, Cole and Taryn had their heads bent together as they whispered to each other. Ethan was laughing and Lark was giggling like a schoolgirl. Their happiness scraped across his last nerve.

And Belle...his little sister was nowhere to be seen. The little shit had disappeared barely fifteen minutes into this PR farce. Her untimely disappearances were really beginning to piss him off. He was stuck here, miserable, so why the hell wasn't she?

Dash stared at the gathered crowd. The street was filled. The air rife with happiness and good cheer. Apparently the cocoa had worked, because not a single citizen mentioned the flying car. Although, he'd never doubted. Noelle was one of the most powerful witches he'd ever met.

Just the thought of her had him fighting the urge to double over in pain. He'd lost her. Again.

Determination twisted through his gut. The difference now was that he wasn't willing to let her go. If he had to follow her to D.C., camp on her front porch and tail her on every single job, he'd do it. He'd give up everything for her. Because she was the one thing he couldn't live without.

He was about to tell Cole he was leaving, but before he could, a disturbance erupted at the edge of the crowd. The sea of humanity split. People leaped out of the way as a swirling dynamo forced her way through. A few people grumbled. A couple squeaked protests.

Noelle didn't seem to notice. She had a destination in mind and she was getting there. God, he loved when she was on a tear. His body reacted even as he worried all that seething energy was about to be pointed straight at his head…and not the one that was excited to see her.

As if she could sense his scrutiny, her head jerked up and her gaze slammed into him. Her eyes roiled with emotions, but she was too far away for him to decipher the mess. Her skin was flushed pink and her shoulders were tight and straight.

He held his breath as she approached the platform a couple feet off the ground. Cole and Ethan had both spoken, expressing their appreciation for Gingerbread's support of Evergreen Industries and offering a toast—and a sizable donation—to the entire town. The PA system was now turned off, and they were hobnobbing with the important people.

Without even bothering with the steps, Noelle pressed

her hands to the floor and vaulted up onto the platform. God, she was gorgeous.

Every eye was trained squarely on the mesmerizing vision of her. Not that he blamed any of them. He couldn't force his gaze away from the petite dynamo that halted in front of him either.

Noelle glared up at him, her eyes flashing in a way that had dread settling thick and heavy in his belly.

At least she'd bothered to tell him she was leaving this time. Not that that offered him any comfort.

Dash braced. But while he waited for her to utter the words sure to slice straight through him, the anger slowly drained from her face. Placing a soft hand against his face, she went up on tiptoe and pressed a gentle kiss to his lips.

That was not what he'd expected at all. His heartbeat stuttered in his chest, hope blooming even as he tried to tamp it down.

Pulling back, Noelle stared up at him, attempting to fill her expression with a harsh sternness, but failing miserably. "If you ever lie to me again, Dash Evergreen, I'll hurt you. And we both know I can back up that threat."

Dash simply nodded, biting back a grin he knew would earn him some form of punishment.

Apparently satisfied, she wrapped her arms around his neck and pressed her body tight against his.

"I love you, Dash, and have ever since you found me curled up on the sleigh. Do you remember?"

How could he ever forget?

He'd gone into the barn, already in the process of learning the job he'd one day take over. The place had been quiet and, he'd thought, deserted. Until he'd looked inside Santa's sleigh and found Noelle curled up asleep on the seat. Her skin had glowed perfect and pale in the faint light. Her dark hair fanned out across the dark red velvet.

He'd had to touch. He'd only meant to wake her. At least

that was what he told himself. But the moment her warmth trickled into his body he hadn't been able to stop himself. The curve of her shoulder, the slope of her collarbone, her cheeks and eyelids and lips. He'd wanted to touch all of her, even back then. The need had been an interminable ache.

And when she'd opened her eyes, so vivid and blue... he'd been a goner. Especially when she smiled at him, all drowsy and flushed and tempting.

He'd started falling for her in that single moment.

"I love you, too, Elle," he whispered, his voice gruff with choked emotion.

"You don't have to lie to me to get me to stay, Dash. All you have to do is ask."

"Please, Elle. Don't leave me. Not again. I don't think I can survive without you."

Brushing her lips against his ear, she whispered, "You don't have to," and then punctuated the words with a sharp nip of his lobe.

He groaned and tightened his arms to crush her harder against his body. Damn all the people.

Somewhere behind him someone giggled. Someone sighed, a kind of perfectly happy sound. Cole and Ethan clapped him on the back. Gabriel's voice boomed, "You better damn well marry the girl again, Evergreen."

Dash pulled back and grinned down into Noelle's perfectly blue eyes. "I don't have to. We're still married."

The shocked expression on Elle's face was priceless.

"Elle didn't rescind her vows before she left. And I sure as hell didn't. I knew there'd never be another woman for me. The year and a day is long gone, so she's stuck with me whether she likes it or not."

Her fingers tangled in the hair at his nape and tugged. "Oh, I like," she said, right before her lips found his. The kiss left them both breathless. A cheer went up around them, followed by a loud cough when it went a little too long for public consumption.

"We'll discuss you keeping that piece of information to yourself, Mr. Evergreen, as soon as we get home."

"Whatever you want, Mrs. Evergreen. I rather like it when you lose your temper."

Elle made a rude noise in the back of her throat, passion and the promise of retribution glittering in her gaze. Her mouth thinned, and he knew she was about to start the argument early, but he didn't give her the chance.

Sweeping her into his arms, Dash stalked to a dark corner and apparated them both home.

He took his time undressing his wife, cherishing the way she looked at him, lust and love, comfort and hope all twining together in her gorgeous blue eyes. Dash felt the echo of those emotions pumping erratically through his own bloodstream.

She reached for him, slipping her soft hands beneath his clothes, searching for skin. The feel of her sizzled through his system.

Slowly, deliberately, she popped each button free, her gaze devouring every inch of his skin she revealed. No one but his Elle had ever been able to make him feel this way, desperate and deliriously happy at the same time.

Bending down, Dash used his mouth to worship her, memorizing and discovering every inch of her body until they were both panting, need held barely in check.

They'd been hot and desperate for each other for days. But tonight, now, was different. Better. Deeper.

Entwining their fingers together, Dash pressed their joined hands into the bed beside Noelle's head. She arched up to him, opening herself and offering him everything.

With the easy, deliberate glide of hard flesh into soft, Dash reclaimed his wife. Noelle met the moment with a

Andrea Laurence is an award-winning contemporary romance author who has been a lover of books and writing stories since she learned to read. A dedicated West Coast girl transplanted into the Deep South, she's working on her own happily-ever-after with her boyfriend and five fur babies. You can contact Andrea at her website, andrealaurence.com.

SILVER BELLE
Andrea Laurence

To Vicki, Rhonda and Kira, the ladies I shared this awesome experience with—

Working on *Jingle Spells* with you guys was great. Probably the most fun I've ever had plotting and writing a story. Thank you.

Seven Days until Christmas Eve

Belle hated cocoa. Even when it had fluffy homemade marshmallows or fresh whipped cream on top.

It was a dark secret she would take to her grave or else risk being ostracized by her family and friends. At Evergreen Industries, the witches, wizards and elves that made Christmas magick all drank cocoa. That's just how it had always been. There were no coffeepots in the building, at least none that anyone knew about. There was an emergency Keurig and a stash of pods hidden away in Belle's bottom file drawer. But that was it.

As far as Belle was concerned, their casual dismissal of coffee was a crime, and one that forced her out of the building every day to visit the local coffee shop, A Cup of Cheer. Her emergency brew couldn't hold up to the deep, rich flavors of the coffee she could get at the shop. It was only a few blocks away from the Evergreen corporate offices and worth it for her much-needed jolt of daily caffeine. This close to Christmas it was the only thing that helped her maintain her holiday cheer. Not even Ethan's sparkly, enchanted ornaments worked on her anymore.

Rolling over in bed, she spied the broad, bare shoulders

of Nick lying beside her. But it wasn't all bad. She supposed she should really thank her cocoa-imbibing brethren for driving her out of the office each day. It was during those daily visits to the coffee shop that she met local contractor Nick St. John. The successful businessman was tall, dark and undeniably sexy. What had started as a casual flirtation each day turned into more, and before Belle knew it, they were getting their coffee to go and heading to Nick's place.

It wasn't easy being the youngest Evergreen and the only girl, to boot. Her older brothers were nosy, overprotective and could make her life miserable if they wanted to. Dating was impossible. She had her own apartment at the lodge, but it was on the same floor as her parents and her brothers. There would be no comings or goings from her place that someone in her family didn't observe and report.

Belle wasn't supposed to date a human, but they'd made it all but impossible to date a wizard. Besides, two of her three brothers were dating outside the Winter Clan, so she didn't want to hear a word about it.

It wasn't like she and Nick were dating, anyway. It was more of a mutually beneficial arrangement with no strings. Judging by the sore heat between her thighs, the dull throb of her belly and the raw scratchiness in her throat, today was one of their more adventurous mornings.

She watched Nick's shoulders move gently with his soft breathing. The poor guy had worn himself out working so hard to please her, and she appreciated his effort. He was by far the best lover she'd had, and that was saying a lot considering many wizards used magickal trickery in the bedroom. Nick didn't have a crutch like that to lean on, so he had to work hard for every gasp of pleasure that came from her lips.

Belle wanted to reach out and run her palm across his bare back. She wanted to weave her fingers through the dark curls of hair at his neck. With each passing day she was tempted to stay longer. To learn more about the man that ruled her mornings. But she couldn't do any of those things.

Instead, she flung back the sheets and swung her legs out of bed. She moved around his bedroom collecting her clothes from where they had been hastily discarded. Belle had only managed to slip on her red lace panties when Nick rolled over and frowned at her.

"Leaving already?"

"You know I have to go." She tugged her tweed slacks up over her hips and reached for the matching lace bra she'd worn today for Nick's sole benefit. He was very appreciative of her fine lingerie. "I'm already infamous around the office for taking the longest coffee breaks in history."

Nick sighed and sat up, letting the sheets pool low around his waist. *Good gumdrops*, he had a beautiful body. Every inch of Nick's physique was hard, wrought by building homes. Lifting wooden beams and sanding drywall did a body good.

Belle was so distracted by the sight, she buttoned her blouse crooked. She didn't notice until Nick arched a dark, amused eyebrow at her, and she looked down to see what he was looking at. "Oh, *snickerdoodle!*" she cursed, unbuttoning and re-buttoning her top.

"You're so sexy when you talk dirty." Nick slid out from under the covers and walked nude across the room to where she was standing. Judging by his proud, aroused state, he wasn't kidding when he told her that her second-grade swearing vocabulary turned him on.

Nick wrapped his arms around her waist and pulled her close. The press of his firm heat against her belly stirred new pangs of arousal in her. She wanted to strip off all her clothes and waste away the afternoon in his bed, but she couldn't. She had to get back to work. It was a week before Christmas, and things were about to get crazy at the office. Maybe in January she would have enough free time to take off a whole day and indulge in the pleasures Nick had to offer.

Belle lifted the loose strands of her hair between her fingertips and pulled them back into a ponytail. Nick took advantage of her movement, and his lips met with the sensitive skin of her exposed neck. The tingle traveled down her arm and along her spine, tightening her skin into goose bumps and making her tremble slightly in his arms. "Stay," he whispered into her ear.

His rough hands glided across her skin as he started to convince her to stay a little while longer. And then her phone rang.

"Damn it," Nick cursed and stepped away.

"I'm sorry." Belle picked up her phone from the nightstand and frowned. It was her brother, Dash. "Yeah," she said, bypassing any pleasantries.

"I don't know where you are or what kind of slow roast Sumatra coffee you're waiting on, but you need to get your jingle bells back to the office right now."

She planted her hand on her hip in irritation. "Since when did you become my boss, Dasher Evergreen?"

"Would you rather Cole be the one to call? He's in a foul mood, but I can ask him to relay the same message if you're going to be stubborn."

"No, thanks." Her oldest brother Cole was the CEO of Evergreen Industries, so in fact, her brother *was* the boss of her. But given a choice of being chewed out, she'd take Dash any day. "What's the big emergency?"

"I don't think we should talk about it on the phone."

"What? Why?"

"Because we've got a Code Red here, and this line may not be secure."

Dash's words were like a splash of icy water on her libido. A Code Red was the highest alert at the office, reserved only for Santa-related emergencies. Given everything that had happened the last few weeks with Kris and his midlife crisis, she wasn't surprised. But she was concerned. Christmas was only a week away.

"I'll be there in ten minutes."

"No. You need to *apparate*, now."

Belle glanced over her shoulder at Nick. He was tugging on his jeans and trying not to listen in on her discussion. "Now is not the best time for that."

"Then find an alley or go into the ladies' room or something because *Santa is gone*!"

The line went dead, leaving Belle to wonder if she'd heard him right. Santa was gone. That couldn't be right. She'd seen Kris just this morning. Or was that yesterday morning?

"Trouble at work?" Nick asked.

"Yes," she said with a weary smile. "There's a big emergency I need to get back for. Working with family is always special. And this time of year is so busy for us that everything is a crisis of one sort or another."

"I understand. We'd both better get back to work. I've got to install all the cabinets at my latest house today. Same time tomorrow?"

"That's my plan. I'll text you if it changes."

Nick leaned in to kiss her goodbye. The moment his lips met hers, she could feel her head start to swim. He had potent powers over her body. Every nerve lit up at his touch.

Belle pulled away reluctantly and picked her coffee cup up off the nightstand. "I'll see you tomorrow," she said.

Nick waved at her from the front door wearing nothing but his blue jeans. She had to take a deep breath to force her feet down the street toward her office building. Once he shut the door, she looked around for any humans. The street was pretty quiet, but she couldn't take any chances. She ducked between two houses and with one last look around, she flicked her wrist and disappeared.

Nick's truck rumbled over the icy gravel of his latest construction site. He pulled up alongside the van and car of two of his employees. Ben should be inside priming and painting the drywall, and Tom was working on plumbing fixtures. His task today, as he told Belle, was cabinets. He had to get those in so Tom could put in the sinks and faucets.

His heavy boots crunched through the yard until he stepped up over the threshold into the house. There was a large stack of cabinets on the floor, each wrapped with a protective outer layer. Nick had picked them up from the supplier early that morning and dropped them off before going to meet Belle. He pulled a pocket knife out of his belt and set to work unwrapping them all.

He had the base cabinets screwed into place when Ben came into the room behind him. "Hey, Nick. How are the cabinets going?"

"Good so far. Where are we with priming?"

"The downstairs is all done. I've got one bedroom left upstairs. Then I can start the base coat. I painted two coats on the kitchen and bathroom walls yesterday so you could get the cabinets in. I'm expecting to have everything painted with trim and crown molding by Christmas Eve. I thought that was a good stopping point before the holiday."

Nick frowned. Was Christmas really that close? He tried not to pay that much attention, despite the fact that Gingerbread was destination Christmastown, USA. Being surrounded by Christmas all year actually seemed to dull the impact of the real holiday. At least in Denver, he knew when the lights and decorations went up that it was getting to be that time. "How long until Christmas?" he asked.

soul-deep sigh of acceptance and wonder that did everything to make him feel invincible.

This amazing woman was his.

They came together slowly, milking each stroke, caress and kiss until they were both drowning in sensation, their bodies quivering with release.

"I'll never get enough of you," Dash reverently murmured against her skin.

Hours later, weak sunlight was seeping around the dark curtains when they finally fell asleep, blissfully tangled together.

A loud pounding startled them both awake long before their exhausted bodies were ready. Dash groaned and rubbed at his scratchy eyes. Noelle vaulted out of bed. Her bare feet landed silently on the floor even as her hand groped uselessly at her side.

Recovering first, she threw on a robe and padded over.

The elf waiting on the other side shifted nervously from foot to foot as he wrung his hands. Horror and dread filled his eyes as he blurted out, "Kris and Merry are gone!"

* * * * *

"A week," Ben said. "Time just flies, man. I've still got to go get a gift for my wife at Baubles. She wants some fancy charm bracelet she saw on television. And of course my kid wants an impossible to get toy from Santa, so I've got to start haunting the internet for that. You got any fun plans this year?"

The answer to that was a resounding no, but Nick didn't tell people that. If folks thought he would spend Christmas alone eating a frozen dinner, they would feel bad and want to invite him to their family dinners and parties. He wasn't interested. He didn't dislike Christmas. Nick just didn't care for the commercial hype that went with it.

This, of course, as he custom-built Christmas-themed bungalows for wealthy snow bunnies. The irony was not lost on him. But that didn't mean he wanted to get all wrapped up in it, either. "Yeah," Nick said. "I'm going to drive up to see my folks in Denver."

"That's great." Ben smiled. "I'm going to haul in the last of my primer and get that bedroom knocked out."

Nick watched his employee disappear into the yard and focused his attention back on the cabinets. He snorted quietly to himself as he thought about the idea of actually spending Christmas with his parents. He couldn't imagine a more stressful, awkward holiday experience.

About six years ago, when he'd first started his business, he'd been too busy to go home for Christmas. The next year, it seemed like a good excuse to use again. Then he moved to Gingerbread, and the lie perpetuated itself year after year. No one seemed to miss him. They just sent a generic fruit basket like he was one of his father's clients. He was pretty sure they got the same cellophane-wrapped dome of apples and oranges he did.

Christmas had become just another day, and one where he couldn't even get food from a drive-thru at that.

Nick did wonder what Belle would be doing for Christmas. She hadn't mentioned anything, although he was certain the holiday was a big deal in the Evergreen household. Her family was famous for their Christmas ornaments, and her brother Ethan was a holiday fixture on television. They donated a small fortune to the community and other charities. But aside from that, no one really knew much about them or their company. You could sit outside the building for hours and not see a single soul go in or out. And aside from Belle and her brothers, Nick didn't know another person in town that actually worked there. It was a factory. There should be hundreds of community residents working for Evergreen Industries.

The Christmas cynic in him wondered if they secretly shipped in all their ornaments from a plant in India or Mexico and just claimed to make them here. Anything was possible when nothing was really known about them.

Despite the fact that he'd spent every morning with Belle for the last six months, he didn't have much more insight than anyone else.

At first, Belle's silence was refreshing. They were both very busy professionals. Their time together was fun and easy. She never lay in bed and bored him to tears with stories about the banalities of her day or how she broke a nail opening a pickle jar.

She also didn't demand quality time with him outside of their daily interludes. They hadn't been on a single date by his recollection. They'd never even shared a meal aside from the occasional scone with their coffee. Belle never called and rarely texted. It was the perfect relationship for him as he poured every ounce of energy into his company. Most women he'd dated hadn't understood how much time and effort it took to be successful, and they eventually gave up on him. Usually, that was just fine by Nick.

And yet…he'd found himself wondering about Belle. At first, he thought he'd hit the woman jackpot. She showed up daily for hot sex and was out the door before he could make up some excuse for her to leave. But over time, he found himself wishing she would stay even as she disappeared. She was the first woman he dated that left him wanting more, but he was too respectful of their arrangement to push for anything more substantial than what they had. He didn't want to be like the women that had always pressured him to give more than he could.

But it did make him curious about his elusive lover. Why didn't they ever go back to her place? He didn't even know where she lived. Hell, she could be married for all he knew. And what were all those calls and texts about that sent her scuttling off from his bedroom each day? Yesterday was a security problem and today, some emergency. What kind of emergency could she run into at an ornament manufacturing company? Nick couldn't come up with much. He knew one thing, though.

He couldn't wait for 10 a.m. tomorrow morning.

Belle reappeared in her office half a heartbeat after she vanished from Nick's neighborhood. She was dizzy for only a moment and didn't spill a precious drop of her double-shot latte with peppermint. As the details of her office came into focus around her, she took a deep breath. *Apparating* was not her favorite form of travel, even if it was the most efficient. She enjoyed the occasional brisk walk through the cold winter air. It helped clear her mind. But time was not on her side today.

Once she got her bearings, she slipped out of her coat and dumped it and her purse onto her desk. She picked up her tablet and walked over to the mirror on the back of her office door. Whenever she came back from Nick's, she had to make sure her appearance didn't give any signs of what she'd been up to. A quick glance confirmed that her golden-blond hair was still neatly slicked back into a low ponytail. Her makeup looked fine, although she could use more lipstick. Her clothes looked just as neat and professional as they had when she left the office. All was well.

Then she frowned. Leaning into the mirror she focused on a dark smudge just below her ear. She rubbed at it with her finger, but it didn't disappear. Then she realized what it was. Nick had given her a hickey. Of all the things... Belle groaned and dug in her purse for some concealer. She blotted the mark with the makeup, and then readjusted her scarf to cover it. Her brothers could not see that. Santa emergency or not, they'd be all in her business.

That done, she could finally go in search of Dash to find out what the *holly* was going on with Kris Kringle.

It wasn't hard to find them. She only had to follow the loud voices down the Hall of Santas to Cole's office. All three of her brothers were there, frowns lining their faces. Sitting in the corner was Dash's ex-wife, Noelle. By some weird twist of fate, they were dating again, but she didn't look blissfully in love today. Not that she ever did. Noelle was an intense person. She'd left Evergreen to join the CIA, returning earlier this year to fill in for her ailing father as the head of security.

Today, Noelle appeared even more unapproachable. Her dark brown hair was slicked back into a severe bun. Her normally bright blue eyes were tired and bloodshot with gray circles beneath them. She looked as if she had been up all night. And not in a good way.

"Belle, you're here. Good. Sit down," Cole said, gesturing to the empty chair in the office.

The three brothers all turned to Noelle, mostly ignoring their sister. "Okay, now that Belle is here, start from the beginning."

Noelle took a deep breath. "Late last night, I ran into Merry in the hallway. She had luggage with her, but I was too distracted to think about what that meant. Dash and I had a fight, and I was considering leaving Gingerbread. Merry talked me out of it, and then she left. I ran back to apologize to Dash. It wasn't until this morning when we found the Corvette was missing that I realized I had caught her midflight and didn't know it."

"Merry is gone?"

The four other heads in the room turned to look at Belle. Apparently, she was behind the curve. "Dash only told me that Kris was gone," she explained.

"They're both gone," Noelle clarified. "They took off last night in the Corvette. We have no way of knowing if they're ever coming back."

Belle's jaw dropped open. This was a Code Red if she'd ever seen one. Santa was MIA. It was no wonder she was summoned back. The minute any employee issue arose, it fell into her territory to work on the problem, be it an elf strike or inappropriate wizardry in the workplace.

"We have to replace him immediately," Cole decreed.

"Wait a minute," Belle argued. "We don't know he's gone for certain. He might have just needed some air to clear his head. We know they've been having marital troubles. A couple days away together might be what they need to come back and rededicate themselves to the job."

"Yes, but all of their troubles have revolved around his role as Santa," Ethan argued. "He would sacrifice that for Merry and the sake of their marriage. He's not coming back. I can feel it. His Christmas spirit has fizzled out."

"But what if Kris does come back? Once the new Santa puts on his suit, the magick is severed, and Kris can never be Santa again. This is a huge step to take, and we can't go back. Did they leave a note? Anything to let us know what their plans are?"

"There was no note," Dash said. "But Kris left this behind." He held up the holly pin that Kris always wore on his lapel. The shiny brooch had three solid-gold holly leaves

and a cluster of diamond-and-ruby berries in the center
that were more than one carat each. It was handed down
from Santa to Santa, an antique so priceless, any collec-
tor would kill to have it. *If* they knew it existed. "It was on
his desk. That's a pretty clear sign to me that he's done."

"Belle, you need to find a new Santa. It's only a week
until Christmas. Six days, if you consider Christmas be-
gins in the Pacific twenty hours before Gingerbread. We
can't waste any time."

Belle eyed her oldest brother as she twisted her lips in
thought. Kris had been Santa for twenty years, almost her
whole life. He was the only Santa she remembered. Choosing a new Santa was a monumental task, and one that only
happened every other generation.

The role of Santa was always filled by a human, and he
was selected by the Winter Clan's magickal means. Even if
the person wanted to be Santa, and sometimes they didn't,
it wasn't easy. She tapped at her tablet and pulled up the
checklist that would need to be completed before a new
Santa could drive off in the sleigh. The assimilation of a
human into Gingerbread alone could take nearly a month
if all went well.

"It's impossible," she said, shaking her head. "We'd do
better to send out a team to look for Kris and bring him
back. If we can convince him to do one more Christmas,
we'll have a whole year to get his replacement ready."

"What if he won't come back? Or we can't find him?
Are you willing to risk Christmas, Belle? Because if we
don't get someone on that sleigh in less than a week,
Christmas won't happen. If he comes back, great, but I'd
rather have too many Santas than too few."

Six Days Until Christmas Eve

Belle had been dismissed from the meeting so she could immediately get to work. But she wasn't as convinced as Cole was that they needed to select a new Santa right away. If she could get a Santa ready in seven days, six wasn't much more of a hardship, and it bought her a day to try another tactic. Instead, she'd pegged two of her assistants, Ginger and Holly, for a special assignment.

Kris didn't know that Dash had put a GPS tracking system on the Corvette last week. It hadn't been intended to stalk Kris, but to track his Christmas flight and ensure they could recover the car if it was stolen. Kris had demanded that Dash enchant the convertible so he could fly it on Christmas instead of the sleigh. If by some chance Noelle's cloaking device failed and a human got into the car, they couldn't risk it accidentally flying through the air with them trapped inside.

None of the brothers had mentioned tracking Kris, but that was because they'd given up on him. Belle hadn't, at least not yet. She hoped that Kris and Merry were coming back. It wasn't like them to leave everyone in a lurch like this. But like Ethan, she knew in her heart that Kris had lost the joy of his work. She understood how he felt, but that said, if Ginger and Holly could find him, Belle wasn't above coercing him into one last trip around the world. Then she would happily replace him if that was what he really wanted.

Right now, the GPS was showing the Corvette was in Arizona and continuing south. She wouldn't be surprised if they were headed to Mexico or even South America and its warmer climate. Ginger and Holly were gone in search of them by midafternoon.

Belle had hoped to hear from them soon. Like that evening. But it was the following morning, and there was no word from her assistants yet. She needed to take a two-pronged approach and start the new Santa process, as well.

She made her way down the hallway to Santa's office. Belle rarely came into this room at Evergreen. If all went well, there wasn't any reason to. It was normally Santa's retreat, the place where he could work and think without constant interruption.

With a swipe of her security card, the heavy golden doors swung open, allowing her inside. The large space was filled with wondrous antiques and magickal artifacts from years of Christmases past. Large shelves along one wall housed a massive collection of leather-bound books. Some were first editions of beloved Christmas tales like *A Christmas Carol* and *A Visit from St. Nicholas*, but most were the naughty and nice archives from back before they went digital. Another wall was lined with all the gifts children had left him over the years. Milk and cookies were the American standard, but on the occasion that a child left Santa a drawing or a coffee mug, it was always brought back and kept here.

Santas, as a general rule, were very sentimental. They couldn't throw away anything a child gave them, be it a

popsicle stick reindeer they made in school or a flashlight to help him see in the dark.

Belle continued through the office, stepping around several large burgundy velvet bags overflowing with mail. She frowned at the sight. Kris had not been reading his mail from the children like he was supposed to. He'd been too busy jogging and juicing lately to do his job. She would have to get Taryn to send down someone to log the gift requests in the system since she was the new head of the IT department.

At the back of the room was another door. Belle swiped her card to open it, revealing the most secret and sacred of rooms at Evergreen Industries. In tall, lighted, glass cabinets were Santa's clothes from Christmases past. The uniform had changed over the years, and when an outfit was retired, it was displayed here as a revered museum piece. She stopped to admire one of her favorites. The old Father Christmas style included a long, dark green, velvet, hooded cloak lined in soft, white fur. It was hand-embroidered with a holly pattern; the gold thread and tiny gemstone berries made it sparkle in the light. It was beautiful. Much more festive and true to the spirit of Christmas in Belle's eyes.

Beside it was the original red-and-white suit from the early 1900s. It wasn't their decision to go with the style, but once popular culture set an expectation of what Santa wore, they had to follow along. A newer design was beyond it, modernized by the Coca-Cola styling of the thirties and forties.

A rack just beyond the cases held several replicas of the current Santa suit. It was still red and white, but the style was more modern, and they had made some technological advances to it over the years.

On the far wall was Belle's destination. The delicately carved curio cabinet was the home to the most sacred of the Winter clan's heirlooms. The side panels were inset with stained glass depicting falling snowflakes in blue, white and silver. The front was clear glass with a door-knob made of one gigantic sapphire.

Belle grasped the knob and opened the door. There were four shelves inside holding a variety of treasures. The wand of the Winter clan's founding mother was there. The heavy, leather-bound copy of the original naughty and nice list was there. As was the snow globe.

The large glass sphere was nestled in a sterling-silver base. All around the bottom were intricate Christmas scenes of the past. Silver reindeer antlers curled around the glass globe like talons keeping it in place. Inside was only snow. No snowman figurines, no quaint villages. Just snow.

This was what she had come for. She grasped the snow globe with two hands, surprised at how heavy it was. This was how the next Santa was chosen. An enchantment was placed on the snow globe hundreds of years earlier. It had the power to see into the hearts and minds of every person on the planet. It would choose, with over 99 percent ac-curacy, the perfect new Santa. With just a shake, the face of the chosen replacement would appear.

This was the first time Belle had needed to use it. Ner-vously, Belle gave the snow globe a good jostle, then held it steady to watch. The snow danced furiously inside, a mini blizzard swirling and sparkling with the faint blue magickal glow. When the flakes settled, a man's face slowly appeared. It was clear as day. The dark hair, the chocolate-brown eyes, the mischievous smile.

It was Nick.

No, Belle argued with herself. There had to be some-thing wrong with this thing. Nick was about as far from Santa material as they came. He was too young, for one thing. Santas were usually in their forties at least, and Nick was barely thirty if she remembered correctly. Nick was sexy and hard-bodied, not cheerful and soft. He was career driven and health conscious. She'd never seen him so much as put a packet of sugar in his coffee, much less eat ten thousand sugar cookies in one night.

And frankly, she didn't get the touchy-feely vibe from him. She'd never seen Nick around kids, but she imagined he'd hold one at arm's length with suspicion in his eyes.

Belle frowned. Somehow, the snow globe had made a mistake. She gave it another shake, erasing Nick's image with a flurry of snow. She waited, her heart pounding in her chest as the next image slowly formed.

Nick's smiling face continued to stare back at her from inside the globe.

Her heart dropped into her stomach with a nauseating ache. This couldn't be right. At least, she didn't want it to be right. Maybe he was secretly soft-hearted and good with children. Maybe he secretly adored cookies, but stayed away to keep in shape. Belle didn't know as much about Nick as she thought. And that had been by design on both their parts. Their secret rendezvous were supposed to be easy, casual fun. A little stress relief in their crazy, busy lives.

And now she would lose him, like everything else, to the holiday machine.

Belle loved Christmas. And she loved her work and her life in Gingerbread. But sometimes…she needed to get away from all of it. She wanted to spend time with someone who didn't curse with Christmas slang and thought elves were make-believe.

Her mornings with Nick were her escape. The time she spent with him kept her sane. He was her daily dose of normal in a world of magick and merriment. And with one shake of a snow globe, she'd lost it all.

A chirp sounded at her hip. She placed the snow globe back in the cabinet and shut the door before looking at the screen of her phone. It was her fifteen-minute reminder of her standing coffee break appointment.

Belle sighed and put the phone back in her pocket. Nick was going to get a little more than a cup of coffee and some lovin' today.

Belle was late.

Nick sat at a corner table, nursing his grande black-drip coffee. He checked his cell phone again, but there were no texts saying she was running behind. Belle was punctual to a fault. It made him wonder if yesterday's emergency was just a rouse to leave. He'd never been with a woman so emotionally disconnected from sex. Was this her not-so-subtle way of brushing him off?

He got his answer when the front door opened and Belle blew into the coffee shop. She turned to him and gave a short wave before ordering her coffee. Nick got up from the table and waited for her at the counter where the barista would leave her drink when it was ready.

There was something odd about Belle today. He picked up on it almost immediately. Her smile wasn't as bright, her green eyes were wary. Perhaps the emergency was real and more serious than he thought. She seemed to be carrying a heavy burden on her shoulders.

"Hey, Nick," she said with a weak smile as she approached.

"Decaf non-fat grande latte." Her cup was passed across the counter to her. She slid it into the cardboard sleeve and popped a lid on the top.

Decaf? Belle never ordered decaf. Something was definitely going on, but he didn't want to ask her with so many other people around. "Are you ready to go?" he asked. They usually didn't loiter long.

She nodded, and he held the door for her to step outside. They walked quietly down the block, sipping their coffee.

She wanted to tell him something. He could tell. Perhaps she was about to break it off.

"Is something wrong?" he asked, once they were clear of the street traffic and on the quiet road to his subdivision.

"Wrong? No. But we do need to talk about something today. It's kind of important."

Nick's heart stopped. The breath was sucked from his chest in an instant as his brain pieced together the clues. Decaf coffee. Tired. Nervous mood. Important discussions. Belle never wanted to talk about anything.

"Are you pregnant?" he choked.

Belle's eyes grew wide at his question. "Pregnant?" she repeated, her voice sharp with surprise. "Of course not. Why would you think something like that?"

Nick closed his eyes and took a deep breath. It was as though he'd been jerked back from a cliff, and his whole life was about to change if he fell. She wasn't pregnant. Great. He wasn't opposed to children, but he wasn't exactly in that place right now. Especially if it meant having them with a woman he really knew nothing about. "I'm sorry," he said. "You were acting nervous, drinking decaf, wanting to talk…you never want to talk, Belle."

She smiled and shook her head. "I'm sorry I scared you. I am definitely not pregnant. I was up early, and I've already had one cup too much caffeine to deal with everything going on. My nerves are on edge. But I do have a uh…*business proposition* to discuss with you."

Business proposition? "Do you need a house built?"

"Not exactly." Belle paused at his doorstep, and he unlocked the door to go inside. "Let's sit down."

For the first time, they didn't head down the hallway to his bedroom, but turned right to the living room and kitchen. Belle sat down on his brown leather sofa and tucked one leg beneath her. Nick followed suit, sitting on the other end of the couch and turning to face her while he sipped his coffee.

"So what's going on, Belle?"

"That emergency yesterday was kind of a big deal where I work," she began.

"How bad of an emergency can you have at an ornament factory? Someone lose a hand or something?"

"No, but still very bad. We lost a very important member of our staff unexpectedly." Belle reached into her coat and pulled out a small silver flask. She sat it on the coffee table.

"Are we drinking? It's a little early."

"No. That's just my back-up plan."

Nick frowned. "Back-up plan?"

"Nick, I need to tell you a secret. It's a big secret that only a few people in the whole world know about. I have deliberately kept it from you for your own good, but I've been given no choice. I have to tell you the truth."

"You're a spy?" he joked.

"No, I'm a witch. And you are going to be the next Santa Claus."

Nick was glad he didn't have a mouthful of coffee or he would've made a mess of Belle's cream-colored blouse. He was on the verge of laughing at her joke when he realized her expression was deadly serious. "So, will the Easter Bunny be joining us later?"

"No. Spring isn't my territory," she retorted without missing a beat. "We're from the Winter clan. My family is responsible for Christmas. We use our magickal powers to make Santa and his reindeer fly, deliver toys around the world in a single night and spread holiday cheer."

Nick was beginning to think he liked Belle better when she didn't say much. Now that she was talking, he was sad to realize she was batshit crazy. "Did you skip some important medication today?"

Belle's lips tightened into a firm line. "I have to show you, don't I? You're not going to believe it until you see it."

"See what, Belle? Are you going to use your magic wand to make me into Santa Claus?"

"Something like that." Belle stood up. Reaching inside her purse, she pulled out a long, thin piece of wood, like a conductor's baton. She tapped it a few times against the palm of her hand, sending a few tiny, sparkling snow-flakes out of the tip.

"What the hell?" Nick stood up and took a step back.

Belle flicked her wrist and pointed the wand to the bare corner of his living room. A surge of white, glittering light shot from it, and in an instant, there was a seven-foot Christmas tree in the corner. With another swipe, a silvery swirl wrapped around the pine branches, leaving lights and ornaments behind it until the tree was completely decorated.

"Are you more of a star or angel kind of guy?"

"What?" His heart was pounding too hard in his chest to grasp what she was asking him.

"A star, I think." A quick jab of her wand conjured a shining silver star on the top of the tree. When she was done, she slipped her wand back into her purse and calmly sat down on the couch.

Nick swallowed hard and stepped backward from the tree and its conjurer until his back met with the brick of his fireplace. "What is going on?"

Belle sighed and patted the couch beside her. "I'm sorry for the theatrics, but I need you to listen and believe what I'm telling you. We don't have much time. Christmas is less than a week away."

Christmas. Witches. Santa. Magick. The words swirled in his mind as he tried to make sense of it.

"Nick, please sit down. I'm not going to hurt you. I'm

the same person you've seen every day of the last six months."

"Not exactly," he sputtered.

"Yes, exactly. We just didn't talk much about ourselves."

"If we had, would you being a witch have come up?"

"No. We can't tell humans our secret. It's for our protection as much as yours."

"But you're telling me now."

"Only because I have no choice. You are the chosen. The next Pere Noel, Sinter Klaas or Babbo Natale. If you choose to accept this honor, you *will* be Father Christmas."

"And if I don't accept your crazy offer?"

The light faded from Belle's green eyes. "If you decline, you need only take a sip from this flask. You will remember nothing about this offer or anything that you saw. It will be as though it never happened. It will also be as though *we* never happened. The next time you see me on the street, I will be just another stranger."

There was a sudden, restrictive tightness in Nick's chest. He didn't think he wanted to be Santa Claus, but he didn't want to lose Belle, either. "Wait—can't we just go back to yesterday like this conversation didn't happen?"

A small smile curled Belle's lips. "No, I'm sorry. I assure you that I am as disappointed as you are by this development. There are only two choices. You come with me now to Evergreen Industries and become the next Santa Claus, or you drink from the flask, and you and I are done."

Nick eyed the flask and slowly eased back down onto the couch. "What's in that thing?"

"Cocoa."

He arched a dark brow at her. "Just cocoa?"

"It's a special batch."

Nick sank back into the cushions. "If I turn down the job, what happens on Christmas Eve?" Part of him couldn't believe the words coming from his own mouth.

Santa wasn't real. Flying reindeer didn't exist. His parents bought all his presents. He remembered the crushing disappointment when his father told him the truth. The magick of Christmas had died for him in that moment, leaving only a hollow, commercial shell behind. And yet there was enough of a spark in his mind to wonder what would happen if what Belle said was true.

"I'm not sure. We've never had this happen before. I'll go back and see if a new Santa can be chosen in time. If not…" A shimmer of tears formed in her emerald eyes. "…I failed. And for the first time in hundreds of years, there will be no Christmas."

Nick wanted to reach out to her and comfort her. Belle had always been so even-keeled. She came off as a no-nonsense businesswoman with her sharp suits and slicked-back hair. This was the first time he'd noticed a crack in her emotional veneer. "What happened to the previous Santa Claus? Is he…uh…" He hesitated to ask a teary woman if Santa was dead.

"He's fine," she said with an irritated tone lacing her words. "Kris disappeared in the night, leaving us high and dry with days left until Christmas. We've looked everywhere for him, but we haven't had any luck yet."

Santa went AWOL? This job might not be as merry as it seemed. "Will you excuse me a moment?"

Belle turned to him with concern, but nodded. She probably thought he was about to sneak out the back door but was polite enough not to follow him, anyway. "Of course."

Nick brushed past her and slipped into the guest bathroom. Hovering over the sink, he splashed cold water on his face. He braced his arms on the porcelain edge and looked at himself in the mirror.

Was it possible that Santa Claus was real? Disappointment and disillusionment had hardened him to the season. It was supposed to be about love and family, giving and sharing. Instead, it had become about Black Friday sales and the latest, impossible-to-find toy. People would spend the whole month gorging on cookies and candy and turkey, while tossing a token can of expired peas into the food drive bins at work.

That's why Nick had mentally checked out. If he just pretended Christmas never happened, he wouldn't have to face the reality of what it had become.

But maybe he was wrong. Maybe there still was some magick left in the season. If there was any chance that he could have back the holiday of his childhood, he would take it. But even with wands and elves, was it even a possibility? Was his own heart too hardened to embrace Christmas again?

His own dark eyes reflected to him, a faint shimmer of tears blurring his vision. Perhaps it wasn't too late for him or for others like him.

He snatched the towel from the nearby rod and dried his face before going back into the living room. Belle was still sitting patiently on the couch when he returned.

She stood up and turned to face him when she saw him walk back into the room. Belle had such a fragile beauty about her. There was something about the golden waves of her hair, large jewel-tone eyes and creamy, blush cheeks that reminded him of a china doll. He'd thought at first he might break her, especially considering he was a foot taller and at least eighty pounds heavier. But Belle had a spine of steel and enough ambition for two or three people. He loved the contradiction of her.

For the last six months, she had been the highlight of his day. Even before he laid a hand on her, he'd timed his breaks so he would see her at the coffee shop. She was always so businesslike and proper. He had wanted to see her wild and free. And he had, many times. She was never as beautiful as when she came undone in his arms. But Belle had never let him see all of her. She held so much back.

He never expected her secrets to be so earth-shattering. And yet, once the panic subsided, the truth had suited her so perfectly. This was the puzzle piece he was missing. The mysterious details of Belle's life that he'd craved all this time. And he'd only gotten a tiny taste of the true woman. He wasn't ready to drink the cocoa and let her go just yet.

"Do I have to decide right now?"

She shook her head. "We still have some time. I can take you to the Evergreen offices first. I'll introduce you to the clan and show you around. It will give you a better idea of what you're signing up for. It isn't all like the children's books, but it's still quite magnificent. Then you can decide."

Nick could deal with that. If things got too weird, he could always drink the cocoa, walk out and go back to being his old, cynical self. "Let's go, then." He grabbed his coat and keys off the kitchen counter. "Do you want me to drive? I don't even know if you have a car."

Belle smiled brightly for the first time today, and it made his heart feel lighter to see her happy again. "We don't need a car."

Nick frowned. "It's a long walk. What are we going to take? A broom?"

Belle chuckled. "Only the Autumn Clan rides brooms. We're going to *apparate*. It's faster and one of the only ways to get inside the building with our extensive security system." She reached out and took his hand.

Nick wasn't sure he even knew what *apparate* meant.

"You don't get motion sickness, do you?" she asked.

"What?" Nick said, turning to her with concern.

And then they were gone.

Sixty-Three Hours until Take-off

Belle looked at her cell phone and frowned. She'd just received a text from Holly. Apparently, she and Ginger had a bit of an issue at the Mexican border and had missed their chance to intercept the Corvette. Since neither of the girls had ever set foot out of Colorado, they were unable to envision the location in their mind. And witches and wizards could only *apparate* to locations they had been before.

Awesome. The longer they waited, the farther Kris and Merry traveled without them.

Things weren't much better at Evergreen Industries.

Cole stuck his head into Belle's office, the stress of the last few days visibly lining his face. "Has he signed yet?"

"No, he hasn't signed yet," she snapped. He'd asked her this question at least ten times since Nick came. "We've started the orientation process to get ahead of the game, but Nick hasn't signed the contract or tried on the suit."

Cole rolled his eyes and bashed his forehead forcefully against the door frame. "Remind me why I was chosen to be the CEO?"

"Because you're the oldest Evergreen and the most responsible of the four of us."

"And you're the baby," he noted, "and everyone does what you want. So get out of this office, find Nick and do whatever it takes to convince him to take this job. Today."

Belle watched Cole disappear down the hallway in a huff. Usually, Cole was a lot more easygoing. If any of the Evergreens were going to send wizards and witches fleeing from the sight of them, it was usually Belle. She was tiny, at five-foot and an angel's hair tall, but feisty enough that her size didn't matter. She could intimidate the smallest elves and tallest wizards alike.

She didn't like to think of herself as intimidating. That's not what she wanted to be. She kept the employees of Evergreen Industries happy, but productive. Christmas was no small undertaking. There were procedures to be followed, checklists to tick off and policies to uphold. If that made her come off as strict, she'd live with that for the sake of the children. She didn't have time to waste on silliness.

And she didn't have time to waste on Nick, either. When she said he didn't have to decide right away, she thought a tour and a couple of hours would do the trick. It had been two days and so far, nothing. It was a big decision, but it was now or never.

Belle grabbed her tablet and headed out in search of Nick. He'd spent the morning touring the underground toy and ornament production floors with Ethan. The security system showed his last badge swipe was the cafeteria. They'd gotten him a temporary card to move around the facility and get comfortable. It had proven to be a useful tool in keeping track of him, as well.

She summoned an elevator and headed to the cafeteria to find him. As she entered the large dining hall, she stopped short. It was lunchtime, and the room was quite full, but it took only a moment to locate Nick. The six-foot-two construction manager was seated in a green plastic chair more suited to an elf. His knees protruded over the top of the table, so he had to lean in between them to reach his tray of food. It looked miserably uncomfortable. Belle could hardly stand to sit in those chairs, and she was one of the tiniest witches in the building. Despite all of that, he was smiling and chatting animatedly with the crowded table of elves around him.

Belle couldn't help but smile. Despite her reservations, the snow globe knew better. Perhaps Nick would fit in here just fine. Now it was only her selfishness motivating her reluctance for him to become Santa.

Honestly, she didn't know why she cared. Whether he became Santa or not, Belle had lost her morning coffee breaks. If he left, he wouldn't remember her. And if he stayed, things between them would be…complicated to say the least. She certainly couldn't continue her affair with him as Santa. That was just wrong on so many levels. And she had no intention of being the next Mrs. Claus, either. She couldn't bake or knit, and the idea of doing either bored her to tears.

Her only real choice would be to sit back and watch as another woman took her place. Maybe a human, maybe a witch. Their Santas usually came married, so it wasn't an issue they had dealt with in her memory. It was miserably selfish, but Belle knew she would rather Nick leave and Christmas be ruined than to watch him with another woman for the next forty years. She didn't realize she had such a jealous streak, but it seemed to run deep where Nick was concerned.

Either way, in the end, Belle was left with nothing. Well, not *nothing*. She still had a job to do. They needed a Santa, and Nick needed to make a choice.

Nick turned in her direction and noticed her watching him. He waved, and all the elves at the table turned and waved, too. Despite the pain of losing Nick, Belle knew she had to smile and wave back. She didn't want her feelings on the situation to influence Nick's decision. This was his life on the line, not hers, even if it felt that way at the moment.

Nick said a few things to the elves, and then stood up from the table with his lunch tray. He weaved through the tiny tables to where she was standing. "Afternoon, Belle."

"Hi, Nick."

"I was thinking about you when the glockenspiel chimed ten this morning."

Belle couldn't help the blush that instantly colored her cheeks. "Shh…" she whispered. "No one knows about all that."

"We're in a crowded, loud room. Who's going to hear us?"

"Elves, Nick. Those big ears aren't just for show. If you're done eating, dump your tray, and we can go somewhere more private to talk."

They went out into the hallway, and Belle gestured for him to follow her to the nearby Cranberry conference room. She shut and locked the door behind them. Nick immediately rounded the large meeting table and walked to the wall of windows that looked out over Gingerbread. "It's hard to look at this town and see things the same way I did three days ago. I drove by this building every day and never imagined there was a toy production facility run by elves fifty feet below my tires. And do you know how many times I've gone hiking or mountain biking on Mistletoe Mountain? And to think there's an entire wizard village up there, and I never knew it."

Belle sat at the edge of the table and crossed her arms over her chest. "You weren't supposed to know. Not everyone is allowed to see."

"That's a shame," he said, turning from the window to face her. "Most people could use a little more wonder and magick in their lives. Adults, especially. They lose the childhood wonder too soon."

"We do what we can," Belle explained, "but most adults have lost their ability to believe."

Nick nodded and took a few steps closer to her. "Despite all the wonderful things I've seen and learned, I've still missed you these last few days."

Belle straightened up a bit, stiffening at his approach. She had wanted to keep this discussion professional. "I've been here the whole time."

He leaned into her, pressing his palms into the hardwood table. Nick loomed over her with his large frame, forcing her to lean backward or find herself in a compromising position on the conference table. If she caught one of her employees like this, they'd find themselves in her office getting a reprimand.

"It's not the same," he said, his dark eyes focused on her lips while he spoke. "I've been able to touch you, taste you, nearly every day for months. Then all of a sudden, everything changed."

His voice was low, his words like a verbal caress. Belle was too close to Nick not to respond to him. The warm scent of his cologne teased at her senses and took her back to his house. To the smell of him on the pillowcases. It made her want to inhale deeply and keep that part of him with her when she lost the rest. An ache of need gnawed at her center, forcing her to clamp her thighs tightly together. A lot of things may have changed in the last few days, but her body hadn't gotten the memo.

Nick frowned at her silent rebuff of his advances. "What's the matter, Belle? Have I lost my appeal now that I'm not the unsuitable boy from the wrong family? Is the thrill gone if I'm a part of your world permanently?"

She had thought that once. The thrill of seeing Nick had to be because of the secret, forbidden nature of it. Belle swallowed hard, and his eyes focused on the movement of her throat. Her breath was rapid and quick, moving in time with the desperate beating of her heart.

She was wrong. Nick knew all her secrets, had nearly become an integral part of Evergreen operations, and she wanted him more than ever.

Nick leaned in closer, his lips a whisper away from her own. Any movement would bring them together, and Belle knew that if she kissed him, she wouldn't be able to stop.

"I'm sorry, Nick."

"For wha—?"

Before he could finish his question, Belle vanished and reappeared on the other side of the room. Nick stared at the empty table in front of him for a moment, not quite sure what to think.

"For that," she said.

Nick jerked to face her direction. She expected him to be angry, but his lips twisted with amusement. His dark eyes watched her with appreciation, although he didn't approach her again. "You know, our affair could be that much more interesting for all the new tricks you could bring to the bedroom."

"Nick…" Belle began, not quite sure what to say to him. *I can't date you if you're Santa* seemed silly.

He didn't wait for the words. Instead, he crossed his arms over his chest and widened his stance. "So if you didn't come to see me for a jolt of caffeine, what do you want, Belle?"

"I need you to make your choice."

"You said I had time."

"I said that two days ago, Nick. It's December 21. You have to choose. The suit or the cocoa."

"That depends," he said. "You said the cocoa would make me forget you."

Belle was afraid he would focus on that. "And everything else you've seen and heard while you were here," she reminded him.

"So if I go home, I won't remember anything I've seen, and you and I are done."

She nodded.

"And if I stay?"

"You and I are still done," she said, as much as the words pained her.

"Why? Is there some sort of conflict of interest? Are we forbidden to be together if I'm Santa Claus?"

"No."

"Okay. I know it's not a human-witch thing. I've seen two of your brothers roaming around the building with human women. So what is the problem? Will my hair turn white and my belly get flabby the instant I put on the suit?"

"You'll age normally. Your appearance will be a direct result of your lifestyle like anyone else."

He ran his fingers through his dark hair in irritation and considered her words before he spoke again. "So I was right before. You were just using me as an escape from your world. Now that I'm a part of it, you don't want me."

"That's not true."

His dark gaze pinned her in place, his voice low. "Then you *do* want me."

A shiver of desire ran down her spine at the deep rumble of his words. She did want him. But that didn't matter. "It's complicated, Nick. Once you become Santa, things will change. I would be the village outcast if people found out that we were having an affair."

"What if we were dating?"

Belle narrowed her gaze at him. "You're splitting hairs."

"No, I'm not. Meeting up for sex once a day in secret isn't dating. Dating involves dinner. Talking to one another and getting to know each other."

"To what end?"

Frustrated, Nick threw up his hands and turned his back to her. "What, Belle?" He spun back and took a few large steps toward her. "Do you think that if we really date and people know about us that we'll end up married? Is the idea of being Mrs. Claus so terrifying that you won't even consider it?"

"Being Mrs. Claus is different than just being Mrs. Nick St. John. It's not what I've pictured for my life."

"And you think being Santa Claus is what I pictured for *my life?* Come on, Belle. My whole world changed with a flick of your wand. Don't you think I'm having a hard time adjusting to this new reality, too?"

Belle dipped her head and gazed at the berry-hued carpet. He was right. She wasn't taking his feelings about this into consideration like she should. "You're right. I'm sorry. But I don't want your choice to be a reflection of whether or not we're going to be together. Being Santa is a huge commitment. You can't just change your mind and return to your normal life. What if we break up a year down the road? Then what? If you choose to be Santa, you need to want to be Santa in your heart, with or without me."

Nick's brown eyes looked her from top to bottom as he processed her words. The heavy inspection brought heat to her cheeks and her belly. How would she survive life with Nick here, unable to touch him the way she craved?

"Okay. I've made my decision. I will accept the job offer on one condition."

Belle's breath caught in her throat. This was the moment. Yes or no, Christmas depended on his answer. "Yes?" she managed in a hoarse whisper.

"You have to agree to go out to dinner with me tonight."

Dash offered to drive Nick back to his place that afternoon to pick up some of his things. After Christmas, they would worry about selling his house, moving all of his belongings up to the lodge, and dealing with his company.

Nick called the members of his crew, gave them paid vacation through the New Year and had Ben close up the house they were working on. They were thrilled. It didn't cross their minds that he wouldn't be back. He was hoping to sell his company to one of the guys. That way everyone could keep working. "Are you going to miss construction?" Dash asked from the living room.

"Not really. I was getting tired of it, but I'd worked too hard to quit." Nick tossed handful after handful of clothes into the large duffel bag Dash gave him. No matter how much he put in there, the bag still had room for more. "What's with this bag you gave me? It won't fill up."

"Yeah," Dash chuckled, coming down the hallway to peek into the bedroom. "It won't. It's the same kind of thing you'll use at Christmas. How do you think we get toys for every child into one little bag?"

It would take Nick a while to get used to having magick as a part of his daily life, but it certainly was handy. He moved faster, not being as discriminating about what he put in now. For his own amusement, he grabbed a lamp off the dresser and watched it disappear into the bag. "Amazing."

"What are you going to tell your family?"

Honestly, he hadn't given a lot of thought to it. "I'm not very close with my family. We don't get together much. I think the snow globe knew what it was doing when it chose me. No one is going to miss me."

"No one? Were you dating anyone?"

Nick eyed Dash to see if he was fishing for information about Belle, but he seemed genuinely curious. "No."

"Okay. That sucks for you, but it's fewer loose ends for us to deal with. I'm sure you'll find some attractive and willing witches interested in you before too long."

Nick tossed the last of his shoes into the bag and lifted it up. It was ten pounds at the most, and it had nearly all of his clothes, shoes, suits, belts and toiletries in it. And the lamp. "Speaking of willing witches, can I ask you something just between the two of us?"

"Sure," Dash said. "Shoot."

"It's about your sister."

At that, a grin spread across Dash's face. "Good luck with that, man. Belle is probably the least willing of them all."

"What do you mean?"

"My sister doesn't date. She says it's because Cole, Ethan and I chase all her suitors off. I think we just have high standards for our little sister. I haven't seen her so much as flirt with anyone for months."

If nothing else, that made Nick feel good. They made no promises of exclusivity, but in that moment, the thought of her being with someone else while they were involved made him want to punch his fist through the drywall. "I asked her to dinner tonight. She said yes, but I feel a hesitation. Do you know why she's so—" he searched his mind for the term at least one woman had flung at him in anger "—emotionally unavailable?"

Dash reached out to pick up the duffel bag and gave Nick a pat on the back. "My sister is like a tiny drill sergeant. She's a lot like our mother that way. She could probably run Evergreen single-handedly if she tried. But don't let the suits and tight ponytails fool you. I think if you get to know her, you'll find she's a marshmallow on the inside. For a while, Ethan and I thought she might actually be in love and keeping the relationship a secret. We could never figure out who the lucky guy might be, but we might be wrong. You might stand a chance with her."

Dash's words haunted Nick all the way to the lodge. There was a nervous excitement in his stomach as they made their way up the mountain. He couldn't tell if it was because he was getting to see their home at the top of Mistletoe Mountain for the first time, or realizing that Belle might be harboring secret feelings for him.

Both thoughts vanished from his head as they approached a dead end. The road ended at a sheer rock face that stretched up a hundred feet in front of them. Hikers typically pulled over and parked around here. But instead of slowing down, Dash turned to him with a wicked grin and slammed his foot on the gas. Nick clutched the armrest of the SUV and braced himself for the impact, but it never came.

When he opened his eyes, they were in a dark tunnel that ran through the mountain itself. "You scared the crap out of me, man."

"I know," Dash said with an evil laugh. "I love doing that to people."

Reaching the end of the tunnel, the road curved to the right and revealed a small cabin, similar in size to the bungalows he built in town. He expected Dash to drive past it to the lodge, but instead, he parked at the house.

"Home sweet home," Dash said, getting out of his SUV to unload Nick's bag.

"This is the lodge? Where all the Winter clan live? Are there more than three of you?" Nick had expected something massive and grand like a resort in Aspen.

"The thing about magick is that you can't always trust what you see."

Nick eyed the house with suspicion. It looked just as real as that wall of rock they drove through earlier. He followed Dash through the front door and froze dead in his tracks. He'd stepped into a small cabin, yet he found himself in a massive five-story open atrium. Dark wood beams arched across the ceiling, framing a stone fireplace that roared on the far wall. It was large enough that he could stand inside it without hitting his head. There were people everywhere, sitting at leather couches talking, having drinks in what looked like a lounge. It was incredible.

"Now this is more like I was expecting. Although in my mind, it was made of gingerbread with candy cane beams and gumdrop roof tiles. How does all of this fit into a tiny little cabin?"

Dash smiled. "Magick. Your room is on the third floor now, but that's temporary. Santa's suite is on the sixth floor with the other Evergreen suites. We've got to track down Kris and ship the rest of his things to him before we can move you there."

Nick followed him to the elevators and down the hallway to his room. His badge from Evergreen opened the door, and Dash sat his bag just inside the doorway.

"There's a red button on the phone. If you need anything, press it, and the front desk will help you out. I'm sure Belle will be by shortly to continue your orientation."

Nick noticed a thick notebook sitting on the kitchen counter with a yellow note that said "Read this" stuck to it. "I think she's already left me my homework."

"Good. Read up. Tomorrow we're going to do some work with the reindeer and check out your skills driving a sleigh."

What skills? Until that moment, Nick hadn't really, truly, considered that he would be flying the sleigh. Being Santa was still a nebulous concept to him, but reality got clearer with every day. Flying. He hated airplanes, but wouldn't admit that to Dash. Hopefully, there wouldn't be turbulence. "Thanks, Dash. I'll see you later."

"Good luck with dinner tonight," Dash added, his voice heavy with doubt, before slipping out the door.

Left alone, Nick roamed through the two-bedroom apartment. It was nice. Well furnished. It had a massive plasma television mounted on the wall, so he couldn't complain about that. He walked to the sliding glass door that opened to a small balcony. From there, he had a view of the entire Winter clan settlement. In the distance, he could see the chimney smoke and rooftops of the elf village. Several small buildings and businesses lined the tiny streets with wizard-owned shops and specialty stores. Elves and witches mingled in the streets below. In a clearing to the right, there were reindeer grazing on fresh hay. They were a lot bigger than he imagined, even from a distance.

It was amazing. He wanted to blink his eyes and make sure it was real. But it was. And now it was home. He had signed on the dotted line and was officially *Saint* Nick now.

But his agreement came with a price, and he intended to hold Belle to her end of the bargain. Tonight they were going to the Crystal Snowflake for dinner. It was the nicest restaurant in Gingerbread and *the* place to go for a romantic evening. He hoped it would be just the thing to melt Belle's resolve. If Dash was right, and she was hiding her feelings for Nick, she might warm up to the idea of seeing him again. He'd never taken a woman there before, but if he was only going to get one date with Belle, it was going to be a good one.

Fifty-Four Hours until Takeoff

Belle was falling fast and hard.

She'd agreed to this dinner because it was a small price to pay to have a Santa for Christmas this year. But she would be lying to herself if she didn't admit that at least a small part of her wanted to go on the date with Nick. Belle just hoped she would be strong enough to resist him while she did what had to be done.

That wasn't happening. It was impossible in a restaurant like the Crystal Snowflake. It was dark and romantic with candles and a roaring fireplace. Tiny LED lights in the ceiling glittered overhead like twinkling snowflakes falling over them. The booths were small and intimate, the dinner designed to be shared by two. Once the wine started flowing, Belle was lost.

Dessert was done, the check was paid, and she found herself watching Nick intently as he told her a story about college. He had been right when he'd said dating was different. There were so many things she didn't know about him because they didn't share much more than idle pillow talk. Nick was smart, funny, ambitious, passionate and lonely.

Belle hadn't anticipated the last. She knew he was a workaholic like she was. It was easy for family and friends to fall to the wayside when every moment went to being successful. That had become painfully evident to Belle the last few weeks as she watched each of her brothers find love. Maybe that was why she'd been so resistant to losing Nick to the red suit. When Christmas was over and the family gathered together to celebrate another successful year, she didn't want to be the only one that was alone.

Nick seemed to be growing weary of his breakneck pace, as well. As he spoke about his family and his time alone in Gingerbread, she sensed a sadness. Their coffee breaks had become more important to both of them than they had planned. *Nick* had become more important than she had planned.

"What?"

Belle refocused on Nick with raised brows. He finished his story, and she'd missed something by getting lost in her own thoughts. "I'm sorry?"

"You were staring at me with an odd look on your face. Do I have chocolate soufflé on my face?"

"No, I think this wine has finally hit me." She smiled, hoping he wouldn't question it.

"So, after a great meal, decadent sweets and plenty of wine, are you feeling relaxed and content?"

Not exactly. She was well fed, but her mind was swirling with thoughts, desires and doubts. After tonight, Nick would put on the suit and become Santa. What happened between them after that was uncertain. But for now, he was just her Nick. He was a bit more educated about her life, but still just Nick St. John, the guy that captured her attention at a Cup of Cheer by holding the door for her and flashing his charming smile.

There were a lot of reasons why she should thank him for a lovely night and return to her room alone. But she wouldn't. This was her last night with Nick, and she wanted to make the most of it, even if it would just make it hurt more to lose him later.

Belle eased closer to him in the curved booth for two. "If I didn't know better, I'd think you were trying to ply me with wine and chocolate to soften me up."

Nick scooted over and wrapped his arm around her shoulder. "Absolutely not," he whispered in her ear. "It's a blatant attempt at seduction."

Belle scooped her clutch up and looked at Nick through her lashes. "It worked. Take me home."

"Absolutely. Wait inside where it's warm while I have the valet bring the car around."

"No," Belle said. "We can come get it later. I want you right now."

"In the restaurant?" Nick laughed.

"Not even a witch could disguise that. But…" Belle took Nick's hand in hers and looked around the restaurant. Everyone was wrapped up in their own romance, the servers well trained to be scarce. Taking the opportunity, in an instant, they were gone.

Nick tightened his hand around Belle's as he adjusted to the unexpected trip. It took a moment for him to stop swaying on his feet and realize they were in Belle's suite at the lodge. They'd always gone back to his place, so there was a sudden, unexpected thrill at finally being in Belle's home.

They were in her bedroom. The large master suite had a king-size, four-poster bed in the center of the room. It was made from a dark wood with intricate etchings in the headboard and the posts. Dark green velvet curtains draped around it, held back with twisted ropes of gold thread.

"You really need to warn me when you're going to do that."

"I'm sorry," Belle said, unbuttoning his shirt and slipping her hands inside to roam over his bare chest. "But I couldn't wait any longer."

Nick let his blazer and dress shirt slip off his shoulders to the floor. He bent down to caress Belle's face in his hands and capture her lips with his own. It had only been a few days, but he was desperate to taste her again. Usually, there was peppermint mocha on her lips, but tonight she tasted of crisp chardonnay and her own, natural sweetness.

Belle wrapped her arms around his neck, reaching to pull him closer. She had worn some fairly high heels to dinner, but it wasn't enough to close the gap between their heights. He slid to his knees at her feet, parting from her lips only when he had to. For once, he was looking up at her. She had worn her hair down tonight, and the lights from overhead backlit the loose golden waves making her almost glow like an angel.

Nick's eyes didn't leave hers as he untied the belt of her wool trench coat. Beneath it, his hands made contact with the sapphire-blue lace of her dress. The short sheath dress was completely layered with lace. The floral design of it was nice, but it covered too much of her. It barely exposed the skin beneath, only hinting at the swell of her breasts and shapely legs. He sought out the hem, pushing the fabric higher and exposing inch by inch of her smooth thighs.

He dipped his head to press his lips to her skin. Belle quivered as the dress moved up, and his mouth followed the trail. When he reached the sheer fabric of her panties, his fingertips hooked beneath them and drew them down her legs. She stepped out of them and shrugged her coat off.

Nick slid off each of her heels before his hands roamed over the smooth skin of her legs as they traveled back up her body. He placed a searing kiss at her hip, then the soft skin just above the cropped golden curls of her sex. Belle gripped Nick's shoulders for support as his fingers slid over the delicate skin between her thighs. She gasped softly as he probed her, stroking the wet heat that beckoned him. She was ready for him, but wasn't going to rush. If this was the last time he made love to Belle, he was going to make certain neither of them ever forgot tonight.

Nick used his thumbs to gently open her up to him. His tongue immediately sought out her swollen, sensitive flesh, wrenching a desperate cry from Belle's throat. He moved quickly to brace her hips with his hands as her knees threatened to give out beneath her.

"Nick," she gasped, her cries growing more desperate as his mouth devoured her flesh.

She was on the edge, and he intended to push her over. Holding her steady with one hand, he used the other to dip inside her. The combination was her undoing. Belle threw her head back and cried out, her body thrashing against him with the power of her orgasm.

When it was over, Belle slid to her knees in front of him. She lay her head on his shoulder, gasping and clinging to his biceps with both hands. Nick took the moment to reach for the nape of her neck and unfastened the button at the top of her dress. She eased back and lifted her arms over her head so he could pull the lace dress off.

Belle hadn't worn a bra beneath it. Her creamy breasts were instantly exposed to him. The back of her dress was open, so he should've anticipated it, but the realization sent a surge of white-hot desire to his already aching groin. He covered one with his hand and sucked the hard pink tip of the other into his mouth.

"Yes-s-s," Belle hissed. She buried her fingers into his hair, massaging his scalp and pulling him close. "Oh, Nick," she panted in his ear.

He couldn't wait much longer to have her. It already felt like it had been weeks instead of days since he'd found oblivion in Belle's enticing body. "Hang on," he instructed, wrapping his arms around her waist.

Belle clutched his neck, wrapping her legs around his waist as he rose from the floor. He carried her to the massive bed and eased her back onto the soft coverlet. She watched him with flushed cheeks as he unbuckled his belt and slid out of the last of his clothes. He pulled a condom from his pocket before he dropped his pants to the ground and quickly sheathed himself.

She slid back toward the headboard, her green eyes dark and inviting. Nick followed suit, climbing onto the bed and covering her body with his own. Belle opened herself to him, and he slowly pressed into her welcoming heat. A surge of pleasure rushed through his body. Being with Belle was the most divine experience he'd ever had. He eased back and thrust into her again. He was tempted to close his eyes, but he couldn't. Not this time. Not if it were the last.

Nick tried to memorize every expression on Belle's face, every gasp, every sensation. No woman had ever affected him like this. She drove him to distraction, starred in his every fantasy. How could he possibly walk away from her, even if it meant leaving his whole life behind? He couldn't. Wouldn't. And he would do everything in his power to convince her not to give up on them.

Belle bent her legs and pulled them back toward her chest. The movement shifted him deeper inside her, wrenching his focus from anything but the throbbing ache of mounting desire. Nick buried his face in Belle's neck and wrapped his arms behind her back to pull her tight against him. Her cries rang out in his ears as he drove into her body with desperation.

"Yes, Nick!" Belle gasped as she found her release again.

The tightening flutter of her body wrapped around him as it climaxed, coaxing away the last of his restraint. He buried himself hard and deep one last time and he was lost.

A burst of sublime pleasure surged through him, racking his body with the violence of his long-awaited orgasm.

Nick closed his eyes, hovering over Belle and savoring the moment. He didn't open them again until he felt a cold prickle along his back and legs. He turned his head to look around them and saw snow. It was snowing in Belle's bedroom.

"Are you doing that?" he asked.

"Not intentionally," Belle admitted. "That's what tends to happen when I completely let go."

He propped onto his elbows and arched a brow at her. "You were holding back the other times?"

"It was a struggle, believe me. More than once a few flakes fell and I had to focus so hard to make them stop before you rolled onto your back."

"Well, let it snow," Nick said with a laugh, shifting his weight to lie beside her on the bed. He pulled a blanket up over them and rolled onto his back. Belle curled up beside him and rested her head on his chest. They sat silently for a few minutes, watching the sparkling flakes until they finally dwindled away to nothing. "This is nice," Nick said at last.

"What's nice?" she asked.

"You don't have to leave. You've always run out the door. And tonight I get to keep you right here." He protectively wrapped his arm around Belle's shoulders. In his mind, he was still expecting her to run off, even though this was her place.

Belle snapped her fingers, and the lights in her bedroom went out. Now there was only the moonlight from the window, sending a silvery cast to everything in the room.

The darkness and warmth worked quickly to lure them both toward sleep. "I'm glad you chose to stay here, Nick," Belle mumbled into his chest.

Nick held her close and lay quietly, waiting for her

breathing to become soft and even. "I chose to stay here to be with you." He whispered the words into the strands of her golden hair before finally drifting off to sleep.

Belle couldn't sleep, and for once in her life, it wasn't because of too much caffeine. It was guilt.

For a while, she thought she'd imagined what Nick said. She'd been teetering on the edge of sleep until the low rumble of his voice made his chest hairs tickle at her nose. Suddenly wide awake, she wasn't certain if he'd really said the words or it had been a fleeting dream.

The longer she lay there thinking, the more convinced she was that it was true. It rang true to her ears. Nick would make a great Santa, she had no doubt of that now, but if he only did it to be with her...

Nick had given up everything for her. His successful business, his home, his friends and family...all gone because some snow globe told her he was *the one*.

Her stomach ached with dread almost as badly as her chest ached with longing for him. She was torn.

A quick glance at the clock confirmed it was the early hours of December 22 now. In about forty-eight hours, they would be loading the sleigh and taking off for the kickoff of Christmas in the South Pacific. Last she heard, Kris and Merry were somewhere in Belize, and it didn't seem likely they were coming back in time. Nick was their only hope of pulling Christmas off. She knew that.

But that didn't make her feel better about it. Later, all of this would be her fault. When Nick became restless and unhappy in his role as Santa, Belle would be the recipient of his blame. Just look at Kris—he willingly signed up to be Santa, and yet he'd walked off the job a week before Christmas.

How long until Nick's white fur collar started to chafe?

Belle slipped silently out of bed, pulled on her warm,

flannel robe and went down the hallway. She flipped on the kitchen light and made herself a cup of decaf with her Keurig. The warm drink helped her think; but she didn't need any help staying awake. When she opened the refrigerator door for cream, she spied the silver flask of cocoa sitting beside the carton.

She had intended to dump it out after Nick took the job. There was no reason to keep it. And yet, there it was.

Drinking the cocoa wouldn't do much good since he signed the contract. He might forget, but come Christmas Eve, he would technically still be Santa, just the amnesiac version. That would just make dealing with him harder.

But how could she get him out of the contract? It was signed, notarized and sealed with magick. The only way to terminate the contract was if Nick quit, which he wouldn't do. Or…if he was fired.

The idea was like a bolt of lightning straight down Belle's spine. *She could fire him.* As the head of Elf Relations and Evergreen staffing, she was one of the only people that could. That would release him from the contract, and the cocoa could wipe his memories clean. It could work, but the timing would have to be just right. If she fired him first, he would never drink the cocoa. And if she waited too long to fire him after he drank it, he might remember her and the lodge.

But if she moved all his things back to his house while he was asleep, she might be able to give him the cocoa, fire him and transport him back to his own bedroom fast enough that all of this might be like some fuzzy dream he couldn't piece together.

Belle's chest ached as she looked at the cocoa, but she knew what had to be done. This wasn't fair to Nick, and she needed to put things right. He wouldn't suffer. He wouldn't know the difference. She would be the one left with the memories and the fallout of her actions.

After she finished her coffee, Belle changed into a pair of jeans and a sweater. She slipped Nick's access card from his wallet and went to his suite. He hadn't unpacked much, so it didn't take long to load his things back into the bag and return them to his house. She tried not to loiter in his home. They had too many memories together there. Instead, she put away his things as quickly as she could and returned to her suite before sunrise.

Belle waited, tense, until she heard a stirring in the bedroom. She quickly heated the cocoa and poured it into a mug.

"Good morning," he said as she came into the room. Nick pushed himself up in bed. His hair was charmingly messy, and his eyes more closed than open with the sunlight streaming in the window.

Belle sat on the edge of the bed and pasted a smile on her face. "Good morning, sleepyhead. Here, I made you something." She held out the mug to him, filled high with warmed memory cocoa.

"What is this?" Nick asked, frowning at the cup.

"It's cocoa. It's all folks drink around here, remember? That's why I go to Cup of Cheer every day. Maybe after you finish training with Dash today, we can go into town for some real coffee."

"This won't mess with my head, will it?"

"No," Belle lied. "Only Noelle's special brew does that. This is just plain cocoa. Try it. You might like it. Everyone else around here seems to."

Either she was too good a liar or Nick had placed too much trust in her. His concern immediately faded away. Belle held her breath as Nick brought the cup to his lips and took a tentative sip.

"This is pretty good," he said, taking another large sip. He then lowered the mug into his lap, his expression confused for a moment, and then the tension in his face melted away as his mind stopped fighting the magick. His dark gaze was blank, his memories of Mistletoe Mountain, Evergreen Industries and Belle, fading away.

Moisture welled in Belle's eyes, but she didn't dare to hesitate. "Nick, you're fired. As staffing manager of Evergreen Industries, I do hereby nullify your employment contract."

And then, with the flick of her wand, he was gone, and Belle burst into tears.

Seventeen Hours until Takeoff

Nothing felt right to Nick. It must be the holidays throwing off his routine. He'd given the guys the week off, so there was no work to be done on the house. His family had accepted his excuses not to drive up to Denver. He had free time, and Nick never had free time. He couldn't come up with anything that he needed to do, and yet he had this nagging anxiety in the back of his mind that insisted he was missing something important.

A beep chimed in his back pocket. It was his cell phone alert for his daily break. It was almost ten when he walked down to Cup of Cheer for some coffee. Maybe that was what he thought he should be doing. He went nearly every day, so it was a fairly ingrained routine. But for some reason, he didn't want to go there today. And they were closed on Christmas Eve and Christmas day. He'd just have to make his own coffee at home for a while.

And yet something still felt wrong. His house seemed unfamiliar. He recognized it and all his things, but nothing seemed to be quite where it should be. He opened his sock drawer and found underwear. His shoes were lined up neatly in the closet when they were usually in a jumble on the floor. His toothbrush was in the wrong hole of his toothbrush holder. It was as though someone had scrambled all his things while he slept.

Nick had woken up yesterday with one hell of a headache, and he'd been in a fog ever since then. He didn't remember what he'd done the night before, but it must've involved tequila if he felt like he did. He'd rolled out of bed around noon, taken an aspirin and tried to distract himself with television, but every channel he turned to had a Christmas program on it.

While he didn't care for the holiday, the shows seemed to make him more irritable than usual. Almost angry. He couldn't figure out why he was in such a bad mood. It must've been the dreams he had the last two nights. He couldn't remember them, but every now and then he had a flash of one thing or another. The first night, he recalled a sexy blonde, a rustic mountain hotel…and Christmas elves. There definitely had to have been some tequila involved if he was dreaming of elves.

Last night he was certain he'd dreamt of the blonde again, but had a feeling the dream had taken a decidedly naughty turn. When he woke up, thinking of the blonde made him crave coffee so badly, his throat ached for it like a man in the desert without water.

"I'm going stir-crazy," he said aloud to his empty house. "I need to get out of here."

Maybe he should go get that coffee, anyway. Nick tugged on his coat and decided to walk into town. It didn't take him long to reach Main Street. It was a Sunday, and the day before the Christmas holiday, so things were pretty quiet. He popped into A Cup of Cheer for coffee, then carried it out with him to drink while he walked.

Nick wasn't sure where he was headed, but he pressed on. The crunch of the fresh snow and the bite of cold air against his cheeks were soothing somehow. He didn't stop until he found himself standing across the street from the high-rise building of one of the local businesses—Evergreen Industries. He wasn't sure why the building had drawn his attention. He knew they made nice ornaments. He'd mailed one to his parents once as a gift. But that was it. They looked closed today, too. Nick supposed they had several months before the rush of production started for Christmas again. By now it was all over.

Nick turned to continue down the street, but he stopped again. He fought the urge to cross the street and this time, his eye went to the top floor of the building. For a second, he thought he saw a silhouette of someone watching him from one of the windows. But again, he was imagining things. There was no one there.

Cold and frustrated, Nick spun on his heel and headed back to his house to get his tools. He may have given his guys the time off, but he needed to occupy his hands and his mind if he was going to get through this holiday.

"You fired him?" Cole yelled at Belle. And he never yelled at anyone.

She deserved it, though. Belle had let her guilt ruin Christmas for every child on the planet. She would get coal in her stocking this year, if anything at all. As it was, she'd put off this moment as long as she could by telling Dash that Nick got food poisoning at dinner and couldn't go out yesterday. She'd hoped her stalling tactic would help her think of a plan. When she woke up this morning, she had no ideas and still, no Santa.

"I had to," she insisted. "But I'll get out the snow globe and we'll pick a new Santa."

"Today? We'll pick one today? It's December twenty-third, Belle. Santa is scheduled to take off around 3 a.m. tonight. Pulling off a new Santa in a week was a miracle."

Cole looked down at his watch. "Fourteen hours is damn near impossible."

Belle was already teetering on the verge of tears. She'd given up the man she loved for his own good, ruined Christmas and made everyone hate her in one swift move. She couldn't take much more. One wrong word and she was going to start bawling again. "Make Dash do it."

"Dash can't be Santa," Cole argued with her.

"He knows how to fly the sleigh. He works with the reindeer. I'm sure he can figure out the rest. If anyone could fill in as a last-minute replacement, it's Dash."

Cole sighed and leaned back in his leather executive chair. "You go to Santa's office and try to conjure a new replacement. I'll have Dash ready on standby. If nothing else, maybe he can go along and drive the sleigh for the new Santa."

For the first time since Nick vanished from her bed, Belle started to feel a lift of encouragement. Maybe they could really pull Christmas off without Nick.

Today when she went into the back room, a freshly cleaned Santa suit was hanging on a hook by the door. Two shiny black boots were on the floor beside it. The outfit was ready to go for Christmas Eve, even if Santa wasn't.

Belle brushed past the costume to the magickal cabinet and pulled out the snow globe. Once again, her heart raced as she shook it and waited for the snow to fall again. A face appeared.

It was still Nick's image.

This couldn't be right. In the past, when a Santa quit, the globe showed a replacement immediately. It should be the same with firing Santa. "What is wrong with this thing?" she yelled, shaking it again, harder.

When Nick's face showed up again, Belle clutched it to her chest. She backed against the wall and let herself slide to the floor. The tears flowed in earnest now with nothing to stop them.

Christmas was ruined. Dash could fill in if he had to, but that would only solve the trouble this Christmas. If she shook the globe tomorrow, would Nick's face still be there?

"Belle?" Ethan stepped into the room.

She couldn't move fast enough to hide the fact that she was on the floor, crying and clutching a snow globe. So she didn't bother. Instead, she set the globe aside, sniffed and wiped her eyes with the sleeve of her suit coat. "What?"

"Are you okay?"

"Do I look okay, Ethan?" Belle said the words and immediately felt bad for it. Ethan was in charge of Christmas spirit, not to mention her brother. Of course he'd be concerned to find her crying at Christmas. "I'm sorry."

"Don't be sorry," he said, sitting down on the floor beside her. "Tell me what's going on. Is this about Nick?"

Just the mention of his name sent the tears flowing again. She nodded, silently crying. Ethan put his arm around her and hugged her to his chest.

"He's the one you were in love with, wasn't he?"

Belle was too exhausted and emotionally spent to deny it. If her brothers knew it, she might as well come to terms with it herself. "Yes," she sniffed. "He did it because he didn't want to lose me. But I couldn't let him give up everything for me."

"How do you know that he was? Nick seemed like a great guy. He might have made the perfect Santa and been happy to do it. Especially with you by his side."

"Me, Ethan? Mrs. Claus?"

Ethan shrugged. "Did you imagine I would end up with the most outspoken Christmas cynic on the planet? Or that Cole would find the woman he had to leave behind all those years ago? And Dash and Noelle? I never saw that reconciliation coming. But love is a funny thing. And just like it helped turn Lark from a cynic to a believer, it could turn you into the perfect Mrs. Claus. You don't need to knit and bake like Merry if you don't want to. You could give it your own spin."

Belle appreciated her brother's encouragement, but this talk was a few days too late. "He's forgotten all about me now, so this is a pointless conversation."

"Well, just don't give up on love yet. That's all I'm saying."

Belle nodded and sat up. "What are we going to do about Christmas? Nick's face is the only one that will come up."

Ethan climbed to his feet and held out a hand to help Belle up. "We go out there and make Christmas happen. We're Evergreens. That's what we do."

One Hour until Takeoff

"Put on the suit."

"I don't want to put on the suit," Dash snapped. "I will drive the sleigh, I will handle the reindeer, but someone else is putting on the red suit."

It was 2 a.m. Christmas Eve morning, and Belle had had a very long day with virtually no sleep since Nick left. She had a headache that wrapped around her skull like a vise. With every hour closer to Christmas, it seemed to grow tighter. The toys were nearly loaded in the sleigh. The reindeer were hitched up and ready to go. The naughty-and-nice list was downloaded into the control panel on the dashboard display. Everything was set. Except for a Santa.

"Please, Dash."

"You know what? You fired Nick. You wear the suit."

"How about *I* wear the suit?"

Belle was about to yell at her brother when another man's voice came from behind her. She turned and froze in place, her eyes disbelieving what they saw.

It was Nick. He was standing by Blitzen, casually feeding the reindeer a handful of oats and patting his neck. It was like he was meant to be there. Like the cocoa and the last forty-eight hours never happened.

"Nick!" Dash exclaimed. "Thank goodness you're here. Are you ready to fly, man?"

Nick nodded, but his dark eyes didn't leave Belle's. There was an intensity in his gaze. She couldn't tell if he was angry with her or ready to devour her. Either way, he shouldn't even know her. Or this place. Or anything about Santa Claus and Mistletoe Mountain.

"I'll get everything ready to go," Dash said, making a quick exit.

Belle finally found her voice as Nick slowly made his way through the snow to where she was standing. "The cocoa worked," she said, shaking her head. "You forgot."

"I did forget. I walked around for two days trying to figure out what was bothering me. Something felt wrong. I was at the job site yesterday, installing closet shelves. One of my guys left a radio there, so I turned it on to drown out the doubts nagging my brain. The station was doing a live reading of *A Visit from Saint Nicholas*. Normally, I would've changed it, but I couldn't. As I listened, the pieces started coming back, one by one."

"How is that possible? The cocoa has never failed. Maybe it was a faulty batch."

"Absolutely not!" Noelle interjected from the other side of the sleigh, where she'd been testing the cloaking device and other security systems. Belle hadn't even realized she was there, or listening. Years in the CIA had paid off. "There wasn't a thing wrong with that cocoa. Nick just stumbled into the loophole."

"There's a loophole?" Belle said, her eyes wide. How did she not know this?

"It's a minor thing." Noelle shrugged. "The only way someone can remember us after drinking the cocoa is if they really, truly believe in their heart in the magick of Christmas. Most people, adults especially, don't believe. But even without remembering what he saw, Nick believed."

Nick turned to Belle and nodded. "I had this feeling deep in my gut that told me it was all true. Then I remembered that I was Santa Claus. And that I lived here on the mountain. I remembered you. And what you did."

Belle felt her heart sink. She was hoping her betrayal would be the one thing he wouldn't recall. "I didn't want you to do this for me."

"I know. And I want to thank you for caring enough about me to make the hard choice. But—"

A loud honking noise interrupted them. Everyone looked around before finally peering into the night sky and seeing what looked like a falling star headed straight toward them.

"What is that?" Nick asked.

The light glowed brighter and more yellow in hue as it came closer. The honking noise continued until she could spy the shape of…a Corvette convertible. "You have got to be kidding me!" Belle shouted at the sky. "It's Kris and Merry."

"He doesn't look like Santa Claus," Nick noted.

"Neither do you."

The canary-yellow Corvette made a dramatic landing, skidding in the snow and coming to a stop a few feet away. Kris and Merry climbed out, suntanned and dressed more for a beach holiday than a Colorado winter.

"Hey, everyone!" Kris shouted. "We're back." He turned to Dash, who'd just stepped outside carrying the Santa suit. "The flight mods to the car worked great. We made great time coming back from Belize. Just in time, by the looks of it. Say…" Kris frowned. "What's with the suit?"

Dash turned to Belle. "Tell him, sis."

Belle shot Dash eye daggers before turning to Kris. "Kris, we didn't know where you were or if you were coming back. You left your holly pin behind, so we thought you'd quit."

"Quit?" Kris said. "I left the pin in my office so I didn't lose it on the trip. It's too valuable. We left a note." He turned to Merry. "You left a note, didn't you?"

Merry frowned. "I thought *you* were leaving the note, Kris."

"Aww, fudge. We're sorry, guys. We just needed to get away for a little time just the two of us. We always intended to be home in time for Christmas."

Belle glanced back and forth between her two Santas, not quite sure what to do. She'd gone from no Santas, to too many in just a few minutes' time.

Cole pushed through to the front of the crowd of elves and witches with Taryn by his side. He surveyed the scene with an expression nearly as bewildered as Belle's. "Nick is back. *And* Kris is back."

"That's what it looks like," Belle agreed.

Cole nodded. "Kris, I'm sorry to say we replaced you. Or we did until Belle fired your replacement." He turned to Nick. "I don't know why you're back here or why you're not at home in a cocoa coma. I know this has been a whirlwind of a week for you, Nick. Since you haven't tried on the suit, you're under no obligation to stay. Kris is still technically Santa. With him back, Christmas can go on without you."

"And what if I want the job?"

Cole seemed mildly surprised by the declaration. He turned to Kris. "Are you ready to retire, Kris?"

Kris hesitated for a moment too long before Merry sent an elbow into his ribs. "Ooof," he gasped as he bowed over and nodded. "Let the kid have the job. You all can hire me back as a part-time consultant until he gets up to speed. I'll even ride with him tonight and show him the ropes."

"If you want the job, Nick, you've got it."

"I want it."

"Excellent. We'll deal with the paperwork later. Right now, you need to go with Dash and put on that suit to make it official. The elves are about finished loading, and we've got to get you to the South Pacific before it strikes midnight there."

Belle watched Nick disappear inside with Dash. Things were happening so fast, she wasn't quite sure what was going on. Their conversation got interrupted. She didn't know if Nick was angry with her or where they stood. He'd thanked her and followed it with an ominous "but" before Kris showed up. Now she could only mill around the launch site and wait.

Nick returned a few minutes later, dressed for the first time in his official Santa Claus attire. The suit adjusted to fit the Santa, but somehow the red velvet and white fur looked so much sexier on him than she ever imagined it would.

"Departure in ten minutes," someone announced.

Belle frowned and clutched her tablet to her chest. Christmas was the first priority. Her talk with Nick would have to wait.

"I need to say something before I go."

Belle turned to see Nick standing behind her. "Yes?"

"I wanted to tell you that I truly want to be Santa Claus. And not just to be near you. This is my chance to reconnect with the magick of Christmas. I lost it so young, and I've mourned that loss my whole life. Now I not only have the joy and excitement of the season back, but I get to spread it around the world. How could I possibly turn that down?"

"You're going to be a great Santa, Nick." And Belle meant it. No matter what happened between them, he had been born to wear the red suit.

"Thanks. And I think you're going to make an excellent Mrs. Claus."

Belle started to argue the point with him, but shut her mouth when Nick dropped to one knee in the snow.

"Belle, you have turned my life upside down. And despite your attempts to put things back the way they were, I wouldn't change a thing because I wouldn't love you the way I do. This job and this place are all the more special because you're here. I want to spend the rest of my life spreading Christmas cheer, and I want you to do it with me. Will you marry me and be my Mrs. Claus?"

Tears stung Belle's eyes. She had always thought that she didn't want that for her life, but Ethan had been right. She could make it whatever she wanted it to be. And the moment Nick asked, she couldn't think of a single thing she wanted more. "Yes," she said. "I will marry you."

Nick stood up and covered her hands with his own. "I wanted to get you a ring, but all the jewelers were closed. The day after Christmas, I'm going to get you the most beautiful ring you've ever seen."

Belle didn't care about a ring. She threw her arms around his neck and pulled his lips to hers. Falling into the arms of the man she loved and almost lost was more precious than any metal or stone. The days of anxiety and sadness faded away, and she let her body melt into his. Christmas wasn't ruined, and Nick wanted to marry her. The only thing that would feel better than this moment was when he got back and she could make love to him again.

Nick pulled away. "Belle? Is it snowing or is that you?"

She looked around them at the shower of sparkling

flakes coming down only in their immediate surrounding area. "It's me. I've just never been so happy."

"Nick!" Kris called from the sleigh. "Let's get a move on!"

"I've gotta go," he groaned, reluctant to let her go.

"I know. Have fun tonight," Belle said with a smile. "They say you never forget your first Christmas as Santa Claus."

"I know I won't. But what I'll remember most is the moment you said yes." Nick kissed her again, this time pulling away to jog off toward the sleigh. He climbed inside beside Kris and spent a few minutes with him going over the controls.

Nick turned one last time to give her a wave before calling out the reindeers' names and taking flight. He looked... as excited as a kid on Christmas morning.

The reindeer started moving through the snow and a few seconds later, they were gone. Left behind, as always, were the workers that had made Christmas possible. Now was time to clean up, to go to bed and start resting up for another year.

Belle was the last to stay outside. She watched the sleigh's streak shoot across the sky and disappear into the darkness. Her work here was done for now. With nothing else she had to do, she was overwhelmed with the sudden urge to bake snickerdoodles. Unfortunately, she hadn't the slightest clue where to even start.

"Congratulations," Merry said, joining her outside.

"Oh, thanks, Merry. Congratulations on your retirement."

Merry laughed softly and shook her head. "It was a long time in coming, and it got a little rocky toward the end, but things worked out for the best. Now I can pass on my book of cookie recipes to you and work on perfecting the perfect piña colada, instead."

"Do you have a recipe for snickerdoodles?" Belle asked.

"Absolutely." She put her arm around Belle and led her back toward the lodge. "What do you say we go make some right now?"

Belle smiled and eagerly followed Merry inside. "That sounds wonderful."

Christmas Eve, One Year Later

"This is the first Christmas in over twenty years that you haven't had to work," Merry noted. She buried her toes in the sand that was still warm despite the darkness that had swallowed up the tropical heat several hours earlier.

"Retirement is awesome," he said, taking a sip from his frothy, tropical drink. "And Christmas in the southern hemisphere is even better."

"I'll drink to that," Merry agreed. Belize was amazing. Their beach bungalow was perfect for two retirees looking to spend some quality time together. "After so many years in Gingerbread, I almost can't believe I'm spending Christmas in shorts and flip-flops. No sweaters, no turtlenecks..."

"I'm glad we decided to come back here. Christmas cut the trip short last time."

Merry had jumped at the chance to move to Belize after Nick's training was completed. She had enjoyed their road trip, but Belize was where they had really reconnected. They had spent their honeymoon here, and it was where they had started their marriage over again. After twenty-five years of marriage, most of which was dedicated to

Christmas, it was nice to just be a couple again. There were no sexy, Italian ski instructors to distract them. Kris had let the artificial color fade from his hair and grew out his beard, returning both to the silky silver waves she remembered and loved. There were no more tricks, no more games. Just an appreciation for one another that they had lost along the way.

"It's almost time," Kris said, eyeing his watch.

They both looked up at the sky, waiting to catch a glimpse of Nick on his first solo flight. Dash had sent them a Christmas card and told them to watch. He'd added an exciting new feature to the sleigh that they were sure to love.

"There it is," Merry said, pointing toward the silver streak that stretched across the sky over their heads. To their amazement, the twinkling stardust it left behind started falling toward them. A moment later, they found themselves in a tiny blizzard with magickal snowflakes falling around them. It was an amazing sight considering the humid tropical climate of Belize. Each flake danced through the air, disappearing the moment it touched the smooth sand.

They had found a way to give everyone a white Christmas, even if just for a brief moment. It was beautiful. Mesmerizing. Enchanting. Just as Christmas should be.

"Dash has outdone himself this time," Merry said.

"Indeed he has." Kris took her hand and lifted it to his lips. "Merry Christmas, my darling."

"Merry Christmas, Kris."

* * * * *

Debbie Herbert writes paranormal romance novels reflecting her belief that love, like magic, casts its own spell of enchantment. She's always been fascinated by magic, romance and gothic stories. Married and living in Alabama, she roots for the Crimson Tide football team. Her oldest son, like many of her characters, has autism. Her youngest son is in the US army. A past Maggie Award finalist in both young adult and paranormal romance, she's a member of the Georgia Romance Writers of America. Debbie has a degree in English (Berry College, Georgia) and a master's in library studies (University of Alabama).

SIREN'S TREASURE
Debbie Herbert

As always, to my husband and parents
for their support.

To my agent, Victoria Lea,
Aponte Literary Agency, for her faith in my
writing, and to Harlequin Nocturne editor
Ann Leslie Tuttle, who gave me a publishing
opportunity.

I also want to thank the amazing copy editors
and proofreaders at Harlequin who whip my
manuscripts into shape and make them shine.

Away down deep in the 'Bama bayou,
You'll find a mysterious Gothic brew
Where Spanish moss drapes ancient oaks,
And sea-slithery lizards and gators croak.
The swampy water creeps ever in,
And lured down many a man has been
By magical, whispering, haunting sounds
Where not another soul is found.
Stay out of the water, whatever you do,
Ain't no telling what will become of you
If you can't resist a quick little dip.
Let me give you a tiny tip:
Should you feel a tug at your feet,
It mightn't be the tide pulling underneath.
Be wary, human, you must beware—
For some say mermaids lurk down there.

"Siren's Song," old folk tune,
Bayou La Siryna, Alabama

Prologue

Placing second or third? Not good enough.

She *had* to win the Undines' Challenge this year at the Poseidon Games, had to discover the reason other merfolk shunned her.

Jet whipped her tail fin and surged forward through the turquoise water—pushing, pushing—speeding through the sea like a rocket, streams of bubbles in her wake. Only one goal consumed her.

Winning.

The adrenaline rush, combined with Jet's superior strength and determination, propelled her ahead of the other merfolk within the first minute. She took a quick peek over her left shoulder and found Orpheous mere feet behind and rapidly closing in.

Her nemesis was gaining.

Jet sped past the Dismals, a barnacle-ridden limestone outcropping, and toward the next hurdle of the race. At the entrance of the honeycombs she cast a quick glance backward. Orpheous grinned, displaying jagged, pointy teeth. His long cobalt hair and teal tail fin distinctly marked him as one of the rare full-blooded members of the notorious

Blue Mermen Clan. Ruthlessly aggressive and muscular, his kind usually won most sporting events.

Jet slowed as she slid through the first opening of a large coral with a series of slender gaps. Although beautiful, the hot-pink coral was razor sharp and could gash exposed flesh and scales, causing painful injuries. Each contestant had to maneuver through the marked portals without any part of their body touching the coral. If they did touch, one of the judges on the sidelines would blow a conch shell, signaling the contestant must start over.

Halfway through the coral maze, the muted bellow of conch blasted. Jet's heart tripped. She hadn't touched, had she? She looked at the judges perched on a rock ledge twelve feet away, but they pointed to Orpheous and signaled him to exit and start over.

"Liars!" he screamed, ignoring the stream of blood spiraling upward from a gash on his arm. "I did not touch. You are prejudiced against my clan."

Jet resumed swimming through the narrow twists and turns. She would win and take her place among the strongest and most skilled. Surely then they would respect her.

A quarter mile ahead, the Wrath of Mer loomed. Already, her breath grew shallower in the methane-laced water and her gills flared, struggling to suck in more of the declining oxygen. A methane vent disturbed the water's buoyancy under the mile-long towering rock ledge.

The bubbling fields let Jet know what to expect. As her body hit the area, she propelled forward, as if powered by jet fuel. What a rush! Better than any runner's high she'd experienced on land in human form. She luxuriated a moment in the sensation of near weightlessness.

A mass of black stone was suddenly three feet ahead. She'd miscalculated.

Jet abruptly swished her tail fin to turn but it was too

late. She slammed into the rock with her right shoulder and tail fin taking the brunt of the blow. Searing pain radiated from her shoulder down to her fingertips and she drifted downward, fighting unconsciousness. The metallic scent of blood prickled her nose. Jet surveyed her body but didn't see any open wound.

Orpheous is near.

He shot through the swirl of bubbles, almost slapping her face with his tail fin. He leered at her briefly, his hair a storm of blue, before shooting away.

Jet clenched her jaw and thrust both arms forward. Her shoulder pain transformed to a numbing sensation. *Keep going. Don't stop.* She swam out of the methane trap and came to the roofed cavern, selected for its strong cross-currents.

Piece of salmon cake.

Orpheous entered the cavern and purposely whacked his tail fin against its walls before racing out. The wall appeared to disintegrate as dozens of disturbed gulper eels oozed out of its crevices, their long snaky bodies slithering into the churning water.

Great. She would have to swim through a mass of pissed-off eels.

She made it through without slowing. With her speed, she could overtake him en route to the Devil's Well, an ancient, dormant volcano. But once inside, he would have an advantage.

Jet kept up the rhythmic pattern of swimming that best suited her—extending her arms forward first, then crunching her abs and thrusting out her tail fin. At the volcano's tip, she dived into the narrow passage with Orpheous close by. The light quickly dissipated and Jet extended an arm along the side wall to keep her bearings. Each contestant had to swim the five hundred feet to its bottom and collect a piece of lava rock.

Halfway down, she realized something was wrong. Orpheous had stopped swimming and was moving upward. "Chickening out?" she asked. She swam closer to his vibration until she could make out the blue-white of his teeth.

He exposed his jagged molars in a grin that was half snarl, half glee and held up something in his hand.

Jet fumbled in the darkness until she found his fist, which was closed over a smooth, flat piece of lava rock.

"I've got my token."

Jet's mouth dropped open. "But how? We haven't reached bottom yet."

"I brought it with me. Rules are for losers. Better luck next year." He turned his back, dismissing her.

Anger shot up from the tip of her tail fin to the top of her scalp like an electrical burn. Jet surged forward, bent her body in two and whammed her tail fin into the back of his scalp. A bubbling *argh* sound filtered down. The lava rock loosened from his grip and fell.

"I won't let you cheat me again," she shouted, racing down with Orpheous hot on her tail.

His voice vibrated close behind. "Ever ask yourself why winning means so much to you?"

She frowned. "It just does."

"Look at you." His tone was amused, condescending. "Hair so black it shines blue in the sun. So strong, so competitive. You're nothing like Lily."

"Leave my sister out of it." She hated hearing Lily's name on his foul blue lips. "You're trying to delay me with stupid chatter."

"True." His voice was closer. "But the two of you look nothing alike. Ever suspect you are one of us?"

One of the Blue Clan? Impossible. "Never," Jet hissed.

She swam faster, all the while expecting Orpheous to grab her tail fin and drag her down into the black abyss. At the volcano's craggy bottom, she extended her fingers until they scraped hardened lava and extracted a loose nugget. Jet surged upward, passing Orpheous moments before he touched bottom.

She pushed on, free of the volcano. Ahead, a crowd of merfolk perched on rocks, waiting for the winner to leap over Rainbow Rock and claim the golden trident.

Jet had envisioned this moment for years. She gathered speed, dived downward and then thrust upward, breaching water. As she crested the rock, she savored the moment—the drops of water coating her naked breasts, the dark blue and purple tail-fin scales glinting in the afternoon sun and her sleek, muscled torso poised in a perfect arc before diving under the sea.

She slowed and came to a halt at the winner's platform, a tall, flat boulder where the head judge sat upon a chair of abalone shell, trophy in hand.

She'd done it! Finally she'd won the grand prize.

Jet held out her hand. Firth, a Blue Merman and former winner, was the honorary head judge. He examined the rock and scowled, blue lips twisting over sharp, pointy teeth.

She looked past him and spotted her mother and cousins seated in the first row, smiling and waving.

Orpheous swam to her side and Firth scowled at his fellow clan member. "You dishonor us. Yet, I must perform my duties." He addressed the crowd. "Jet Bosarge is the winner," he said flatly, then thrust the golden trident into Jet's right hand.

Her arm was still numb from the injury but she managed to close her fist over the solid gold trident, which nearly matched her height. Jet stomped the base of the trident in the sand three times and chanted, "As descendant of Poseidon, I claim my reward."

Instead of the thundering cheer Jet expected, the whistling and applause was decidedly lukewarm. Large swarms of merfolk swam away, moving on to the highly anticipated Siren Song event. Even her mother's chair was now empty.

"You know how this works," Firth said, nodding at the trident. "On land, the trident will shrink to the size of a charm pendant. It contains a onetime wish, good for one year."

Jet bowed her head, eager to get away and watch Lily win the siren contest, but a strong hand closed over her arm. She frowned at the green talons and long fingers resembling seaweed.

"Not so fast," Orpheous said, rubbing her arm suggestively. "Come with me and meet others in your clan."

His breath smelled like fish guts and Jet tried not to visualize those jagged teeth ripping apart some tasty amberjack. "Go away, you thug fish."

Orpheous was seriously getting under her skin. Damn it, she was a Bosarge woman, descended from a long line of mermaids well-known for exceptional beauty and intelligence.

He shrugged. "Deny all you like, but I see Blue in you."

Jet smacked his midsection with her tail fin and he doubled over. She swam as fast as an eel and made her escape. At the crowded Siren Song competition, she saw her family had not saved a place for her at the front of the stage.

Jet regarded her mother and the rest of her family with new eyes. Every one of them was gorgeous, even by mermaid standards: petite, curvy bodies, pale, gleaming skin, lovely pastel hair tints and varying shades of blue eyes spanning from the lightest ultramarine to the deepest cobalt. All dripping with feminine allure and charm.

Not for the first time, Jet considered her own black hair, cut short to prevent drag in the races, and eyes so dark only a hint of brown radiated from the irises. Mom had even chosen the name "Jet" because of their color. No, she wasn't a precious gem like Ruby or Sapphire or Pearl. Jet was nothing more than fossilized wood that had fallen into stagnant waters; so common it could be found on most beaches.

Clearly, she was no delicate aquatic flower like Lily.

A hush swept over the crowd as Lily swam to the front of the rock and took her place. Lily raised a hand and the crowd hushed again.

It was hard to call what came out mere singing. It was a symphony of sound, the epitome of tone meeting strength. Judges swam a hundred yards away, measuring the distance of the sound vibrations.

Jet closed her eyes and let the notes wash over her. Even though Lily could charm humans above, her voice was at its purest undersea with the crystal notes melding in the currents.

Jet gave a little shake and studied the seascape. All the hard training had been for naught. No one cared that she'd won the Undines' Challenge. She scanned the crowd, all in awe of Lily.

At least she had the trident. She would return home, and when Mom arrived later, she would use the trident's onetime wish. Jet tried to catch her mother's eye to wave goodbye, but Adriana's gaze was locked on the fair Lily. Typical.

She pictured Orpheous's leering face. *You are one of us.*

Was this why most merfolk shunned her? Why she felt like an outcast even among her own family? Could it be that her bloodline was mixed with the shunned Blue Clan?

Soon, she would demand the answer.

Chapter 1

Perry's back. Two words that shook Jet's world, but not in a good way. She'd returned home from the Poseidon Games two nights ago, exhausted, when her cousin Shelly had broken the news.

Jet sighed as she scanned the bored, impatient crowd packed inside the government-services waiting room, its ambience a curious mixture of sterility and shabbiness. The old building was painted an institutional green and smelled faintly of disinfectant, mold and stale coffee. In the lobby, cheap metal folding chairs were set up in rows.

Outside, the morning rain beat down in gusting sheets. Jet eyed the few people roaming Main Street, searching for a certain build, that certain shock of brown hair and chiseled profile.

Stop it. You'll see Perry soon enough. And oh, how she'd make him pay. That rat would get on his knees, by Poseidon, and beg her forgiveness before she sent him on his way.

Oh, no. Huge mistake. She shouldn't have pictured him in that position, those brown eyes staring up at her naked body with hunger. Jet squirmed. *Think of something else.*

She closed her eyes, imagined swimming the warm waters of the Florida Keys and scooping up antique cuff links and coins sunk in ships hundreds of years ago, like a child picking up dropped marbles on a school playground.

It wasn't helping. Jet placed a hand over her stomach. Sexual need fierce as a knife wound seared and twisted her guts. Damn, she hated that part of her mermaid nature that intensified sexual hunger. It could be a hindrance if she saw Perry after this meeting as she'd planned. But she had to face him eventually and see what he wanted. She would have to keep her sexual need under control and send him away with the tongue-lashing of the century.

Ugh, tongues lashing. Now she could taste his lips and tongue in her mouth, his long, slow, languid kisses that made her frantic with desire in nanoseconds.

There she went again. She was the biggest fool on the planet to pine for Perry's kisses. He'd been out of prison for weeks. If he'd been languishing in a jail cell for the past three years, missing her and regretting his betrayal, he'd have shown up long before now. Forget him—he'd done the unforgivable.

"Jet Bosarge," the receptionist called out.

She grabbed her backpack, and the man seated across from her frowned. "I've been here longer than you," he grumbled.

She shrugged. "Take it up with them." Jet marched down the labyrinthine hallway until she found a door marked IRS. No one answered her knock, so she opened it and stuck her head in.

The office was tiny and contained an old wooden desk. A metal folding chair, identical to those in the waiting area, was positioned across from it. The IRS could have sprung for better accommodations; it collected enough money to do better than this bare cubbyhole. A cheap, utilitarian clock hung on the wall; its secondhand clicked inconsistently—slow, fast, fast, slow—as if it were spitting out Morse code. She paused, wondering if she were in the right place, until she spotted the nameplate that read Landry Fields.

She dropped her backpack by the chair and stood at the lone rectangular window. Quite a show played outside with the swirling rain pounding the parking-lot pavement.

Jet pressed her face against the cool, damp pane. She loved the rain. Loved every pore on her body drenched in raindrops. The only thing better than land-walking on days like this was swimming undersea during a thunderstorm. She'd swim close to the ocean surface, watching raindrops bounce on top of the water and meld into a white, bubbling cauldron of energy while underneath, the pull of the tide crested and heaved in response to the wind. And if a rain shower coincided with the night of a full moon, the energy was electric with intensity.

She closed her eyes and touched her palms to the glass, imagined swimming under the rain's onslaught right now. Her body came alive, prickling with sensation—

"It's a mess out there, isn't it?" came a voice, low, rumbling and way too close.

Jet jumped and spun around. Her eyes bored into a pinstriped suit covering a broad chest. Her gaze traveled upward, taking in a strong jaw and ice-blue eyes that pinned her as if she were a trapped butterfly the man wanted to dissect.

"Mr. Fields?" she guessed. Her voice came out a touch squeaky and she cleared her throat.

He extended a hand. "Miss Bosarge?"

His grip was firm and brief, but far from impersonal, at least on her end. Her palm tingled from the contact and she had a wild urge to curl her fingers over his hand and never let go.

Insane. Jet hastily withdrew her hand and crossed her arms over her stomach. Fields gestured to the folding chair, his face reflecting no sign that their contact had affected him at all. "Have a seat."

She sank into the chair, feeling underdressed. She usually sported black yoga pants, a T-shirt and sneakers, perfectly fine for helping Lily at the salon or working out at the gym. In honor of this visit, she had slightly altered her normal attire by wearing jeans, a purple long-sleeved top and a purple-and-red scarf. Jet wished she'd taken more time with her appearance and played with Lily's boxes of lotions and potions. At the very least, she could have styled her asymmetrical bob. Oh, well, she had remembered earrings. Maybe her five-carat diamond studs would deflect attention from her plain, unadorned face. Humans seemed to care inordinately about such things.

Under his probing gaze, Jet readjusted the scarf to ensure it completely covered her three-inch gills, which extended from the top of the collarbone to her windpipe on each side of her neck. Although the slotted marks in her flesh were faint, she was careful to keep them covered to avoid questions by any observant human. And this guy looked way too sharp. Jet mentally noted to grow her hair out a few more inches so it would be long enough to cover the gills by the time summer arrived, when scarves and turtlenecks would appear odd. Since her hair grew an inch a week, it should be plenty long enough at summer's advent.

Fields pulled out a single file from the front drawer and placed it on the desk's otherwise bare surface. He opened the file and glanced through it, as if refreshing his memory.

"Your letter stated you only found an irregularity in my tax records," Jet volunteered.

"Mmm-hmm." He kept reading, never looking up, even when the printer kicked up an odd whirring sound, as if a hive of angry hornets had swarmed to life. The noise ended as suddenly as it had started.

Jet stifled an exasperated sigh and started swinging one crossed leg. The small room was stifling. The man's mere presence completely engulfed her senses and she stared at his large hands with the clipped, clean nails. No wedding band, but he wore a ruby ring set in a gold band on his right hand. Some kind of class ring, probably from an elite college. His clothes looked tailored and his facial features bore a patrician vibe. The harsh planes of his face, strong jaw and chilly eyes made him appear stern.

The man certainly didn't fit in with the shabby surroundings. Jet admired his clean, crisp aura and sniffed discreetly, picking up a lingering scent of soap, as if he'd just showered and dressed. And didn't *that* make her squirm. Hell, what was wrong with her today? She didn't even know this man. News of Perry's arrival must have unsettled her more than she first suspected.

The silence got on her nerves. "Since when did our town warrant an IRS office?" she asked. "I don't remember ever seeing one here before."

His gaze stayed fixed on her file as he answered, "It's a temporary field office for tax season. We'll close by the end of May. It's all part of our agency's public service."

Public Service? More like a public nuisance. What was so interesting about her tax records? True, she had bucketloads of money in trust funds, but her inheritance was legit. Her ancestors had always been careful to hire the best attorneys to cover where the real money originated—

from expensive undersea trinkets strategically sold in bits and pieces over decades.

He finally gave a small nod and faced her. "I remember viewing your file now. The first thing that caught my attention was the income fluctuation in two of your businesses. Four years ago, you claimed a net annual profit of over fifty thousand dollars with The Pirate's Chest. The business is still listed as open, yet no more profits have been claimed. Then three years ago, another business of yours, The Mermaid's Hair Lair, reported steady profits until it shut down last year. For the past six months, you've been earning an income solely from the interests and profits of various trust funds and stocks."

She couldn't help but notice the slight, contemptuous curve at the corners of his mouth. Jet bristled; it rankled when people assumed she must be some sort of privileged society girl. She'd worked hard to contribute to the Bosarge family fortune with years of physically exhausting and high-risk ventures, reclaiming sea treasure with the rat-bastard Perry Hammonds. Not that she could tell this numbers nerd *that* particular bit of information. "Is inheriting money against the law? It's not like I intend to live off the trust fund forever. I'm reopening The Pirate's Chest. I've already purchased a downtown building and I'm stocking inventory. A big shipment of antique furniture should arrive from Mobile tomorrow."

The auditor remained unruffled and silent while rain splattered the window, loud as a knocking at the door. The beating rain outside created a cozy sense of intimacy in the small room and Jet fantasized what it would be like to lean over the desk and kiss Mr. All-Business-Man until he lost that aloof self-control and had his way with her... Jet shook her head slightly and blinked. This had to stop.

Against her better judgment, she spoke up again, eager

to get her mind back on track. "My sister, Lily, and I jointly owned the salon. She's taken an extended leave of absence to travel. We might open it again one day, though." Jet bit the inside of her lip at the white lie. Not likely the beauty shop would reopen; Lily seemed happiest living undersea and using her siren talent to attract mermen.

Fields wasn't interested. "Okay, moving on. In reviewing your inventory and sales at the antiques store, I noted you sold maritime artifacts, some quite rare. Are the manifests for these items on file?"

Jet swallowed. As far as she was concerned, once a ship sank, whatever cargo sank with it became the property of the merfolk. What good was all that treasure sitting at the bottom of the ocean? The sea belonged to the merfolk, not humans, and they could keep it or sell it to dirt dwellers as they chose. But she could hardly tell him that, either. "Of course, I have paperwork," she said coolly. "I also have an excellent accountant who filed my taxes. Perhaps I should have brought either him or my attorney with me. However, your letter phrased this meeting as discussing an irregularity and not a full-blown audit."

"You're always welcome to bring an attorney or accountant. That's perfectly within your rights as a citizen." He studied her, no emotion showing in those frozen eyes. His face was stern, his manner stiff and formal. "Moving on to your stock portfolio," he said, as if she hadn't voiced a concern. "Over twenty percent of your stock is invested in one company, Gulf Coast Treasures and Salvage, LLC."

Damn. She and Perry had sold, without papers, plenty of shipwrecked, illegal items to that very company. In return, they were given cash, which they used, in part, to purchase stock in the salvage company. Jet kept her mouth shut and merely raised an eyebrow.

The silence between them stretched, but she refused to be the one to break it this time.

"These types of ocean recovery companies are very risky," Fields continued. "Even if they do find treasure, they must have a profitable way to recover items and bring them up to land using approved archaeological methods. And if all *that* is accomplished, there's the thorny issue of who gets a share of the profits—the state, foreign governments, the originating ship's company, distant heirs of the original property—"

So maybe all this wasn't about her, she decided with an internal whoosh of relief. It was about the government clamping down on these industries, making sure they got their own profit cuts. A treasure-salvage company in Tampa had been in the news recently when it recovered over five hundred million dollars worth of silver and gold coins from a colonial-era wreck near Portugal. Naturally, the Spanish government filed an immediate claim of ownership and refused to pay the company any salvage fee.

Jet hated worrying about pesky ownership issues. The mermaid philosophy of finders keepers seemed fairer. She was relieved to be out of business with Perry and leave that aspect of her life in the past where it belonged.

"So call me a risk-taker," she replied with a shrug. "I think it's a good investment. There are over three million known shipwrecks. It's a potential billion-dollar industry." She couldn't resist showing off a little and letting him know why she suspected the IRS had a sudden interest in the maritime salvage industry. "Especially since an American salvage company found three billion dollars worth of platinum on a World War II merchant vessel."

He ignored her mention of the platinum discovery. "But of those millions of shipwrecks, only thirty thousand of them are believed to have valuable lost cargo."

Jet shrugged again. "Your point?"

"We're taking a closer look at these companies. You have a huge amount of money invested in Gulf Coast Salvage, a disproportional amount of your assets."

She surmised it must be difficult for a stodgy man like him to understand people willing to take risky ventures, and suspected the auditor was about to go down a path she didn't want to follow. Jet stood. "Thanks so much for your concern about my portfolio. Warning taken."

He rose also and frowned. "Sit down, Miss Bosarge." This time his voice had an edge as sharp as a stingray's barbed stinger. "Only a couple more questions."

She reluctantly planted her butt back in the cheap chair.

"Are you acquainted with any of the officers of this company?"

"No."

Perry had handled all aspects of their treasure sales to Gulf Coast Salvage. She'd checked the company out on the internet and they'd seemed legit. Her accountant had warned her not to put so many eggs in one basket, but he'd also found the company aboveboard. But if it was being investigated and about to go under, she'd better pull out quick.

"How did you hear of them to start with?"

Jet again stood. "They're large and well-known. I live on the coast and have always been fascinated by treasure. Why wouldn't I pursue my interest? I haven't done anything wrong. I may be an incompetent judge in picking stocks—" *damn you, Perry* "—but that's it. If you have any more questions, I'd prefer to exercise my right to have an attorney or my accountant present."

He nodded and rose. "No need to be on the defensive. If I need more information, I'll get in touch."

Easy for him not to be upset—he wasn't the one being

drilled. Why did they always have to go after the little guy anyway? Plenty of hedge fund investors and private equity firms, with tons more money than she'd ever see, had been flocking to invest in increasingly specialized treasure ventures.

Fields walked with her toward the door. "Much success on reopening your antiques store. You already have employees hired?" he asked. His previously intense manner, combined with his sharp, wintry eyes, mellowed to a casualness that she suspected was false.

"No. Not yet," she admitted.

"I see. Well, I wish you much success."

His body was close to hers. Too close. The soapy, clean smell was strong. Jet swallowed and licked her dry lips. "Thanks."

She swept around him and into the hallway, inhaling the stale air deeply, ridding her lungs of the auditor's masculine, clean scent.

"Miss Bosarge?"

Jet whipped around.

"I'll need to take a look at the manifests for all the items you and your business partner sold to Gulf Coast Savage."

"All of them?"

His mouth curved upward, but those arctic eyes gleamed with sardonic amusement. "Every last one."

She frowned. The gleaming teeth made her think of a shark. Perhaps Landry Fields was as lethal on land as a shark was at sea. Only the faintest curling at the ends of his light brown hair ruined the predatory image. "I'll have my accountant call you and make arrangements to send the paperwork."

"No need for all that. I'll drop by your store to collect them, or your home if you prefer." His smile widened, but she wasn't fooled by the offhand manner with which he requested the paperwork or by the way he casually leaned against the doorframe, arms crossed.

Jet scowled back. She most certainly *didn't* prefer Landry Fields inside her house. The whole thing reeked of unprofessionalism and an interest that went beyond the norm of an IRS audit. What was his real game? "Give me a couple days and come by the store. I'll have them."

"Thank you so much for your coop—"

Jet turned and scrambled away before he could finish the insincere thank-you. As if she had a damned choice, as if he wasn't issuing an order.

The rain outside felt wonderfully fresh and she didn't bother with an umbrella, unlike the few humans venturing outdoor in the storm. The contact of water on skin some-what calmed her agitation and Jet smiled ruefully. How desperate was she that a number cruncher like Landry Fields could affect her body so deeply during an IRS audit? The man was probably as passionate as cold pudding and would laugh his ass off if he guessed her errant thoughts.

She lifted her face to the rain one last time before getting in the truck, absorbing moisture as if it were sustenance. The water fortified her. At least Mr. Conservative-Government-Man provided a convenient excuse to con-front Perry today. Her pride no longer demanded she sit and wait for him to show up again.

Perry was the one with the contacts at Gulf Coast Sal-vage and had insisted the company provided a perfect cover for selling their stuff without bothering with legal hoopla. Did he personally know the company owners or major stockholders? Did it have a reputation for playing fast and loose with maritime-reclamation laws? She had never asked him.

That was what you got for trusting someone. It always came back to bite you in the ass.

* * *

What an unusual woman.

Landry Fields stood at the window, watching Jet Bosarge in the parking lot as she lifted her face skyward, closed her eyes and smiled. Rain ran down dark eyelashes onto an elegantly sculpted nose, lush lips and then down her long, pale neck before disappearing in cleavage. The wet purple cotton shirt molded to the curve of her breasts. Abandoning his usual professional detachment and gentlemanly manners, Landry leaned forward against the windowpane, curious if there might be an outline of nipples.

Damn, she was too far away to tell. He ran a hand through his hair, which annoyingly curled at the ends, despite his best efforts to comb it down straight. Bosarge wasn't easy to peg, and he liked to classify people he interviewed into categories within minutes of meeting them: Con Man, Bad Guy with Attitude, Psychopath, Injured Wife, Slutty Girlfriend, or—more rarely—the Innocent or Unknowing. All part of his job as an FBI agent.

Too soon to know what type of woman he was dealing with. And the sexual tension crackling between them played havoc with his normal analytical observations. It made no sense. He'd never before had chemistry with someone he interviewed and Bosarge was unlike any other woman he found physically attractive. She was dark-haired, tall and athletic, deep-voiced and a bit edgy. His usual type was a petite, curvy blonde with a soft voice and an easy, uncomplicated smile.

The woman jumped into a battered red pickup truck and pulled out much too fast, tires squealing on the wet pavement. The corners of his lips involuntarily tugged upward. What kind of woman wore diamond earrings and drove a beater jalopy? She could easily afford a Rolls-Royce.

Everything about Jet Bosarge was a contradiction. Dark

hair and eyes contrasted with pale skin and deep red lips. She dressed casually, as if she'd thrown together an outfit with no thought, but the choppy haircut and diamonds gave an air of natural, feminine elegance. At first, she gave one the impression of an overgrown tomboy with her lean, muscular body, short hair and direct mannerisms. Yet, her long legs and low, throaty voice had distracted him so much, only his considerable willpower had allowed him to remain professional during the interview.

He'd studied photographs of the woman, but those cold prints didn't do her justice. Something about Bosarge in the flesh was vibrant and pulsing with energy. It was as if the rainy day had been nothing but gloomy shades of gray until she'd walked into the office. The effect was akin to when Dorothy in *The Wizard of Oz* tumbled out of the ruined Kansas farmhouse and stepped into an explosively Technicolor alternate universe.

Landry shook his head at the direction of his thoughts. The woman most likely was a thief and a liar. Getting personally involved with her would be inappropriate and potentially damaging to his career. He was here to do a job and at last things were moving. He'd spent a whole week in the bayou doing nothing but watching Perry Hammonds and reviewing, yet again, the case files with which he'd grown sickeningly familiar. Evidently, the suspect had been in a holding pattern like him. Hammonds did nothing but bum around his rental cottage drinking beer and watching television.

If there was one thing he despised more than deceit, it was sloth. Laziness should be one of the top sins; there was no excuse for sloppy living. You might fail, but at least you got up every morning and made your own way in the world. That belief had helped him rise above a childhood of poverty and emotional chaos.

He'd been about to approach Hammonds directly when Bosarge had returned from out of town. Past experience taught him it was always easier to get to the girlfriend, or ex-girlfriend—whatever the status of their relationship happened to be—and dig around for preliminary information.

Bosarge's records were most unusual. She possessed a staggering family trust fund. The interest alone provided a comfortable living without her ever having to dip into the fund's capital. And almost every dime she'd earned from selling maritime artifacts with Hammonds had been donated to various ocean-related charities: Save the Dolphins, Save the Whales, Save the Oceans, Save the Manatees.

Could be she was a spoiled princess who got involved with Bad Boy Hammonds for excitement. The philanthropy could be a smoke screen or a means of assuaging her guilt over stealing. Because it *was* theft if the collection site was close to shore. That salvage technically belonged to the government and the taxpayers. And Hammonds and Bosarge hadn't owned an expensive vessel with all the bells and whistles needed for deep-sea extractions.

Landry picked up the fake tax file and shoved it into a drawer. She'd bought his accountant act hook, line and sinker. The important files were locked in his desk at home. He turned off the printer before opening and checking it for jammed papers. Nothing appeared wrong, as usual. With a sigh, Landry turned his attention to the clock and reset it to the correct time. He held it to his ear and picked up the slight hum of the battery he'd installed yesterday.

Finished with his afternoon ritual, Landry retrieved a jacket and umbrella. No need to hurry; he knew exactly where she was heading.

Sure enough, ten minutes later he drove past Hammonds's cottage and spotted her red truck pulling into the driveway, splashing mud like an angry beast. Landry gripped the steering wheel tightly until the cottage was out of sight. He flipped on public radio, trying to lose himself in a news story, but it was no good. He couldn't help wondering how the post-prison reunion was unfolding between them. No doubt they had once been lovers and not merely business partners. He'd been privy to many pictures of them embracing or kissing on board the boat they sailed in search of maritime artifacts.

Forget her. He had an investigation and he would concentrate on doing his job. His real focus was on Hammonds. Their past crimes, if they were guilty, were fairly small in the grand scheme of things—he had coworkers covering billion-dollar drug-smuggling rings, after all—but the FBI took notice when Hammonds was released early from a South American prison. That early payoff had been financed by one Sylvester Vargas, a known crime figure with a reputation for dabbling in foreign intrigue. Hammonds had wandered aimlessly for weeks until Vargas's men collected him and put him on a one-way flight back to Alabama. Now Hammonds was back in the States, and the coupling of maritime salvage with foreign investors and criminal activity was a red flag.

The woods grew denser as Landry passed into a less populous area of Bayou La Siryna until he reached home. He climbed the wooden staircase to the humble cottage set up on stilts like many others in the remote bayou.

The plain door gave way with its customary squeak of rusty hinges. Most things eventually corroded in the salt air. If he took up permanent residence, his sleek BMW would have to be traded in for the ubiquitous pickup truck. Seemed Bosarge was onto something after all with her rusted truck.

The smell of lemon and ammonia mixed with brine

meant the maid had come by today. He'd used the same one for years. The first time Landry returned to the cottage after Mimi's death, the scent of musty decay had been depressing, so he had his real-estate agent hire someone to clean and air out the rooms before his visits. Now that he'd moved in for the next few weeks, he'd been able to keep the same cleaner.

His grandmother had taken great pride in maintaining the tiny place. The scarred pine floors were always waxed, the air-dried bedsheets were crisp and smelled of the ocean, and the cheap linoleum-tiled kitchen had smelled of corn bread, pecan pies, roasts or shrimp boils.

Mimi had spoiled him every summer, as if compensating for his shitty life with a careless mom and her string of increasingly sorry boyfriends. His mother's house was filled with half siblings from stepfathers that came and went, and constant drama from financial pressures. Every new romantic relationship of his mother's had created new sets of problems and complications.

Landry placed the car keys on a table in the den and surveyed the interior with satisfaction. Most of the furniture he'd replaced over the years. Mimi's sofa had been upgraded to a modern leather sectional. He'd kept what he could. The leather couch was draped with one of her crocheted afghan throws, a patchwork of rainbow colors against a sleek sea of black. Her old wicker rocking chair remained in the same spot. The bathroom, however, had no sentimental value and he'd gutted and expanded it the first year after Mimi's death.

He hung his suit jacket in the bedroom closet and stepped out of the black leather loafers. Back in the den, he adjusted a glass cat figurine on the battered sideboard. The cleaning company knew his peculiarity for detail and sameness, but they weren't perfect. His fingers accidentally brushed against a red sequined coin purse and he re-coiled, as if the haunting memories associated with it could transfer into his heart. It had been one of Mimi's treasured possessions but he had never liked the purse openly displayed. After Mimi's death, he'd taken it off the sideboard but then wandered about the cottage, unsure of an appropriate resting place for the ghostly memento mori. In the end, Landry had returned it to just where Mimi had left it.

After a few more minor tweaks to the figurines display, he slipped open the glass doors and stepped onto the wooden deck.

The scent of salty brine swirled in the early-April wind. He inhaled deeply and leaned over the wooden railing. Mimi's house could best be described as quaint—or ramshackle to be more precise. But here lay its secret charm—the million-dollar view. Located at the bend of one of the bayou's fingers, Landry could look over the pine and cypress trees hugging the shoreline and see the vast expanse of the Gulf of Mexico.

A tiny flash of orange darted at the base of a tree.

"I'll be damned," Landry muttered. He hurried inside and found the binoculars in the sideboard drawer, rushed back out, then focused in on the orange patch. A ginger tabby nestled in a bed of pine needles. Closer examination revealed a swollen belly. Landry set the binoculars on the rail with a sigh. The feral cat population was alive and thriving. It was a losing battle, but he'd try to entice the mama cat into a trap and do what he could to find the kittens a home.

His eyes scanned the ocean. The waters were calm, a blue-gray sheen with a few scatterings of tame whitecaps.

But despite its calm facade, Landry secretly suspected that beneath its placid surface lay a foreign world teeming with mystery and creatures beyond most humans' imaginations.

He knew. He'd witnessed it with his own eyes.

No, don't go there. Landry ran a hand through his hair and dismissed the foolish memories. He'd been a kid. A scared, ridiculous kid with a huge imagination. Nothing more to it. He reentered the cottage and made his way to the kitchen, determined to change the direction of his thoughts. He opened the fridge for a drink. His hand drew back abruptly at the sight of the porcelain cat figurine sitting on the shelf by the soda cans.

The same figurine he'd straightened on the sideboard less than ten minutes ago.

Damn. It was getting worse.

Chapter 2

*S*tay strong.

Jet repeated the phrase like a mantra as she sped through the rain-sloshed streets. Although it was not yet night, dark storm clouds blanketed the bayou. The town square was a jumble of small shops clustered around an old courthouse, much like any small Southern town.

But the life-size mermaid statue in the middle of the square was a departure from the norm. Rainwater streamed off the mermaid's stone-and-steel form, giving the impression that the siren had just emerged, dripping, from the nearby gulf waters. The etched half smile on her face bespoke secrets buried deep within the mysterious body that was part sea creature, part human.

Bayou La Siryna's founding fathers might have bought into the mermaid myth—old newspaper articles recorded local sightings—but nowadays, the natives scoffed at such nonsense. Most didn't even recollect that the town's name was given in recognition of the sea sirens.

Which suited Jet fine. With modern science, if humans suspected the old tales were true, mermaids would be hunted down and subjected to who-knew-what kind of experiments.

Her heart quickened as she rounded the curve on Shell Line Road with its row of rental bungalows nestled in thick pine and cypress. Lights glowed on porches and behind curtained windows like a promise, beacons of love and comfort that pierced her with longing. At one time she'd dreamed of fitting into this human world, since the mer-folk didn't have much use for her.

There it was. Third cottage on the left, where Perry had once lived. Light glimmered inside and a red Mustang was parked in the driveway, the kind of flashy car Perry would drive.

Three years. Three freaking years with no phone call, no letters, no nothing. She'd waited for an apology or any expression of remorse, had hoped incarceration would lead to introspection and recognition that he needed to change and beg her forgiveness. Stupid, stupid and more stupid. The memory of the last time she saw him replayed in her mind. During an expedition, Chilean marine police had caught them unawares. If only she had still been under-water, she would have heard the boat engine miles away. But after hours of bringing up the day's catch, they'd taken a nap.

At their capture, Perry had pointed a finger at her, de-claring it was her boat and her stuff. He'd even told them she was a freaking mermaid, a claim they laughingly dis-missed. She'd had no choice but to jump overboard to pro-tect her kind from possible exposure. The bleat of the horn and the shouting above had given way to the silence of the sea. But the usual numbing cocoon of the deep fathoms had failed to silence her despair.

In many ways, it still haunted her thoughts.

I've never gotten over it. All the pain of that betrayal

churned inside her like a giant tidal wave as she pulled in behind the Mustang. Perry probably thought they would get back in business together. Hell, why wouldn't he think she'd run back to him? In the past, she'd always done so, had overlooked his faults and dalliances.

She'd thought they really had something, until Shelly and her fiancé, Tillman, became a couple. Their trust and acceptance of one another had been a revelation. Jet realized that all along she'd wanted something Perry was incapable of giving—love.

She got out of her truck, hardly noticing the rain pelting her body as she strode to the door and rapped loudly. Deep inside came the muffled sound of a television. The volume lowered and footsteps approached. The door creaked open and there Perry stood.

White teeth flashed as he gave an easy grin, leaned his tall, sculpted body against the doorframe and crossed his arms. Jet reluctantly drank in the familiar image. Being near her former lover, with all their physical history, churned up memories and feelings she'd rather forget.

Don't even think about it. Jet lifted her chin and met his amused smile. *Conceited ass.* Perry's shoulder-length brown hair curled in waves, while a faint bit of stubble lined his jaw.

He gave a slow, knowing wink. "You are as beautiful as ever."

"Prison seems to have suited you," Jet snapped.

Perry's smile didn't falter. "Direct as always."

"Aren't you going to ask me in? I'm getting soaked out here, in case you haven't noticed."

"Since when has water ever bothered you? I remember you love rain." He stepped aside and waved an arm. "But do come in," he added, as if offering the keys to the palace.

She swept past, careful not to brush against him. Still,

she caught a whiff of his designer aftershave, which smelled of male skin warmed by the sun. Unable to pronounce the Italian product's name, Jet had dubbed it Aqua de Sexy. It tugged at memories of them together, her face pressed against his chest.

But the memory didn't devastate her as she expected. Instead, Jet recalled Landry Fields's soapy after-shower scent: simple, unpretentious and casually masculine. No use dwelling on *that*. Fields was not potential boyfriend material. Besides, getting seriously involved with anyone would mean again confiding that she was a mermaid, which compounded the risk of their secret race being exposed to scrutiny.

Jet drew a deep breath. "I've just come from the IRS office. The auditor asked all kinds of questions about my investments with Gulf Coast Treasures and Salvage."

Perry shrugged.

"Has anyone from the IRS contacted you?"

"Nope. The only good thing about prison is that there's no paperwork to file. I haven't had an income to report in years, so there's nothing they could question me about."

"You were sentenced to ten years. Why did you get released early?"

"Good behavior." He lowered his chin and waggled his eyebrows. "You know how good I can be."

He crossed the distance between them, but Jet turned away and walked to the window. She was too unnerved to handle the closeness. "How well do you know the owners of that company?"

He scowled. "Who said I knew them?"

"*You* did. When we first started selling stuff we pulled from the ocean, you claimed to know a company willing to accept our merchandise with no questions asked."

"I heard about them from other divers and met up with

a couple of them a time or two." Perry laid his hands on her shoulders and guided her toward him.

Jet clenched her jaw, willed her body not to respond to the steady pressure of his palms.

"We have far more interesting things—" he gave a smoldering once-over gaze from the top of her body to the bottom "—to discuss."

"Like how you tried to screw me over three years ago?"

He ran a hand through his long brown locks. "Yeah, that."

Jet shook off his hands and paced. The cottage was sparsely furnished, like most rentals, but clean despite a dirty dish on the kitchen table and a newspaper spread out on a coffee table.

"I only told the police you were a mermaid to protect you."

Jet stopped in her tracks. Somehow, he always managed to catch her off guard, like he had since they met five years ago. He'd reeled her in like a dumb, hungry fish. She'd been so lonely, so damned grateful he accepted her shape-shifting body. And when Perry went away, Jet was left gasping and flailing on land, like the same stupid fish she'd been all along.

Her jaw dropped and she snorted in disbelief. "You did it to *protect* me?"

Perry clasped her arms in one swift movement, his eyes a mask of concern. "I knew if I didn't piss you off, you'd stay with me out of stubbornness. No sense both of us going to jail."

She found herself drawn into an embrace. "Stop it." She pulled away and inhaled deeply. "If I'd been captured and interrogated, my fate would have been far worse than your jail time."

"Nobody would have believed me."

"Not at first. No. But if they probed enough, saw holes in our story of how we accidentally found treasure, ran background checks on our enterprises…"

"I wouldn't have told them anything else," Perry insisted.

"And what if I'd gotten sick and they had a doctor find freaky things in my medical tests? Or what if the police had thrown me into the sea to test if I changed? You didn't put only me in jeopardy. You put my entire race at risk of exposure."

He gave a disarming grin. "Ah, come on, sweetie. Don't get melodramatic on me now."

Of all the nerve. "You really are a son of a bitch, you know that? You knew about my nightmare."

His brow crinkled, then cleared. "The aquarium thing?"

Jet dug her nails into her fists, concentrated on the painful half-moon indentations in her fleshy palm, recalling one of the few times she'd shown her vulnerability to Perry. She'd awakened one night from that recurring nightmare, gasping for air, and spilled all about it. "Yeah, that thing," she snapped.

"Never going to happen. But if it does—" he flashed a grin "—I'll rescue you like a knight in shining armor."

Right. Perry would be a hero only if it suited his own purposes. Jet sucked in the pheromone-filled air of the tiny room. The man grinned so confidently, as if the past three years had never happened. As if he'd been some noble person when he'd ratted her out.

"Why are you here?" she asked.

"Why wouldn't I come back?" He ran a hand down her hair and neck, pausing slightly as his fingers brushed the trace of her gills. "I missed you." His lips brushed her forehead. "Missed this." His lips dropped to her mouth.

Jet gasped as Perry's hands cupped her ass and drew her

against his body. It would be so easy to surrender, enjoy the moment before—

"No." Jet tore away and drew in a few ragged breaths, unexpectedly grateful for the IRS meeting earlier. Landry Fields's questions served to make her more wary of Perry's lies and manipulation. "I need to set you straight on a few things."

Perry scowled and flung himself onto the sofa. "I explained why I told the police you were a mermaid. What else do you expect me to say?"

"For starters, how come I didn't hear from you the whole time you were locked up?"

"They wouldn't let me post mail."

"Bull. And you've been out for weeks before showing up here."

Perry narrowed his eyes. "How do you know when I was released?"

"You don't know?" No reason not to tell him. "The deputy sheriff, Carl Dismukes, told me. You remember him."

Perry slapped his palm to his forehead. "Of course, the crooked cop. But how did he know I got out?"

"I'm not sure. Maybe because your last driver's license listed you as living here in the bayou and they notify law enforcement when an ex-felon is released."

"Well, we aren't paying him shit anymore. He had a lot of nerve, blackmailing us for his silence. I don't know how he figured out what we were doing."

Jet bit her tongue. Dismukes might be despicable, but distant merblood ran in his veins, and she wouldn't betray his secret to a human. The deputy knew everything that happened on land and guessed a great deal about what happened undersea.

Perry narrowed his eyes. "Do you hear me? Dismukes gets nothing."

"Obviously. There won't be anything to split. You and I are history."

"Come on, baby." His voice grew husky. "Let's do one more job together. Give me a chance to prove I love you."

Her stomach clenched in response to Perry's gruff, low tone and his familiar declaration of love. *Stay strong.* "After what you've pulled, I'd be crazy to do it."

"I told you, babe! I honestly thought it was the only way to get you to jump ship and save yourself."

Liar. Could he learn to love someone other than himself? Her thoughts shifted from Perry's dark brown eyes to the ice-blue eyes of the IRS agent. Those penetrating, no-bullshit eyes that cut through her defenses. Landry Fields would burn through Perry's charming facade like dry ice on tender skin. Too bad her eyes didn't have a similar effect on Perry.

And why was she thinking of Landry Fields anyway?

"Please, Jet," Perry wheedled in that tone he used when he wanted something. "One last big haul to help me get back on my feet."

Her mouth widened in surprise. "What do you mean? You should have plenty of money socked away from all we've collected."

He hung his head. "I, um, had lots of lawyer bills and stuff."

"What about your fancy Mercedes-Benz? Your jewelry?"

"Gone." His face tightened. "I bought everything on credit and when I got thrown in the slammer, everything went to shit with my finances. All that stuff got repossessed."

Jet gave a low whistle. This was the real reason Perry had returned, of course. The guy was broke and needed her. Angry as she was, Jet couldn't help feeling a little sorry for him. "Maybe there is some way I can help," she answered evasively. Perhaps she could buy him off and get him to leave her alone. "What did you have in mind?"

He brightened and Jet tried to ignore the gleam of triumph in his chocolate-brown eyes.

"There's a site with a huge potential profit at Tybee Island, Georgia," he answered promptly.

"Never heard of any shipwreck there."

"It's an old Spanish ship supposedly loaded with gold and silver colonial coins."

Jet frowned. "Seems I would have heard about it. What's the ship's name? Do you have the cargo manifest?" It always amazed her that Perry got such great tips on treasure sites.

Perry waved a hand dismissively. "Leave all the research and details with me."

"I'll think about it." Jet bolted for the door. She had to get out quick, before he suckered her into a commitment. That would be colossal stupidity on her part.

Perry overtook her and laid a hand on the door. "Don't make me beg. All I'm asking for is one more job."

Jet swallowed hard and stiffened her spine. He'd left her hanging for years with no word. She could make him wait a day or two. Let him be the one to sweat it out. She had to get out of the cottage and think over everything rationally. Despite the years of silence, Jet knew Perry wasn't finished with her—she was much too valuable for him to completely abandon. Without her, he'd be back in the same boat he'd been in before they met, living a hand-to-mouth existence with the few treasures he could scavenge alone.

There must be some way to get Perry out of her life without agreeing to another treasure excavation. If she turned him down flat, there was no telling what he'd do for spite. "I said I'd think about it." She yanked the door-knob, sending Perry stumbling back a few steps. "See you around."

She stepped into the swirling rain and made her escape.

Jet was no fun anymore.

Perry kicked over the coffee table. She was playing a game. Trying to show who was boss, especially when he'd tried to stop her from leaving. Damn her abnormal mermaid strength.

But that freaky bitch still wanted him, would eventually cave in, and they could pick up where they'd left off.

Or maybe not. Sylvester Vargas claimed this Tybee Island thing was BIG. Enough money in it for all of them to live easy the rest of their lives. With enough dough, he'd move far away to someplace that didn't stink of bilge and shucked oysters like this bayou.

And then he wouldn't need Jet. At first, it had been fun, an ocean salvager's dream come true. She knew where the nearest, best stuff lay on the ocean floor. And once he got over his initial revulsion about touching a mermaid creature, the sex had been great. But slowly, Jet had changed, had begun to stifle him like any other woman he'd slept with more than a few times.

That woman-animal-sideshow-thing believed she had the upper hand. But he was the one with the contacts to sell the shit.

The sharp trill of his cell phone went off and he glanced at the screen: *Sylvester Vargas*.

Damn. The timing couldn't be worse.

"I see your girlfriend just left," said a heavily accented Spanish voice. "When can we set the date?"

Wow. Are they watching everything I do? Perry cleared his throat. "She's a little miffed at me right now. But she'll come around," he added quickly.

An ominous silence settled on the connection.

"I'm getting impatient."

"Yes, sir." He should have contacted Jet long before now but he'd had so much fun reacquainting himself with post-prison pleasures. The days had sped by with his indulgence of booze, women, gambling and partying.

"My company paid to get you out of that hellhole prison in South America. I'm beginning to think you're stringing us along with your wild tales."

"No, no. Not at all. Haven't you checked out what I told you?"

"That's the only reason I agreed to get you out of jail. I don't believe in that mermaid shit, but I can't deny how incredibly lucky you've been with sea finds. I contacted the managers of my salvage company you used as a front. They said you were their most reliable supplier."

"Told you so."

"No doubt something *fishy* is going on down there." Sylvester barked out a laugh at his own pun.

"And don't forget the police report."

"All it stated was that a female went missing during the arrest and is presumed dead."

"She jumped off the damn boat! That's why she went missing."

"From that I'm supposed to believe that your Jet grew a tail and swam hundreds of miles to some backwater Alabama bayou?"

Perry swallowed an angry retort. Sylvester was not a man to antagonize. He forced himself to speak with respect. "I need another week or so to convince Jet to go along with us."

"You have until the end of this week. If she doesn't agree by then, we'll have to use force."

Perry's mouth went dry. He wasn't sure if Sylvester was threatening *him* or Jet.

Or possibly both of them.

"Jet will come willingly. No need for force," he said with false confidence.

But the line was dead.

The library was quiet and musty-smelling with an antiquated vibe only punctuated by the sparse number of elderly people at reading tables with magazines. All eyes turned to him. Landry gave a rusty smile that he suspected looked more like a grimace. Where was that woman? She'd entered ahead of him just minutes ago. Surprisingly, she had not stayed long at Hammonds's rental.

"May I help you?" a middle-aged librarian asked, tilting her head slightly downward to examine him better with her bifocals.

"No, um…" He noticed the stairs to his right. She must have slipped up there. "I'm fine."

The carpeted steps muffled the noise of his entrance. Despite the room's small size, he couldn't see her. But she was there. Ripples of energy stirred his senses, just like in the office earlier. Landry walked to the rows of bookshelves and spotted her running a finger over the spines of several titles. Time to up the pressure on Jet today and ask more direct questions.

"Find what you're looking for?" His voice boomed like a firecracker in the muted space.

She jumped and nearly dropped a load of books cradled in one arm. "What are you doing here?" Dark eyes narrowed. "Are you following me?"

"Why would I do that?" He folded his arms and leaned against a shelf. "I mean, you're not a criminal or anything." Landry arched an eyebrow. "Are you?"

"Of course not." Red flushed her pale cheeks. "What do you want from me?"

He wanted… Unbidden, he imagined the woman in his bed, naked skin against naked skin. Something about her stirred him deeply, in ways he didn't understand. "Answers," he said. "I want answers."

"I'll get those stupid papers to you."

Landry leaned in close enough to read the book titles clutched against her like a shield—*Treasure Hunting in the Gulf, Shipwrecks in the Panhandle, History of Tybee Island* and— He snorted at the last title. "*Little Women?* Aren't you a little old for that one?"

Her chin lifted an inch. "Never. It's a wonderful book about family sticking together through hard times."

"A fairy tale."

"You're a cynical man, Mr. Fields. Got family issues, huh?"

To put it mildly. His family was a disaster, had been since The Incident when he was five years old. Not that home had ever been exactly harmonious, but at least it had been stable up until that time. Landry pushed down the bitter taste of those childhood memories. "Doesn't everyone have family issues?" he said with elaborate casualness. He didn't talk about that past with anybody. No sense rehashing something he was powerless to change. All he could do now was try to prevent it from happening to anyone else.

The tight set to her lips relaxed a fraction. "I suppose you're right, to some degree. But in the end, family's all we have."

Then I am so screwed. "I depend on myself and nobody else."

"Guess you're never disappointed, then." She lifted a shoulder. "But it sounds a bit lonely if you ask me."

"Hardly." Landry stiffened. He had his share of women,

had a few male acquaintances from work that he got together with for the occasional beer and football-game parties. Sure, a family would be nice, but you could live a perfectly fine life without them. He was proof of that.

"If you say so," she said in a tone that conveyed she didn't believe it.

Landry shook his head. *Wait a minute.* This conversation had taken a turn into the unexpected. He was supposed to shake *her* up, rattle *her* composure, not the other way around. He pointed at the book on shipwrecks. "You said you were through with the salvage business. But it looks like you're still interested in treasure hunting."

"It's a hobby. You should get your head out of your ledgers and find one." She turned and stormed toward the end of the aisle.

"A hobby?" He overtook her, blocking the exit. "So you didn't meet with your ex-partner today after you left my office?"

She drew her breath in sharply. "How did you— You *are* following me."

The flash of fear in her eyes made him want to pull her to him, to kiss her until she couldn't even remember Perry Hammonds's name, to protect her from her own dangerous impulses.

What was wrong with him? She crackled with spirit and a unique beauty that was downright unnerving. He'd never felt such a strong pull to a complete stranger. Especially a woman clearly on the wrong side of the law. But just how far had she gone? And was all that truly in her past?

Her eyes hardened. "Not that I have to explain anything to you, but my ex-partner is just that. An ex. I'm done with him."

He wasn't used to hostile female suspects. Most fell over themselves to be cooperative and friendly in the hopes of being left alone. Then again, Bosarge thought he was an IRS accountant.

Those people sure got no respect.

"I hope that's the truth," he said, meaning it. Bugged the hell out of him that he couldn't pin Miss Jet Bosarge into his usual tidy categories of good or bad. He wanted to believe she had no involvement with a ruthless criminal like Vargas. But if she knew something, a cooperative informant in the investigation would be useful before the agency closed in.

"You don't believe me," she said flatly.

Landry shrugged. "Time will tell."

"Look, whatever you may think of my past business dealings—"

A clamor erupted behind her and they both stared at the pile of books that had fallen and lay helter-skelter on the floor.

"I must have accidently knocked them off the shelf," Jet said, forehead scrunching in confusion.

She bent down to pick them up at the same time he did, their hands touching as they picked up the fallen books. He glanced up, startled, and Jet's face was mere inches from his own. He didn't move—couldn't if he wanted to anyway. Their breath joined and he felt absorbed in her impossibly dark, wide eyes. If he believed in magic—which he most certainly did *not*—he'd swear she was a witch casting a spell.

She broke contact first, swooping up the books and piling them haphazardly on the shelf. He stood, resisting the impulse to reshelf them in the correct Dewey decimal order. Keeping his own world in tight order was work enough. No need to take on librarian duties.

"As I was saying," Jet said, standing with her arms crossed. "I've been out of that line of work for three years.

Maritime salvage is a cutthroat business filled with lots of gray areas about what is and isn't legal. I'm done with it. I've dabbled in a few other ventures since quitting and now I'm reopening my shop."

Must be nice to *dabble* for years, courtesy of a wealthy family. He sure hadn't had that luxury. Landry shoved the thought aside. It wasn't her fault she'd been born into a family with advantages unimagined by his parents and siblings. Sometimes life just screwed you that way.

"Tell you what," he said, as if coming to a quick decision. "I've got some photographs I want you to look at."

Her brow wrinkled. "Right now?"

"Yes. While digging into your finances, my audit has broadened to other people and companies."

She followed him to the unused computer in the corner and watched as he logged in and uploaded a photo from his personal email account. It wasn't the greatest picture. Too bad he couldn't display the mug shot on the FBI site. Landry scrutinized the photo along with Jet. Sylvester Vargas was standing with a group of men by the docks and wore a hat, but the lower half of his face was fairly visible. If she'd met him before, she'd recognize him in the photograph.

"This guy look familiar to you?"

She leaned in and he inhaled her scent—fresh and invigorating like cooling rain after a long drought. Except her closeness felt anything but cool. His gut clenched at the fierce stab of longing that washed through him.

"No," she said, her breath sending tempting wisps of desire by his ear. Her arm brushed against his shirt, and even through the cotton fabric, heat spread over his entire body.

Landry fought not to squirm. If just being near her and not touching got him this aroused, what would it be like to have her in his arms? In his bed? He cleared his throat. "Are you sure?" Damn, his voice sounded husky and strained.

"I'm sure."

He glanced up in quick surprise. She sounded out of breath.

Bosarge straightened and patted her black hair in place about her long, slender neck. Must be a nervous habit, because she did the same thing this morning when he questioned her.

So much for getting anywhere with a photo identification. Landry signed off the computer with a sigh and stood. He hadn't gained a thing in this second meeting. All it had done was reemphasize the strange attraction to this woman. She met his gaze head-on, direct and unflinching.

"Your name matches your eye color," he blurted. Hell, what a stupid remark.

"Really?" Her upper lip curled. "Thanks, I didn't know that."

Sarcastic witch. "Is that any way to talk to the man auditing your tax records?"

"It's about as appropriate as a government employee commenting on my personal appearance."

She had him there. "Touché." He nodded before delivering a parting shot. "I look forward to examining your complete records in excruciating detail."

Jet hadn't planned on visiting Dolly tonight, but evidently her subconscious was in charge. She'd driven on autopilot, consumed with the day's meetings with two very different men. One a stranger, the other a man who knew her secrets.

But Jet didn't think of loam-brown eyes so similar to her own; rather she recalled blue eyes sharp as barbed wire. She didn't think of the casually familiar bearing of an old boyfriend, but the tight, controlled precision of an auditor. Most surprising, she didn't continue mulling over the long distances and spaces that marked her past relationship. Instead, her mind and body focused on the unexpectedly cozy intimacy of a library's book stacks.

It was all very confusing.

She parked by the only other vehicle at the water park, Dusty's old Cadillac. Jet beeped the horn in three short blasts and grabbed a tote bag from the backseat.

"Glad you made it today," Dusty said as she approached. "Our girl is a bit down."

Although his merblood was distant, Dusty had inherited a special feel for sea life. Jet impatiently shifted the weight on her feet until at last his gnarled fingers released the gate's lock.

She swept past him to the restroom, changing into a tank top and bikini bottoms. When she emerged, Dusty was mopping inside the office. He nodded before turning his back.

At the pool's edge, Jet bent down and slapped the water's surface. In seconds, over four hundred pounds of sleek silver-blue dolphin breached the water in a graceful arc before swimming like a torpedo toward her hand. Dolly playfully pushed against Jet's palm with her bottlenose beak and squeaked out a greeting.

Jet grinned. "I'm coming in for a swim." This was exactly what she needed. To hell with the complex human male species. She shed the bikini bottoms and slid into the water, legs instantly fusing into a long, shimmering tail fin.

A whiff of urine and feces assaulted her. Andrew Morgan, the park's owner, wasn't using the equipment properly. Damn, he had no business keeping a wild mammal from its natural habitat. The saltwater pool felt sterile, so unlike the ocean, which teemed with everything from gigantic blue whales to tiny microorganisms like plankton drifting in the ever-flowing currents.

She reigned in her distaste and anger. Dolly sensed emotions and Jet didn't want to add to her unhappiness. She ran a hand down her sleek side, fingers lightly tracing deep scars. Dolly was lucky that when she washed ashore on the bayou banks with severely lacerated flanks, a group of locals banded together to help save her.

Andrew, to give him credit, had provided a healing home as Dolly recovered. But instead of releasing her back to the sea, he discovered that Dolly's popularity brought in enough money to refurbish his formerly run-down park.

Dolly clicked and chattered, leading Jet to her favorite toy, a purple beach ball. Once she reached it, Dolly tossed it to Jet with her beak. Jet dived down in the water and flipped it back to Dolly with a flick of her tail fin. Back and forth it went for several minutes.

But something was off. Dolly didn't have her normal energy, her jumps weren't quite as high, and her turns and underwater maneuvers were a tad slower, too. Jet swam closer to Dolly for a better look. The dolphin tossed her head, pointing it toward the deep end of the pool, where Andrew kept the food buckets.

"Is that all? You hungry, girl?" Relief bubbled inside Jet. The dolphin couldn't be too depressed if her appetite was strong. Jet obligingly dumped a bucket of food for Dolly, who ate as if she were starving. Jet frowned. Time she had a talk with Andrew.

Dolly seemed energized after the meal and ready for play. She blew air from her blowhole, casting underwater rings. Jet gracefully swam through the bubbling circles, as eager as Dolly for companionship. She had precious little of it, since her family lived in near isolation. Oil spills had run off the few full-blooded mermaids who had lingered in the gulf. Lily had been at sea for months and Shelly was preoccupied with Tillman and their upcoming wedding later this summer.

Jet stifled a familiar pang of loneliness. She was happy for Shelly. It wasn't her cousin's fault that her relationship with Tillman was a constant reminder of what Jet lacked in her own life.

Yet again, Dolly tired quickly and floated, nuzzling her beak in Jet's palm with a slight clacking sound that could have been a sigh or a whimper. Despite the dolphin's appearance of a perpetually smiling mouth, something was definitely amiss.

Jet sang a lullaby, wishing Lily was here to soothe Dolly with her magical siren's voice. Dolly floated as Jet stroked the rubbery-smooth flanks, careful not to touch any old injuries.

A tiny wave of motion rippled the underside of Dolly's lower flank, so subtle Jet almost missed it. Her hand stilled on Dolly's thick skin, and there it was again. Something inside Dolly was alive and flipping. Awe and understanding dawned.

Dolly was with calf.

"No wonder you're so tired and hungry," Jet cooed, doing some quick calculations. Dolly had been here six months, so she was at least halfway through a dolphin's twelve-month gestation period. She laid a cheek against Dolly's warm-blooded body. Dolly should be with other females in her pod, who would aid her during labor and later share mothering duties.

"I'll get you out of here somehow," Jet whispered.

Dolly faced her sideways; one small black eye gazed into Jet's. Comprehension emanated like a wave of intelligent words. Dolly understood her heart's intent.

"I promise," Jet vowed.

Chapter 3

The crunch of gravel lifted Landry out of his musings on Jet Bosarge. He didn't know many people in Bayou La Siryna, preferring to keep to himself. Life was simpler that way, more predictable. Only a couple of old ladies at the humane shelter even gave him a casual nod of recognition. Landry went to the window and drew back the curtain.

Damn. He frowned at the battered Plymouth Duster. Only one person in the world owned that classic piece of shit. He rubbed his jaw, then stilled when two people got out of the car instead of one. And—oh, hell—they were unloading dozens of bags from the trunk.

He slipped a pair of sneakers on and walked outside. In the deepening twilight, Landry focused on the tall, lanky teenager. Which of his many half siblings was this one?

"Seth, say hello to your brother." His mother banged down the trunk, the sound echoing in the lonely gloom.

The kid regarded him sullenly.

This was the youngest of his mother's brood and the one he knew the least. She'd asked him if he could stay a few days this summer. Give Mom the tiniest opening and she'd bulldoze through it.

He eyed their cargo with mounting unease. "What's with all these bags?"

"Seth's here for a visit." She stuffed some into his arms. "Help us get this stuff inside."

"A *little* visit?" Between the three of them, there were over a dozen such crammed bags.

His mother stalked toward the porch before Seth found his voice. "You can't make me stay here," he complained. "This place looks like a shit hole and it stinks like one, too."

His mother whirled around as if the words were a knife launched into her spine. "You're staying. I've had all I can take of your stealing. And your mouth."

"Stealing?" Landry asked, looking back and forth between them.

Seth kicked at the gravel with a pair of frayed sneakers. "It's no big deal."

Landry suppressed a sigh. "What do you expect me to do?"

She crossed her arms. "You work for the FBI, don't you? Be a positive role model. He's got no father to speak of."

A flush of anger darkened the kid's neck. "I've got a dad," he said hotly.

His mother raised her hands and spun in a half circle, looking around the deserted stretch of bayou. "Really? Where is he?"

"He's oil rigging. Making money."

"Which we see precious little of," she snapped.

Sounded like old times. Five minutes with his family and his stomach was knotted. He'd been on his own for so many years he'd lost tolerance for the past drama of Life With Mom.

Landry gave a time-out signal. "Truce. Let's go inside and discuss this over dinner."

His mother stalked off again. "I'm not hungry," she called over her shoulder. "I need to get home real quick-like."

"Well, *I'm* hungry." Laundry motioned for Seth to follow them. At first it appeared the kid wasn't going to budge from his slouch against the old Plymouth, but with a sigh worthy of a Shakespearian actor, he dragged his feet forward, shoulders slumped and head down.

Inside, his mother threw her load of bags onto the couch. "Nice setup. This place used to be a real dump when your grandmother was alive."

Landry faced Seth and got his first good look at the kid. His chin-length brown hair hung in oily locks that partially shielded heavy-lidded dark eyes. He wore an olive camouflage jacket two sizes too large and a pair of faded jeans. "I'm grilling steaks. You hungry?"

"I'd rather have a hamburger. Can't we just go to McDonald's?"

Landry suspected the fast-food preference was a ploy for Seth to get rid of their mother faster. That had to be one tense ride from Mobile to the bayou. Landry grabbed his car keys and tossed them to Seth. In two seconds, the kid was out the door.

"You're taking a mighty big risk with your expensive car," his mother chastised.

Landry rounded on her. "I can't believe you showed up like this."

She had the grace to appear somewhat sheepish. "You agreed to a visit this summer."

"It's early April, not summer. And I'm in the middle of an investigation," Landry growled. "For Christ's sake, isn't the kid still in school?"

Her hard eyes clouded with tears. "He was suspended for cutting classes. In fact, he missed so many he might as well stay out of school the rest of the year and make it all up in summer school. Please let him stay. You're my only hope," she sobbed.

The great big ole fake. He knew it, she knew he knew it, and yet it worked every time. Landry tried to remember her the way she was before their lives were destroyed. He'd lost more than a sibling that dark day; he'd lost his mother and father, too.

Landry groaned and threw up his hands. "Okay. *Okay.* He can stay a few days. I'll try to talk to him but there's no guarantee it'll do one bit of good."

Mom hugged him tight with a smug smile she couldn't entirely hide. "You're my anchor."

"Just this week," he reiterated.

Jet riffled through the stack of invoices and moaned. Paperwork sucked. Tomorrow would be much more fun when the delivery from Mobile came in.

A sharp rap at the front door startled her. The shop wouldn't open for a couple more weeks. The front windows were taped over, so she couldn't see who'd knocked. She stuffed her feet into a pair of flip-flops, went to the door and unlocked it.

Crap. If she'd known who it was, she wouldn't have bothered. "Sorry, we're not open for business yet," she said quickly and began shutting the door.

"Not looking to buy anything," Landry Fields said, stepping inside before the door closed. His sharp eyes roamed the mostly empty space. "When do you anticipate opening?"

Jet inhaled the soapy-clean male scent she remembered from yesterday. "Not for a few more weeks. I've got a big shipment of furniture coming tomorrow. It'll take some time to get everything arranged." She resisted the urge to touch a curling tendril of light brown hair grazing the auditor's stiff white collar. His hair was slightly damp, as if he'd just showered or combed his hair down in a failed attempt to flatten the curly ends. Jet shook her head at the sight of his gray jacket and trousers. "You keep wearing suits like that and by next month the humidity will eat you alive."

"I'm from Mobile. I'm used to it." Landry didn't even give a polite smile, bearing an air as formal and reserved as his attire.

It only sent Jet's imagination into overdrive, fantasizing about what lay beneath the conservative clothing. She tried to convince herself Landry was probably pasty-white and about as fit as a dead June bug but as he walked away toward the front counter, something about the energy of his movements refuted that theory.

Landry stopped at the huge mahogany bar that served as a front counter and ran a hand down its gleaming, nicked surface. "Nice. You don't see these kinds of large pieces anymore."

Jet nodded, unexpectedly pleased at the compliment. "It's the reason I bought this space to begin with. Came with the property." She closed the door and walked to him. "I don't have the manifests yet that you requested."

Landry sat on one of the counter bar stools, as if settling in for a long chat. "How could you?" he asked with a wry smile. "I didn't specify how many years back I wanted you to go."

Jet scowled. "Years?"

"Correct. I want the documentation on all the salvage property you sold to Gulf Coast Salvage."

"I didn't think about it while I was in your office, but the company should have a record of that. Can't you get it from them?"

"You should have a copy, as well."

Landry didn't look at her, instead he riffled through the invoices she'd left lying on the counter. Nosy man. Her pleasure quickly turned sour. "What are you doing?" she asked tartly.

He laid down a paper and faced her. "Just curious. I find everything about you curious and fascinating."

A warm glow settled in the pit of her stomach at the words. No one had ever called her fascinating before.

"I want to satisfy my curiosity about you and your business associations." His eyes returned to the icy-blue she remembered from their first meeting. "Especially your association with one Perry Andrew Hammonds. The third, to be precise."

The warm glow died, replaced by a sharp chill up her spine. Damn. She knew it; Perry had somehow brought this fresh hell into her life. "What about him?"

"Now that Hammonds is out of prison, do you plan on resuming the treasure-hunting business with him?"

That was the million-dollar question. Jet opened her mouth, but no words came out. She'd had a sleepless night, debating whether to help Perry one last time. Maybe if she did he would make enough money to go away and leave her the hell alone. "I don't know," she answered truthfully.

"If you're serious about operating this store, you won't have time for long excursions." His eyes honed in on the help-wanted sign by the door. "Hired any employees yet?"

So, he was trying to see if she was truly making a run at this venture or if it might be a front to shelter money. "No." Jet crossed her arms and changed the subject. "What about your plans? You said the IRS field office here would only be around for tax season. When do you go back to Mobile?"

The blue chips in his eyes thawed a bit. "Trying to get

rid of me? I was actually thinking of staying in Bayou La Siryna permanently and commuting."

She almost laughed. "Why would you want to do that?" Mr. Sophisticated-Government-Man would die of boredom. Nobody visited their town and stayed. The bayou was an acquired taste—you were either born and raised in it, so that over the years the place settled into your blood and bone and brain like a fever, or you married a local. A disturbing thought hit her. "Are you seeing somebody in town?"

"No. But I have roots here."

Jet narrowed her eyes and scrutinized him. "What roots? I've never seen you before." She'd sure as hell remember if she had.

"I used to visit my grandmother most summers growing up, out by Murrell's Point."

"Hmm, thought I knew most everyone in these parts. What was her name?"

"Claudia Margaret Simpson."

Simpson, Simpson... Jet ran the name through her mind's inner database but came up blank. "How about her husband's or children's names?"

"What is it with people in small towns and the need to identify someone's family history?" he grumbled. "Doubt you ever crossed paths. Mimi kept to herself a lot."

"A family trait?" Jet observed wryly.

Landry tipped his head slightly in assent. "Could say the same about your family. In spite of the fact that your kin is one of the wealthiest and oldest in Bayou La Siryna, the Bosarges have a reputation for being aloof and reserved."

"Can't deny that." Jet grinned, until it struck her that he was prying again for tidbits of information about her. "Are all IRS guys as nosy as you?"

"If they're any good—yes."

What was good for the goose... "All right, then, since you seem to know so much about me, what are your grandfather's name and your mom's name?"

"Edward Fields. He died before I was born. And Mom's name—get ready for this—is Clytie Sands-Fields-Riley-Johnston-Hogge-Riley-Grimes."

Jet raised a brow. "Two Rileys?"

"Married and divorced twice."

"Ouch." Jet snapped her fingers. "It's coming to me now. Did your grandmother live in that blue cottage on Adele Avenue and drive a yellow Continental?"

"That's the one. Impressive memory."

"We all knew her as the crazy cat lady." Jet clamped a hand over her mouth. She really needed to get a mouth filter one day. She quickly grabbed a bunch of scattered invoices and stuffed them into a folder. Normally, it took a lot to fluster her, but something about Landry Fields kept her off-kilter.

A warm, large hand lay over her right arm, near the elbow. "It's okay."

The touch, combined with his low, husky voice, made Jet quiver even more than she had at the library. Her eyes slowly traveled up his forearm, across lean muscle and a coating of light hair that was so...damned...sexy. How could a man's *arm* be sexy, for Poseidon's sake? She met his eyes—so blue, so deep. As deep as the ocean she swam on summer nights. Landry leaned closer and Jet shut her eyes, wanting nothing more than to smell his clean scent and feel his lips on hers.

The bells above the door jangled and a cool draft lifted the hairs at the back of her neck.

"Well, shit," Landry muttered. "It's Perry the Pirate."

"Huh?" Jet abruptly opened her eyes and blinked. She'd been so totally wrapped in Landry's spell that the worldly intrusion caught her off guard. In a nanosecond, Landry's eyes returned to their previous remote chill. She stepped back and faced Perry.

He sauntered in, smiling easily, dressed in a white shirt and white jeans, just as he had the day she first met him at Harbor Bay. The Greek-god look, she'd laughingly dubbed it. Only now it looked more like a poor imitation of Don Johnson in an old rerun of *Miami Vice*. And since everything Perry did was calculated for effect, Jet wondered at the significance of his attire. His dark hair was artfully, yet casually, combed back and he sported a day's growth of hair on his chin and jaw.

"That your BMW parked out front?" he asked Landry.

"It is," Landry said stiffly, not returning the breezy smile.

"Classy car. A little conservative for my taste, though. I drive a red Mustang."

Yeah, a rented one. The flashy clothes and cars gave a false impression of wealth, and Perry was dead broke. Or so he claimed.

"Sporty car. But a bit too lame on the engineering for my taste," Landry remarked drily.

Perry pulled Jet to his side in a propriety gesture that made her want to give him a good kick in the shins. His Aqua de Sexy cologne did nothing for her after being so close to Landry minutes earlier. Everything about Perry now struck her as synthetic and fake.

It could never work between them again after all that had happened and the years apart. Still, letting go was like a little death. For too long, she'd clung to the hope they could be a real, loving couple, and dreams like that didn't die easily.

"Perry, this is Landry Fields, the IRS auditor that I spoke with yesterday."

"Nice to meet you. I'm Perry Hammonds."

Perry held out a hand, and for a moment Jet wasn't sure Landry was going to shake it.

But Landry played the gentleman. "I know the name. You were once in business with Miss Bosarge." Landry withdrew his hand. "Until you were sent to prison," he added.

Perry's smile flattened. "How nice of you to bring that up."

"I believe in laying out all the facts."

"Spoken like a typical accountant," Perry observed. "Bet you're a blast at parties."

Landry crossed his arms. "Yep, we nerdy types also believe in having plans. What's your game plan? Must be hard finding employment with a felony record."

Perry shrugged. "Something will come up. It always does. Besides, I'm doing my best to talk my girl into going back into business with me."

His girl? Jet stepped away from Perry's overly tight hold.

Landry swept his hand over the room. "Looks to me like she's got other ideas for earning an income. Guess Miss Bosarge could always hire you temporarily to help with shipments and inventory as her supplies arrive."

Jet almost snorted. Perry work as a lowly stock boy? Not happening.

"I have a higher standard than that," Perry scoffed.

The air between the two men crackled with animosity, all pretense of politeness worn thin. Time to break it up. Jet headed to the door, motioning to Landry. "I'll have that paperwork for you no later than tomorrow," she promised. Of course, she had access to the papers. The problem was that most of them were bogus.

Landry followed her while Perry leaned an elbow on the front counter and watched them.

At the door, he handed her a card with his phone number. "My teenage brother is staying with me a few days. A temp job would give him something to do while I'm at work. Think about it and give me a call later if you'd like to meet him."

Suddenly, Landry bent down and whispered in her ear, "Don't do it. Don't go back into business with that guy. You're better than that."

Jet gasped at the feel of his hot breath at her ear, the touch of his cheek as he temporarily pressed against her neck. Even with the protective scarf to hide the gill markings, the silky material only served to make the contact more provocative.

Landry pulled away, his blue eyes inches from her own, intense and full of warning. Without waiting for an answer, he abruptly exited.

"Looks to me like that IRS dude is interested in more than your tax returns," Perry drawled after Landry shut the door. "What gives?"

"None of your business," she snapped. "Why did you come by?" She sat on a bar stool next to Perry and rubbed her temples.

Perry smoothed back her hair behind one ear and ran a finger along the marking. "Let him get too close and he'll wonder about this."

Jet slapped his hand away, hard enough that Perry winced slightly. "That your way of saying I should stick with you since you know my deep, dark secret?"

"It should weigh in my favor that I know all about you and it doesn't bother me."

"Of course it doesn't. If I weren't a mermaid, you'd

still be collecting penny-ante treasure crumbs all by your lonesome."

"That's not true. I want us back together," he said huskily. "The way it used to be in the beginning. Remember?" He leaned in and softly kissed her lips. "I remember. And while I was in that stinking prison I thought about you every single night."

It wasn't true. He'd never written or called. And when he got out, he took plenty of time getting back to the bayou. He nuzzled the tender flesh of her neck and rubbed her shoulders. "I missed you. C'mon, baby. Give me another chance."

Don't do it. You're better than that. Landry's whisper drowned out Perry's coaxing. Jet sighed. "We can never be business partners—or anything else—ever again."

His eyes narrowed. "Is it because of that accountant nerd? I saw the way he looked at you."

Jet's heart gave an odd tug at the idea. "Don't be stupid. We just met."

"Doesn't matter. I heard him ask you to hire his brother. That's his way of keeping an eye on you."

"We were talking about us." She took a deep breath. "It's over." There, she'd said it.

A deep red flush lit his pale face and his jaw clenched. "You don't mean it."

Jet stood. "Yes, I do." She held out her hand. "Good luck with whatever you decide to do in the future."

Perry grasped her hand. "Do this one last job with me. Help me get back on my feet."

"No, but I'll help you out." Jet shrugged out of his grasp and lifted her backpack from a shelf. "I'll write you a check. Enough for you to move and set up in some new business."

Perry's mouth dropped open and Jet smiled inwardly.

He'd obviously expected her to fall into his lap. She found a pen and opened her checkbook.

Perry grabbed her writing hand. "I don't want your money. I want you to go with me to Tybee Island."

Jet jerked her hand away and gazed at him in surprise. "Since when do you not want my money?"

His flush deepened. "I like to earn my money and this is a big deal at Tybee."

"I don't have time for this. I'm opening the shop back up and moving on with my life."

He rolled his eyes. "Bor-*ing*. You'll be stir-crazy in two weeks."

"Shows how little you know me." She signed the check with a flourish and handed it over.

"I told you I don't want your—" Perry read the dollar amount and paused. "On second thought, I'll take it. Thanks." He grabbed the check and stuffed it into his white jeans. "But I still need you for this job."

Jet snorted. What had she *ever* seen in this man? "I gave you enough money to start over doing something else."

Perry stood. "This is your last chance. Say no, and I'm never coming back."

"Have a good life."

Perry's lips clamped together so tightly a thin white line edged the rims. "You'll be sorry," he warned.

"Get out," she said flatly.

He stared at her with an unfathomable expression. At least he didn't stoop so low as—

"I love you, Jet." His eyes softened. "And I'm begging you. Let's go now, right this minute. Forget your shop."

Don't do it. Landry's whisper echoed in her brain. *You're better than that.*

Yes, she was.

"No," she said firmly.

He stiffened. "If that's the way you want to play it." Perry slapped the countertop. "But you'll regret that decision before the week is out. Consider yourself warned."

Chills skittered down her spine at his set face. There was something there behind the words, something twisted. Something more than Perry believing she would miss him.

She picked up the invoice stack Landry had looked through, determined to get right to work and set her mind on business instead of worrying. A strong scent of baby powder tickled her nose and she lifted the papers to her face. Hmm, why would paper smell like powder?

The shop door slammed shut as Perry left, chimes exploding in a riot of discordant clangs.

Jet no longer cared. Landry's expressed faith in her character harmonized in her heart, outweighing Perry's threat and pique.

Chapter 4

A long rock guitar riff assaulted Landry's ears as he entered the house.

"Hey," he shouted. "Turn it down."

Seth sprawled on the sofa, lost in the music, a crumpled bag of chips and half a sandwich by his side. Landry winced at the thought of meat grease staining the expensive leather.

He unplugged the cord and Seth jumped at the resulting quiet. "Wha—"

"Little loud for me. Is this what you've been doing all day?"

Seth sat up straight and stretched. "I got up about two o'clock, fixed a sandwich and listened to my iPod. Jeez, it's so boring out here."

"What do you usually do all day now you're out of school?"

"Hang out with friends. You know."

No, he didn't know. He'd worked nights and summers since he was sixteen and put himself through college. And after college he'd been busy with his career. "What's your game plan until summer school starts?"

Seth gave an elaborate shrug. "More of the same, I guess."

The kid would drive him nuts. "We need to establish a few house rules." Landry pointed to the food refuse. "Pick up after yourself and get in bed by midnight. Or at least turn the TV on low or read a book."

"Read a book?" Seth snorted. "Yeah, this week is going to be a blast."

Oh, hell, he could make more of an effort to be hospitable. A few days wasn't forever. Landry regarded Seth's bored, impassive features and sighed, trying to remember what he liked at that same age, besides the all-consuming testosterone-raging obsession with girls. He'd been a serious kid, always retreating from his noisy family and working jobs for some cash.

"How about a temporary job? I know a lady who might be interested in hiring you."

Seth grimaced, as if tasting sour lemon. "Why would I want to do *that?*"

Right, whatever you want you can shoplift. "It's not so bad. Be nice to have your own spending money."

"Nothing I really need."

"What about a car or money to take out a girl?"

"Don't have a girlfriend and I could never save up enough for a car. Guess I'll try to join my dad on the oil rigs in a couple of years. Might as well be a bum while I can."

Landry thought quickly. "You could save up enough for a used car. Tell you what, whatever you save in the next six months, I'll match it."

It was easy to read the mistrust in Seth's eyes. "Why would you do that?"

"You're my brother."

"Half brother," Seth corrected. "And I haven't seen much of you in the last few years."

Landry fought down the guilt that flared in his gut. "You should take the job. She needs a temp to stock. There's a shipment of goods coming in tomorrow, so she'd need you right away."

"Oh, all right," he said with a complete lack of enthusiasm. "I don't see why she can't do it herself, though. Is she old or something?"

Landry snorted. Jet Bosarge was the complete opposite of old and frail. "She's younger than me by at least five or six years."

"She your girlfriend?"

The question took him aback. Jet's sharp features sprang to mind. She was way too...*intense* for his taste. There was a storm in her eyes, a tightness and electricity in her every move that was disturbing. Everything in her manner suggested a hard, unbending nature. Despite it, there was no denying most men probably found her type alluring. He wasn't one of them. He liked women that were more nurturing with soft, curvy bodies that promised a hot night in bed. And out of bed, he wanted the kind of woman with whom he could relax at home on quiet evenings. God, he sounded like a chauvinist. No wonder he was single.

"Well?" Seth asked. "Is she your girlfriend or not?"

"Not. Definitely not. I only met her yesterday," he said way too loudly, pushing aside the memory of how they had almost kissed in the shop. "And I need a favor. Don't tell her I'm with the FBI. She thinks I'm an IRS auditor."

Seth scowled. "Why'd you lie?"

"It's not a lie—it's an undercover job."

"Uh-huh. So you want me to spy on her."

Landry's jaw tightened. "Of course not." Did the kid think the worst of everybody? He hadn't considered it but... "If you do see anything weird, you could let me know."

Seth snatched up the chips bag and stalked toward the kitchen.

Landry followed him, picking up a used drinking glass and an empty box of crackers. "And speaking of weird— have you noticed anything unusual going on around the house?"

"No. What do you mean?"

Landry felt the back of his neck heat. "Like things not being where they're supposed to be and strange noises. Stuff like that." Seth's blank face reminded Landry why it was always better to just keep his mouth shut. "Never mind. How about we go out? We could swing by Miss Bosarge's house so she can meet you, and then go to Mobile for pizza and a movie."

"I guess."

His brother's lack of enthusiasm was irritating, but at least he hadn't refused. During the fifteen-minute ride to Jet's, Landry looked at Bayou La Siryna with new eyes. Much as he appreciated the lonely, mysterious swampland, which suited his own loner nature, it didn't offer much for a teenager. If Seth stayed the whole summer, he might lose his mind from boredom. Landry pulled into the Bosarge driveway, glad Perry's Mustang was nowhere in sight.

"Cool house," Seth commented, sliding out of the BMW. "She rich?"

"Yep. Her family has a whole lot more money than we'll ever earn in our lifetime." The thought rankled. Jet's wealth was one of a dozen reasons why he shouldn't get involved with her. They were from different planets. Everything he had, he'd earned through hard work and disciplined savings, while she'd been raised in a life of ease.

They walked up the steps onto the wraparound porch of

the large Victorian home. Wicker rockers graced the open space and large ferns hung from wooden rafters. The place didn't reflect Jet at all, much too girlie. He rapped on the pale blue door and waited.

Loveliness, incarnated in human form, opened the door. She had long blond hair, green eyes, perfect skin and full, lush lips. Seth sucked in his breath beside him and Landry smiled. This must be Jet's cousin Shelly, because Jet's sister, Lily, had been gone for months. Whereabouts unknown. "I'm here to see Jet," he said.

Those ocean-green eyes widened a bit. She opened the door and waved them inside. Some *thing*—some mixture of rat, possum and hellhound—scrabbled his way over, barking and snarling.

"What is that?" he asked.

"Our dog, Rebel." Shelly commanded him to sit and the thing complied.

Landry looked at him closer. "What's wrong with him—besides the mange? He's covered in cuts and scars."

Shelly scratched his hairless ears. "He doesn't have the mange. He's a Chinese Crested Hairless. Jet and I rescued him. We found him tied to a tree where a group of kids were stoning him to death."

"Glad you found him in time." No creature, no matter how hideous, deserved that fate. He followed her into the den. "Nice place," he commented. Now, this was more like Jet, especially the collection of swords over the fireplace. "I hope we haven't come at a bad time."

"Not at all. I'll get Jet." She smiled warmly at Seth, who still looked a bit dazed. "Have a seat. Can I get you a Coke or something?"

"No, ma'am." His voice squeaked and he sat down quickly.

Landry shook his head and sat, as well. What had he

been thinking yesterday about wanting to be younger? Seth made him remember that adolescence sucked sometimes.

"This place is cool," Seth said, eyeing the swords.

"Then you ought to like working for Jet." Landry ran a finger over a brass antique compass lying on a coffee table. The magnetic needle jerked and spun frenetically in circles and he hastily stuffed his hands into his pockets.

Seth's gaze turned from the Confederate sword he'd been studying. "This is the kinda stuff she sells? I thought it would be clothing or makeup crap."

"I promise no makeup crap," Jet's voice rang out.

The air in the room crackled as if a high voltage of positive ions had been released, like a smell after a heavy rain at the beach, bracing and refreshing. She wore a pair of cutoff denim shorts and a gray T-shirt with Alabama Crimson Tide stamped across the front.

Landry stood and pulled Seth to his feet. "Hello again, Jet. This is my brother Seth."

"Half brother," he mumbled.

Jet shrugged. "Whatever. I could use some help tomorrow with a big shipment of furniture from Mobile. I'd only need you a day or two. You up for it?"

"Guess so," he muttered.

"Tell me what time you need him at your shop," Landry said.

"About ten o'clock."

Seth's mouth dropped open slightly. "That early?"

Landry elbowed him. "He'll be there."

Shelly walked up beside Jet. "What about school, Seth?"

Seth straightened and a dull red flush crept up his neck. "I'm done for the year."

Shelly absently swirled a lock of honeyed curls. "I see. Since you're at loose ends for a bit, I've got someone I want you to meet. Do you swim?"

Landry shifted uncomfortably, hoping Shelly wouldn't ask him the same question because he hated lying. What thirty-five-year-old man couldn't swim? It was ridiculous. Yet he sank like a stone every time he tried to learn.

"Of course I can swim," Seth answered.

"Then I want you to meet Jimmy Elmore at the YMCA pool. His grandmother Lurlene is one of my senior clients."

Shelly turned questioning eyes to Landry. "Mind if I introduce them? Jimmy's a good kid. You'll see."

"Sure. Seth could use some company his own age."

"I'll set it up now while you two talk business." Shelly steered Seth out of the room. "Let's call Jimmy now and work out a time." Her voice became fainter, from the kitchen. "Then I want to show you our knife collection. Some of them are over one hundred years old—"

"My cousin loves kids," Jet said. "Looks like she's taking Seth under her wing."

Landry couldn't tear his eyes from Jet. For the first time, he noticed her dark eyes were rimmed with flecks of gold and green, like chips of orange citrine and emeralds. He stepped closer, watched them widen with a sudden wariness.

Jet fingered a red scarf draped on the sides of her slender throat as she inched backward. "Why are you staring at me?"

Good question. What the hell was he doing? Jet was a possible felon and might be involved in some big-time scam if she and Perry Hammonds were working with Sylvester Vargas. He had never—ever—looked twice at a woman with a shady background. They were persona non grata in his rule book.

"I'm not," Landry lied, running a hand over the back of his neck. This was inexplicable and frustrating. Everything about this woman was a mystery. And he hated mysteries.

Or so he'd once believed.

"I have those documents you wanted." Jet walked away and he watched her long, slender legs cross the room. She leaned over slightly to yank open a drawer in an old roll-top desk. He stared at the slight curve of her hip framing a heart-shaped ass. The rest of her tall body might be thin and muscled, but her bottom was lush. He imagined gripping a handful of cheek and—

She spun around, an armload of paper cradled at her side, and frowned. "You're staring at me again."

Caught red-handed.

Landry pointed at the papers. "Those for me?" Nothing like a little deflection when denial was pointless. What was the matter with him? He didn't go around gawking at every pretty girl that crossed his path. Yet around her, all he could think about was drawing her body to his.

"Every freaking year accounted for." She marched to him and held out the stack. "All yours."

"How did you get them so quick?" Damn. Hounding her about the paperwork was merely a ploy to test the waters about her relationship with Hammonds. Good thing she'd hired Seth, so he'd have an excuse to hang around her shop. He riffled through the stack—each item had a provenance form with date of origin, location found, date sold and more. On the surface all appeared normal, but how could one woman be so lucky finding sea treasure? He discounted Hammonds as a factor in their success. Perry the Prick was nothing but a useless hanger-on. Anyone with half a brain could see that within minutes of meeting him.

Except Jet.

She folded her arms and matched his stare. Only now, the veiled hostility of yesterday was missing. Her expression was hard to fathom, a mixture of curiosity, sensuality and challenge. Maybe she, too, remembered that moment in the shop when their mouths had been inches from kissing.

He tried to remember all the reasons why this woman was off-limits, but he couldn't name a single one. Everything about Jet fascinated him and stirred his sensual appetite like it hadn't been in years. The pale glittering skin, full lips and unusually dark eyes framed by black hair were so different from any other woman, especially his blonde, blue-eyed ex-fiancée.

No, screw that memory. The past would not haunt him anymore.

Jet crackled with energy and a directness that cut through his usual barriers and demanded sole focus on her own unique qualities.

She leaned closer, a glint of desire sparkled like pixie dust in her enlarged pupils, and Landry's jaw clinched at his body's immediate tug to draw closer. "What did you tell Perry today?" he ground out in a voice harsh from the tightness in his lungs and chest.

Jet blinked. "I told him we were done."

"You really mean that?" If she was truly finished with Hammonds, maybe they could be together. He hadn't found anything—yet—that proved Jet was involved with Sylvester Vargas or had plans to illegally salvage something on a large scale.

She gave a lopsided grin. "Cost me a few thousand, but he finally accepted I won't do any more treasure hunts with him."

Landry frowned, fingers curling into his palm. "Don't tell me you had to pay Hammonds to get rid of him." What a low-life scum bucket. Someone that mercenary and manipulative had no ethics or morals. Someone like that was dangerous. He hoped Hammonds would take the check and leave town, but instinct and experience warned there was little possibility of that scenario playing out.

"Forget I said it, then." Jet shrugged and her eyes again shone with heat. "The important thing is that it's over between us." She touched his chest with one hand, and even through his thick cotton shirt, the heat of her skin traveled downward, and his stomach clenched.

All reason fled. He had to feel her, taste her, claim her—

Landry lowered his face and kissed the top of Jet's scalp, inhaling her warm, earthy scent. If he'd read the signals wrong, she could back away now. But she didn't rebuff him. Instead, Jet wrapped her arms around his waist and pulled him closer, setting his groin on fire.

His body hummed with need. Landry tightened his hold on her before at last claiming her lips. They were as soft and yielding as he'd imagined. Their mouths parted and he tasted liquid warmth as their tongues danced, tentative at first, then with increasing urgency. He ran his hands down her lean, tight back before palming that cute ass he'd been eyeing moments earlier. The contrast of the lushness there, compared to the muscled tightness on the rest of her body, made the soft flesh even more enticing.

Jet let out a noise somewhere between a moan and a sigh and the sound inflamed Landry's senses. He had to explore another area of soft flesh. His hands reached under the flimsy T-shirt until he palmed both breasts, which— thank goodness—were harnessed only by an athletic bra that he easily pushed upward and out of the way.

Although many men might prefer bigger breasts, Landry found Jet's perfect, exactly suited for her tall, athletic frame. He trailed kisses down her throat, reckless with need.

A door slammed shut and the sound of voices entered the hall. *Shit.* Abruptly, Landry pulled Jet's bra down over her breasts and stepped back. He inhaled deeply, trying to control his heavy breathing. Jet appeared stunned by his sudden withdrawal and wrapped her arms across her chest.

"So bring your swim trunks and a few towels—" Shelly entered first, glanced at them both sharply and resumed talking "—because Jimmy will meet you at the Y as soon as you get off work tomorrow."

Landry slowed his heavy breathing with an effort, incredulous at his lack of composure. This woman's effect on him was downright uncanny.

Seth came in directly behind her, running a hand through his wind-tossed hair. "Cool." He grinned at Shelly, looking happier than Landry had seen him since he arrived at the bayou. "It'll be awesome to have someone to hang out with."

Huh? Little brother could actually be agreeable and talkative. It hadn't even occurred to Landry to try to introduce Seth to guys his own age; he'd only been concerned about getting through the visit without the two of them wanting to kill each other. Landry shifted uncomfortably at a little pang of guilt. He didn't know anyone around Seth's age, and besides, Seth would go along with anything Shelly suggested. The kid was obviously spellbound by her looks.

"You can leave work whatever time you want," Jet said to Seth, settling down on the sofa and crossing her long legs. "The schedule's flexible."

Landry stole a glance at her from the corner of his eyes. Jet appeared cool and composed, like she had when they first met. Only the faint darkening of her lips indicated she'd been thoroughly kissed.

To hell with always following procedure and all his rigid rules and preconceived ideas about his perfect type of woman. He'd thought his ex was perfect for him. All those quiet evenings spent at one another's place watching television or reading books. There'd been no drama, no fights. So what if it had been a bit dull? They had settled into a comfortable companionship he imagined would last forever until the day she texted and told him she'd found someone more exciting.

Landry took a deep breath. Nothing about Jet would ever be boring or fade to a companionable kind of relationship. He dropped his gaze to those shapely, smooth legs and wanted to lick his lips. He could almost feel them wrapped around his back as they made love. Maybe once that happened he could regain control over his traitorous body and stop mooning over Jet.

Soon, very soon, he promised himself.

Chapter 5

Seth's thin forearms and biceps knotted into muscled cords as he and the deliveryman carried a Duncan Phyfe sofa into Jet's shop, The Pirate's Chest. Despite his slightly sullen attitude around Landry, Seth had proved to be a hard worker. The teenager's chin-length hair was washed and shining and he'd shaved the face stubble. No doubt the sudden interest in grooming was to impress Shelly, whom he seemed quite taken with last night.

Last night. Little sparkles of happiness tap-danced along Jet's spine whenever she thought of Landry's kiss. Amazing that chemistry ignited when they were together, considering how and why they met. He'd been so antagonistic at first. Yet, even then, she'd been drawn to the crisp blueness of his eyes and the solid strength he emanated. Biology was a very weird thing.

"Set it over here in this corner," Jet directed Seth. The floor space was filling up quickly, yet several large pieces remained on the delivery truck. Funny, her stockpile of nautical salvage hadn't looked so gargantuan in the huge industrial warehouse.

Shelly, perched on a bar stool reclaimed from an old

ship, shook her head as she surveyed the ever-increasing piles of stuff. Ripples, like sun bouncing off water, shimmered through her golden curls. "You should have measured everything first, like I suggested."

"Nobody likes people who say 'I told you so.'" Jet lifted a handful of her sweaty black hair to cool her neck and then remembered the nearby strangers. Drat. She let go and arranged some chunks around her neck to cover the faint outline of gills. Too bad all humans weren't like Eddie, Shelly's soon-to-be brother-in-law. Around Eddie, she didn't have to worry about any oddity. "I'm not worried about the space," she added. "Once I hang up some of the merchandise, there will be plenty of room in the aisles for customers to browse."

Eddie stood as unmoving as an ice sculpture in the middle of the chaos. His head was thrown so far back, only his long neck and the tip of his chin were visible. Jet followed his gaze up to where a four-hundred-pound chandelier glimmered with thousands of prisms, each casting variegated dots of pastel hues on the coppered ceiling.

"Rainbow," Eddie pronounced.

Jet nodded. Eddie was wrapped up in his own autistic world, but when he spoke, he often had a unique perspective.

"So, are you expecting Landry to stop by today?" Shelly asked with a knowing smile. "Maybe y'all can finish what you started yesterday."

Her cousin was far too perceptive. After Landry had left last night, Shelly had gone on and on about what a nice guy he was, such an improvement over Perry, he had such a safe, secure job, etc. The biggest positive, in Shelly's eyes, was that Landry demonstrated a caring nature, since he took his little brother under his wing—much like Tillman watched over his kid brother, Eddie.

Jet sighed; she'd been hoping for Landry to contact her all morning but hadn't heard a word. "No, I haven't seen him, but Perry's called a few times. I didn't answer the phone."

Shelly's green eyes darkened. "That bastard," she hissed.

"That bastard," Eddie mimicked, eyes still glued upward.

Jet laughed. For Shelly to use that language was unusual, especially around Eddie.

"Very funny." Shelly rolled her eyes. "Hope he doesn't repeat it around Tillman later."

"Even if he did, Tillman wouldn't care. He thinks you are Miss Perfect." Jet bit her lip, hoping Shelly didn't catch the whiff of bitterness. Her cousin was one lucky woman and deserved every bit of happiness. She had been through hell last year after witnessing a serial killer dumping a body at sea. The killer had hunted her down, but Shelly and Tillman defeated the man and fell in love in the process. By the time Tillman had discovered Shelly was part mermaid, it didn't stop him from loving her and proposing a lifetime together.

Shelly snapped her fingers as inspiration struck. "Hey, want me to have Tillman run Perry out of town? As sheriff, he could find a way to do it."

"I can handle an ex-boyfriend," Jet said with a sniff. She didn't mention the desperate measure of paying Perry off to get rid of him. Humiliating enough that she'd slipped and admitted it to Landry last night.

As the movers loaded a ten-foot-high mahogany armoire onto a dolly, Jet glanced around, assessing where to best make room. The only hope for it was to take the sofa and move it into a middle aisle so the armoire could be placed against the far wall. She hoisted the sofa, raising it a good two feet off the ground. As she walked forward, she spotted Seth and the deliveryman, who had both stopped rolling the furniture and stared at her, mouths agape. Behind them, Shelly grimaced at the careless, giveaway slip.

Uh, oh. After spending weeks doing nothing but training undersea and attending the Poseidon Games, she was forgetting all the little subterfuges necessary to not draw attention from landlubbers. Good thing Landry hadn't witnessed her strength. The man was way too observant for her comfort.

"How did you lift that all by yourself?" Seth's voice squeaked a bit at the end. He cleared his throat. "It took both of us to drag it in."

Jet dropped it immediately. "I wasn't thinking." She placed a hand on the small of her back and sank down onto the sofa's scratchy wool upholstery. "Oh, my back," she moaned, hoping it sounded convincing.

"You're always trying to lift things that are too heavy." Shelly rushed over with a distracting display of concern and bent over Jet. "Your back will hurt for weeks because of this. When will you ever learn?"

"Good job," Jet mumbled in her ear.

"Play along," Shelly whispered back as she put an arm around Jet's shoulder and pretended to support her. "Come sit up front with me. I've got some Tylenol in my purse."

Jet hobbled around the men and waved her hand vaguely in the air. "Fit everything in here as best you can."

Seth and the mover looked slightly appeased, though their male pride had undoubtedly taken a hit.

Once they were both seated, Shelly pointed to a cardboard box on the long, scarred oak counter. "I'm about halfway through cataloging the contents." She patted a stack of papers. "I've already printed out the inventory for all this." She swept her hand over dozens of old coins, cuff links, and other odds and ends. "You can finish going through this box while you are...um...convalescing that injured back."

"Where are you going?"

"Back to the YMCA." Shelly glanced at her watch. "Next class starts in fifteen minutes. My senior swimmers already have a low opinion of the younger generation. Don't want them to lump me in with the slackers."

Jet snickered. "Those old folks adore you. All your clients do, especially Eddie." Her cousin was a popular woman in the bayou. As an aquatic therapist, Shelly helped the elderly and special-needs persons with their challenges. And by the end of summer, she would be married to Tillman. The merfolk might look down on Shelly because she was half mermaid, half human, but she'd come to terms with her shape-shifting heritage, found a man who loved her and established her place in the community.

Too bad Jet couldn't say the same for herself.

She might be all mermaid by birth, but Jet, like Shelly, had never felt comfortable around other mermaids, either. Jet sensed a distance between them, knew that behind her back they exchanged raised eyebrows or knowing looks of disdain. Growing up, she'd attributed it to her mother insisting she and Lily spend so much time with humans in the bayou. But Jet suspected more was afoot and this year she would demand the truth. She fingered the golden trident nestled against her chest on a chain. As soon as her mother came home for their annual family reunion, she'd use her one wish to find out why the merfolk shunned her.

As far as her love life… Jet bit the inside of her lip. *Don't get too excited over Landry. He'll only disappoint you like Perry.* She let out a deep sigh, stifling the depressing thought. It might be foolish, but she couldn't help hoping this time might be different. Landry was the complete opposite of Perry. You couldn't get any more safe or predicable or stable than an accountant. And she was so tired of being alone. Surely there was no harm in yielding to her carnal desires. Landry's pull was magnetic and she didn't want to fight it.

Only two obstacles stood in the way of them exploring a relationship. One, Perry needed to go away and, two, Landry needed to close his audit file. That high-priced attorney assured her everything was in order with her taxes and she had nothing to fear. Landry might be a bit suspicious but he could prove nothing illegal. This whole matter of an irregularity in the tax records should be dropped as soon as Landry reviewed the paperwork.

Seth gazed after Shelly as she left with Eddie. If he was this entranced by Shelly, the kid would be totally lost if he ever met Lily.

Finally, the delivery was complete and they both sank onto chairs by the window.

"I don't know what I would have done without you today," Jet began.

Seth gave a half smile and pulled one leg on top of the opposite knee. "You probably would have lifted everything by yourself and been finished—" he yawned broadly "—by lunchtime."

Jet let the remark pass without comment. Seth might be a teenager, but he was pretty sharp. "Good thing I met your brother."

Seth shrugged. "You done with me? I can help you move shit—" he stopped and reddened slightly "—I mean move *stuff* around."

"I could use some more help. I'll treat you to lunch first. Let me freshen up and I'll be right back."

Seth ambled out of the chair and went to the counter

where she'd laid out dozens of knives that had yet to be cataloged. "These are way cool."

Jet smiled faintly. *Cool* and *awesome* seemed to comprise a large part of his vocabulary.

"Yeah, they're cool," Jet said, sweeping by the display. Once ensconced in the tiny employee bathroom, she retrieved a comb and ran it through her tangled bob. Not her best look, but it would have to do. She'd secretly hoped Landry would show up and go to lunch with them, but he must be busy.

As Jet reentered the store, she halted in surprise at Seth's furtive glance behind him as he held up the dagger he'd admired earlier. Jet noiselessly stepped behind a bookshelf and watched as he hesitated and then quickly stuffed the weapon into an inside pocket of his baggy camouflage jacket. Her heart plummeted. She'd planned on letting Seth pick out one from the collection as a gift before he left town.

Takes a thief to catch a thief. Jet shifted in the shadows, annoyed the thought popped into her mind. She didn't steal anything, only told half-truths in reporting where and how she found sea treasure. *A half-truth is the same as a lie. Don't kid yourself.* How disappointed would Landry be if he knew all her secrets? Of all the people to fall for, it had to be an IRS auditor. He was sure to view the world like he did financial ledgers, with everything either black or white. And she was definitely a shade of gray. Jet remembered his urgent whisper, *You're better than that,* when Perry tried to persuade her to take one last "sure thing" salvage venture.

She shrugged off the battle with her conscience and stepped out from behind the bookcase, prepared to confront Seth. But before she said anything, he took the dagger out of his jacket pocket and laid it back down on the counter.

"Good choice," Jet said crisply. The words seemed overly loud in the cramped space.

Seth jumped and faced her with wide, stricken eyes. "I...I..." He gulped and couldn't say any more, his entire body rigid and unmoving.

She couldn't help but feel sorry for him. "It's okay. I won't tell your brother."

He relaxed only slightly. "I'm...uh...sorry." Seth's face turned red and he stared at the floor. "Guess I'm fired, huh? I'll call Landry to come get me." Still unable to look her in the eyes, Seth walked to the door with his head down.

Damn, she probably felt as bad as he did. "Wait," Jet called out.

Seth stopped, but kept his back to her.

She walked over and motioned for Seth to sit down in a chair by the door. Pulling up another chair and sitting across from him, Jet leaned close. "Look at me."

He crossed his arms, scooted backward and leaned so far over that he balanced precariously on the two back legs of the chair. His brown eyes might be different from Landry's, but he had the same remote expression down pat. The defensive stance screamed you-can't-hurt-me and Jet would recognize it an ocean away, considering this was how she reacted when cornered.

"You didn't take the dagger and that's what matters. We're—what's your word?—cool."

"You're saying that 'cause you have a thing for my half brother."

Observant guy. "Everyone's redeemable," she mumbled.

Seth regarded her blankly. "Huh?"

"What I mean is...what matters in the end are the actions we take." Holy Poseidon, she was talking about her own situation. No wonder Seth wasn't following her train of thought.

She ran a hand through her hair. "Never mind. Let's forget this whole thing happened. You're not fired and I want you to keep working. Now, how about lunch?"

"No need." Seth craned his neck to look past her out the front window. She'd taken down the paper covering on all the doors and windows to let in the sunlight. "My half brother's here."

Jet turned and watched an expensive BMW being expertly maneuvered between two other vehicles as the driver executed a perfect parallel-parking feat.

"Did you two have plans to meet for lunch?"

"Nope."

Landry entered, polished and neat in a navy suit, eggplant-colored tie and crisp white shirt. The atmosphere shimmered with the heat between them. Jet suddenly became aware of how grubby her jeans and T-shirt were. She sneaked a glance in the mirror at the far end of the front counter. Her black hair had sticky spikes shooting out at odd angles and her face had a sheen of sweat that culminated in a drop of perspiration above her lips. She lifted an arm to swipe at her face, but checked the motion. Landry found her attractive as she was; he'd shown that last night. And the sweat was from trying to make an honest living.

Well, starting *today* she was trying to make an honest living. If you didn't count the few odds and ends for sale that were collected from the bottom of the sea.

Landry gave a low whistle. "And to think yesterday this place was nearly barren. You both must be beat." His eyes went immediately to the six-foot-high mermaid masthead hanging on the opposite wall. "Wow. That wasn't here yesterday. It's incredible. Where did you get this?"

The elaborately carved ship masthead was one of her favorite pieces and definitely not for sale. Instead of the dreamy perfection of most artists' mermaid renditions, this mermaid's features were fierce. In her right hand she held a raised sword, as if defying Poseidon himself as the lone protector of the ship she guarded. The bold cut of her features, as well as the detailed carving of her tail-fin scales, were so precise that Jet often wondered if the artist might have once had a close encounter with one of her kind.

She couldn't keep a bit of pride out of her voice. "I have my sources. That masthead is dated from the late 1700s and is carved from suar wood."

He drifted down an aisle toward the masthead, fingering a few select pieces of brass hull plates from salvaged ships, antique dive helmets and rare, colored-glass floats. He swiveled abruptly to Jet. "I'm surprised Bayou La Siryna has enough high-end clientele to support a store with such expensive items."

"We have a few wealthy families. Last time I had the shop open, we drew a significant customer base from Mobile and Pensacola. Nautical-salvage stores are a novelty. Besides, I sell lots of merchandise over the internet too." Jet rose slowly and remembered to put a hand at the small of her back.

Landry immediately strode toward her, frowning. "What's wrong?"

"You should have seen her," Seth broke in. "Miss Bosarge lifted a big ole sofa all by herself. Thing must have weighed two hundred pounds."

Landry arched an eyebrow. "Did she, now?"

Jet went to the front counter, away from those piercing eyes. She pulled out a bag of old coins from the cardboard box and fired up the laptop to enter it into the store invoice. "Seth has been great. In fact, I'd like him to return after lunch and we can discuss the possibility of him working the whole time he's visiting you.

Seth scrunched his face. "I'm not going to be here long."

"What's this?" The low rumble of Landry's voice beside her caught Jet by surprise. A prickle of sexual awareness tingled down her spine. His large hand closed over one of the artifacts scattered on the counter, an old, sheathed dagger.

Jet's gaze traveled up his arm and into his eyes. Damn, it had been much too long since she'd made love to a man—or a merman, either. Her pheromones were in overdrive and the memory of his touch fueled the fire.

She wasn't alone in feeling a sexual tingle. The pupils in Landry's eyes were so enlarged that the irises had shrunk to a razor-thin rim of blue. Her own dilated eyes were reflected in his like a black mirror image of lust.

Her heart flip-flopped in her chest like a tiny minnow caught in the jaws of a shark. She drank in every detail of his face…the squared jaw, the light brown hair that waved ever so slightly at his earlobes. Jet curled her fingers into her palm to keep from reaching up and again exploring the curve of his jaw, the golden tips of his light brown hair, those firm lips. The stinging imprint of her nails inside her palm reminded Jet that right this moment was not the time to indulge her curiosity.

Landry lowered his face a fraction. The same electricity that sparked every time they were together returned stronger than before. She'd put it off as nerves at that first meeting, but after last night she'd been forced to acknowledge that it wasn't a mere case of apprehension. It was him. Something about Landry drew her, excited her, as primitive as the need to immerse her body undersea during a full moon.

"Check this one out." Seth stepped between them and pointed to the dagger he was so taken with.

Landry straightened abruptly and withdrew his hand.

Jet picked up the dagger and handed it to Seth. The slight tremble in his fingers made her inwardly wince. He was trying hard to act as if nothing was wrong.

The rusty squeal of steel brushing against steel rang out as Seth removed the dagger from its scabbard. He reverently ran a finger down the worn, pitted twelve-inch blade. He pointed at the scrolled engraving on the handle. "Is this gold?"

Jet smiled. Every man who entered her store would walk right past the furniture and accessories and head straight to the knives and swords in the display case up front.

"Sorry, it's just brass."

Seth's face lit up for the first time that morning. "Then maybe I can afford to buy it."

Landry frowned. "Might still be too expensive." He turned to Jet. "Is this another one of your antiques?"

She nodded. "It's early twentieth century but I haven't been able to trace the exact origin."

"How much?" Seth asked, eyes wide with interest.

Poor guy. Jet doubted this trinket would be in his price range. "About eight hundred dollars," she admitted reluctantly. "But I could discount it to four hundred if you really want it."

"Nah, that's okay." Seth's thin shoulders drooped as he replaced the dagger in the scabbard.

Landry slapped him on the shoulder. "You're saving your money for a car. Remember?"

"Yeah." The light died in his dark eyes and his lips turned down at the corners, the same mulish expression he wore when Landry had dropped him off in the morning.

"That's great," Jet said, trying to lift the kid's mood.

"All the more reason to work for me while you're in the bayou."

Seth shrugged. "It doesn't matter. I'll never be able to save enough money for a car." He faced his brother. "Even if you really did pay half."

Landry's jaw tightened. "I said I would."

"Whatever."

As Seth went to the door, Landry rolled his eyes and Jet shared a secret smile with him. There was no doubt in her mind, if Landry said he would do something, you could consider it a done deal.

"I came to invite both of you to lunch," Landry said. "Where would you like to go?"

"McDonald's," Seth cut in before she could reply.

Landry gave Jet a wry smile. "I was thinking of something a little more upscale."

This new, easy manner of Landry's, outside the confines of the IRS office, warmed her heart far more than it should. Besides the physical pull, she actually *liked* this man, enjoyed his company. Too bad she hadn't met him before Perry. Bad boys were way overrated.

"I'm not crazy about fast food," Jet admitted. Actually, she couldn't metabolize red meat, and the fries and other stuff on the menu had the texture of sawdust on her mermaid tongue. "There's a restaurant one block away that serves great fried shrimp."

Seth jerked his arms into his coat pocket. "I hate seafood. It stinks."

Landry frowned. "You can't live off of hamburgers and strawberry milk shakes."

Jet tried to ease the tension. "You two go ahead. I'll order something and keep working. Seth, let me know after lunch if you want to work more while you're in town. I've got a ton of stuff that needs to be either shelved or hung on the walls."

Landry reached into his suit pocket and pulled out a set of keys. "You go ahead, Seth. I want to treat Jet to lunch."

Seth grabbed them quickly, a huge grin transforming his bony face. "Thanks, see ya," he said, practically running out of the store.

"Wait." Jet hurried behind the counter and grabbed a key ring. "Take this spare store key in case you finish lunch before we do." She tossed it to him and he deftly caught it one-handed by the entryway.

The stunned look on Seth's face was priceless. "You really giving me a key?"

"I trust you." If he had no conscience, he wouldn't have returned the beloved dagger.

Seth blinked and the usual aloofness in his eyes softened, making him appear like the young teenager he was. "Hey, thanks, dude," he mumbled.

Landry raised a brow. "Jet's a *dude?*"

Seth didn't bother answering and they watched as he eased the BMW onto Main Street.

"How does he stay so skinny the way he eats?" she asked.

"Metabolism," he said decisively. "What I wouldn't give to have a teenager's ability to burn fat."

His body looked pretty smoking hot as far as she was concerned. And it felt pretty damned hot, too. But then she'd suspected all along that beneath his tailored suits and veneer of reserve, Landry was a passionate man.

Jet hoped to find out just how passionate he was.

The sooner the better.

"How did you and Perry meet?"

Jet almost choked midswallow. She set down the water

glass. They'd been having a fun conversation about Alabama football and their mutual fascination with horror movies and Southern Gothic tales until Landry slipped that question in.

"He'd been sailing around the bayou in his Catalina. I'd pulled my motorboat into the harbor at the same time he was securing his boat," she said reluctantly. She flushed remembering how she'd been so taken, so besotted, with Perry that within a week of meeting him she'd rashly confided her mermaid secret, something she'd never done before or since.

"Did you go into business soon after you met him?"

Jet shifted in her seat. "Pretty quick," she admitted, pushing aside her plate. Why couldn't he just finish his audit and let all that go? He kept chipping away at that stone barrier she'd put in place about her past. "What about you?" she asked, deflecting more questions. "How long has it been since you were in a serious relationship?"

"Not very subtle," he said with a one-sided smile. "But I'll play. It's been a while."

"Divorced?"

"Never married, just engaged once."

"What happened?" Jet's hand flew to her mouth, as if to stuff the words back inside. She was as bad as he. "Forget it. You don't—"

"She found somebody else." Landry's features hardened like chiseled stone.

That must have hurt like hell. She lowered her voice. "How long ago did this happen?"

"Five years."

About the same time she met Perry. She wasn't the only person who'd suffered a betrayal of sorts. Jet lightly touched his arm. "I'm sorry."

He shrugged as if it were no big deal. "I can see now

that we weren't meant to be together. What we had was more along the lines of a friendship and we tried to make it something it wasn't. Besides, nothing ever lasts. You can only depend on yourself."

"Right." Jet straightened her silverware. How often she'd made the same remark. But to hear it from someone else's lips…well, it sounded so desolate. And unbelievable. "At least we have our families," she said with a small laugh. "They're stuck with us no matter what."

His eyes shifted to the window. "I wouldn't say that. Don't count on anyone. Not friends, not girlfriends, not family."

"Really?" Jet chewed her lip. What the hell was wrong with Landry? "You can't mean that. Surely there's someone in your life that you love and trust."

Landry shrugged. "The only one to ever fit that bill was my grandmother. And then she died."

The bleakness in his eyes made her want to do something foolish. Like throw her arms around him and tell him she understood.

He'd hate that. Landry probably thought his aloofness hid the loneliness inside. Or, even worse, he didn't realize he carried the hurt like a shield every day to ward off anyone else getting too close.

Just like me. Jet's fingers curled tightly around the water glass. "What about your parents and brothers and sisters?"

"Dad split when I was five and I haven't seen much of him since. Mom is…" He hesitated. "She's hard to explain. I've got six half siblings and about as many ex-stepdads. Easy to get lost in the chaos."

He looked out the window and continued, his voice wooden and hollow. "We were always broke and scraped by day to day with food stamps, child support and the occasional odd jobs."

"That's awful." Made sense he chose a solid, respectable, steady profession like accounting.

She'd taken her own family's wealth for granted, couldn't imagine worrying about basics like food, rent and utilities. Money never had been, or would be, an issue in the Bosarge household. Although they didn't live ostentatiously and often worked stints in landlubber jobs to fit into society and not raise eyebrows, sometimes the immense wealth made her feel guilty. Like when she witnessed the struggles of the bayou shrimping families, eking out an existence that never lifted them above poverty level. The lucky residents worked for minimum wage in the stinking seafood processing plants, gutting fish and shucking oysters all day, every day.

"It must have been hard to live that way," she said at last.

He shrugged again. "I survived."

"After everything you went through growing up, seems like you would be extra close to your brothers and sisters."

"You'd be surprised."

"What about Seth? The two of you must get along pretty good if he comes down here to spend time with you."

"I barely know him. He's staying as a favor to our mother, who's under the delusion he needs a little male guidance to straighten out his attitude. Frankly, I think she's just tired of dealing with him. He's the last kid at home and she's ready for the empty-nest gig."

"A bit harsh, don't you think?" she asked lightly.

"I know her pretty well." His dry tone suggested she back off with that line of questioning. "I try not to judge my mother too much. She's been through stuff no mother should have to suffer." Landry leaned back in his chair and folded his arms. "But enough about my family. What's yours like? I'm guessing it was a whole lot different than mine."

"As far as money, yes. And there was stability at our house. Maybe too much—living in the bayou is pretty isolating."

"Why's that? I spent summers here and loved it. I got to fish and putter around the backwaters all day in my grandmother's old boat."

She could hardly tell him the truth. They lived between two worlds. Humans weren't allowed to get too close for fear they would learn their secret. Her mother preferred they lived on land, so Jet didn't get to spend much time with the merfolk. Although she suspected there was some other reason the merfolk didn't offer her their friendship, even before Orpheous's poison words during the Games.

Her kind shunned Shelly as a TRAB—a traitor baby born of a mixed couple—and Jet found the exclusion infuriating. But at least she understood that the merfolk viewed all TRABs in the same biased light. Yet they adored Lily and wanted nothing to do with Jet. Was it because Lily was gifted with a siren's voice? Or was there more to it than that? Orpheous's blue face flashed again in her mind. *Ever suspect you are one of us?* Jet fingered the golden trident, her key to the answers.

"Jet? You okay?" Landry's voice cut through her errant thoughts.

"Oh, sorry. I was thinking how best to explain my family. Like you, my dad never played a big role in my life." *Ha.* Mermen were notoriously promiscuous and free-spirited. Most never acknowledged or knew their offspring. "My mom traveled a lot." She didn't mention her mother often took Lily along, but seldom herself. Her excuse was that as a siren, Lily attracted too much attention with landlubbers and needed periodic escapes at sea. "When she was gone, different aunts and older cousins took turns watching us."

"So you didn't have the idyllic family, either."

"But I have a sister, Lily, that I'm close to. My cousin Shelly came to live with us in our late teens when her parents died, so I'm pretty close to her also. Maybe you and Seth will grow closer during his visit."

"Doubt it. There's a huge age difference between us and I've never been around him much. Tell me more about your mother."

"Of course, I love her," Jet answered much too quickly. *Even if I'm not the fair-headed golden girl she loves best.* Being known as the older, ugly sister of Lily Bosarge—both on land and at sea—wasn't easy. "She's an amazing woman—smart, beautiful, confident. The kind of person who walks into a room and takes charge." She couldn't believe how easy it was to open up to Landry; it was something that did not come naturally to her.

"Lucky you." Landry pasted on a grim smile. "No point rehashing childhood memories." He leaned across the table and whispered, "Who's that old lady behind you that keeps staring at us?"

Jet deliberately dropped her napkin. Bending down to pick it up, she casually straightened, eyes traveling slowly upward until they slammed into a pair of brown eyes nearly as dark as her own. Wearing her signature purple turban, the woman was as exotic as snow in the bayou. She gave an almost imperceptible nod to Jet with a mysterious half smile twitching the corners of her round face.

Jet nodded back in acknowledgment and faced Landry. "That's the one and only Tia Henrietta, the bayou's own voodoo queen."

Chapter 6

"Ah," Landry said with a grin, "a voodoo priestess. I should have guessed. The resident psychic I've heard about over the years."

"Or local crackpot, as most people call her."

Landry tapped a finger against his lips. "What do you make of her? Do you believe in the supernatural?"

Jet almost choked on a bite of shrimp. "Me?" she gasped out. She swiftly reached for her glass and gulped down water to clear her throat. "I have an open mind," she managed. "Things might not always be as they appear on the surface." *Ha.* "I don't suppose you would agree. You seem to view everything in terms of black-and-white—which I guess is a useful trait for an accountant."

A shuttered expression settled on his face. "My profession doesn't define me."

Just when she thought she had him pegged, wham, Landry threw a curveball. Jet gave a one-sided smile. "So you do believe in the possibility of magic? Maybe I should have guessed it when you mentioned Edgar Allen Poe and Stephen King are your favorite authors."

"Magic? No." Landry's face tightened. "I wouldn't go

that far. Most times, if something is out of the ordinary, there's a perfectly logical explanation."

"Most times? But you aren't saying there's *always* a natural explanation."

"Not always," he agreed softly. "Have you ever encountered something that defied all logic?"

Her heart thudded painfully against her rib cage. *You have no idea.* "Yes. And you?"

He rubbed his jaw and gave her a considering look, as if debating whether to tell her.

"Go on," she encouraged. "I promise not to laugh or call you nuts."

"Okay." Landry folded his hands on the table. "But remember you promised not to laugh."

At her nod, he continued.

"When I was about twelve, I fished almost every day at an inlet three miles from Murrell's Point. As much as I enjoyed the freedom and quiet, I mostly fished because each afternoon when I went to the small island, I'd find presents left for me on the sandbank, sometimes old coins or bits of sea coral. The best gift was an antique spyglass from the early 1800s. I'd like to imagine it was used by a pirate."

All gifts from the sea, she noted uneasily. "Why do you think they were presents meant for you? They could have been things that just washed ashore."

He shook his head. "No. Every day they were placed in the same spot where I tied up my boat. And each gift was left in a carefully crafted circle of seashells."

"Maybe your grandmother put them there as a treat." She didn't believe it, though.

Landry snorted. "She never set foot in that old boat. Said with her luck, the motor would die and she'd get stranded at sea."

"Oh." Jet licked her dry lips. "Then yes, I'd say you had unexplained weirdness in your childhood."

"I haven't got to the really weird part yet."

"You haven't?" Her mind spun in dizzying swirls. Had he actually seen a mermaid? What would she say if he did? Should she deny the existence of her race and scoff at his story?

"One day I went out on the boat when I shouldn't have. The wind had kicked up and a storm was predicted. But I told myself I had time for a quick ride to the sandbank to check and see if there was a gift waiting for me.

"Big mistake. That trinket, can't even remember now what it was, damn near cost me my life. Instead of riding out the storm on the sandbank, I got back in the boat and headed home. My grandmother had forbidden me to go out that day but I'd snuck out anyway when she took her nap."

Holy mackerel. I see where this is heading—

"Anyway, I never would have made it home except…" He hesitated a moment before plunging on. "Except I wasn't alone. Someone or something below the boat guided it to shore."

"Divine providence?" she whispered.

"Maybe," he acceded. "That's what I've tried to tell myself over the years anyway. I was young, I was scared and too imaginative for my own good."

"Imaginative?" That didn't fit him.

"What kid dreams of being an accountant when he grows up?" Landry's smile was wry. "I was quite the fanciful kid who retreated into daydreams to deal with… things."

"Makes sense. But you've done a hundred-and-eighty-degree turnaround since then."

"By high school, I knew that if I ever wanted to rise

above a hand-to-mouth existence, the key was to make good grades and get a college scholarship."

"Admirable." She meant it. Without a clear motivation to do well in school, she'd merely drifted. Outside of school Jet pursued subjects she was interested in, like marine biology, maritime history and cartography.

She leaned forward in her chair. "Sorry, I can't stop thinking about your story. What do you think guided your boat that time—do you have any theories?"

"I know it sounds preposterous but I thought I saw— just for a couple of seconds—a sea creature that was half-human." He shook his head. "I can't believe I'm telling you this. I've never told anyone before."

The air pressed in on her and her lungs felt as porous as a sea sponge. *Deep breaths. He doesn't know my secret.*

His brows drew together. "You okay?" Landry's hand ran up and down her chilled forearms, his touch thawing some of the frozen slush in her veins.

"You sure it wasn't some kind of illusion?"

"Must have been. Crazy, huh? Goes to show what a wild imagination can dream up when your body is flooded with adrenaline."

Jet clenched her jaw to stop her teeth chattering and managed a tight smile. "Right, crazy," she agreed, ready to change the subject. "Well, aren't you full of surprises?"

"Honey child, we are *all* full of surprises."

They both looked up, startled, at the deep, gravelly voice by their table where Tia Henrietta stood in all her eccentric glory. Jet had forgotten all about the old woman. Jet inwardly winced, hoping Tia hadn't heard the crack-pot reference.

The old woman clutched at the gold shawl draping her olive-colored skin and smiled with an amused glint in her black, faintly almond-shaped eyes.

Jet regarded her curiously. She'd seen Tia around town, but the old woman had never struck up a conversation, and Jet had never driven down the bayou back roads to Tia's cottage, where she reportedly eked out a meager living reading palms and tarot cards.

Tia was an enigma, although she'd lived in Bayou La Siryna since anyone else could remember. No one knew where she came from or if she ever had family. Indeed, no one could even determine Tia's ethnic heritage; with her deep olive skin and almond eyes, it was possible Tia was distantly related to the many Vietnamese who worked in the fishing industry. Or she might even be Creole or African-American, or some mixture of several races.

"Yes, ma'am," Landry said, rising from his chair. He motioned to the empty chair at their table. "You're welcome to join us."

Jet approved the respectful gesture. Landry was a true Southern gentleman, a quality sorely lacking in Perry.

"Thank you kindly, but I must be moseying on."

Jet tried to pinpoint the accent, which itself was a regional hodgepodge. Southern, Gullah, Cajun... None of it quite fit Tia's arresting, unique voice.

"Besides," Tia added, "y'all need lots of alone time together if you're ever gonna figure out each other's secrets."

Jet's jaw tightened. No matter how much time she and Landry spent together, it would be a dry day under the sea before she would again tell another human her biggest secret. Honesty was not always the best policy, even if the man already believed in mermaids. "A woman's got to have a little mystery," Jet said, raising her water glass in mock salute to the elderly woman.

"No one would ever say Miss Jet Bosarge is lacking in mystery." Tia Henrietta made an odd clucking sound with her tongue. "And as for *you,* Mr. Landry Fields, things aren't always what they seem on the surface."

Landry's eyes narrowed a fraction before he offered a glib smile. "And how many secrets do you have, ma'am?"

She laughed a deep, throaty clucking noise that made Jet picture a demented chicken. "I'm right nigh filled to the brim with my secrets and the secrets of all the bayou people who visit me with their problems and questions."

Landry signaled the waitress. "Everybody wears a public mask," he said lightly. "Hardly any earth-shattering supernatural observation."

Jet studied him closely and noted an edge of white around his compressed lips. The genial, Southern manners were being used to suppress a show of annoyance. What could Landry possibly have to hide? He was probably right; Tia merely spouted basic truths of human nature under the guise of psychic revelation. If it kept the old woman entertained and provided a means of supplementing her Social Security check, let Tia have some fun. If she really knew what she was about, Tia would have singled her out, not Landry. After all, she was the one who led a secret life.

Tia Henrietta waggled a long, bony finger at them. "Day of reckoning coming soon. Mark my words." She grinned broadly, exposing a gold crown on one front tooth. She patted Landry's shoulder. "By the way, she's trying to communicate with you, you know. But you refuse to listen."

Landry froze and Jet leaped to his defense. "He does listen to me when I talk."

"Not talking about you, child," Tia said, her eyes glued on Landry. "I'm talking about the spirit of a little girl long dead."

Jet expected Landry to laugh off the preposterous claim but the grim set to his jaw and the wintry gleam in his eyes were more pronounced than when he'd first questioned her business records.

Tia faced her. "And I am no crackpot." With that parting sally, she exited the diner, her bold, Egyptian-printed sarong swishing mightily over her considerable girth and chunky bracelets rattling.

Crazy witch, Jet thought ruefully as Landry paid for their meal. But even crazier, Tia had zapped the fun out of their lunch as much as Landry's mermaid story. His playful attentiveness was again shuttered behind icy-blue eyes. "Let's go," he said in a clipped voice.

Jet raced to keep up with his long stride as they walked the downtown streets. Their return to The Pirate's Chest was somber, despite her attempts to lighten Landry's mood. They had actually been having *fun* until Tia Henrietta squashed it with her cryptic remarks. He'd let her glimpse his feelings behind the steel shell he presented to the world. She'd recognized the lonely child whose grandmother's love had provided a haven, because she had experienced the same sense of separation with her own mother. And even though his mermaid story made Jet uncomfortable, it demonstrated Landry could be open to that which was hidden.

A little girl long dead. It couldn't be. He didn't believe in spirits and ghosts and wanted nothing to do with hocuspocus nonsense. He'd buried that side of him as a child, choosing instead to focus on the real world, on what could be seen with the eye and touched and heard. As an FBI agent, Landry relied on facts. Concrete, observable data that lead to logical answers and correct decisions. It had served him well over the years and he'd trained his mind to strictly focus on only the present reality, smothering any reminders of the past.

Those painful memories needed to stay buried deep in his psyche, as deep in the dirt as his sister's grave.

But…what about the porcelain cat in the fridge, books falling off shelves, weird electrical malfunctions…?

Coincidence, he insisted to the inner whispers. *Coincidence, coincidence, coincidence,* he repeated grimly, until the whispers evaporated under the blistering assault of his will. "Coming back to the bayou this time was a mistake," he muttered.

"Why do you say that?"

Landry started at Jet's question, hadn't realized he'd spoken aloud. That old lady had really gotten to him. Somehow, she had made the connection of his grandmother's name and the crime from long ago. Fakes like Tia found information and used it to convince the gullible to fork over money for messages from The Other Side.

"Never mind," he said nonchalantly. "Carnival acts like the one we just witnessed from that old woman are a pet peeve of mine."

Jet gave him a sharp glance. "Hit a nerve, did she? Must be a reason her comments got under your skin so bad."

"Nonsense."

"Keep an open mind. After all, you did have a supernatural experience once. Who's to say there aren't more unexplainable phenomena in the—"

"Like I told you, the whole thing was some stress-induced illusion."

He shouldn't have told her. What the hell had gotten into him lately? He'd never even told Mimi what he'd seen that afternoon. Jet must think he was loony tunes. He even questioned his own sanity when he recalled that childhood experience and tried his best to suppress the memory.

And since when did Jet's opinion of him start to matter?

He was in Bayou La Siryna to catch a criminal, not find a lover. Worse, Jet was still technically a person of interest.

But he didn't believe that anymore. The woman had gone so far as to pay Perry Hammonds off in a desperate attempt to get him out of her life. Jet Bosarge was a decent, caring person who loved her family, donated a small fortune to charities protecting animals and the environment, and was starting a legitimate business when she had no need for gainful employment. During lunch, she'd opened up and admitted to some painful childhood memories of her own.

Landry walked briskly, brewing over his newfound loquacious streak. Matters had gone from tricky grounds to eerie nether regions when old Tia what's-her-name told Jet he had a secret. How was Jet going to take it when she found out he wasn't the IRS auditor she thought he was? She'd think he was a liar, that was what. A crazy one to boot.

"Slow down. I can't keep up with you." Her voice was breathless from trying to match his pace.

"Sorry." He stopped momentarily as she slipped her hand into his. Her touch felt good, right. As natural as if they belonged to one another.

"Don't let Tia Henrietta ruin your day." Her deep brown eyes were bright with worry. "And don't deny that she did. You were in an awful hurry to pay the bill and leave."

They were a mere block from her shop. Landry was filled with a sudden urge to tell her everything. All about the weird incidents that plagued him and that had reached an alarming pitch since his return to the bayou this year. The fact that he wasn't who she thought. Landry opened his mouth and then snapped it shut. Just a few more days. Time to concentrate his efforts on finding the Vargas/ Hammonds connection. Time to confront Perry head-on.

Time he sent her idiot ex packing—and cancel payment on that check she wrote him if it wasn't too late.

"It's okay," Jet said at his hesitation. Her eyes slid downward a microsecond. "Like you said, we all have our secrets."

Landry ran a finger across her full red lips. He'd love to pry Jet's every little secret from those tempting lips, wanted everything bare and open between them. "Tell me yours and maybe I'll tell you mine," he said lightly.

She gave a shaky smile. "You go first."

"I'm not so easily fooled."

"Me, either."

The longer he put this off, the harder it would be when she discovered the truth. This was a small town; word always managed to get out.

He would do it.

"Okay, me first. The thing is, Jet…" He took a deep breath and looked past her right shoulder, avoiding eye contact. Didn't want to see the kindness in her eyes return to the antagonistic contempt of when they first met. "I need to clear up—" His mind registered the fact there was a county sheriff's car parked in front of Jet's store. "What the hell?"

Jet followed his gaze. "I wonder what Tillman's doing here?"

Out on the sidewalk, the sheriff talked to Seth, a stern expression on his face.

What had the kid done now? He never should have let his mother talk him into letting Seth stay. He sent her a hefty sum of money every month, had done more than any other of his siblings. Wasn't that enough?

Of course it wasn't; it was never enough. Landry raced down the street, past gawking store owners and people milling on the sidewalks. Even through his anger, he worried Seth would say or do something stupid that would aggravate the situation. If Seth just kept his mouth shut, he might be able to help him, ease things over with the local law enforcement and get him an attorney. Whatever was needed.

His brother was in trouble.

Chapter 7

"What did you do?" Landry asked as soon as they got within fifteen feet of The Pirate's Chest. His voice was loud enough that several people passing by shot them curious glances and slowed down to check out the commotion.

Seth didn't respond, his face stoic with what Jet imagined to be false bravado.

Tillman nodded at her in an all-business manner. "Let's go inside and talk this over."

She quickly unlocked the door and pushed it open, the three men following her inside.

"Tell me what happened," Landry demanded as soon as the door closed, pinning Seth with a withering gaze.

Jet wanted to shiver and back away from the frost in his eyes and couldn't fathom what Seth must be feeling under the stern condemnation.

"Nothin'," Seth mumbled. He didn't go so far as to roll his eyes, but his stiff posture and unrepentant expression screamed "stoic teenage boredom" in the face of whatever disaster brewed.

"Why don't we all have a seat at the front counter?" Jet suggested, trying to ease the tension.

Everyone ignored her.

Tillman's hands went to his hips. "It might be nothing at all." He got straight to the point. "I got an anonymous phone call this morning from a man who would only identify himself as a curious citizen. He claimed that a new employee here, named Seth, had stolen valuable knives and coins and hid them inside his jacket."

"That's a lie!" Seth said, bursting out of the indifference act. "Who said that? No one even knows me around here."

"Officer, I'll reimburse Miss Bosarge for the costs of any stolen items," Landry volunteered in a tight voice.

Tillman held up a hand. "I don't know if it's true or not. I came down to talk to Jet and found this young man attempting to enter with a key. I asked if he would mind a few questions."

Seth's face flushed in anger. "And I said *no way*."

"Be quiet and let me handle this," Landry warned.

"But I didn't—"

"He's a minor," Landry said to Tillman, dismissing Seth. "Surely you can—"

"I'll prove I didn't steal nothin'." Seth took off his jacket and threw it to Landry before turning the pockets of his jeans inside out. "C'mon, you can search me."

Jet pursed her lips as she studied Seth, noting that he cared more about proving his innocence to his brother than the sheriff.

"Damn it, kid. We'll talk about this later," Landry muttered.

"I didn't do anything." Seth turned beseeching eyes to Jet. "I swear it."

She wanted to believe him, had imagined they'd established an understanding before lunch when she'd caught him with the dagger. But why would someone call the sheriff's office and report a false crime? It didn't make sense. Who would do such a thing if it wasn't… A flash of red whizzed by in her peripheral vision. Jet narrowed her eyes and looked out the front window, catching sight of a red Mustang whipping around the corner, a block from the siren statue.

Perry.

Perry had found out Seth worked here and he didn't like it.

And in that moment, Jet knew Perry would never give her up. She was too valuable to him. He viewed her as a lifelong meal ticket. She took a deep breath, feeling claustrophobic, as if she were lying on a bed of sand and the weight of the ocean pressed on her lungs.

"Well, look what we have here," Tillman said, pointing to a glint of brass poking through the torn lining of Seth's camo jacket. He reached over and pulled out an eight-inch knife, sheathed in brass, which gleamed golden under the store's chandelier. Several gold and silver coins spilled onto the floor from the ripped lining, the metallic sound clanging loud as cannon fire in the sudden silence.

Jet eyed the knife, relieved it was *not* the dagger Seth loved. If Seth was going to steal something, it wouldn't be this item.

"I'm getting you an attorney," Landry said, breaking the appalled quiet.

"There's no need for a lawyer," Jet spoke up. "I'm not pressing charges."

Tillman narrowed his eyes. "Sure that's what you want to do?"

Seth took a step back. "You can't arrest me! My half brother's with the FBI."

What brother? Jet looked at Landry for clarification. He'd told her over lunch that he had half a dozen siblings, so it must be one of them.

Landry ran a hand over his face before facing her inquisitive gaze. He didn't say a word, his face composed, impassive.

Oh, hell. Landry was the FBI agent. Bits and pieces from their first meeting flashed through her mind: her initial impression that he didn't fit with the shabby surroundings, his questions about Perry and Gulf Coast Salvage, and his insistence on a personal follow-up meeting.

Jet felt as if she'd been rammed in the solar plexus by a giant swordfish. She'd been falling for the guy, especially after their talk at lunch when she'd glimpsed the loneliness beneath his tough exterior—so like her own. And there was his belief that she was above the low-life Perry, his sharp intelligence and, until this moment, what she thought to be his honesty.

Not to mention those hot kisses that flamed her insides. Would she ever learn not to trust humans?

She pulled herself together and turned to Tillman. "Of course I'm not pressing charges. I gave the dagger and coins to Seth as a gift."

He lowered the brim of his sheriff's cap and frowned at the obvious lie. "Why are you protecting—"

Jet started forward, swiftly passing Seth's incredulous face and Landry's inscrutable blue eyes.

"Where are you going?" Tillman asked, but Jet never turned as she headed out.

"Jet, wait," Landry called.

She ignored him, too. As she exited, she overheard Tillman berate Landry for not having the professional courtesy of letting him know a fellow law-enforcement agent was in town.

Outside, she sucked in the windy, briny air and kept walking, hoping to burn off steam. Tia had tried to warn

her at lunch. *You don't know each other's secrets yet...
Day of reckoning coming soon.*

She wondered if Landry had any more secrets. At least
her own secret was still safe, her mermaid nature hidden as always. She smiled with no mirth. Landry might
be the only person in the world she could tell about her
shape-shifting, since he'd seen a mermaid before, as much
as he tried to deny it to himself. Jet halted at the base of
the siren statue and looked up at the mysterious face that
was no doubt modeled after an early ancestor seen by a
human and now immortalized. Had this ancestor ever been
in love with a human? Ever been disappointed by falsely
placed trust?

Jet reached through the spraying water at the statue's
base and touched the cold, wet edifice, closing her eyes.
The forewarned day of reckoning had come early. She
tried to convince herself it was better this way, better to
know the truth early before her heart invested too heavily.

Landry Fields was a rebound thing, she tried to convince
herself. She'd been in emotional turmoil over Perry's return,
and for a brief moment, Landry had felt like a safe harbor,
like someone strong, steady and good in the midst of cor-
ruption, chaos and callous betrayal.

Had he been playing her all along? Pretending an attraction to unearth more about her less-than-stellar past
with Perry? Sure, she'd played fast and loose with the humans' maritime and reporting laws, but what she'd done
was small-time compared to larger salvage companies and
huge corporations with their overseas tax shelters. And
why now, years after any wrongdoing, was the FBI digging into all this?

The fountain's mist sprayed cool drops of water on her
arms, neck and face, providing a touch of liquid comfort.
What she desperately needed at the moment was a good

swim at sea, to immerse her body in Earth's amniotic fluid and swim with the fish. Or she could pay Dolly another visit. Scratch that. Dolly's predicament was too sad to deal with at the moment. The dolphin would pick up on her churning emotions, not good for Dolly or her unborn calf.

A good, long swim might be in order. She hadn't swum much since returning from the Poseidon Games. It would be good to have an activity in which she had the utmost confidence in her abilities. Swimming was something she excelled at, something at which she depended only on her own strength to succeed in.

Forget fitting in with humans. She should turn her attention back to her own kind again. Now that she'd won the golden trident, she'd finally have an answer about her heritage. Her mother couldn't refuse her request for information if she gave up the trident's one-wish magic to know *why*. Why she never fit in anywhere, not at sea nor on land. Why other mermaids pulled away from her, why Lily was the favored one with the gift of the siren's song and why Jet looked nothing like her family or other mermaids. If she knew why, perhaps she could fix whatever was wrong and spend more time at sea—away from lying human men.

If she had those answers, Jet believed she might discover a way to fit in better with her own kind and find some peace. Shelly and Lily maneuvered happily between land and sea, but maybe that wasn't her path.

So why wait? She could swim southward tonight and perhaps meet Mom and Lily returning home from the Games. The store opening could be delayed. It would give her a break from her problems and during the long swim she could devise a plan for getting Perry permanently out of her life. If she was lucky, maybe Landry Fields would lose interest in her and go away. For an FBI agent, there had to be bigger fish to fry. She groaned inwardly at the unintentional pun.

As if her thoughts had summoned Landry, Jet sensed him approach. Landry had an aura of power and stability that was unmistakable. She kept her eyes closed, not sure she could keep the hurt from shining through. The clean scent of water, soap and male pheromones enveloped her like a refreshing wave. Emanations of solid strength drew closer until at last a tentative hand touched her shoulder blades.

She wanted to lean back, sink into the warmth of human skin, feel his hands running through her scalp and caressing the sweet, vulnerable spot at her nape. Jet tilted her head back, enjoying the cool spray of water on the front of her neck and the heat of Landry's hand on the sharp plane of her right shoulder blade.

If she left tonight, this might be the last time she saw Landry. Anything could happen while she was away. The possibility this might be their final meeting made her chest tighten painfully.

"Look at me."

Jet felt the rumble of his voice vibrate down her spine. Two hands were on her bare arms, gently guiding her toward him. She kept her eyes closed, chin tilted upward. He laid a finger over her lips and then his own brushed against hers. "Jet," he whispered, part question, part regret.

She opened her eyes and stared into the burning blue of his, frozen-hot like the sting of ice on bare flesh.

"What do you want from me?" She'd intended for the question to be confrontational, but instead it escaped from her mouth like a sigh of defeat. Everybody wanted something, some little piece of her soul.

Landry hesitated.

"The truth," Jet insisted, calm yet firm.

He removed his hands from her arms and indicated a nearby park bench. After they sat down, each stared ahead at the statue.

"I didn't mean for you to find out this way. I apologize."

"Then what Seth said is true? You're an FBI agent?"

He reached into his back pocket, pulled out a billfold and flashed a shiny badge. It glinted like a silver talisman of doom in the midday sun.

"Why are you after me?"

Landry ran a hand through his wavy hair with the light brown curls at the edge of his collar. "It's not so much you," he admitted grudgingly. "It's Perry Hammonds."

Jet swallowed hard, a knot of fear in her stomach. Had Perry managed to do something spectacularly stupid only a few weeks out of prison? Was he trying to draw her into danger? "Because of our past business venture?" she asked, hoping Perry wasn't presently involved in anything sinister. But she'd heard prisons were training grounds for criminals to learn and graduate to ever more serious felonies. Perry didn't deserve her sympathy, but she only wished him gone—not in serious trouble.

He waved a hand dismissively. "That's not so important." His brows drew together in disapproval. "It's true there's something strange about your past treasure findings and sales." He paused, as if waiting for her to deny it. When Jet kept silent, he resumed talking. "Look, I don't believe you've knowingly committed a major crime or have ever been involved in a crime ring. So I'll tell you what I'm really investigating. Three weeks ago we received a report that a known international gangster had arranged to spring an American citizen out of a Chilean prison. Ever hear of Sylvester Vargas?"

She shook her head.

"Vargas owns Gulf Coast Salvage, the company you did business with and own substantial stock in."

Jet's fingers curled into her palms. Perry had picked the company and handled the administrative end of their ventures. It felt as if she would never be free from her past. "I don't know anything about this. Have you questioned Perry about it?"

Landry regarded Jet through hooded eyes. "Not yet," he conceded. "I've been observing him, gathering additional information from known associates and waiting for him to make a move. What has he told you about his future plans?"

"He wants us to work a site near Tybee Island, Georgia. I told him no. Even though I gave him enough money to start his own business, he still might not give up trying to make me change my mind."

Landry's eyes chilled. "Time I confronted him."

The continuous spray of the water fountain gurgled and stopped momentarily before suddenly shooting up a stream twice as tall as the mermaid statue, as if an underwater geyser had exploded. She'd never seen that happen before.

They both watched until the stream became a normal-size spray once again.

Jet shrugged at Landry's threat to confront Perry. It sounded as if they didn't have much to go on yet. But maybe the questioning would scare Perry off for a while.

So Landry was an FBI agent. Had he lied about anything else? She'd been so worried about protecting her own secrets that she didn't suspect he might harbor a few of his own.

Jet was hard to decipher. When he'd found her by the statue and she opened her eyes and looked at him, the vulnerability and sadness he glimpsed lashed him like a whip. He'd fully expected her to be furious and scald him with righteous indignation at his misrepresentation as an IRS auditor.

Misrepresentation? It was a downright lie. Jet had every right to be angry. He'd never apologize for the undercover work; that was his job. But he shouldn't have let it get personal between them until the case was resolved. Yet instead of anger, she looked defeated. His guts churned at the sadness in her eyes. At their first meeting, he'd thought of her as invulnerable and much too cocky and prickly. And yet he was drawn to her despite it. When she let down her guard, Jet was irresistible. She brought color and vitality into his black-and-white, rigid world.

Jet's spine suddenly stiffened, as if a new idea had struck her. "Now I see."

"See what?"

"You planned on using me to find out what Perry is up to." She folded her arms across her chest. "Why expose who you really are when I can do the dirty work?" Her full lips twisted in a scowl.

This was more like Jet. He'd much rather deal with her anger than hurt. "Something like that. At first anyway."

Her dark eyes flashed in challenge. "What's changed?"

Indeed. What had Jet done to him? Everything was changing. She'd gone from being a suspect of possible criminal mischief to a woman he cared for and wanted to protect from danger. Damn, the admission made him squirm. "What's changed is that I got to know you," he admitted. "I don't believe you have any idea what your ex-lover is up to."

Jet's shoulders slumped and she let out a deep sigh. "Thank God for that at least."

What kind of a jerk did she think he was? "If I thought you were a criminal, I wouldn't have—" His voice drifted off and he gazed down at her lips, dropping his eyes to her chest, where her shirt was slightly damp from the fountain. He remembered the evening before, the feel of her breasts and her hard body pressed tight against him. "Well, I wouldn't have kissed you, touched you." He swallowed hard, fighting the impulse to draw her to him immediately, in broad daylight in a public place. But if he did, he was afraid he couldn't stop at a quick hug or peck on the cheek.

Her eyes widened and her pale face flushed, either remembering the shared passion or guessing his thoughts. Landry wasn't sure which.

Jet abruptly pursed her lips and asked, "So now what? If you planned to have me trick Perry in some way and lure him to a convenient confession, then you're on the wrong track. Perry and I are done."

He felt a lightness in his body at the words.

Jet held up a hand with crossed fingers. "On my end anyhow."

"What's that's supposed to mean?"

"It means I want Perry out of my life but I don't think he'll ever cut me loose."

"Why not?"

She hesitated only the briefest of moments, but Landry had interviewed enough people over the years to recognize that pause as someone carefully crafting their words. "Because Perry needs a job, an income."

"He can find another treasure-salvage company," he said harshly. "The man at least has an uncanny knack for locating sites."

Jet stared at the mermaid fountain, seemingly transfixed by her fractured reflection in the rippling water.

"Unless," he added slowly, "*you're* the one who found the best sites."

She didn't face him. "At lunch, you mentioned a supernatural encounter, something unexplainable by human logic."

Landry stilled, almost not daring to breathe. "Go on," he urged.

She turned to him. "I'm the one who finds the shipwreck sites. Not Perry. He's nothing without me."

"Figures Perry didn't contribute much to the partnership, besides his connections and shady sales." He leaned closer. "Tell me how you find treasure."

"Let's just say I have a sixth sense."

"Let's not."

Her brows rose.

"Sounds a bit far-fetched. You trying to say you take out the boat, wait for some mysterious vibe and then dive to explore?"

Jet jumped to her feet. "Of course it's not that simple. I study history, oceanic maps, old ship cargo manifests—all the things others in the business do."

Landry rose off the park bench. "Go on. What's your special edge? I admit I've been curious."

"Forget I said anything. You'd never understand."

"Try me."

Jet didn't move and he stood stock-still, afraid of scaring her off. The fountain splashed and gurgled in front of them, children shrieked at play and cars drove by, usual sounds at the park, but they seemed far away, as if he and Jet were at a precipice. An island of two where no one and nothing else mattered.

A strong breeze blew back a chunk of her shiny black hair and lifted her loosely tied scarf. Jet adjusted it quickly, but not before he noticed a few distinctive white scars on both sides of her neck. How odd. If he didn't know better, he'd say they resembled fish gills. A chill settled deep in his bones.

She wet her lips and a ghost of a smile danced across the sharp planes of her face. "Why should I explain? You've given me no reason to trust you." With that parting volley, she spun and strode quickly back toward the downtown shops.

"Wait a minute." Landry caught up to Jet and held her arm. "How did you get those scars on your neck?"

She flinched and jerked her arm from his grasp. "Childhood accident," she mumbled.

"Don't go back to work. Let's talk this thing through."

"I'm done talking and I'm not going back to work. I'm going home."

"But what about the shop?"

"Seth has the keys. Let him close up." Jet opened the door of her rusted truck. "And give the kid a freaking break. Families should stick together. You were awful rough on him. He didn't steal anything."

"How can you be so sure?" Of course, Jet didn't know Seth had stolen before. He should never have suggested Seth working for her. This was his fault.

"Don't be so quick to judge, Landry. We all screw up. Just because someone makes a mistake in their past doesn't mean they'll make bad choices the rest of their lives."

"Are we talking about you or Seth?"

She regarded him with pursed lips. "Haven't you ever messed up big-time?" she asked.

"Of course, but I've never stolen from anybody."

"For Seth's sake, try not to come across as such a self-righteous prig when you apologize."

Heat flushed his face. Prig? That was harsh. "Why should I apologize? You don't know all the facts. This isn't the first time—"

Jet cut him off. "If Seth had stolen anything, it would

have been the dagger he admired earlier. Your brother was framed."

That didn't make sense. No one even knew his brother was here. "By whom?"

"Perry, of course. He was parked across the street the whole time watching Tillman bring Seth into the store. He's desperate to drive a wedge between us. Some FBI agent you are." Jet slammed her door shut and drove off in a cloud of noxious fumes.

Landry coughed and rubbed the back of his sweaty neck. Maybe he *had* been too hard on his brother, too quick to jump to conclusions. Had he really turned into a prig? The label stung. He returned to The Pirate's Chest, the door chimes jingling behind him.

Seth was unpacking boxes behind the counter and continued working without glancing up. The sheriff was already gone, irate that Landry hadn't shared information on why a federal agent was in Bayou La Siryna. This was the sheriff's jurisdiction. But Landry knew Tillman was engaged to Jet's cousin and wouldn't risk the FBI investigation by testing the man's loyalty to family.

Landry cleared his throat. "Seems I owe you an apology." Seth still didn't look up. This wasn't going to be easy. Landry tried again. "I know you didn't steal anything."

"Great. *Now* you believe me? After the cop leaves? Thanks a lot."

"Sorry. But you can hardly blame me, since Mom said you've stolen before."

"So I'm automatically guilty the rest of my life?"

Almost the same words Jet had used. "No. It's just that in my job I see the worse in people. I'm paid to be suspicious and prove a case against them."

Seth paused unloading the box. "What made you change

your mind?" He shook his head and went back to work. "Jet must have stuck up for me."

"She did. Said Perry Hammonds, her ex-boyfriend, set you up."

"Why? He doesn't even know me."

"It's not about you. He's doing what he can to keep Jet and me apart."

"Glad to see you finally admit she's your girlfriend," Seth said sarcastically.

"She's not my girl," he automatically denied. "Okay, recent development."

Recent history, more likely, now Jet knew he'd lied about his job. It was way past time he interviewed Hammonds.

"She's too good for you," Seth mumbled.

"I didn't know you were such a fan."

"She isn't as hot as her cousin but she's nice."

Landry leaped to Jet's defense. "She's just as hot as Shelly. Hotter, actually." What a stupid conversation. Seth was dragging him down to teenager level.

"Mom says you'll be a bitter, single man the rest of your life 'cause of some girl that dumped you for another guy."

The hits just kept on coming today. "Ouch."

Seth regarded him from the corner of his eye as he continued pulling out merchandise from boxes and unwrapping newspaper casings. "Sorry I spilled your secret. Is Jet mad at you?"

"Furious." Landry sighed and pulled up a chair. He grabbed a pair of box cutters and sat beside Seth. "I'll give her a little time to cool off and then go see her tonight."

They worked together silently while Landry brooded on Jet's markings. Those scars were too symmetrical for an accident. Not only that, there were identical scars on both sides of her neck.

The memory from age twelve arose for the second time today—the one he'd never forget, had dreamed about a million times.

He hadn't told Jet every detail. For a few seconds he'd seen the invisible force that had guided his boat to shore in the storm. Seconds burned into his brain forever when a sea creature had slipped out from under the boat and he saw it…her. A pale face gazing at him through a foot of salt water, blue eyes unblinking. Long, white hair had fanned upward and a torso had morphed into a glittering tail fin where legs should have been. Tiny flaps on the sides of her neck opened and closed, while her lips stayed clamped together and curved upward in a secretive smile.

Those neck markings were the same size and location as Jet's.

Landry put down the box cutters and rubbed his jaw. Was Jet like that long-ago creature who'd saved his life? If so, was it possible for someone to live both on land and at sea? Sure would explain her uncanny ability to find sea treasure.

He arose and paced the shop, examining antique coins, daggers and an eclectic mixture of maritime-themed knickknacks. A familiar flash of red sparkled on a low shelf and he came to an abrupt halt. What the hell? It wasn't hers; she hadn't owned the only red sequined coin purse ever made. But as Landry picked it up and opened the tiny clasp, he knew damned well what he'd find inside.

Sure enough, the letter *A* was etched in black marker on the purse's white lining. A child's large and wobbly penmanship to mark the purse as unmistakably hers. It held one corroded copper penny, dated 1979.

The year of her death.

Landry rounded on Seth, holding up the child's purse, which was nearly engulfed in his fisted hand. "What's this doing here?" he bellowed. "Did you bring it from my house?"

Seth came over and took a look. "Noooooo—" he said, drawing out the word, as if talking to a deranged asylum escapee. "I've never seen it before." He frowned. "Are you accusing me of stealing or something?"

"No." Landry slowly lowered his arm and stuffed it into his pants pocket. "But it doesn't belong here."

"Okaaaay," Seth drawled, evidently back to thinking his older brother was an idiot. "Whatever."

Landry turned away from him and rested his elbows on the front counter, his breath shallow and rapid. A few moments to collect his composure and then he would get on with his federal case and make a little side trip to try to get to the bottom of this weirdness.

Why was all this happening again? He'd packed away the past and stuffed the memories into a trunk, like an old woolen sweater. Now someone or something had unpacked that trunk. The smell of mothballs was in the air and the threads were unraveling.

His fingers brushed against a stack of business cards by the register with the store's name printed in large blue letters. The Pirate's Chest, indeed. The words conjured images of a seventeenth-century Blackbeard kind of rogue. He tilted his head up and observed the mermaid masthead mounted on the wall above him. The determined, passionate set of the carved face favored Jet.

Could Jet be a mermaid?

Preposterous. Besides, *everything* reminded him of Jet these days. Couldn't possibly be true. He was losing it to even consider the possibility that Jet could jump into the ocean and transform into a mermaid.

But in some dark area of his mind, questions whispered like tiny yet pesky ghosts.

Chapter 8

By the time Landry arrived at the rental cottage, his anger hadn't cooled. If anything it had escalated as he replayed two images frozen in his brain: Seth's crumpled posture of defeat at his false stealing accusation, and Jet's scathing indictment of his deceit that shone in her dark abyss eyes.

All Perry Hammonds's fault. And right now, Landry couldn't control his need to confront the bastard. It overrode years of law-enforcement training and his own sacred creed of following the rules—work hard, obey protocol, keep it impersonal… FBI regulations he'd slowly allowed to become law in all areas of his life.

Until now. Until Jet.

He bounded toward the front door, catching sight of Hammonds peeking through a set of blinds. Before Landry could knock, Hammonds unlatched the door a crack and stared out with bleary eyes, as if he'd just been awakened from a nap.

Landry pushed on the door and Hammonds's wobbly legs careened backward. He entered the den and glared at the man who'd dare threaten Jet and Seth. "Don't you ever come near or say a word against Seth again," Landry said with a growl.

Hammonds managed a smile of bravado. "Who's Seth?"

"Don't play games with me." He grasped and twisted the collar of Hammonds's stylish dress shirt.

Hammonds threw up his hands and gave an unsteady laugh. "Whatever. We're cool, dude," he said, trying to placate him.

Landry let go and stepped back, breathing hard. "By the way, it didn't work."

"What didn't work?" Hammonds sank onto the couch and rubbed his temples.

The guy looked as if he could use a beer and some BC Powder.

"Cut the innocent act. Jet saw you taking off when Tillman and Seth were inside the shop. That red Mustang stands out like a scream in the night."

Hammonds switched tactics, brows drawing together as if in anger. "Why are you after Jet? I was with her first. She's mine."

"She doesn't *belong* to anyone. Jet's her own person."

He pasted on a grin that held no mirth. "Jet loves me. Always has, always will."

Disgust gurgled like burning tar in the cauldron of his gut. "Bullshit. She paid you to leave town. Why haven't you?"

A flush of color tainted Hammonds's pretty-boy face and Landry was unsure if he was furious, embarrassed or perhaps a mixture of both.

"That check she gave me was for new equipment and setup costs for the new site we're going to work together soon."

"Is that so?" Landry drawled, instantly on the alert. Maybe he could draw him out; Hammonds mistakenly viewed him as nothing more than a meek bean counter, a mild nuisance. "What kind of work did you have in mind? Jet's busy opening up her shop at the moment."

"None of your business. Go back to your books."

He regarded Hammonds thoughtfully. "Jet's through with the marine-salvage business. Just as she's through with you."

"You poor, deluded sap." Hammonds rose, putting his hands on his hips. "Jet could never be content with someone like you. She craves adventure, passion—things you can't provide."

Landry wanted to knock the sneer off the guy's face. Wanted to shake, shake, *shake* him until he took back those words and spilled his guts about what he and Vargas were plotting. Some last-recalled shred of FBI protocol stayed his hands, which he fisted at his sides. He hadn't blown his cover yet, but if he stayed much longer, Landry wasn't sure he could keep his temper in check. Some glimmer of uncertainty on his part must have slipped out because Hammonds advanced toward him.

"I know things about Jet that no one else does. We understand one another."

Landry kept his features guarded, refused to give credence to Perry's words of poison. "Stay away from her and my family."

Hammonds snickered. "Or else what?"

Landry leaned in, his face inches from Hammonds's. "Or else I'll have my revenge," he whispered in a voice as frigid as a glacier. To his surprise, Hammonds didn't say another word as Landry turned and exited the cottage, slamming the door behind him for emphasis.

Landry got in his BMW and turned on the engine of the sleek machine, a few degrees less angry than before he'd confronted the jerk. To be fair, and Landry was excruciatingly honest with himself, all of today's recriminations weren't entirely the fault of one Perry Hammonds. Some of the fault was his own. He'd failed to be a stand-up kind of brother for Seth and he'd failed to level with Jet once he believed she was no party to whatever Vargas had planned.

He vowed to do better in the future.

Jet sat at the kitchen table and scribbled a terse note for Shelly, explaining she was going out for a long swim and might be gone a day or two. No sense upsetting her cousin by an unexplained absence, although Shelly was so caught up in planning the upcoming family reunion that she might not notice Jet was gone.

No, that wasn't fair. Shelly was kindness itself. It was Jet's own damned fault that being around the happy couple Shelly and Tillman presented only emphasized her own loneliness. Jet took another bite of a protein bar. She needed the high-calorie sustenance for the prolonged swim.

The crunch of ground shell in the driveway made her jump. Had Landry followed her home? She squashed the involuntary tingle of anticipation running up her spine. More than likely it was Perry. She stole a cautious glance out the window. If it was Perry, she wouldn't answer the door. He couldn't get in with all the new dead bolts and other security precautions they'd taken after last summer's break-in by the killer.

Shelly's golden curls sparkled in the midday sun as she ran up the porch steps. Jet groaned. She'd been only five minutes from a clean getaway. What she needed was physical exertion to burn off the hurt and anger churning in her gut. Talking it out, sharing her emotions, was Shelly's thing, not hers. What good did talking do? She'd kept the pain of Perry's betrayal to herself and she would do so with this latest. She had her pride to protect.

Her cousin burst through the door and hurried over. "I came as soon as I heard the news. Are you okay?"

Jet folded her arms across the front of her body. "Let me guess, Tillman told you all about the little scene in my store."

"Tillman's furious that an FBI agent came to work in Bayou La Siryna and didn't have the professional courtesy to check in with him."

"Yeah, well, he's not the only one who's angry."

"I know it looks bad that Landry lied about being an accountant." Her green eyes widened with earnest concern. "But I'm sure he had a really great reason."

"Sure he did," Jet spat out. "He was investigating my old treasure-salvage company. Evidently, Perry's into some scheme with scary, big-time criminals."

"And his return to the bayou made it look like you might be a part of it." Shelly shook her head in disgust. "That jerk's been nothing but bad news from the start."

"Took a while, but I finally figured that out for myself. Look, there was no need for you to rush home." Jet nodded at the note on the table. "I'm taking off for a day or two."

Shelly bit her lip. "Don't go. Remember you have a mighty big secret yourself that Landry doesn't know about. Talk to him instead of running off. He—"

"You mean well but I don't want to talk with anyone. Even you."

"It's not good to keep your feelings bottled up like you do, Jet. Don't rush off without giving Landry a chance to explain."

"None of that matters," Jet cut in. "He lied to me and led me on, just when I was starting to fall for the nice-guy act."

Shelly put her hands on her hips. "How do you know it's an act? You wouldn't know a nice guy if he bit you on the ass—" Her face reddened. "Um, you know what I'm trying to say."

"You're defending him because you're desperate to steer me away from Perry. Don't worry—I wouldn't go back to that slimeball for anything." Jet started for the back door.

"That's not the only reason." Shelly followed, undeterred. "Think of his positive qualities. First, he's in law enforcement, so we know he's moral and—"

"Like our fine deputy sheriff, the corrupt Carl Dismukes?" Jet snorted.

"And *second,* we know he cares about family or he wouldn't have taken on Seth."

Jet stopped at the door and faced Shelly. "Don't you see what you're doing? The outer circumstances are so much like Tillman's that you mistakenly believe Landry has all the qualities you love and admire about your fiancé."

Shelly's jaw slackened. "Guess you might have a point," she admitted grudgingly.

"Bye, Shell. I won't be gone long." Jet hurried to the shed before her cousin thought of more reasons to delay her. Jet *needed* the swim, needed the water's caress to soothe the hurt.

"Hey," Shelly called out as she neared the shed. "What about your store?"

Jet cupped her hands over her mouth. "Seth can do more of the setup work if he wants."

She unlocked the shed and quickly slipped inside, kicking off her sandals. Leaning her back against the door, Jet sighed as her toes curled in the sandy floor. *Alone at last.* The sound of lapping water called to her from the secret portal where, for centuries, Bosarge women shape-shifted between land and sea. What appeared from the outside to be an ordinary shed actually housed the portal and served as a changing room.

Quickly, Jet stripped naked and approached the small opening, about the size of a manhole on a city street. She inched in her legs and they instantly morphed into a glittering tail fin. Jet admired the mixture of pastel and bold teal sparkles before plunging into the narrow tunnel, part of an undersea cavern, which led to the sea.

Down she went for several feet until the tunnel emerged into open waters. She pushed onward past their vegetable garden of sea cucumber, kelp and water chestnuts and the deep, winding roots of turtle and wigeon grasses lining the bayou banks. Sea turtles feasted on a colony of sea grapes. Jet plucked the green fruit and popped it into her mouth, savoring its peppery flavor. She grabbed a handful and stored them in the sporran she always wore belted at her waist. In it, she kept a knife in case of sudden predators who might view her as a tasty meal.

Jet swam south, fighting against the gulf current pulling her eastward. She might spot Mom and Lily returning from the Games for the family reunion. She kept up the rhythmic pattern of swimming, crunching her abs and thrusting out her tail fin. She knew the action reflected an effect like undulating ripples of sea grass. Fish brushed against her, attracted by her large, sparkling tail fin.

At last, her tattered emotions were lulled by the physicality of movement, the beauty of swarming fish and the antics of dolphins. Poor Dolly. What fun it would be to have her swimming alongside her. Jet lost sense of time, not sure if she'd been swimming an hour or ten hours. Without the protection of other mermaids, she'd had to pay careful attention to the thrum vibration of boats. But all she heard was the constant cacophony of marine life: the high-pitched clicking of dolphins, sand crabs scurrying along the ocean floor and schools of fish cutting through the sea in constant search for either mates or a meal.

Moonlight danced shadows on the waves above and a huge colony of lantern fish glowed like fallen stars. Jet relaxed and drifted in the current, peaceful for the first time in days. The salty sea enveloped and cradled her weary body, the eternal thrum of the ocean undertow a lullaby to her low spirits. She was used to being alone and lonely. No big deal.

But the lie chaffed. Until she met Landry, she didn't realize how hollow and superficial her life had become. She'd existed as a shell of her former vibrant self, betrayed and cast aside by someone she thought she'd loved. But she hadn't known the meaning of love until she'd seen the genuine love Shelly and Tillman shared. Until Landry came along and the hope of new love erased some of the past pain and gave her the strength to resist Perry.

What was Landry doing right now? Was he thinking of her as she was of him? The earlier anger was spent, burned somewhere in the gulf waters.

Yes, he had lied to her, same as Perry. But his reasons weren't for selfish monetary gains. Checking her out and scrutinizing her business had been a necessary part of his job. Landry was on the right side of the law. Shelly had a point there.

The sight of lobsters jolted her out of her musings. Hundreds of them marched single file along the ocean floor—like ants on land—which might mean a storm was brewing. They formed a long line, positioned head to tail, stirring up tiny sediment particles. She dived closer and observed a few stragglers. Those would most likely be the next meal for parrot or triggerfish. Jet eyed a lone, stray lobster, its antennae swaying in the current. She was *really* hungry.

She reached out a hand, hovered it over the unfortunate creature.

No, she couldn't do it. Most mermaids ate raw fish and other seafood, but she stuck to kelp and other sea vegetables while undersea. On land, she had no compunction about cooked seafood. Mostly raised as a dirt dweller, Jet blamed her mom for her weak mermaid stomach.

"Guess you're safe," Jet said, sending bubbles gurgling from her mouth. She pivoted and swam to an area abundant with kelp. Not delicious, but it would have to do. She picked a handful and ate, regretfully watching the lobsters march away.

An eight-foot octopus oozed close and she scowled. A few more feet and the thing would be able to reach her with one of its long tentacles. She studied it closely for any sign of agitation but it didn't change color or exhibit papillae over its dark, horizontal pupils. When erect, the papillae resembled horns, giving it the appearance of a gelatinous devil.

But this one seemed merely curious. Jet relaxed and slowly extended her hand, knowing it wanted to taste her with its suckers and detect what manner of creature she was. "Don't you dare give me a case of giant hickeys all over my arm," she warned. Whatever would Landry think if he saw this? She laughed. He was so full of surprises and so open to the supernatural, he'd probably think it was cool.

Its right eye swiveled in its socket, as if weighing potential danger. Jet didn't doubt its huge brain contained a highly intelligent being. All those millions of neurons must serve some kind of intelligent purpose. If an octopus's life span were as long as a dolphin's—twenty, instead of only three years—it might have evolved into the ocean's smartest life-form.

The octopus reached out one of its eight tentacles and wrapped it around her arm. It probed, caressed, tasted, trying to figure her out.

A sudden sizzle in the water set Jet's sonar sense ablaze. The giant octopus released its hold, turned red and shot away. From the west came a conglomeration of light and sound unlike anything she'd encountered in all her travels. She'd heard tales of what disturbed jellyfish were like, but doubted she'd ever witness such a scene.

Bolts of electrical flashes lit the indigo water like a lightning show on a Kansas prairie in the dead of night. A colony of angry jellyfish lashed at one another with thousands of poisonous tentacles, producing a bioluminescent display worthy of the grandest Fourth of July fireworks exhibition on land.

"Holy Triton," Jet muttered. She was more used to moon jellyfish colonies floating like white, placid bubbles in oceans of blue, or like clouds in the summer sky. But true of most things undersea, the more beautiful something was, the deadlier it was. Best to keep her distance from the warring turmoil.

Jet veered northward toward home, disappointed to have heard nothing from Mom or Lily. If they'd been anywhere near one another, Jet would have heard Lily's magical voice singing, its crystal purity riding the currents for miles. Same old story. So many times she had swum out as a child, hoping to hear her family returning—only to go home alone.

That old sharp pang from the memories didn't pierce as deeply. Landry had faced far worse. Opening up and swapping stories with him had helped. Perhaps Shelly was right. It was good for her to talk about what lay buried in her heart.

And maybe—just maybe—she'd been unfair to lash out at Landry. Time and expended energy had gained her perspective and she viewed the revelations in a newer, calmer light.

Besides, it wasn't as if she'd been entirely truthful with him. She had her own secrets.

Chapter 9

Landry shook his head in bewilderment at the plethora of sea-treasure sites. He was accustomed to using the computer for criminal or missing-person searches, not for shipwrecks. Astonishing the number of wrecks caused by war, error or weather over the centuries.

He kept looking, determined to discover what Perry was so intent on finding with Jet. He didn't believe the con man for a minute when he claimed Jet wanted to keep working with him and that the check she gave him was for purchasing supplies. But it felt like a gut punch when Perry confidently claimed that Jet still loved him and always would.

Maybe Jet couldn't help herself; maybe she was one of those women drawn to the bad-boy type. He'd met many over the course of his career. Landry shook off the disturbing thought. He was giving Jet a chance to cool off a bit while he continued his investigation. She didn't have any more information on the Sylvester Vargas/Perry Hammonds connection. He'd call her again later today. He'd tried to reach her last night but she wasn't returning his calls. Her anger and shock should have melted considerably by now. He'd go to her house tonight.

He concentrated on the search. Tybee Island had a rich history, as the French and Spanish had fought to obtain the barrier island. Pirates, including Blackbeard and Captain Kidd, were also frequent visitors to the Georgia and South Carolina coastlines. Despite being a well-known treasure-hunting site for avid amateurs who searched for Spanish galleon, none of the known wrecks around Tybee indicated a huge, unclaimed treasure awaiting discovery.

Landry rubbed his jaw. How did Jet find so much treasure? She'd been close to revealing her secret method. If only Seth hadn't spilled his own secret about being an FBI agent. Landry glanced over at the sofa and frowned at the pristine cleanliness. No potato chips lay scattered across its black leather, no cans of soda littered the coffee table and no sandwich crumbs marred the gleaming, waxed floors. In fact, there were no signs anyone lived here but himself.

In the past, this would have pleased him. Now the place seemed hollow and empty. Seth was spending most of his time with Jimmy Elmore, the kid Shelly had introduced him to. This should have thrilled him, yet he missed Seth's companionship, strained as it had become after the false shoplifting accusation. They'd struck a truce, but Landry still felt guilty for not believing Seth at first. Their mother had made him out to be a lying, no-good nuisance who couldn't be trusted. Jet had shown him that wasn't true.

It was way too quiet. He pushed back his chair and went for the TV remote, turning the volume high to soak up the silence.

Much better. Landry returned to the Tybee Island search and almost scrolled past a web link until the word *bomb* caught his eye. Quickly, he pulled up an old newspaper article from 2011 about residents at a special town meeting airing concerns of an old hydrogen bomb jettisoned near the island in the 1950s and never recovered.

His pulse raced. The makings for a dirty bomb would interest Vargas. If he found it, no doubt some foreign country would pay hundreds of millions to get their hands on such a weapon. But was there really a bomb nestled in the ocean floor? And if so, was it even feasible to find and recover it? The whole thing reeked of intriguing conspiracy theory, wrapped smartly in military history and glittering with the shiny gold bow of a treasure hunt.

He scanned everything he could for quick answers. Yes, it had really happened. On February 5, 1958, a B-47 bomber collided midair with an F-86 fighter jet during a simulated combat mission. The pilot jettisoned the H-bomb so he could land the plane without crashing with the bomb on board. His action prevented a nuclear explosion on the barrier island, which was less than twenty miles from Savannah.

Navy vessels and divers searched the ocean for ten weeks before the military declared the bomb irretrievably lost. It was now one of the dozen or so nuclear bombs commonly known as Broken Arrows.

As recently as 2001, the United States Air Force reported the bomb was probably buried anywhere from five to fifteen feet in silt and posed no hazard if left undisturbed. The area where the bomb was believed to have dropped was extremely murky and no radiation readings were ever obtained by navy divers in the initial search.

If left undisturbed. A mighty big *if,* in Landry's mind. There was so much new technology developed since the '50s, he was surprised the government didn't search again. Maybe recovering the 7,600 pound bomb, labeled Number 47782, would be prohibitively expensive even for Uncle Sam's deep pockets.

But researching further, he read that the estimated recovery costs, if the bomb was found, would be roughly five million dollars. Not cheap, but certainly doable, if nothing more than to reassure Savannah citizens that possible uranium leakage wasn't contaminating their public water system. If he lived there, he'd be worried about heavy-metal poisoning.

And what about the environmental danger for marine life? He remembered Jet's frequent visits to the dolphin at the water park and her substantial donations to Save the Oceans and other such charities. She would be appalled to know that a potential menace to the entire gulf was buried in less than twenty feet of silt.

Suddenly restless, Landry got up, poured a fresh cup of coffee and grabbed his binoculars before walking out onto the cottage's second-story deck. As he did at least twice a day, he aimed it at the cage across the bay where he put out fresh fish daily, in hopes of luring the pregnant feral tabby. Yet again, the cage door was open and the fish gone. He shook his head and grinned. Damned smart cat. Even if he couldn't tame and spay her, at least she was getting food for herself and the unborn kitties.

The sea surface gleamed with millions of rainbow prism droplets swaying from underwater currents. Number 47782 was one of the earliest thermonuclear devices, designed to be a hundred times more powerful than the Hiroshima bomb. What kind of devastation would erupt from an underwater mushroom cloud? How many species of aquatic plants, mammals, fish and other creatures would be boiled alive—wiped out forever?

He wasn't a scientist, couldn't begin to guess how all that would affect human lives as well as… The creature of his youth came to mind. For the first time in ages, Landry stopped trying to fight remembering. Too much had happened in the past couple weeks to keep discounting the possibility that something lay beyond the ordinary. Whatever the creature had been, it had seemed human, a sentient, sympathetic being. Who knew what lurked far into the ocean's uncharted depths? It was as mysterious as any galaxy light-years away.

Countless times he'd stood on this deck, staring at miles of watery realms. The sea had depths no human had ever entered, its deepest ocean floors more mysterious than the moon. It held power and mystery, could be savage or serene; each wave held an enormous store of energy as it crested. There might be any number of sentient beings that existed undersea.

It stretched farther than his eyes could encompass, yet Landry strained to search beyond the point where ocean met sky in a flat line of mixed blues and grays. A pang of loneliness squeezed his chest.

Where was Jet?

He needed to hear her voice. At once.

He tried calling again, but got no answer. It had been nearly two days now since she'd discovered his lie. Plenty of time for her to recoup from the surprise and hurt. He hated the way she'd found out, but he'd been doing his job the best way he knew how and he'd make Jet understand that. Filled with resolve, he grabbed his car keys and headed to the Bosarge home.

During the short drive, Landry worked himself into a state of agitation. Jet claimed she had a sixth sense for finding sites. What if Hammonds and Vargas wanted to exploit her talent to find the missing hydrogen bomb? He pulled into their driveway and quickly skidded to a stop, overcome with urgency. Her red truck was there, a good sign. He rapped at the door sharply, but was disappointed when Shelly appeared.

"Where's Jet?" he demanded.

"She's not here."

Dread prickled the back of his neck. "Where is she?"

"Jet's gone," Shelly answered evasively, moving to shut the door.

He grabbed the handle. "Hold on a minute. What do you mean, she's gone? Do you know where she went?"

It was the kidnapping nightmare all over again—the defining incident of his childhood. That damned red sequined purse was the last physical link, an albatross from the past that warned life could be snatched away in an instant. One unguarded moment and all was lost forever.

Panic and despair from years ago washed through him. What if he never saw Jet again? He'd have to live the rest of his life with the memory of the hurt in her eyes when she'd found out he was an FBI agent. Wasn't it bad enough he'd lived through this same kind of hell once before? The gods were surely punishing him for some unfathomable reason.

Shelly frowned. "Why? You come to arrest her? Jet's done nothing wrong."

"No. Of course not. I'm worried about Jet. When is the last time you saw her?"

She stiffened. "Are you questioning me in an official capacity? 'Cause if you are, I'm calling Tillman to—"

"No," he interrupted hastily. "I just want to make sure she's okay." Landry swallowed hard. "Please."

Shelly's face softened. "She's okay. You really care for her, don't you?"

He started to deny it. But the idea of Jet going missing had frightened him to his very core. The memory of The Incident from his childhood washed over him. "You're sure she's okay and not in any danger?"

"Positive." Shelly's eyes narrowed. "Now answer my question. Do you honestly care about Jet? If you're using her to get at Perry, I promise Tillman and I will make you regret it."

"I care." The admission made him uncomfortable. He'd have to deal with those emotions later. What was important was making sure Jet was safe. "Tell me where she went."

"She's on an out-of-town trip."

"When will she come back?"

"I'm not sure. Anytime now."

Shelly was insufferably evasive. Never mind, he'd dig up the facts. Landry nodded at the red truck. "She didn't take her vehicle."

Shelly blinked those wide green eyes and said nothing.

He'd check the Mobile flight lists when he got back home. He'd also need to notify his supervisor about the Tybee Island bomb possibility. The bayou would probably soon be swarming with officers from both agencies. It wouldn't look good if Jet was MIA in the midst of it all.

Landry's frustration built. His duty was clear—notify his boss about his suspicions. But how could he do that if it meant Jet would be treated as a suspect when he knew she was innocent? She'd never forgive him for an ordeal with the federal government.

A more sickening thought assailed Landry. If Perry couldn't sweet-talk Jet into the Tybee Island excursion, he might force her to cooperate. A deep fury pounded through his veins at the very idea. Low-life scum like Perry were capable of anything, especially when desperate for money. "Look, Shelly," he said urgently, "Jet could be in deep trouble."

Her eyes widened farther. "What kind of trouble?"

He pulled his very best officer intonation. "I am not at liberty to say."

"It's Perry, isn't it?" She put her hands on her hips and sighed. "We always knew he'd be back one day, causing more problems."

"Then help me help Jet."

Shelly bit her lip. "I'm really not sure when she'll come home. Like I said, it could be anytime."

"I need to find her immediately and warn her of a possible danger."

The sound of a door slamming shut drew his attention to a shed located about thirty feet from the side of their house. As if he'd conjured her from his own desperation, he saw Jet had returned. She was dressed in a white terrycloth robe; her black hair clung to her neck as if she'd just emerged from water. She adjusted a lock on the shed door and then turned toward the house, walking slowly, shoulders slumped, as if she'd finished a million-mile marathon.

How odd. Landry looked around the yard, puzzled. What had she been doing in a shed? There was nothing in her hands to suggest she'd gone out for a tool or some other necessity. Instead, it appeared she'd had a shower and was exhausted. At least he knew she was okay. The relief nearly made him weak in the knees. He knew Perry was in town, but one of Vargas's men could have easily slipped her away. Landry silently vowed to keep an eye on her until all this was resolved.

Shelly quietly closed the front door, but he stood rooted on the porch, eyes on Jet. Her pale, wet skin shimmered under the Alabama sun.

He'd never seen a more beautiful sight.

Through an exhausted haze, Jet's skin prickled with awareness. She was being watched. She raised weary eyes and found Landry's frosty eyes pinned on her. Had he seen her come out of the shed? Of course he had, she admonished herself.

The long swim had drained all her mental and physical energy. All she needed now was sleep and lots of it.

Landry hurried toward her, face grim and harsh.

"Where the hell have you been?" he demanded as he bore down on her.

She shrugged. "What does it matter? I'm back."

He grabbed her shoulders and hesitated, as if debating whether to shake her or hug her. Concern etched worry lines in his brows and the corners of his eyes. "Don't ever do that again," he said gruffly.

"Do what?"

"Don't leave me."

He pulled her to him and pressed her tightly against him. She rested her head on his shoulder and let him support her weight. It was the first time in days Jet had felt such calm comfort. It struck her again that Landry's touch was like finding an oasis in the desert. She hoped it wasn't all a mirage.

It sure felt real.

She listened to the steady thump of his heartbeat and felt her own heart hammer like a resounding metronome in perfect time with his. If she could, she'd curl into a little ball and slip into the crook of his arms, her face resting against his chest. The sound of his heart and the echo of waves in the background felt like a perfect union of land and sea—like a home she'd always wanted and never had.

"Okay," she mumbled into his chest. "I won't leave again."

He held her out at arm's length. "Promise?"

She was bereft without his hold, chilled in the middle of a hot, humid Southern sky. "Promise," she agreed quickly, needing his arms around her again.

He complied with urgency, a quickness that was stunning. What had gotten into him? Jet inhaled the soapy, male scent that she loved. The why didn't matter; she needed him now and was too drained to ask questions. *Later,* she promised the last questioning voice in her brain that didn't want to be quieted, until at last it shut up and left her in peace.

The sun's warmth, coupled with Landry's body heat, made her groggy. She was safe at last.

"I'm sorry I had to lie to you about my job," he whispered into the top of her scalp.

"It's okay. I don't like it, but I understand."

Landry gave her a quick squeeze. "Thank you," he said simply.

"Uh, um, Jet." Shelly's voice broke through her reverie. Jet reluctantly raised her face away from the haven of Landry's chest to find Shelly holding out an overnight bag.

"I think you're going to need this," she said.

"What do you mean?"

Landry took the bag and nodded at Shelly. "She'll be safe with me."

"What the hell are you two talking about?"

Shelly gave her a quick hug. "I packed several days' worth of clothes, your charged cell phone and all the essentials."

"I'm not going anywhere except to bed." At Landry's raised eyebrow, she flushed. "To *sleep*," she elaborated. "I'm dead on my feet, in case you all haven't noticed."

"And starving, too, no doubt," Shelly said. "Call me later," she added, before walking away.

Landry guided Jet toward his BMW, but she dragged her feet.

"Where do you think you're taking me?"

"I know you love shrimp. What would you say to a shrimp-and-lobster smorgasbord?"

Her mouth watered and her stomach grumbled. "But I'm not up to going out," she said regretfully.

"Who said anything about going out?"

She gave up and followed him, taking the path of least

resistance. At the car, he opened the passenger door and tucked her in as if she was precious cargo. She sank into the soft leather.

He came around the other side and started the car. "I'll grill the seafood and boil some corn on the cob. I think I have the makings of a salad, too."

"No need for all that. All I want is shrimp and lobster."

"You got it."

Jet laid her head back on the headrest and soon the steady drone of the car tires was like a lullaby. She sighed, slipped out of her sandals and placed a hand on Landry's right thigh. Beneath her fingers, his muscles felt strong and tight. A small smile escaped. And to think that when she first met him she'd imagined his body would be soft and flaccid like a geek's. Landry was full of surprises.

She rather liked that.

Chapter 10

Jet awoke and blinked in unfamiliar darkness. Through deep shadows she looked around the small, pristinely neat room. She would have called the style minimalistic except for a collection of neatly piled quilts at the foot of the bed. On the nightstand a lamp sat atop an old-fashioned doily that was slightly yellowed with age.

Under the nightstand she at last saw a familiar item, her blue overnight bag. Memories besieged her brain like pieces of a quilt—returning from that long swim, Landry overtaking her on the lawn, Shelly handing her the bag.

She stretched, grateful for the peaceful sleep on a mattress instead of some sandy shore. Jet swung her long legs over the side of the bed.

Her long, naked legs.

Jet's hands flew to her chest. Gone was her old terry-cloth robe; she was completely naked. She groaned, searching in the shadows for her robe. She spotted it folded neatly in a chair on the opposite wall.

Had Landry seen her naked? Her skin heated and flushed until an even worse realization hit. He might have seen her exposed gill scars. She tried to quell a surge of fear. Surely most men would be much more interested in other parts of a woman's body than their *neck,* for heaven's sake. No, he wouldn't have undressed her. She must have taken off the robe herself but was just too tired to remember.

Quickly, she donned the robe, turning up the collar as best she could. Her nose led her from the hallway to the kitchen, where Landry stood at the stove, his back to her. The light illuminated streaks of gold in his hair. He seemed competent in the kitchen, as he did in every situation.

Jet inhaled deeply as she entered the room. "I hope it's time to eat. I'm starving."

He didn't even turn around, as if he was able to merely sense her presence. "Have a seat. Everything's almost ready."

She sat at the kitchen table, already laid out with plates and condiments, then poured a glass of water from the pitcher and drank. She tried to quell the nervous fluttering in her stomach. The man was probably going to grill her with questions. Maybe even want to know what was wrong with her neck. She considered going back to the bedroom and sinking into oblivious sleep.

"Where's Seth?" she asked.

"Staying with Jimmy Elmore, the guy Shelly introduced him to. They really hit it off."

"Is that his room I slept in?"

Landry snorted. "No way. His room is disgusting. Bed unmade, dirty clothes on the floor." He shook his head. "Hard to believe we're brothers."

Landry set a platter of shrimp and lobster on the table.

"I don't know what you like to eat with them, so there's a little bit of everything here." His hand swept the table. "Melted butter, cocktail sauce, ketchup—"

Jet eagerly filled her plate and began eating, trying not

to make a fool of herself and gobble it up too quickly. But all too soon, the plate was empty. She reached for more and caught Landry's bemused eyes upon her.

"How did you work up such an appetite?"

The questioning had begun. Jet shrugged and carefully dunked a shrimp in butter, eating slower. "Swimming."

He nodded. "Where at?"

She waved a hand. "Oh, a good ways south of Bayou La Siryna."

Landry nodded again and proceeded to ignore her as he ate.

The silence began to unnerve Jet until at last she had to know. She pushed away the plate. "You said I was in danger. What's happening?"

He rose. "Let's sit out on the deck and talk."

She picked up her plate and headed for the kitchen sink to wash it, but he stopped her.

"I'll get those later."

She gave him a half smile. "Must be serious if you don't want to do dishes first. Your house is immaculate."

"I do like to keep things in a certain order."

"Then let's clean up. It won't take long with both of us working together."

Working together. Had a nice ring to it, Jet mused. She took in details of the kitchen and den as she rinsed and loaded the dishwasher. In spite of the overall modern ambience, there were whimsical touches that seemed out of place: old canning jars lined against the backsplash, cat figurines in a curio cabinet and kitchen towels trimmed with crocheted embellishments.

She picked up one of the mason jars and read the label aloud. "Ginger-peach jam. Who canned these for you?"

"Mimi, my grandmother. She left this cottage for me when she died."

Ah, that explained the homey touches. "How long ago did she die?"

"About seven years ago."

Landry possessed a sentimental streak to hold on to her things for so long. She liked that about him. At least he'd loved one person in his life. She secretly watched him as he efficiently put condiments back in the refrigerator and wiped the table. "Did you enjoy every summer you spent with her?"

"Every single one. I used to count down the days during the school year. Mom's house was always full of too much drama."

No wonder the guy loved order and solitude.

He reached under her and took out some dishwasher detergent from the lower cabinet. "Go on outside while I start the dishwasher. Want some wine or beer?"

"What kind of wine do you have?"

"Merlot okay?"

She nodded. "I'll get it. Tell me where everything is." Jet poured a glass and briefly returned to the bedroom to change into shorts and a T-shirt Shelly had packed in the overnight bag. She retrieved her wineglass before stepping into the warm night air swirling on the balcony. Nice view where the salty gulf waters edged the property. She sat in a rocker and the nerves from dinner dissipated. The warmth, the full stomach and the gentle rocking soon had her yawning. It would take a couple more days of deep sleep to recoup. She set the merlot on a coffee table and closed her eyes.

A scrape from the sliding glass door had her bolting upright. Landry's tall figure emerged from the shadows and he eased into a chair across from her.

"Did a little research today on what kind of shipwreck

might be off the coast of Tybee Island," he began, direct as always.

Jet sipped the merlot, curious as to what he'd discovered. She'd never bothered to read that library book or search the internet. Opening the shop and manufacturing the manifests Landry had requested had taken all her free time. Besides, she'd had no intention of going anywhere with Perry again. "What did you find?"

"Something highly unusual." The glacier chips of his eyes glowed in the darkness. "Nearly eight thousand pounds worth of unusual."

Jet snickered. "You think Perry wants to excavate the remains of an entire ship? We—that is, *I*—don't have the right equipment to excavate something as large as a ship's hull."

"Exactly. I don't think he intended for the two of you to work alone."

She tilted her head to the side, recalling Perry's words. "I don't remember him saying we'd work with a crew. We never have before."

"You really don't know what lies buried out there, do you?" He paused, gazing at her thoughtfully. "What about your, um, special abilities?"

Jet stiffened, not sure if he was mocking her. "That's only good once I'm in the water. Not before."

"How good are you at finding something buried several feet in sediment?"

"It would be harder, but I could probably do it." Her mermaid sense of smell was even stronger than her excellent night vision. Highly developed sight and smell were necessary for navigating murky or deep waters. You had to know what danger might lurk.

He whistled. "Impressive."

She took a long, fortifying swallow of the rich wine,

savoring its tang. "Now tell me what's going on. You said I'm in danger."

"I can't prove anything yet. But after a little digging I discovered there's a missing hydrogen bomb believed to be buried offshore."

"Bomb?" She gave a disbelieving laugh. "How the hell could that happen?"

"A military mishap from the '50s. Navy divers tried to find it, but had no luck."

She shook her head, setting down the drink. "And you think Perry wants us to find this? What the hell would we do with a bomb?" The notion was ludicrous.

"It's worth millions to the right buyer."

"Maybe. But neither of us has international connections. Everything we did was fairly small-scale."

"Until now," Landry insisted stubbornly.

"Coincidence." Jet stood and walked to the edge of the deck railing. The news of a bomb rattled her inside. "Do you think so little of me that you believe I'd sell a bomb to the highest bidder?" she asked, her back to him. Her hands gripped the railing as she fought waves of disappointment.

The scrape of wood on wood was loud as he rose from his chair. "Not you. I can believe anything of Perry Hammonds. But not you."

The pressure of his hands suddenly rested on her shoulders, searing her with heat.

"I told you before," he began, hands lowering to her hips as his mouth found her neck. "You're better than that," he whispered. His breath sent tingles of desire exploding through her body.

Jet leaned back, sinking into Landry's steel chest. She closed her eyes, inhaling his clean scent while she listened to their heartbeats and the ocean waves pound in an inevitable union. She started to turn in his embrace but as she did so, a flash of orange across the lagoon drew her attention. Jet narrowed her eyes, adjusting to the darkness, until she made out details.

An orange-striped tabby—extremely fat—stared back, eyes aglow. Even at this distance, the cat had zoomed in on her with its acute, predatory olfactory sense. Damned stray cats followed her everywhere she went in town. How long had it been watching her? She allowed her nictitating membrane to lower a fraction for better vision. The extra eyelid was useful undersea as well as on land at night. She spotted the outline of a gray cage.

Outrage pushed aside passion. "There's a caged cat out there." She pointed at it.

Landry squinted in the direction she pointed. "How can you tell in this darkness? I can't see it."

"I have perfect vision." *To put it mildly.* "Why would anyone trap a cat? We've got to help it."

Landry ran a hand through his hair, as if composing himself. "Guess I better go get it, considering I'm the one who set the trap."

"Why would you do such a thing? I hate seeing animals in cages!" Her nightmare pricked in the back of her mind.

"I'm trying to help it. She's a pregnant feral cat. I'd like to see the kittens be adopted at the shelter."

"Oh, I see." If only it were this easy to help Dolly and her calf.

Landry started toward the door. "Let's go get her. It won't take long."

Jet hurried after him as he sped downstairs for the carport. She heard him mumble something about *damn cat* and *why now of all times.* "I'll wait for you here," she called out.

He was walking across the lawn to a small fishing dock

with an old johnboat attached to it. "Come with me," he said, waving an arm toward the boat. "Won't take long."

"But I'll get wet."

He turned at that. "The first day we met it was pouring rain and you lingered outside with no umbrella. Now you're worried about getting wet?"

Jet struggled for an excuse. If so much as a drop of salt water landed on her legs, the gig was up and the freak show would begin. "I feel like I'm coming down with a cold," she offered lamely. Desperately, she scanned underneath the carport, at last spotting a pair of knee-high wading boots. That should do the trick. "I'll borrow your boots." She hurriedly put them on. Landry started the boat motor as she clumsily made her way to shore.

He raised a brow at the boots but didn't comment. He threw her an orange vest and grabbed another for himself. "Put this on."

As if. "Don't need it."

He frowned. "It's the law."

"Seriously? It's just you and me in the middle of nowhere. Besides, I have an *in* with the local sheriff." She gave him a wink. "We're good."

His fingers stilled on the jacket straps. "What if the boat tips over?"

All hell breaks loose, that's what. She wanted to go back inside but didn't want to draw questions about her motives.

"If it tips, we swim," she answered grimly. What a relationship killer that would be.

"The thing is…" Landry spoke hesitantly, his voice trailing off.

Jet glanced at him sharply, surprised to see a flush of red in his cheeks. "What?"

He slowly snapped closed the jacket fasteners. "I don't swim."

She gaped at him, astonished. "Why not?"

He expertly guided the boat out toward the cat. "I can't, okay?" he answered testily.

She couldn't imagine not knowing how to swim; it would be like a human saying they never learned to walk. Of course, she'd heard some people couldn't. Shelly even taught a few adults at the YMCA who'd never learned how.

They continued in silence until they reached the bank on the opposite shore. Jet carefully maneuvered out of the boat, avoiding water as best she could, even with boot protection. Landry squatted down in front of the large, wire cage. "We meet at last, little mama," he said in a soft voice. "You put up a good, long fight, I'll give you that."

Jet bent over, eyeing the tabby, which instantly hissed and began growling.

"She was fine a moment ago," Landry said, brows knitting.

"I have this weird effect on cats. Sort of a mutual non-admiration society."

"I thought you loved animals. Anyone that could love that ugly mutt of yours—"

"Leave Rebel out of it," she warned in mock sternness. Reb couldn't help the cruel joke nature had played on his appearance.

Landry picked up the cage, the tabby crying and spitting its disapproval. "Sorry, girl. The ride over won't be fun, but we've got some leftover shrimp you're going to love."

Although Jet did her best to not even look at the cat on the boat ride home, the thing mewled like a banshee from hell. At the dock, Landry donned a thick pair of rubber fisherman's gloves before picking up the cage and hauling it to the cottage.

"Smart thinking," Jet said, watching the cat flay its claws out the cage slits, ready to do damage.

"It's not the first time I've done this. I'm fighting a one-man battle to end the bayou's feral cat population."

"Why?" she asked in surprise.

"Because most end up living short lives filled with both disease and serious fight wounds, or else they starve."

She followed him upstairs. "Where you taking her?"

He set the cage down in a small utility room. "I'll take her to the shelter when I get a chance. They can take care of her until she has the kittens." He left the room. "Be right back. I promised her shrimp."

Jet dropped to her knees and eyed the tabby, which glared and hissed in response. "You better start acting lovable," she warned. "Nobody wants a wild hellion."

The tabby growled louder and spit.

"I see no progress has been made," Landry observed, carrying in a plate of shrimp and a bowl of water.

"How do you plan on getting that in the cage without being clawed?"

He shrugged. "I don't. I'm letting the cat out." He got down on a knee beside Jet and set down the food and water. "Maybe you should back away. You seem to make her more agitated."

"Fine." She rose and watched as Landry opened the cage latch. She expected the cat to dig in on the peeled shrimp, but the tabby backed into a far corner, eyeing them with suspicion.

"Thought you said wild cats were usually starving. She's not acting hungry at all."

Landry rose, grabbed a large plastic container and filled it with kitty litter. "Be patient. It takes time. When I check on her in the morning, the plate will be empty." He turned to the door. "Let's leave her in peace to get used to her new surroundings."

Jet's mouth dropped open. "But you can't leave her locked in here!"

His mouth twisted in a wry smile. "Better here than in a cage at the shelter anyway."

"Then maybe she's better off in the wild." She folded her arms across her chest. "Let's release it."

He leaned against the doorjamb, eyeing her with curiosity. "What is it with you and caged animals?"

"It's just…" Her mouth went dry and she swallowed hard. "It's just like this dolphin at the local water park. She's with calf and instead of being with her pod, she's trapped and alone."

"You mean Dolly?"

She gave him a sharp glance. "You know her?"

"*Know* her? That's an odd way to put it. I visited the water park once. You go there a lot so I wanted to see the main attraction. I still don't see your objection."

"Never mind, you wouldn't understand." She went to the door, but Landry blocked the exit.

"Try me," he said.

She lifted her shoulders casually. "I have a recurring dream where I'm stuck in a tank, er, I mean a cage."

He nodded wisely. "Probably a guilty conscience symbolically urging you to break all ties with Hammonds before you end up in prison."

"Don't analyze me with that FBI profiling crap," she snapped. But then she caught the stirrings of a smile playing at the corners of his mouth. She ran a finger along the edge of his strong jawline. "Whoever would have thought the uptight FBI man had a sense of humor behind that stiff exterior?"

The amusement faded. "Is that how I come off?"

"Most definitely," she assured him. "Serious, hard-working and uptight."

"I'll show you uptight." He pulled her against him and kissed her long and hard, until Jet was breathless with need.

"I retract my statement," she whispered in a shaky laugh.

His hands lifted her T-shirt and caressed her breasts. He cupped them, thumbs brushing her nipples. Sexual need hot as lava erupted in her core. But in spite of the erupting desire, Jet was conscious of the gill markings.

"Let's go to your bedroom," she gasped.

He drew back, incredulous. "That's so predictable," he said. "Now who's the uptight one?"

But he picked her up in one efficient, effortless move and carried her to the last bedroom down the narrow hallway. Once inside, he flipped on the lights but at Jet's protest turned them back off.

"Never figured you as the shy type," he said huskily. "I wanted to see you. All of you."

"Later," she promised. She wanted to see his naked body, too, but didn't want their first time marred by probing questions. All she needed tonight, truly needed, was to merge her body with his. From the first time they met, Landry had stirred her passion. Something about the penetrating chill of his blue eyes made her want to fuse it with her own heat.

He laid her gently on the bed. Jet flung off her shorts and T-shirt in the darkness, heard the sound of metal scraping metal as Landry unzipped his pants and the whooshing of fabric against skin as he ripped off his shirt. She scooted over and he eased down alongside her, stroking her breasts and then the plane of her abdomen. She'd never considered her stomach an erogenous zone, but Landry's hands on her flat abs inflamed her body's internal temperature even more.

Jet placed one leg over his, running the tender flesh of her instep along his sleek, muscular thighs. Beneath his conservative attire, Landry hid a body as hard and muscular as a professional athlete. The man was full of surprises. She snuggled closer, the small mounds of her breasts pressing against his broad chest. Curly hairs tickled her nose as she inhaled the fresh scent of soap and clean skin.

His hands moved upward and her scalp prickled as Landry ran his fingers through her short hair. In the darkness she couldn't tell where he would touch her next and that added to the excitement. Everywhere he touched sent her nerve endings tingling with fever. Each moan and ragged breath Landry released was amplified and echoed, as if they were alone in some deep, black cave.

But what amazed Jet most of all was the tender eroticism of his caresses. All her senses surrendered to his touch. His hands moved from her scalp and traveled down her spine until he located the curve of her hip and gently pushed her back against the mattress. Landry kissed the hollow at the base of her throat, his tongue lapping the indentation before trailing his mouth over her breasts, kissing and licking. When Jet thought she couldn't wait another second, he pursed his lips over the soft bud of one nipple while he gently squeezed the other between his thumb and forefinger. Her fears and insecurities gave way to raw desire.

Burning spasms of need flared between her legs, as if a hidden toggle switch existed between her nipples and core. Jet moved her hands to his erection, wanting him to be as desperate as she for release. His manhood was hard, ready. Landry groaned and pressed into her exploring palms.

"Let's do it," Jet whispered in a ragged whisper. "Now!"

"So soon?"

"There's always next time for more foreplay," she promised.

He made a noise that was half moan, half chuckle. "You bet."

Landry parted the folds of her core and entered slowly.

He was driving her crazy. She needed him now, would shatter into a million pieces if he took his time. She bucked her hips underneath him and he increased his pace. Tension coiled in her stomach, an unbearable need.

Jet flipped Landry so that he was on his back, she astride him. She cringed at his quick inhale. Damn, she'd shown too much of her inhuman strength. She hardly dared move, waiting for Landry to demand an explanation.

"Don't stop," he groaned. He placed his hands on either side of her hips, urging her to continue.

He was as desperate as she for release. Jet momentarily reveled in the knowledge before rocking her core and taking in his manhood, until all thought abandoned her mind once again. The only thing that mattered was the gathering storm at the apex of her thighs. "Landry," she cried out, needing the sound of his voice, her orgasm crashing like tidal waves against a granite cliff.

"I'm with you, baby," he assured her, body taut and straining as he matched her quickened pace.

Jet knew the instant he found his own release as he moaned and shuddered before lying completely still, breathing hard and fast. She laid her head against his chest, listened to his deep breathing as he stroked her hair.

"That was incredible," he murmured against her ear.

"Mmm," she agreed, suddenly too tired for conversation. Landry rolled her over and rubbed her legs in relaxing massage strokes. Exactly what she needed. Every muscle ached from her swimming binge. "Oh, that feels so good."

"Relax and take a little nap," Landry encouraged. He chuckled. "I want you well rested for next time."

"Whatever," she said, concentrating on the muscle relief. She'd probably agree to almost anything right now.

"And next time—" he lightly patted her ass "—it will be with the lights on."

Momentary alarm flared at his words, but Jet decided to deal with that problem later. Right now was pure bliss, the aftermath almost as incredible as the sex—something she'd never before experienced.

His hands continued their magic, comforting and healing Jet. She snuggled against the pillow, breathing in Landry's scent as he massaged her body, all the way down to her toes. Who knew toes needed love and attention, too? Landry, that was who. She nestled her face into the pillow. Her breathing slowed and grew deeper under Landry's expert touch. Jet experienced the same sensation as when she swam under a full moon—her body was fluid, responsive, in the flow of being exactly where it needed to be.

Sweet Triton, she never wanted to leave Landry's bed.

Chapter 11

Landry eased out of bed, careful not to awaken Jet. He pushed open the bedroom door and light from the hallway spilled into the room. Her pale skin seemed to shimmer in the semidarkness. He leaned over to smooth a lock of hair from her face and again noticed the faint etchings of some past trauma that had left small white scars on the sides of her neck, so eerily like the mermaid of his past that it disturbed him. Jet's ebony hair framed the patrician features of her face. Full red lips were curved as if she were having sweet dreams. She looked like a dark angel, he decided. A very *sexy* dark angel.

He frowned at the direction of his thoughts. Jet Bosarge was getting to him. Getting to him *bad.* First, he went into overprotective mode to keep her from Hammonds. Second, the news she was missing had scared him shitless. And then tonight when they'd landed in his bed, he'd been flooded with mixed feelings of tenderness and passion. It was so much more than mere physical need. Frankly, it made him nervous as hell.

He grabbed his discarded clothes from the floor and left the room, shutting the door quietly behind him. Jet appeared to be exhausted from wherever the hell she'd been. Time enough to question her later. He still needed more concrete information before he went to his supervisors.

Something had been tickling the back of his brain. Something he couldn't quite catch, like trying to remember a dream fading away as soon as you awakened.

Landry quickly dressed, booted up the computer and read more on the hydrogen bomb. After nearly half an hour of reviewing the material, a name jumped out at him—Brian Tindol, copilot of the plane that scuttled the H-bomb to land.

He'd heard that name before today, Landry was positive. It was unusual enough to catch his eye. But where? He pulled out the files on Vargas and Hammonds, searching for a connection. He would try Hammonds's phone list first, since there were fewer names and numbers to scan. Twenty minutes later, Landry neatly tucked the phone records back in the Hammonds file and determinedly started on Vargas's records.

Bingo! Vargas had been in extensive communication with one Jim Tindol. He'd bet his house that Jim was related to Brian. Satisfaction settled deep in his bones now that he had a connection between the H-bomb and Perry Hammonds. He'd call his supervisors in Mobile in the morning and let them run a background check to confirm the Tindols were related. The sooner he laid this case to rest, the sooner he and Jet could put Hammonds behind them.

Perry smirked, his brown eyes taking on the sly look of a fox that had cleverly sneaked into a chicken coop to survey the easy prey. "You're mine. All mine," he said in a singsong chant. "Forever and ever."

Bubbles of frustration spewed in Jet's gut, before rising and clogging her throat in a stifled scream. Not again! She couldn't, wouldn't be tricked by Perry and turn into his treasure-hunting slave.

"There's no escape. Mine, mine, mine."

Jet jumped off their boat and swam from his voice as fast as she could, but had only gone a few yards underwater when something sharp grabbed her ankle. She kicked, but even her strength was no match against that steel grip. She turned, staring into Orpheous's blue-green face with its smile exposing sharply pointed teeth. "Told you I'd find you one day and make you mine," he said with a leer. "You belong with me and the Blue Clan. Together, we will mate and produce fine specimens. Our sons will become elite warriors and our daughters fitting mates for Blue Mermen. Our family will be pivotal in forcing other merfolk to serve our cause—domination of the seven seas."

Jet's limbs were useless appendages, as paralyzed as her vocal cords. *No, you deluded maniac,* she tried to protest, but no sound emerged. Orpheous shook her like he would shake seaweed off a dead fish before biting into its flesh with his jagged teeth. But instead of biting her, Orpheous flung her deeper undersea. Jet found herself in some kind of pit where electric eels encircled an invisible border she could not cross without being stung.

Beautiful mermaids passed, pointing and laughing. Even their cruel laughter held a beauty, an allure that she could never attain. Jet glanced down. Her beautiful mermaid's tail had transformed into pale human legs. It was all wrong; she shouldn't be human down under the sea. She was more of an outcast than ever.

"You don't belong," one voluptuous mermaid sang out, and the others immediately joined in a chorus. *Don't belong, don't belong, don't belong.*

Again she struggled to move, and this time she was rewarded with a reconnection to her limbs.

Soft sheets rubbed against her naked flesh and she opened her eyes, staring into a strange room. Confusion gave way seconds later to recognition. This was Landry's bedroom. She stretched out an arm and found the space beside her empty. Quickly, she found her cast-off clothes on the floor and dressed before she entered the living room. Landry sat in front of the computer, but his hands gripped a framed photo. The profile of his tight jaw and the white knuckles drew her curiosity. He didn't move as she walked barefoot and stood behind his back.

A small girl grinned from a tire swing mounted to a tree. The picture was slightly blurry, as if she'd been in motion when the camera snapped. Something about the blond curls and the shape of her nose and mouth suggested a strong family connection. A daughter perhaps?

"Who is she?" Jet asked, laying a hand on his shoulder. His muscles tensed beneath her palm.

"My sister. Her name was April."

"I caught the resemblance—" Jet paused as the word *was* sank in. "Was?"

Landry carefully set the frame down beside the computer. "She died less than a month after that picture was taken."

"That's...that's awful. What happened? She doesn't look sick in that photo."

"April was kidnapped. Went missing one summer afternoon from our own front yard. Mom had gone into the house for something and when she came back out a minute later, April was gone." He pointed to the photo. "That tire swing was still in motion."

Jet's throat closed up and she couldn't speak. Words

were so inadequate anyway. She rested her chin on the top of Landry's scalp and wrapped her arms around his chest.

"April's body was found a month later by a fisherman, under a clump of pines along the Mobile River."

In the silent stillness, she heard the eternal motion of waves lapping against shore. Lace curtains billowed from the open window like pale ghosts. "I'm so sorry," she whispered.

"My first vivid memory, at age five, is of Mom screaming."

The bleak, deep timber vibrations of his voice traveled from his chest to her fingertips and on up through her arms, past her rib cage and into her heart, where it pinched like a monster sea crab. His sorrow was her sorrow.

"I'll hear it forever," he continued. "Those screams echo in my brain every damn day, with every new case."

"It's why you became an FBI agent," she answered past the ache in her throat. "To stop crimes from happening to anyone else."

"Exactly. When I see this photo, see that happy grin on April's face, it's a reminder that in a minute—a mere sixty seconds—one evil person can snatch a loved one and destroy their life and their family's lives."

Jet moved around Landry's side and sat in his lap, stroking the nape of his neck and the small wisps of light brown curls he always tried to keep combed down.

"It broke up our family," he continued. "Dad moved out three months later, away from the scene of the trauma, the looks of pity on everyone's face. Away from April's dark, closed-off bedroom, her empty chair at the kitchen table. Away from the shadow person Mom became."

"And from you." Jet simultaneously hated and pitied Landry's father. "He deserted you, too." No wonder Landry loved coming to visit his grandmother every summer. It must have felt like a prison furlough from the house of misery, a respite from haunting memories.

He shrugged as if his father's absence were no big deal. "I learned to live with it. Mom's method of coping was keeping a steady stream of new boyfriends and more children." He shook his head with a rueful smile. "Lots of children."

"Keeping busy." She gave a small smile of understanding. "Kids will ensure your mind stays occupied all day."

Landry nodded. "My mother never stopped *doing*. We never sat down in the evening to watch TV or movies like other families. She was always busy—going out, cooking, cleaning, whatever." He fell silent a minute before giving a weary sigh. "But at least she didn't run away, not physically anyway. I try to be patient and remember what she went through, but it hasn't been easy."

How difficult it must have been growing up as the eldest with a slew of half siblings while he was the one that favored April in appearance. Every time his mother looked at him, she must have remembered his dead sister.

"Enough about me," he said resolutely. "I don't know why, but I end up telling you things from my past that I don't speak about with others, and stuff I try not to dwell on even privately. Besides, we need to talk."

Jet groaned and stood up. "Sounds ominous."

"It's serious, not ominous. Go ahead and sit. Want something to drink first? Coffee?"

"It's too late for coffee. Just some water for me."

"Coming right up."

Jet tried not to stare at April's photo as Landry went to the fridge. She was still rattled about the news and her own intense response to his pain. His sister's tragic murder explained so much about Landry—his strong sense of justice, his need for order and his self-contained reserve that she at first mistook for aloofness. Everyone in his past had deserted him in one way or another, so he learned to rely on no one but himself.

Would he ever fully open up his heart again and risk being hurt?

Could she do the same? Fear lanced through her brain as she again recalled Perry's betrayal when the Chilean marine police had sneaked in through the fog and caught them.

The blasting marine foghorn had jolted them awake from a nap. Naked, they had leaped to their feet and tried to cover their loot with an old tarp, frantically kicking the rest of it under the seats. But it was too late. Three skinny officers dressed in navy uniforms boarded their boat, shouting a high-pitched volley of foreign words.

"Americano?" one of them had asked, leering at her breasts. "You speak English?" he'd added in a thick accent. An officer spotted antique jewelry scattered on the deck and pointed. After a moment of incredulous silence, their voices rose in a chorus of excitement. The shortest policeman, who sported a long, twirling mustache, flung the tarp aside. All three dropped to their knees, picking up handfuls of expensive artifacts. She hoped they would take the loot for themselves and leave. But one of the officers returned to the patrol vessel to radio in the find.

Perry pointed a finger at Jet. "It's her!" he'd screamed, eyes wild with fear. "This is *her* boat and *her* stuff. The woman's a freaking mermaid."

Jet had stared at that pointing finger, transfixed at the betrayal.

"Mermaid?" The shortest officer asked, mustache twitching in confusion.

The three spoke rapidly to one another until Shorty beat a hand on his chest and said, *"Sí. Soy el Capitán Hook."*

Jet stood transfixed as they laughed. This was so not a Disney moment for her.

"Captain Hook, *comprendes?*"

"It's true," Perry insisted. "She really is a mermaid, and I can prove it. Capture her and you'll be rich!"

The officer beside Shorty, the one who had been leering at her breasts minutes earlier, pulled out a set of handcuffs.

No way in hell.

If Perry was bailing on her, exposing her secret, she had no choice. Jet had dived off the side of the boat. That long, long journey home had been more physically demanding than ten Poseidon Games races put together. She'd returned to Bayou La Siryna skinny and frail and exhausted and emotionally shattered.

"Here's your water."

Jet jumped at the sound of Landry's voice.

"What's wrong?" he asked, placing a warm hand at the back of her neck.

"Nothing. Just thinking," she said hastily as she sat, gesturing for Landry to join her. No need to dwell on Perry's miserable betrayal. What Landry had been through was so much worse. She opened the water bottle and started to take a sip when she recalled Tia's words. "The little girl who's trying to talk to you!" She grabbed his arm. "It's your sister, April. Right?"

"Maybe," he said with a frown. "I wanted to dismiss the old woman as a charlatan. Wanted to believe that she remembered the old news of my sister's death and used it to pretend she had secret knowledge."

"Why would she do that?"

"I've seen it several times in my career. Fake mediums who—for a price—will help families locate missing children or communicate with a dead loved one for clues on where to find their body or who murdered them."

"You said you *wanted* to think that," Jet noted. "Has something happened to make you believe Tia's telling the truth?"

Landry gave a rueful, one-sided smile. "More crazy stories. You up for it?"

She shook her head at the irony. If he knew he was sitting across from a shape-shifting mermaid… "Nothing would be too left-field for me," she said drily. "Trust me."

Landry stood and picked up something from the sideboard. "Ever seen this before?" he asked.

She squinted at the old red coin purse before also rising and taking it from him. "No," she said. "No offense. But it's nothing valuable." She ran a finger over patches of missing sequins and its scarred clasp. "Oh, did it belong to your sister?"

He took it from her hands and laid it gently back on the sideboard. "It was found on the grass by the tire swing. April carried it everywhere. She drew her initial on the inside and carried a lucky penny in it."

Some luck, poor kid. "Damn," she muttered. "I don't know why you think I've seen it before, though."

"Because it was in your shop a few days ago."

"Impossible."

Landry raised an eyebrow. "Exactly. For the past couple of weeks weird crap has escalated—broken clocks, electrical malfunctions, moved objects, even the scent of baby powder when there shouldn't be any."

"Those papers you touched," Jet said in wonder. "You went through some paperwork in the shop and after you left I smelled baby powder, too."

"April always smelled like talc. Mom put some in an old saltshaker and called it pixie dust. April hoped she'd attract fairies if she sprinkled it everywhere." A ghost of a smile crossed his face.

"You said everything's escalated since you came to Bayou La Siryna. Why now?" Jet asked softly.

"No clue. Creepy stuff happened before, but not as often or as strange."

"You can't dismiss it anymore. Let's find out what April wants."

The twisty back road grew narrower and Landry inwardly cursed. Even driving Jet's truck, the tires whirred ominously in the looser, less-compacted sand. Early-morning sunlight slipped through oak-tree limbs and Spanish moss that smacked and scraped against the truck. "Between the sand and the potholes, we're likely to get stranded out here in the boondocks," he said.

"Better hope not." Jet gave a casual shrug of her shoulders. "There's no cell-phone signal to get towed if we do."

"Terrific. You sure this is the right way? 'Cause I keep expecting to drive into a swamp at every bend in the road."

"I promise we won't end up as gator food. Shelly gave me exact directions."

This was a bad idea. Landry couldn't believe he'd let Jet convince him otherwise. For once, he'd been caught up in the moment and pushed his job aside. Jet's enthusiasm and his own curiosity had temporarily got the best of him. "I'm wasting time chasing ghosts when I should be working. I didn't tell you what I discovered earlier about Hammonds. He and—"

"There's the house," Jet interrupted.

Some house. The clapboard structure more resembled a shack with its tattered roof and dangling shutters. The headlights exposed a maze of potted plants and other assorted junk spread out front. Oh, well. He'd see what Tia had to say and then he and Jet would decide on a strategy before he called his supervisor today. Landry wanted to leave Jet out of everything as much as possible.

He pulled up close and hurried to open Jet's door. "Hold on to my arm so you don't trip. It's tricky with all this crap lying around."

"I can see fine. You don't need to…" She hesitated. "Okay, great."

He guided her through the maze of junk and up dilapidated porch steps. The door swung open with a screech of rusty hinges before he knocked.

Tia beamed at them. "I knew you two were a-coming this evening. Welcome."

Landry's eyes watered from a hit of burning incense as they entered the cramped, yet clean, den. Tia pointed to an old, battered sofa, where a cat napped on a lime-green afghan. "Have a seat."

The cat rose up, arched its back and glared at them resentfully, hissing at Jet before racing out of the room.

"Bad kitty," Tia said, clicking her tongue. "But he powerful good company on a lonely night."

A card table was set up by the sofa. Candles burned at all four corners and a strange game board with symbols and letters lay open.

"What's all this stuff?" he asked as they sat down, Tia across from them.

"The Ouija board. Spirits tells me most of what I need to know through it."

By the looks of her shabby abode, Tia should be asking the spirits for winning lottery numbers.

Jet squeezed his hand. *Open mind,* she mouthed at him while Tia Henrietta shuffled a deck of cards.

"The tarot cards fill in details the spritis may not have or don't want to tell." Tia held out a wrinkled hand, palm up. "Give me April's purse."

Landry's breath caught and the room went fuzzy. He turned to Jet and his vision righted as he watched her pull it from her backpack. She'd been right in thinking to bring it; Tia wanted to touch an object that had belonged to April.

Tia laid the purse on the table. "I just needs to get me a few more details," she said, spreading out a row of colorful cards with pictures of dragons and angels and other fantasy images. "Mmm-hmm, that's what I thought," she mumbled. Tia closed her eyes and hummed, a deep, guttural sound that vibrated the flimsy table.

Landry clenched his jaw to hold back a snicker. The medium act was as hokey as he feared. This woman knew nothing of April other than what she'd heard of the murder years ago. Another minute and he was walking out. This was ludicrous, a travesty, a—

Tia opened her rheumy eyes, the grayish film a shroud over the too-perceptive stare. "I have a message from your sister," she announced in a deep, dark voice that was surprisingly vibrant for a woman of her advanced years. "But first—" Tia fixed her gaze on Jet "—you must leave."

Jet pasted on a smile and stood. "I can take a hint. I'll go sit on the porch."

"Sorry, this won't take long," he promised.

Tia said nothing more until the front door closed behind Jet. "April's skipping for joy she finally got yer attention."

He threw up his hands. "I have no choice but to concede that she's nearby. Too much has happened."

Tia tilted her head to the side as if hearing a voice. "She says you weren't this way when you were both young'uns. Says you both used to try and sneak up on fairies in the garden."

A faraway memory tickled his consciousness. The two of them playing outside, the sun shining on her golden hair, the same shade as his own. Carefree, happy days before everything changed. "Is she—okay?" he asked. Stupid question. April was dead.

"Oh, she's just fine. Don't you worry about her," Tia said. "Your little sister be prancin' about with the angels. Mimi watches over her, as well."

He'd never given much thought to his sister's afterlife. Could only imagine April's last minutes on earth ending in terror and pain. Preventing the same crime from victimizing others was the sole reason he'd become an FBI agent and worked crazy hours every week.

"Forget that last day," Tia said sharply, either reading his thoughts or guessing them. "'Twas a long time ago. That's why she's here. To tell you to move on. She sees the bitter, rigid man whose heart and mind are closed to love and magic."

"I'm not—" He wanted to deny it, but couldn't. Landry cleared the lump in his throat. "Why now? Why after all these years is she communicating with me?"

"Because, way April sees it, you got a mighty big test comin' up. You either pass it or you're doomed to go through life lonely and empty-feelin'."

He tried to lighten the spooky miasma. "Doomed?" he asked, grinning.

Tia's face grew sterner. "Doomed," she repeated.

"I want more details. What test? When will it occur?"

"April says that's just like you to starting cutting straight for the facts." Tia gave a throaty chuckle and handed him the coin purse. "Magic don't work like that." She blew out the candles and rose.

Landry stood also. "That's it? Will April still hang around?"

"She's always around her big brother." Tia moved toward the door, dismissing him.

"I've been an agent for years. Can't expect me to just change," he muttered, digging out his wallet.

"There's plenty things to investigate besides violent crimes round this bayou. Weirdness you ain't never dreamt of," Tia said with a mysterious smile.

Landry slapped a handful of twenty-dollar bills on the table. From the looks of things, Tia Henrietta could use the money. Outside on the porch, Jet stood and gave him a questioning glance. He gulped in the fresh, briny air, his lungs grateful at the change from the smoky interior.

"Everything okay?" Jet asked.

"Fine." In his haste to get away, he forgot to dodge the junk in the yard and stumbled over a collection of conch shells. Damn, no, he wasn't okay. He wasn't sure how he felt about this visit—confused, relieved, intrigued, curious, uncomfortable, but no longer a skeptic. He started the truck and they began the tortuous path out. Driving, even in these conditions, was a familiar, safe distraction.

"Tell me what happened," Jet said. "Did she know why April's trying to get your attention?"

Landry shot her a sideways glance, took in her bright eyes and pale, gleaming skin. Love and magic? He needed time to mull over the evening and process the information. It was too new, too strange. Jet had shaken up his world, made him question his beliefs, forced him to remember the past and the young child who'd been gifted sea treasure and had been saved in a storm by an unknown *something*.

He shrugged, reluctant to share all that Tia Henrietta had mentioned. "Tia said the usual occult things. April is on The Other Side and doing fine. And there's some kind of test or trial coming up soon."

"That's it? No startling world-shaking information?"

He grinned at Jet's disappointment. "I wasn't expecting any. This isn't my first go-round with a medium. We get them all the time at the agency, volunteering their services when news of an unsolved crime gets lots of media attention."

"Don't you believe April's spirit is here with you?"

"I do," he said promptly.

"That's a start," she muttered.

"Start of what?"

"Oh, nothing." Jet looked out the window, avoiding his eyes.

They rode on in silence. A few miles from his cottage, Jet spoke again. "Before we left for Tia's, you said we needed to talk. What gives?"

He frowned, berating himself for losing focus on his job, even if it was for a short length of time. The most important thing for now was to solve this case and keep Jet from danger. Afterward, he could consider April's message.

She raised an eyebrow. "You look as serious as you did when you interrogated me about my tax records." Jet gave a teasing smile. "Should I call my attorney? Am I in trouble?"

He didn't crack a smile. "If you're talking about a few petty, past legal violations in the salvage business, the answer is no. None of that matters. But you are in danger. I've found a connection that directly ties Hammonds with Vargas and the missing hydrogen bomb at Tybee Island. I need your help to stop them."

Chapter 12

It had been hard convincing Landry to let her leave yesterday. What with the annual family reunion and setting up the new business, Jet had no time to be sequestered away from home. Landry worried Perry would whisk her away before he had a chance to prove his case and arrest Hammonds. In the end, she'd persuaded Landry that carrying on as usual would keep anyone from suspecting they were onto their possible plan to retrieve the missing bomb.

Today her place was overrun with Bosarge women. Everyone had returned from the Games for their family reunion, always held after the Poseidon Games to celebrate their victories and spend time together. Mom, Shelly, Lily and a couple of the older cousins lounged in the den while the younger cousins roamed the house, exploring treasure crammed in every bureau drawer from generations of Bosarge hoarders.

Jet took a swig from her water bottle, surveying the den awash with golden hair and luminous, pearlescent skin. All the women wore pastel sundresses with long strands of pearls and abalone-shell earrings. Mother-of-pearl bracelets jingled as each sipped water from delicate antique teacups. Each had model-lovely hands, gracefully holding their cups, opal rings glittering to advantage.

It was like being dropped into a living advertisement for *Town & Country*. Jet stretched out her bare, unpedi-cured feet and inwardly sighed. She wore cutoff jeans and a crimson-colored University of Alabama T-shirt. Her only jewelry was a pair of stud ruby earrings and the golden trident necklace.

"You should have heard Lily sing. I declare, she's more mesmerizing every year." Adriana Bosarge beamed at her youngest daughter. "The other mermaids didn't stand a chance." Her cobalt eyes settled on Jet. "Darling, couldn't you have stayed another couple of hours at the Games to watch your sister? You're always in such a rush."

"I had Orpheous on my tail. Literally."

Mom raised her chin and waved a hand dismissively. "As long as you were with us, in the crowd, no harm would have come to you."

Lily laughed, trilling delicate whimsical notes that made everyone around her involuntarily smile. Except Jet.

"Yes, you should have stayed," Lily said, suppressing a giggle. "The Blue Merman was besotted with you."

Jet shrugged. "Not after he heard you sing."

"That's true." Lily patted the lavender folds of her dress. "I don't think you need worry about him chasing after you for a long time. When we left, he was muttering something about taking you down next year."

Shelly caught Jet's eye and gave her a knowing nod of sympathy. She pointed to Jet's pendant. "Isn't it awesome that Jet won the Undines' Challenge?"

Lula Belle, a great-aunt, set down her teacup, pulled an old-fashioned opera glass up to her faded blue eyes and squinted at the necklace. "I see you haven't used your wish yet."

Jet stared at her mother across the room. "No. But I know exactly what I want to use it for."

Lily hopped up and spun in the center of the room. "Look what I got for winning the Siren's Song again." She held out a conch shell made of solid eighteen-karat gold with diamond dust glittering in its folds.

As everyone oohed and aahed, Jet crossed her arms and watched them cluster around Lily. She had never felt so distant, so left out from her family. No matter what she accomplished, it was never as good as what came naturally to Lily. She didn't fit in. Why, why, *why?*

Jet's cell phone pinged and she checked her messages. Landry had called three times already today, as had Perry. She skimmed Perry's messages, each increasingly desperate for her to meet him, but focused on the last one from Landry.

Did you read my earlier texts? I was called in to the Mobile office today and will return this evening. Respond so I know you're okay.

Jet quickly scanned Landry's previous texts, filled with warnings to stay hidden from Perry while he made the entrapment arrangements they had agreed upon yesterday. Worrywart. If Perry caused her any trouble, she could flip him and throw him to the ground in a second, and well Perry knew it.

A whiff of amber mixed with coriander tickled her nose. Adriana settled into the chair beside her. "What's got you scowling? Trouble already with your new boyfriend?"

"I see you've been talking with Shelly. I wouldn't call Landry my boyfriend yet." Jet turned off her phone.

Worry clouded her mom's face. "Shelly also told me that worthless Perry Hammonds is in the bayou again. Please tell me you aren't entertaining going back into business with the jerk."

"Of course I won't."

Adriana patted her arm, as if Jet was still a five-year-old. "Good girl."

"Mom, we need to talk."

A slight veil shuttered the brightness of her irises. "Maybe later. We're all exhausted from our trip right now." She arose and yawned delicately. "I'm going to take a little nap."

Typical evasive move, but this time Jet wasn't giving up. She waited a good five minutes after Adriana left and then headed upstairs.

Portraits hung on the landing, depicting generations of Bosarge women. Their eyes seemed to follow her movements, like a galley of creepy *Mona Lisa*s. They might as well have been painted with an index finger pressed against their full, luscious lips, a warning to all mermaids to guard their secrets.

Jet studied them in a new light. Interspersed among the blue-eyed blondes were a couple of redheads and a chestnut-haired beauty with kiwi-green eyes. Not a black-haired, brown-eyed one in the bunch.

She rapped softly on the guest-room door before sticking her head in. "Mom?"

Adriana sat up in bed and sighed. "I can tell by the determined gleam in your eye you want to have *that* conversation again."

"Da—" Jet clamped her mouth shut. No need for vulgarity and a lecture from Mom. "Right." She sat next to Adriana. "I can't help feeling there's something you're not telling me. I'm so different from Lily and every other blue-eyed blonde in our family." Jet paused. "Why is that?"

Mom wouldn't quite meet her eyes. "We don't all have

the same eyes and hair color," she argued. "Some have green eyes like Shelly, and I have a great-niece with hair the color of red algae. And remember your aunt Melusina? Her hair was a lovely shade of turquoise."

"I'm not just talking physical appearance. I'm not like any of you. I have no siren skills and I'm freakishly stronger than any other mermaid I've ever met." Jet got up and paced. "Besides, whenever I'm at the Games or around other merfolk, something about the way they look at me and whisper behind their hands, it makes me think something must be terribly wrong with me."

Adriana stoically crossed her arms. "Nonsense."

You are one of us. Orpheous's words ran in her brain like an endlessly looping tape cassette.

Jet tried again. "I've told you before. If I have a different father than Lily, I'm cool with it. I've only seen Dad a few times in my life. He takes no notice of me. I won't be upset if someone else is my father."

Mermen were notoriously neglectful fathers. Mermaids outnumbered the male species of their race almost five to one. As a consequence, mermen recklessly impregnated mermaids and swam on their merry way to the next conquest.

Her mother frowned. "We've been over this a hundred times. If anyone is judgmental toward you, it's because of all the treasure you've taken."

She didn't expect that. Merfolk were taught as children that what fell to the sea belonged to its own. "What do you mean? Everybody does it."

"Not to the extent you have. Not only did you take huge quantities of valuable artifacts, but you did it for Perry's profit. It's not like you needed the money. And if we all did that, there would be nothing left before long. Even worse, it was obvious you'd told him our mermaid secret."

The heavy censure in her voice made Jet inwardly wince, but she wouldn't back down. There had to be more to it. "I'm out of that business now, have been for years."

"Merfolk have long memories," Mom insisted.

"You leave me no choice." Jet unclasped her necklace and held the trident pendant in her palm. "My wish—"

"Stop." Adriana put up a hand. "Don't squander your wish."

"Then tell me the truth."

"There's nothing to tell," her mom said harshly. "Why must you always be so obstinate?"

"By trident's power, my wish is to know the secret of my heritage." There. She'd said it. No mermaid could deny such a request—or else risk merfolk shunning them for being disrespectful of one of their oldest customs.

The pendant floated three inches above Jet's palm. Mother and daughter watched as it glowed red-hot like lava before disintegrating to ash and drifting down to the hardwood floor.

Adriana slowly sank down on the mattress, eyes on the far wall. "I wish you hadn't done that."

But her words held no power. Jet sat beside her and waited. At last, Adriana faced her with distressed eyes Jet had never seen before. It was even worse than when Mom had told them that Shelly's parents had died. Jet laid a hand over her mom's. "Whatever it is, I can handle it. It's time."

"I promised never to tell," she whispered. "Forgive me, Waverly."

Jet raised her brows in surprise. Her aunt, Adriana's sister, had died in childbirth before she was ever born and Mom rarely mentioned her name.

"Waverly was your biological mother," Adriana admitted. "My deathbed promise to her was to raise you as my own."

No wonder she never measured up to Lily, the true daughter. "Okay. But why the secrecy all these years? I don't understand."

"Waverly didn't want you to know about your father."

A premonition of what was to come flooded her senses as she remembered Orpheous's blue lips grinning and asking, *Ever suspect you are one of us?* Jet groaned. "He was one of the Blue Merman of Minch, wasn't he?"

Adriana nodded.

Jet crinkled her nose. "How could she fall in love with one of those crude thugs?"

"She didn't."

"Then how—" Jet paused, appalled at the possibilities.

"Pelagia, your biological father, forced his will on her." Adrianna rose and walked to the window. "Waverly sneaked away from our family one evening during the Games and swam alone. Pelagia found her and took advantage of the situation."

Disgust and horror roiled in Jet's stomach. Poor Waverly. "I was unwanted and she died giving birth. I see why you didn't tell me," she said past the sore tightness in her throat.

"There was no reason for you to ever find out." Adriana came back to the bed and sat. "You shouldn't have made me tell you. We kept it secret from everyone."

"Sorry, I'm not doing this to hurt you." Jet bit her lip and pressed on. "Deny it all you want, but other mermaids must know about my parents, too, because I've felt their distance all my life. Ugly secrets have a way of spilling out no matter how you try to hide them." A sudden thought struck Jet. "Is that why we always spent so much time in Bayou La Siryna growing up? You wanted to isolate me in case someone told."

"I wanted to protect you," Adriana corrected. "And honor my sister's deathbed request."

Chill bumps ran along Jet's arms and legs. She'd hoped— She wasn't sure exactly what she'd hoped. Perhaps that her mom would reveal some truth she could understand or correct and make things right with her own kind. But there was no getting past this.

"That's why I have such a temper," Jet muttered. "Why I'm so strong and impatient and untalented and ugly. I'm like my horrible father. The other mermaids will never accept me."

"Stop it." Adriana's crisp retort surprised Jet. "You are who you are. Ever consider the possibility that your prickly personality is to blame? You don't make it easy for others to approach you."

So much for sympathy and understanding. "Wrong. It's my dark looks. They see me and think I'm part of the Blue Clan. Even though we're all merfolk, it's something they can't get past." Little wonder, given that the Blue Clan, particularly the males, were so bloodthirsty and selfish.

"It's more about your treasure hunting than your heritage at this point. You've been reckless and irresponsible about our need for secrecy."

Jet started to deny it, but clamped her mouth shut. They were right. How selfish she'd been, all in a losing effort to try to win Perry's love. Pathetic. If she were one of them, she'd probably feel the same.

She thought of her unknown mother. She'd have to hunt through some old photo albums later and look more closely at the woman she'd always thought of as an aunt. "Who named me?" she asked suddenly.

"Waverly."

A stab of disappointment squeezed her chest. "Why

did she pick Jet? It's cheap and common fossil fuel. Not exactly attributes one wants in a name."

Adriana threw her hands up in the air. "Beats me. Waverly did love collecting Victorian jewelry. Jet was quite popular in that era." She rose from the bed and fiddled with the chunk of amethyst bracelets on her right wrist. "I hope you're satisfied with the answer you forced me into giving. I may not be your biological mother, but I did the best I could."

Jet's throat constricted. "You did fine." She could have done a whole lot worse with a different guardian. True, she played second fiddle to Lily, but Adriana—whom she would always consider Mom—cared for her in her own way.

Adriana patted her shoulder. "Glad that's over with. I think I'll go rejoin the party." She went to the door and paused, hand on the knob. "Shelly's filled me in on you and Landry. We're hopeful Perry will leave and never come back."

"Not as much as I do. But I'm worried because he knows our secret. What if he exposes us?"

"No one will believe him. He has no proof mermaids exist. Just make sure it stays that way. And if the very worst happens, leave the bayou and stay undersea with us."

"Bet the merfolk would love that," Jet muttered.

Adriana left, shutting the door quietly.

Jet opened a nightstand drawer and retrieved an old family photo album. She flipped through until she found Aunt Waverly—*Mom*—standing on a beach with her three sisters, their arms encircling one another's waists.

"I promise I'll try to be a better mermaid," Jet whispered, running a finger over her mother's image.

She was a beauty, as blonde and blue-eyed as her sisters. Jet could find no physical resemblance between them.

Her mother's fairness only diluted the dark coloring from the paternal side. At least she could be thankful that the distinctive blue skin was a recessive trait.

She flopped down on the bed and covered her eyes with an arm. Didn't she owe it to her family and to herself to find her place in the world? Shelly had done so. But as a TRAB, Shelly's choices had been more limited. Merfolk acceptance was out of the question, and even if they did welcome Shelly, her cousin wasn't biologically suited for long periods undersea. Shelly's choice had been whether or not to reveal her mermaid side to her true love.

If she could have anything she wanted... Jet pictured living at sea and overcoming the problem of merfolk acceptance there. Adriana seemed so sure it could be resolved despite her Blue Clan paternity. Last night she'd even overheard Mom and the rest of the family discuss what amounted to a campaign for her reputation undersea. They'd inform the merfolk that she'd dumped Perry for good and had donated huge amounts of money to various ocean causes. Lily had insisted that the timing for this to work was now while the merfolk remembered her victory in the Undines' Challenge. Jet had snorted and almost given away her presence. The merfolk hadn't seemed too impressed by the feat that she could tell. If her own kind gave her any chance for hope, it would mainly be because of Lily's popularity and the long-respected Bosarge name.

What about Landry? Bet he wouldn't care about a supposedly tainted heritage. Jet pushed aside the question, unwilling to examine her feelings too closely. She'd trained tirelessly over a year for the Poseidon Games in order to discover why she'd grown up living like an exile. Now that she possessed the truth, she felt unsettled, unmoored, adrift with dashed hopes and purposes.

* * *

Landry's fist was raised to knock again on Jet's door when it was suddenly yanked open by a trio of young girls.

"Who are you?" the littlest asked, grinning at him with open curiosity. Another smiled in delight and proclaimed, "You're handsome!" The middle girl giggled and continued licking an orange Popsicle, which was melting and splattered on her yellow sundress.

"Girls," a sharp voice rang out, "I told you to let me get the door." An older lady with arctic-white hair appeared, blinking at him myopically before pulling some kind of old magnifying glasses to her eyes. Enlarged, rainbow-colored irises scrutinized him from head to toe. She let the glasses down. "Are you Landry Fields?"

"Yes, ma'am. And you?"

"Lula Belle Bosarge, great-aunt to your Jet. Come in. I needed to make sure it wasn't that abominable Perry Hammonds come calling again."

Landry stepped into the den, eyes widening at the sight of half a dozen stunning ladies lounging about in light-colored dresses. They looked so much alike with their long, blond hair and graceful figures that he had no doubt they were all intimately related. He searched amid the sea of pastels, honing in on Jet, dark hair and eyes gleaming like a beacon. She gave a bemused smile, as if guessing his thoughts.

He started forward, aware of his audience.

One of the young lovelies arose from the sofa and planted herself in front of him. "I'm Lily, Jet's sister."

He nodded and looked over her shoulder. "A pleasure."

Lily didn't move. "I've heard so much about you." She held out a hand.

He shook her hand quickly and let go. Her voice had a reverberating, musical quality that made him uncomfortable. Despite her bland smile, her eyes had a sly cast. Maybe *sly* was unfair, considering he'd just met her. The kinder word would be…*mysterious*.

"Let him through," Jet said.

Jet's voice, on the other hand, was low, throaty and sexy as hell.

Unexpectedly, Lily began to hum. Was the woman not quite right? She drifted to the piano and idly plucked a few keys, humming louder. A buzzing started at the back of Landry's head, a creeping numbing that felt as if he was being hypnotized. Lily's humming vibrated deep inside, consuming his will so that his only desire was to hear more and…

"Enough, Lily," one of the women cut in sharply.

The buzzing in his brain ceased abruptly and he shook his head. Jet came to his side and introduced him to everyone. He nodded politely, eager to get her alone. "Can we talk somewhere in private?" he murmured in her ear.

She guided him through a dining room and onto a screened-in back porch. They sat next to each other on a metal glider loaded with frilly cushions and pillows. Jet hugged a pink floral pillow to her stomach and leaned forward, eyes closed.

"You might not want to kiss me when I tell you what I've planned," Landry said drily.

Her dark eyes opened and she quirked an eyebrow. "Well?"

Landry stood and paced the long, rectangular room. "That connection I found was between the H-bomb copilot's grandson and Sylvester Vargas. We've been after Vargas a long time. He's behind countless illegal operations here and all over the world. The man uses his wealth to bribe and influence others. He and his men have murdered dozens of people over the years. They'll stop at nothing to get what they want. I called my supervisors in Mobile, who agreed that the next step is coaxing information from the low man in the operation."

"I know, and that would be Perry. I told you I'd help."

"Great. We think—"

"—that I can get him talking," Jet supplied. "I'll do it. I want him out of my life as much as the FBI wants to nail Vargas."

He sat down beside her. "Are you sure? I wouldn't put you through it if I didn't think it was the quickest, safest way to resolve the case." Damn Hammonds for drawing Jet into this dangerous situation. He couldn't rest easy until this was over and she was no longer at risk. "Okay, then. Call Perry and set up a time tomorrow to meet in a public place. I'll have you wired and prep you with a list of questions to ask. I promise I won't put you in any danger. I'll be close by."

"Perry doesn't scare me a bit."

"If he doesn't, then Vargas should," Landry warned. "I'm going to notify the local sheriff what we're doing so that—"

"No! Don't tell Tillman." For the first time, Jet looked alarmed.

"I'm confused. He's practically your family. I thought you liked him."

"I do. It's his deputy that worries me."

"Why?"

Jet sighed deeply. "Because Carl Dismukes is a dirty cop. He blackmailed Perry and me almost the whole time we treasure hunted. Not that we did anything wrong." She squirmed a bit in her seat. "But we didn't want him to bring unwelcome attention to us, either."

His brows drew together. "And Tillman didn't fire him?"

"Tillman doesn't know."

"Then tell him. Or I will. We can't have this Dismukes jeopardize our case."

Jet hesitated. "Let's have Tillman sworn to secrecy. Tell him the feds don't want anyone else local to know about it."

He sighed. "I don't like it. But I suppose that could work." Once this case was over, he'd get to the bottom of why Jet was protecting Dismukes. Right now, he had enough to deal with besides a local crooked cop.

The sound of a piano and singing drifted from inside the house. For some reason, the sound seemed to annoy Jet. "That's Lily," she muttered with a scowl.

"Your sister has a nice voice."

"Nice?" She gave a disbelieving laugh. "*Nice* is for a glass of iced tea in the summer heat. Lily's voice is *spectacular.*"

He cocked his head to the side, listening. "She's good, but I prefer a low alto. Like yours."

Her mouth widened in astonishment. "You're kidding, right?"

"Self-confidence issues?" He chuckled. "Never would have thought that of you."

Her lips twisted wryly. "You've seen my family, the golden ones. I'm the drab flotsam floating among pristine, pure waters."

"More like a black diamond glittering in a sandy stretch of blandness." He felt heat rising at the back of his neck. Hell, he wasn't normally one for flowery words.

Jet's mouth dropped open and he was rewarded with a smile that made the embarrassment worth suffering through. "I'm hardly a diamond," she protested. "You know that jet is a kind of coal, right? Lucky me, named after a lump of fossil fuel."

He tenderly ran a finger down her cheek. "When coal is heated and emerges from tribulation, a diamond is born."

The dark eyes lit with a wonder and happiness he hadn't seen on her face before. "I've been through enough heat and tribulation the last couple weeks to last me forever," she said ruefully, deflecting the compliment.

Surely he wasn't the only man to ever comment on her striking appearance. Landry shifted uncomfortably. "You know you're attractive. You must have had men falling over you all your life."

She launched herself at him, kissing him passionately. He chuckled in surprise. How he'd missed her when she'd left, had fantasized about her back in his bed. Landry returned the kiss, pulling her body closer.

A burst of giggles sounded. He broke apart from the kiss to see the little girls pointing and laughing. He sighed and stood up. "We have an audience again."

Jet shooed them away and stood also.

"Come back home with me tonight," he whispered urgently.

"I can't," she groaned. "Our family is having this huge wingding tonight with Tillman and his family. My relatives live far away and might not be able to travel to their wedding later this summer. This dinner is a chance for everyone to get to know each other better."

"Oh, a reunion? So that's why you have a full house."

They drew close together, foreheads touching, their breathing rapid and shallow.

"I'll slip away when I can, but it will be awfully late."

"I'll be waiting for you," he promised.

Chapter 13

Perry lowered the binoculars and kicked the side of the boat. He'd seen the little girls and that dragon-lady great-aunt of Jet's when they had opened the door for Fields. Looked as if the whole damned house was full of folks, and not an extra car in the driveway. He'd bugged Jet for years about where she came and went when shape-shifting at home, but on that subject her lips were sealed.

He stroked the stubble growing on his chin, deep in thought. Likely every one of those mermaid freaks was strong like Jet and possibly armed. Her family had always despised him. But the little kids wouldn't feel that way; and he didn't recall meeting them before, so they wouldn't recognize who he was. If he grabbed one of those little girls, Jet would do anything to save her. He thoughtfully tapped the side of his face, weighing the pros and cons of this new idea.

No, there was too much risk. Kidnapping a kid would bring way too much publicity and attention to himself.

Damnation, he could see no way around the dilemma except to go with the plan that involved help from Vargas's henchmen. One way or the other, he had to deliver

Jet to Vargas. If only she'd cooperated from the beginning, none of this would have been necessary. They could have been rich together, but no, she'd evidently developed a conscience while he was away and preferred another man over him.

That rubbed him wrong most of all. He'd never—*ever*—been dumped. He was the one who called it quits in a relationship. He didn't love Jet, never had, but it still wasn't right. She deserved everything coming to her.

But the real pisser of it all was that now he might get scuffed up a bit in drawing Jet to Tybee Island. Bitch would pay dearly for that.

Time was up. Vargas had drawn a line in the sand about getting her immediately. Jet hadn't been at The Pirate's Chest for several days, but no matter. Most days Shelly and Seth were in there putting up inventory and preparing for the grand opening. All he had to do was make sure one of them witnessed his fake abduction.

"You're gonna get it now, you freaky bitch," he muttered, hands fisting at his sides. "Nobody dumps Perry Hammonds. Nobody. Especially a damn fish."

Jet sang loudly and off-key in the privacy of her truck, the only place she ever sang. By water nymph's beauty, she wouldn't expose her voice to ridicule at home, not even in the shower. Fingers tapping to the radio, she sped through the bayou darkness. She had hesitated driving over to Landry's; it was so late, she wasn't sure if he'd still be up. But she'd said she would. She'd go to his cottage and if there was a light on, she'd knock on his door. If not, she'd leave him a text message.

The dinner had run late. Anxious as she was to escape and be with Landry, Jet had stayed close to her family, savoring their time together before they again returned to the sea. Although once Landry arrested Perry, she'd be free to join them, if she chose. Easy enough to hire a manager for The Pirate's Chest after it opened for business. She could begin to try to work her way into merfolk acceptance by banking on her victory over Orpheous at the Games.

The thought didn't produce the customary jolt of hope and excitement it usually did.

Jet pulled her truck behind Landry's BMW, shut off the engine and took a deep breath. She would have to make a decision. Land or sea? Could Landry be the man for her?

All men are not like Perry. Some can actually be trusted. She closed her eyes and remembered the sweetness of their lovemaking and his compliments earlier in the day. And especially the way he had claimed to prefer her alto voice over Lily's. He might possibly be the only man on the planet who would do so.

A sharp rap on the passenger-side window made Jet jump. "Oh, it's you," she said in relief as she unlocked the door and Landry slid in beside her.

Up close, the half-moon shadows under his eyes betrayed a weary exhaustion. "Why are you up so late?"

He yawned and rubbed his hand over his face. "Because I was waiting on you. Besides, Seth didn't get home until thirty minutes ago."

"Is he okay?"

"Yeah. He's been having fun with Jimmy and his new friends."

"He should have called you."

"He did. But I couldn't sleep until he came in."

"You're going to miss him when he leaves."

He snickered. "Miss the kid? My house will be free of his mess and loud music. I'll sleep in peace again."

She didn't believe him for a minute. "Shouldn't we be

discussing Perry and the questions you want me to ask him?"

"I'd rather not be talking at all." Landry slid back the satin folds of her dress and placed a large palm on her thigh. "I've never seen you in a dress. It suits you." His hand slid farther up her leg. "Not to mention, it's so convenient."

The contact sent heat shivers into her core. "Got dressed up for the big dinner," she said, gasping. She moaned and arched against his hand as it cupped the curve of her womanhood.

"You're so hot, so damn sexy. The most beautiful woman I've ever seen."

"Really?" Jet's insides bubbled and fizzed with wonder. He'd seen the mesmerizing Lily and the rest of her astoundingly stunning relatives yet thought she more than equaled them in beauty. He saw something special in her that her own family did not.

"Really." Landry ground out the word as he slipped a finger past her swollen folds.

Fire. Heat enveloped her senses until her entire world centered on the hard knot of tension where Landry probed. It was bliss, but still not enough. Never enough. It could never be enough with Landry.

The realization only heightened her desire. Jet whimpered, needing more. Landry slipped in a second finger, gently stretching her insides. She moaned even louder, until he covered her mouth and explored it with his tongue. The intimacy of his tongue and fingers made her wild with need. Her body convulsed and she wrapped her arms around Landry's broad back, holding on. He was a steady anchor while she drowned in waves of passion. She never, ever wanted it to end.

But her body had other ideas. The quivering muscles

relaxed, leaving Jet in a euphoric lethargy. She ran a hand through the slightly curling ends of Landry's hair. "Wow," she whispered in his ear. Could he sense she was starting to fall in love? Her emotions ran as deep and strong as an ocean current. How could he not know?

Landry chuckled and fell back against the car seat. "Been a long time since I shared a passionate moment in a vehicle."

"But what about you?" She squeezed his hand, wanting to please him like he had her, wanting to demonstrate with her touch what she was afraid to voice aloud. "Shall we continue this inside?"

He put an arm over his forehead and groaned. "Seth's still up."

The tender moment was shattered. Jet hastily tugged down her dress. "I hadn't thought about that. Damn."

"Soon," Landry promised. He heaved a resigned sigh and abruptly pulled open the passenger door. "Let's go inside and I'll fix some coffee. We'll go over how to proceed with Hammonds."

"Whatever you say," she said lightly. She trusted Landry.

Chapter 14

"What time is your mom picking you up today?" Jet asked Seth. She fidgeted with an old charm bracelet, finding comfort in the smooth, cool texture of the glass beads. It was only ten o'clock in the morning. At this rate, she'd be a wreck before her lunch date with Perry. Landry and Tillman would have wasted their time with the wire setup.

Seth kept unpacking a box filled with conch shells and other nautical knickknacks. "Supposedly she'll get here by three," he answered, not looking up from his task.

He'd been working steadily for the past couple of hours and showed no signs of fatigue. The many perks of youth, Jet decided. Her days of staying up all night and working eight hours the next were over. While he was completely absorbed in his task, she pulled out a gift-wrapped package from under the counter.

"For you," she said, holding it out.

"Huh?" His eyes clouded in confusion. "What's this?"

"A little something to thank you for helping me set up shop. Figured your brother probably strong-armed you into working here, but I appreciate all you've done."

Seth opened it cautiously, as if he expected a snake

to pop out of a can. Clearly, he wasn't used to surprise gifts. Jet grinned when he opened the box and his mouth dropped open. He lifted the brass dagger out of its case and cradled it in his palm.

"You're *giving* me this?"

"Somehow I knew you'd like it," Jet teased. It was the same dagger Seth had admired the first day on the job and almost shoplifted.

"Wow. I, um, don't know what to say. Thanks, man."

Jet turned away and busied herself with the computer. "You're welcome." She was probably as embarrassed as he at emotional displays.

They continued working in companionable silence until Seth let out a disgruntled snort. "I can't believe this dude has the nerve to show up after what he did!"

Jet whipped around to see Perry getting out of his Mustang. He was two hours early. She'd called Perry last night, saying she'd meet him at noon by the mermaid statue downtown, that she had reconsidered the job at Tybee Island.

She wasn't ready for this encounter yet, emotionally or otherwise. The microphone Landry had given her this morning was still in her pocketbook, and Landry and Tillman wouldn't be listening in so early even if she put it on.

Perry Hammonds was never early for anything. Either he was suspicious of her sudden change of heart, or he was so desperate for money that he wanted to leave immediately. She hoped it was the latter.

"Don't worry, I'll get rid of him for you," Seth said at her dismayed expression.

"No, don't do that. We were meeting for lunch today. He's just way early."

Seth narrowed his eyes. "Does Landry know about this?"

Does he ever, Jet wanted to say. She leaped off the stool and grabbed her pocketbook. "Tell him I'll be out in a few minutes." At Seth's closed arms and downturned mouth, she added, "Landry knows about lunch. It's okay." Last thing she needed was for Seth to run Perry off before she could get answers.

Jet raced to the bathroom. Maybe it was better this way. She'd get it over with a little earlier than planned. She pulled out the microphone clip and pinned it to her bra strap, hands shaking so badly it took four tries before she was satisfied she'd done it right. She texted Landry about the early change of events and dumped the phone back in her purse.

Jet took several deep breaths and surveyed her image in the mirror, checking to ensure the microphone was hidden. Her button-down shirt had been selected because she figured it would cover a lump better than a smooth T-shirt could. She touched the empty spot in her cleavage where the trident pendant had rested for only two weeks. Damn, she could use it about now. Jet tilted her head to the side and tapped a finger to her lips. No, she'd done the right thing using the one wish to discover her true heritage. Perry was manageable, or at least he had been in the past.

Jet nodded grimly at her reflection and stiffened her spine. She had a job to do and she wouldn't disappoint Landry. One last check of her cell phone—no message yet from Landry—and Jet sailed back into the store. Perry and Seth were silent, regarding one another with wary hostility.

"Why so early?" she asked. "Did you miss breakfast this morning?"

"I couldn't wait any longer to see you. I was so glad you called me last night." Perry gave his easy, signature grin, stuffing his hands into a pair of expensive black trousers. His silk shirt was a vivid shade of salmon, a color most men couldn't pull off. But Perry's confidence and bohemian style suited almost any look. His teeth flashed a brilliant white against his olive skin. He'd evidently been working on a tan the past few days. That seemed to be the only job he was interested in pursuing, besides the Tybee Island expedition. Even so, Perry's role had always been nominal during their treasure hunts.

Could this man she once thought she loved really be involved in such an unsavory deal with a man like Vargas? Perhaps he didn't realize the true treasure off the Georgia coast was something altogether different than their shipwreck-salvage ventures. And if he knew the truth, did Perry care? Despite the check she'd written, he appeared desperate for this last deal.

"You're looking hot today," he said, giving her a sensual once-over scan from toes to scalp.

If Perry thought he could win her over with his lame come-ons, he wasn't as bright as she remembered.

"That's what my half brother always says," Seth piped up from behind the front counter. "And Jet's probably not hungry at all. They ate a huge breakfast at our cottage this morning."

Some of Perry's insouciant smile dimmed. "She's with me now."

"Excuse me," Jet butted in crisply. "I'm game for an early lunch."

"You always did have a huge appetite." Perry gave Seth a significant look. "After all these years, I know my girl."

"I'm not your— Oh, never mind. Let's go." She pushed past Perry and exited the front door. The Alabama heat hit her like a wall of fire. "I'm not even walking two blocks. Let's take your car."

"Um, sure."

The subtle hesitation in his voice drew her up in surprise. Jet spun around and caught him looking up and down both sides of the street as if afraid of an unknown danger lurking in the small-town streets of Bayou La Siryna.

"What's wrong?"

"Nothing." He pasted on a smile that didn't reach his eyes. "The Sea Basket diner, right?" He placed a hand on the small of her back and guided her to the Mustang. "Where you'll order your usual shrimp platter." He opened the door and pointed at the car's interior with a flourish. "Your carriage awaits, princess."

Jet placed one foot inside the Mustang and hesitated. He wouldn't do something as foolish as kidnap her, would he? And even if he did, she was wired. Jet settled into the seat and waited for Perry to shut the door before discreetly turning the microphone on and checking her cell phone. Still no word from Landry. Damn.

The loud noise of grinding brakes startled Jet and she dropped the phone back into her purse. A black SUV stopped in the middle of traffic and two unsmiling, muscle-bound men jumped out of the driver and passenger doors. Both wore black polo shirts and were nearly identical but for the ornate sleeve tattoos covering one's arms. They left the doors ajar and headed straight to Perry.

Jet put a hand on her chest, her mind racing with possibilities. Bill collectors? No, these men were too forceful for that. Repo men? Maybe they were going to wrestle away Perry's car keys and take it for nonpayment.

If Perry hadn't paid his bills, he totally deserved to have it repossessed. But Jet knew how much he loved the Mustang—which was probably more than any affection he carried for a real person. Still, she could work out a deal with these men. It wasn't as if she didn't have a ton of money. She'd try to negotiate with Perry—if she paid off his car, he'd give up the Tybee Island deal. That way, maybe Perry could escape from the whole dangerous mess he'd gotten into and walk away unscathed.

The men surrounded Perry and grabbed his arms. A flash of metal glimmered from the exposed waist of one of the men.

A gun? Really? Jet's hand froze on the door handle. These men might work for Vargas. Perry must have angered them somehow and now he was in deep shit. Jet broke out of her paralysis and opened the car door. "Leave him alone," she yelled, charging forward.

Neither man spared her a glance. The one closest to Jet pumped his meaty fist into Perry's stomach with a casual violence that stunned her. She watched, appalled as Perry doubled over and stumbled. The oaf on the other side fisted Perry under his chin and he straightened, wobbling from the blow. Perry surely would have fallen if the two goons weren't gripping his arms. Bright red blood gushed from a cut under his chin and sprinkled the silk coral shirt. *At least he's not wearing his white Don Johnson suit today,* Jet thought, shaking her head to clear the hysterical rambling of her brain.

Reaching one of the men, she wrapped both her hands around the steel band on the biceps of his free arm, yanked as hard as she could and pulled him off Perry. At last she had his attention.

"What the hell?" he sputtered, bushy eyebrows knitting together. "How did you—"

She ignored him, intent on freeing Perry from the other man. Perry's eyes rolled, so that three-quarters of his eyes were white, the chocolate-brown irises hidden behind his upper eyelids. She heard shouts of "police" and car doors slammed as traffic came to a halt. A crowd gathered.

Her hands wrapped around the other goon's arm and pulled, but it was no use. The unmistakable feel of a gun indented the bottom of her back where spine met tail-bone. "There's a crowd. Let's move it," said a guttural voice from behind, the Yankee accent clearly out of place in the bayou. Definitely not local repo men, a tiny part of her brain noted.

The gun was removed from her back and the world tilted as Jet was thrown to the ground. Hot asphalt scraped her knees raw. Bleeding and stunned, she watched the two shove Perry into the backseat of the black SUV. She couldn't see Perry's face through the dark tinted window. The men moved surprisingly fast considering their Atlas-size bodies, maneuvering into the SUV and slamming the doors shut behind them. The vehicle lurched forward, scattering the gaping spectators. It sped off like a mechanical demon returning to the furies of hell.

No license plates, of course.

"Are you okay?" Seth crouched in front of her field of vision, waving a cell phone. "I already called my brother."

A surge of relief flooded her body. "First time you haven't called Landry your half brother," she said, rising to her feet.

Seth raised his brows, an expression so similar to Landry's it made Jet smile. "After what happened, that's all you've got to say?" he asked incredulously.

"Landry will find Perry."

"How can you be so sure?"

"Because he knows where to start the hunt." Jet scooped up the microphone, which had fallen to the pavement during the scuffle. At least the brazen kidnapping would bring down the full attention of state and federal forces like nothing else could have done.

Seth shook his head. "I still don't like the guy but I feel sorry for him. He got sucker punched something awful."

* * *

Pain. So much pain. Those assholes didn't have to rough him up that much to make the kidnapping convincing. They did it for the sheer pleasure of torturing another person. Perry cradled his stomach and wondered if he'd sustained permanent internal injury. Hopefully, it was nothing more than a bruised kidney or spleen or something unimportant like that. At first, he'd thought his jaw was broken, too, but that pain had subsided after a few hours and he was able to swig beer and talk without too much discomfort. His expensive shirt and trousers, however, were ruined beyond repair.

Perry scowled, finally consoling himself that once the job was finished, he could walk into any upscale men's clothier and order a closetful of shirts and suits.

"I don't see why we didn't just take her instead of *him*," the big goon said to Vargas, nodding at Perry. "She would have offered more resistance. That woman is a spitfire."

"She shrugged you off like you weren't nothin' but a seventh-grade science geek," the other guy laughed.

Vargas held up a hand. "Jet Bosarge would attract too much attention. Better to draw her in so she comes voluntarily. Her damn brother-in-law is a sheriff and her new boyfriend's an FBI agent."

"What?" Perry's mouth hung open. "I thought Fields was an IRS auditor."

Vargas puffed a stinky cigar he claimed was Cuban and cost over a hundred of dollars. "Wrong. Let's hope your old girlfriend has some tender feelings left for you. Enough to follow you here to Tybee Island." His eyes narrowed so much they glittered like snake slits. "The deal was for you to deliver the girl."

Perry swallowed an angry retort. "Jet will come," he

answered with more confidence than he felt. "We have a history."

Vargas exhaled a plume of smoke into Perry's face. "If she doesn't, I'm throwing you to the sharks, so to speak."

His two hoodlums grinned inanely and one of them cracked his knuckles, evidently anticipating a longer session of fun mutilating his body. What the hell had he gotten himself into? Frissons of ice traveled his spine. For the first time, he felt the chill of fear. He was in over his head. This Tybee Island thing was Big Time, and if he made promises he couldn't deliver, they would kill him. At the very least, he'd end up with the beating of a lifetime. And growing up with a mean, drunk father like his, that was saying a lot.

Vargas leaned across the table, his face mere inches away. Perry smelled garlic from the man's shrimp scampi at dinner. "Jet's mere presence isn't enough. She has to find that bomb. You think you got troubles? I've got buyers from several countries bidding on that baby." He jabbed a finger into Perry's chest. "Don't disappoint me."

Perry's stomach roiled. He needed fresh air; the small dining room belowdecks stank and he was claustrophobic. Perry rose. Pain radiated from his gut but he refused to let them enjoy his suffering. "I'm going up top for a bit."

Vargas nodded at one of his hulking bodyguards and the big man placed a rough hand on Perry's shoulder, pushing him back into his seat.

"Not yet. We need to make a call first, let your ex know where to find you. I don't care what you have to say or do, but you get Bosarge here—alone. Am I clear?"

A computer monitor was placed before him and he saw his reflection, swollen jaw, unkempt hair and all. Perry ran his fingers through his messy hair but it was no use. Probably all for the best anyway; Jet would totally believe he'd been taken by force when she saw him.

And by God, his pain was nothing compared to what that bitch was gonna get. If she'd come along at first like he'd told her, he wouldn't be in this position now.

You wait, Jet Bosarge. Your time is coming. And I'll bring your whole race down with you if I need to.

Landry lounged against the wall, unimpressed with Hammonds's pathetic act. Nothing the man said rang true. The light from the computer monitor glowed eerily beneath the darkened window. A single moonbeam shone on the monitor, like a stage light at the theater.

"Help me, Jet. Please," Perry begged. "And come alone. They know Landry Fields is an FBI agent."

A tattooed arm came into view and it delivered a punch to Perry's jaw. A paper was placed in front of Perry. He wiped away a trickle of blood from the side of his mouth as he read it. "There's a plane ticket for you in a plain envelope in your mailbox."

"I'm not flying," Jet said adamantly. "I'll drive all night and be there by morning."

Perry nodded. "Just come. Please. If you don't…well, the rest of your family is in danger."

Quite a convincing performance, Landry had to admit. The punch added a nice touch of authenticity. But he speculated the whole thing was a setup to draw Jet to Tybee Island.

With those last, pleading words, the screen went black. Jet stared at the dead blankness, no doubt imagining Perry suffering at the hands of his captors. "I have to go," she whispered. "I can't put my family in jeopardy."

"Absolutely not." Landry's jaw clenched. "It's way too dangerous."

"If I don't go, they'll kill him," she said flatly. "And then they'll come after me and my loved ones."

Did Jet still have some shred of affection for Hammonds? The thought made his stomach churn. "Better him than you."

"Look, as of right now you don't have enough proof to nail Vargas on anything. I'll go and you can wire me up. I'll meet with Perry like we originally intended."

She was right. He had nothing. All he had so far was hearsay on the bomb excavation. Damn, they needed to nail that bastard before he compromised national security. This time, they had to get Vargas in custody and stop him for good. "I won't wire you up again. Vargas is too smart for that. He'd have you strip-searched at once."

Jet paced the cottage den. "Let's leave right now. We can be there in a few hours and get this over with. Thank God your mom picked up Seth today like she promised."

Yeah, after numerous phone calls to her all week. In the end, he threatened to cut his monthly check unless she came. But there was another, more pressing matter to take care of. He folded his arms. "We can't leave right this minute."

"Why not?"

"First, I have to call my boss, apprise him of the latest news, and then he'll have to run everything by the brass to get backup in place. Everything will probably have to be coordinated with Homeland Security, as well. And second, we're not leaving here until you tell me how you find things undersea that no one else can."

Jet abruptly stopped pacing. "What does that matter?"

"I need to know why you're essential to this operation. My job is on the line with this and I need the full story."

"Can't you trust me to handle this on my own?"

He had to know the truth about Jet. He would need to

at least know everything Hammonds and Vargas knew before he set foot on Tybee Island. "Let me turn that question around on you. Why don't *you* trust *me* with your secret?"

"I'm—intuitive. Let's leave it at that."

A mewling like the hounds of hell erupted.

"Saved by the cat's meow," Jet muttered.

Damn that cat; it was as if it had a sixth sense on how to be disruptive. He'd never gotten around to dropping it off at the shelter like he meant to do. That feline better not be having her litter now. Landry beat Jet to the utility room and yanked open the door. Baby Girl, his temporary name for the tabby, stood in the middle of the cramped space and blinked at them. Over the past few days, he'd earned a semblance of trust from her and in return he'd let her roam the house soon. Little steps.

They regarded Baby Girl as she calmly began grooming her derriere.

"She's been making that awful noise a lot lately. She's close to her due date."

"Why haven't you taken her to the shelter yet?"

Good question. Landry shifted uncomfortably. "I haven't had time," he mumbled, knowing it was a lie. The cat had grown on him.

Jet bent down and held out her fingers for Baby Girl to sniff. All she got for her efforts was a hiss.

"She doesn't like you very much," Landry noted. "She doesn't hiss at me anymore."

"You should have let Seth stay to watch over her. We need to hit the road." Jet sighed and whipped out her cell phone. "I'll have Shelly or Lily check on your cat while we're at Tybee."

"There's no need for that. I'm sure this isn't her first litter. She'll be fine." Jet ignored him and tried to persuade one of her kin to cat-watch. Evidently, they weren't into felines, either.

Landry called his supervisor and, as he expected, was informed to stay put until he was granted the green light to proceed to Tybee Island. He slipped outside to the deck and leaned against the railing. The sea was calm tonight but his mind was far from peaceful. He closed his eyes and remembered the young girl/sea creature with long white hair that swirled against the blue-black waters. Her thin, pale arms guided the small boat as she swam below the water's surface. Once he'd reached the shallows, close enough to the shore to walk on land, she had let go of the boat and turned, diving deeper.

And that was when he'd seen it. Where her legs should have been was a long fishtail that glittered like an explosion of crushed mica. It flashed but an instant, but Landry would never forget it, much as he tried to logically dismiss the image from his mind over the years.

April had made sure he could never again simply ignore the supernatural.

He put his head in his hands, recalling again the set of scars along Jet's neck. What if Jet's treasure-finding ability stemmed from her biology, because she was the same kind of creature as that other one? He couldn't deny the facts staring him in the face.

Chills ran down his spine. If, if, *if.* If it was true, he would find out.

Open your mind and heart to love and magic. He wasn't sure he could make that leap yet.

It was a no-go on finding a cat-sitter. Jet laid her phone down and went onto the deck, where Landry stood, head in his hands. The trick was how to rush him. They needed to get Perry.

"Ready to go?" she asked brightly.

"I'm waiting for my boss to call back with clearance. Why are you so worried about Perry? I didn't realize you cared that much for him."

"It's not that," she said quickly. "I just want to protect my family and get this over with."

"You sure that's all there is to it?"

Jet pulled his head down to hers and pressed her lips against his. To hell with words, she'd prove it with her touch. She licked his bottom lip, tasted the slight saltiness from the ocean breeze and that indefinable something that was unique to him. An aching tenderness welled inside her. If he discovered her secret at Tybee, this could be their last night alone.

Perry could wait. The whole world could wait. This moment belonged to them. He sensed it, too; she could tell from the way he pressed her body against his, letting her feel his swelling manhood as it ground into her pelvis.

Jet moaned. She wanted Landry in her. Now. Wanted to be joined with him as they explored and reached that shattering intensity and release together.

Landry pulled back and cupped her face in his strong, rough palms. The lightness of his eyes lit a tenderness inside her that brought tears to her eyes. The things he could do to her with a single look. He ran a finger down her cheek and neck, every nerve of his body in tune with her longing, with her love.

Should she tell him? Jet swallowed away a hard lump of fear and parted her lips to speak. But Landry's index finger, which hovered around the hollow of her throat, rose back up and landed across her lips in a hushing motion. He knew. Somehow Landry always seemed to know her innermost thoughts. Jet's lips trembled slightly. She felt raw, exposed.

"There should be no secrets between us," he said. His voice was gruff. "What are you hiding from me?"

"You don't want to know. Please, can't you let it go, just for now?"

He ran a hand down the back of her scalp, in a gesture so tender she wanted to bury her head against his chest and blurt out the truth. His lips brushed against the top of her head and her resolve slipped. "Later," Jet promised. "Right now I want you to make love to me." When he didn't move, she added, "Please."

Wordlessly, Landry took her by the hand and led her inside. She followed him past his grandmother's knick-knacks in the den, the pitter-pat of Baby Girl in the utility room and the now-barren, tidy room where Seth had stayed. Inside his bedroom, Landry flipped on the light.

Jet turned it off. She hated to keep lying to him about the gill marks on her neck. No way she could relax if he noticed them. And Landry noticed everything.

Landry flipped the light switch back on and rested a palm against it. "The light stays on this time," he said in a voice that brooked no argument.

"But," Jet gulped "but I have some scars—"

"Right here." Landry reached out and drew lines down the sides of her neck. "I know. I've already seen them."

She should have remembered she'd told him about them. "Oh, okay, then." Jet sat on his bed and patted the mattress. A diversion was in order immediately before he asked how she got them.

"We'll talk about all that later," he said, shooting her a look that promised no compromise. "In the meantime—" Landry pulled off his T-shirt and stepped a foot away from where she sat. He picked up her hand and placed it on his right side. "Check out this nasty bugger. Appendectomy from age nine." Her fingers traced the raised, bumpy sur-

gical scar. How painful and scary it must have been for
Landry as a child going through that operation.

The crisp clank of metal rang out like a shot as he undid
the clasp of his leather belt. Jet licked her lips as Landry's
jeans slid to the floor. He pushed her hand down to the
inside of his left thigh. "This scar is the result of a junior-
high shop-class accident."

Jet leaned into the warm, hard muscles of his thigh. "I
don't see anything," she said, her breath exhaling against
the soft blond hair on his legs.

"Here," he bit out in a strangled voice.

She narrowed her eyes and saw the faint curve of a
white scar. She darted out her tongue and flicked it against
the tiny line.

"I'm sure there are many more if you care to look."

Jet smiled at him. "I do care. Take off all your clothes
and lie down."

"Bossy woman," he said, stepping out of his jeans.
Landry peeled off his boxers without a shred of embarrassment and lay beside her. "Examine all you want."

Jet marveled at his confident ease. She stripped off her
own clothes and then started with his chest, where beige
hair curled around his rib cage. She took in the outline of
muscled biceps and triceps before switching her gaze to his
flat abs. Her eyes went lower and stilled. Desire rekindled,
hot and as blistering as asphalt in the Alabama sun. How
she loved every single detail about this man. She longed
to tell him, but she couldn't get the words out.

"Your turn." In one quick move, Landry flipped her
onto her back and drank in the sight of her naked body.
She tried not to flinch when he touched the sides of her
neck. Her ready explanation fled out the window. How
could she explain them?

"We'll talk later," he said. "Like you promised."

Relief washed through her agitated mind. For now, she would enjoy making love with a man she truly loved. He trailed kisses down her neck and stopped at her breasts, circling each nipple with his tongue. And then he went lower still, and his tongue grazed her belly button before finding her swollen folds.

Jet arched into the warm haven of his mouth, utterly wanton. She cried out with pleasure and Landry replaced his mouth with his shaft. Waves of ecstasy crashed and swirled in every cell. She held on to Landry, tight, and moaned with pleasure as he came with her.

Afterward, Jet cuddled against his lean body, her head resting on his sturdy shoulders. One of his large hands rested on the curve of her hip. She'd never felt so safe, so secure.

"It's time," he said, the rumble of his voice vibrating against her cheek.

Jet languidly stretched against the cotton linens. "Time for what?"

"Tell me your secret."

Chapter 15

Jet followed Landry down to the shore, careful to avoid the lapping water. "I don't know why you had to drag me out here to talk," she grumbled, kicking sand. "We should be on our way to Georgia."

"Not until my boss has followed all the proper protocol and not until we get a few things cleared." Landry stopped abruptly and Jet stumbled against him. "How do you find sea treasure?" he asked. The blue of his eyes was as implacable as an arctic glacier.

Jet took a deep breath, inhaling the bayou's ever-present scent of brine mixed with pine-tree sap. Her skin went clammy as the salt air settled on her arms and legs. She'd promised him the truth in a moment of weakness, a delaying tactic while she tried to think of some probable explanation. She thought fast. "You know how some people have a great nose—their olfactory senses can pick up scents other people can't? Or people who have lost one sense like eyesight and then develop a hypersensitive ear as compensation?"

Landry raised a brow and she realized he wasn't buying the direction she was leading. Jet threw up her hands.

"I don't know how to explain it. This feeling comes over me when I'm swimming in the vicinity of old shipwreck ruins. Maybe old coins and jewelry emit a subtle smell or there's some minute kinetic shift in the waters I pick up on. I don't know."

Her feet were suddenly snatched from underneath and she gasped as Landry's strong arms cradled her back and behind her knees. She instinctively wrapped her arms around his neck.

"What are you doing?' she asked, dumbfounded as he waded into the ocean. If a wave broke close to shore and the spray hit her legs— Jet pushed her arms against his chest, frantic to escape. "Put me down," she ordered. This was a fine dilemma. If she got wet, the jig was up, and if she used her strength to outmuscle him, that would be another issue to explain.

He kept walking, the water halfway to his shins.

"Don't make me hurt you," she warned. "I'm stronger than you."

"Maybe. But you won't make any move for fear I'll drop you."

"Don't let go of me!" Jet clung to him like a barnacle to a ship's underbelly. She couldn't bear to see the disgust in his eyes if her legs disappeared and her tail emerged.

"Your secret."

The moonlight emphasized the hard planes of his cheekbones and jaw. Yet his eyes held a soft glimmer of tenderness that he couldn't hide. Not from her.

"You wouldn't dare," she whispered in soft challenge.

Landry abruptly pulled an arm in, leaving one of her legs unsupported. She let out a cry and clung harder around his neck, staring down into the black water, mere inches from the tips of her bare toes. "Okay," she gasped. "You win." Better to tell Landry than have him witness the truth. If she was lucky, he'd laugh and call her a liar.

"Is it so hard for you to trust me?" he asked gently. "I already know the truth, Jet."

She snorted. "You have no idea."

"You're a mermaid."

Her mouth dropped open. Had she really heard him right? The world seemed to tilt, spinning crazily. *He knows. Landry knows my secret.* "It's true," she whispered. Jet stared into his eyes, looking to find disgust. Instead, she found a flicker of hurt.

"I wasn't really going to drop you in the water," he admitted. "I wanted you to tell me yourself." He stared past her shoulder at the wide expanse of sea. "I would have believed you. I told you what I saw when I was twelve. Plus, you know about April's ghost."

Landry turned and waded back to shore, still carrying her in his arms.

"But you weren't sure what you saw. Remember? You said you were a scared kid."

Landry set her down onshore and kept walking, his back to her. Jet scrambled to keep up with him. Of all the ways she'd envisioned him discovering she was a mermaid, never once did she consider he would guess it on his own. "Talk to me. Please." Her voice crumpled at the end and Landry slowly made his way over.

"Don't cry. I hate that." He wrapped his arms around her and she nuzzled into the solid warmth of his body.

"Wasn't going to cry," she lied. Why did she do this? She always had to prove she was strong, that she didn't need anybody or anything. Another whopping lie. She needed and wanted Landry and couldn't imagine life without him. Plain and simple: she loved him. Loved his strong moral compass for justice, loved his loyalty and the way he made her feel safe and treasured. Real treasure wasn't the trinkets and baubles she had hunted, nor was it the golden trident she'd trained so hard for and won, and it certainly wasn't the missing H-bomb lying in the dark depths of an obscure salt marsh.

Here. Right here was the real treasure. More valuable than any pirate's cache of gold.

"Sure sounded like you were about to cry." Landry stroked her back. "Look, I'm sorry. I was an ass just now. I shouldn't have threatened to drop you in the ocean. You can't force someone to trust you."

"But I *do* trust you." The words were muffled against his wide chest.

"Not really. Sure, you realize I'm an improvement over that lying bastard Hammonds. But you could hardly do worse than your ex-boyfriend."

Jet pulled away from his chest and faced him. "Don't even mention your name and his in the same sentence. You're wonderful.... I...I..." She swallowed past the lump in her throat. Damn her misplaced pride. Saying *I love you* was too scary. She wasn't lovable. Even with her own mom—er, aunt—she came in second place to the lovely Lily. He'd come to view her as a freak of nature one day, same as Perry. "How did you guess I'm a mermaid? That's never happened to any of us."

Landry lifted his hands and ran his fingers down both sides of her neck. "The same markings I saw on the other mermaid. I should have guessed earlier but it took a visit with Tia to really open my eyes."

"What did she say?" Jet bit her lip. "Does Tia know I'm a mermaid?" If Tia Henrietta guessed the truth, that meant others might have done the same. With each dirt dweller who knew their secret, the risk of exposure grew exponentially for her and her kin—and for all merfolk.

"She didn't mention you. Tia just cautioned me to be open to the possibility of magic and—" He paused.

"And what?"

"Never mind." Landry dropped his hands to his sides and took a step back. "But between Tia and April, I was forced to acknowledge every inexplicable detail in a new light. Besides the neck markings, there was your eerie ability to find sea treasure, your own admission that you had out-of-the-ordinary means in locating treasure. Combine all that with your abnormal physical strength and night vision, and it wasn't hard to add it up."

Just her luck. An FBI agent who noticed every detail, put it all together and didn't discount the supernatural factor. If only they'd had more time together, she might have been able to break the news to him gently. Gradually have gotten him used to the idea of mermaids. And, most of all, had the time to make Landry fall so madly in love with her that he wouldn't care if she turned into a toad on every full moon.

Everything was ruined now. She'd spare them both a lot of pain and end their relationship at once. Jet couldn't bear to watch him struggle to find a kind way to say goodbye. She gave a short laugh and clapped her hands. "Bravo. Well-done, Mr. Federal-Agent-Man. Welcome to the freak show. Before you dump me, I beg you not to tell anyone about my family. Bosarge women have lived in Bayou La Siryna for generations. I don't want to be the one who screws that up."

"Of course I won't—what makes you think I'm dumping you?"

Suddenly, she was crushed against the long, solid width of his body.

"Don't ever say the word *freak* again," Landry said harshly, his breath hot and sweet on the top of her scalp.

"Like I said before, you're the most beautiful woman I've ever seen."

Deluded man. Jet squeezed him back, her heart tripping with the small hope they had a chance to make this thing work. Landry hadn't run away yet. "I thought you were mad at me for not being up front tonight," she mumbled against his chest.

He tipped her chin up, forcing her to meet his eyes. "I was hurt you couldn't tell me the truth," he corrected. "I went about it all wrong trying to force you to tell me. Forgive me."

He still cares. He knows what I am and it doesn't matter—unless he only wants to use me like Perry. No, she wouldn't compare the two. Landry was ambitious and hardworking but he also actually had some morals. "If that's the worse you ever do to me, we're good," she said with a shaky laugh. "You wanted to know all the facts before we left for Tybee Island."

Jet relaxed in his embrace as the sound of the waves lulled her fears.

Landry sighed. "Speaking of which…we should pack and be prepared to leave as soon as the call comes in from my boss."

She reluctantly stepped out of his arms. "Agreed."

They strode quickly back to the cottage. Worry settled back in Jet's stomach. "If the FBI sends out a bunch of people, Vargas might find out and kill Perry."

"Hammonds isn't important. Your safety comes before everything. I don't want you involved in their bomb scheme."

That wasn't her biggest fear. "What scares me is that Perry may have told these people about the merworld. Although, I don't know how he could convince them we exist without any proof."

"They would think he was nuts. Your past success in locating treasure is reason enough for Vargas to use you, no matter what kind of story Hammonds may have told them."

They hurried up the cottage stairs to pack.

Landry tossed some toiletries in an overnight bag. "I hope you don't have a problem with airplanes. The Bureau might provide one to get us there quickly."

"No way!" Jet shook her head emphatically. "The high altitude messes with my body chemistry. Mermaids aren't built for it." Too much time in the air caused systemic edema, and the swelling and inflammation could be quite painful. To counteract the edema, it was necessary to return undersea for a long period of recuperation. She didn't have the time or inclination now for weeks undersea.

"Good to know." Landry picked up his cell phone. "I'm calling Sheriff Angier. We might need his help in keeping your—your—mermaid nature a secret."

The early-morning sun cracked through the clouds in a blistering haze of red as Jet drove through streets of rainbow-colored cottages dotting the Atlantic shoreline. She scanned the street names constantly until she found the diner Perry had instructed her to stop at when he'd called five minutes ago. Only sheer adrenaline had kept her awake during the six-hundred-mile journey from Bayou La Siryna and she hoped it stayed kicked in until this ordeal was resolved. She glanced in the rearview mirror and although she couldn't see Landry's face through the tinted windshield, it was a relief knowing he and Tillman were close behind in a government-issued sedan.

Behind the lead car, her family tagged along. Mom, Shelly and Lily had filed into a van and hit the road, much to the consternation of Landry and Tillman. Jet managed a wan smile remembering the heated arguments that ensued when Tillman told Shelly to stay home while he joined the Tybee Island rendezvous. Shelly had immediately gathered the family together, and each insisted they might be of help in some way, especially if the kidnappers held Perry on board a ship. Landry was appalled and Tillman resigned. The men sternly warned the trio of blonde beauties to stay out of the way and out of contact with Jet until the situation was under control. They nodded and gave vague smiles, sweetly agreeing to the conditions. Jet couldn't imagine how they might be of service, but knowing they were along for the ride helped quell her nerves.

At last she spotted the Starlight Diner and turned her truck into the parking lot. Jet staggered, stiff-legged, out of the truck and made her way inside. Her stomach grumbled at the smell of fresh-baked doughnuts. Might as well knock back a couple; who knew when or if she'd get a real meal today? But first, she went to the ladies' room and relieved the sharp tug on her bladder. She freshened up and grimaced at her reflection in the grimy bathroom mirror. Dark circles had formed, and her skin looked dry and parched. She needed to return to the sea and rehydrate. First thing when she returned home, she'd slip down the Bosarge hidden portal for a long, cool swim.

Even the thought of swimming refreshed her and Jet opened the bathroom door with a renewed determination to help Landry catch Vargas and save Perry from himself.

A buzzing vibration in her back pocket made her jump. "Probably Landry again," Jet muttered, digging out the cell phone from her purse. He checked in at least every thirty minutes even though he was following her.

Instead of Landry, it was Perry's number on the screen. The phone buzzed again like an angry hornet.

Jet hit the reply button with shaking fingers. "Perry?"

"It's me."

Jet frowned down at the phone in her hand. The connection was so clear it sounded as if—

The firm, warm weight of a man's palm encircled her arm, right above the elbow. Jet gasped and instinctively pulled away.

"It's me." Perry's breath was hot and fervent in her ear as he drew her outside the back door. "They're watching us. Just come with me."

"What? How?" Jet stumbled beside him but had enough wits to stuff the cell phone deep into her back pocket. A family sat at one of the picnic tables, children licking their fingers from the sticky glaze of doughnuts. Seagulls squawked nearby scavenging food near an overflowing garbage can, while a few cars passed on the main road.

It was happening too fast, nothing like what they had planned. Before she could protest, Perry had ushered her into the passenger seat of a waiting car, and she heard the door lock with a click. Jet grasped the door handle.

Only there was no handle. Her fingers grazed the smooth expanse of metal overlaid with vinyl. Son of a bitch. Anger sent her synapses snapping with energy and she lurched toward the driver's side. Cool metal poked the sweaty nape of her neck and the deadly click of a cocked trigger exploded in the sealed vehicle.

"You're not going anywhere this time, Jet Bosarge" came a gravelly voice from behind.

In the rearview mirror she saw the burly man who had tried to snatch her with Perry yesterday. He bore a distinctive tattoo on his arm, a skull with a lightning bolt through it. The dude who'd led Perry away was sitting beside him, smirking.

The hell if she'd give them the satisfaction of seeing her panic. "Three-on-one to capture a woman?" she asked with fake nonchalance. "And you even thought it necessary to bring along firepower. Impressive."

Perry slid in beside her. "Already charming them with your sunny personality?" The wide grin did nothing to dispel a feral gleam in his brown eyes, almost as dark as her own. The stench of Aqua de Nausea was suffocating in the cramped quarters. How had she ever found it appealing?

Jet turned her lips upward in angry reciprocation as she rebuked him with her eyes. "You were never kidnapped. You've been in on the whole thing."

"Were you worried about me, sweetheart?"

One of the men in the back grabbed her arms and pinned them down to each side of her seat. Perry snatched up her T-shirt and shoved his hands down the front of her bra. He squeezed her breasts and ran both hands over her back and inside the waistband of her jeans.

"No wire," he declared, then drove down a dirt road so fast that every pothole made her insides feel as if they were being scrambled.

Did Landry have any idea they'd slipped her away? "Let go of me!" she screamed, trying to twist to see if the government sedan was on their tail.

The man let go of her arms and grabbed the purse off her lap. "Got a phone in there?" He dumped the contents out onto the backseat.

My phone. A frisson of hope shot up her spine. She felt the outline of it crushed against her ass.

"I dropped it when Perry grabbed me," she lied, praying Landry wouldn't call. It had been at least twenty minutes since his last check-in. Somehow, she had to turn it off or press his number without anyone seeing. Jet eased onto her left hip, facing Perry.

"How did you get mixed up with this crowd?" she asked.

"Got lucky."

Jet casually tucked her T-shirt into the waistband of her shorts, inserting a finger into her back pocket. Feeling along the phone's edges, she found the button and switched on vibration mode. Success! She put her face up to the rearview mirror and faked surprise. "I think someone's followed us." All three men spun their heads to face the back windshield. Jet seized the moment to slip the phone out of her pocket and place it under her right thigh.

"I don't see nuthin'," the tattooed man grunted. "We plucked you away from the police right under their damn noses. We knew they were following you to the island."

"My bad, then," Jet said with a shrug. "Where are we going?"

"To the boat." Perry slid a sideways glance at her. "Guess your boyfriend, Mr. FBI Agent, told you all about the missing hydrogen bomb."

"He did. If you're smart, Perry, you'll let me out of here now before you get in so much trouble you stay locked up forever."

"I'd rather die." His fingers tightened on the steering wheel. "Bitch," he added.

Jet kept an eye on the passing road names and landmarks. Landry had put a trace on her phone, but she didn't know how well it would work on this rural road. No telling how far they were from a GPS satellite. "Have you always been such an asshole or did prison bring out the worst in you?" she asked Perry, hoping to keep him focused on their conversation.

"Shut up," he growled, raising his hand as if to smack her. "When we get to the boat and meet Vargas, you better show him some respect."

She placed a hand over her stomach and grimaced.

"What's the matter with you?" he asked, eyes flashing in annoyance.

"Something I ate on the road made me sick." She searched for a button to roll down the side window, but there wasn't one. "Are we almost there yet?" Jet retched, deep heaves that shook her upper torso.

Perry wrinkled his nose and leaned into the driver's side door. "Don't you dare throw up."

"How much longer?" she grated out in between heaves. The pretty beach houses were long gone, the landscape fading to stretches of wild salt marshes.

"Almost there. We turn at the next road. Do I need to pull over?"

"No!" one of the men in back roared. "No stopping. I don't care if she vomits all over herself. She'll be getting in the water shortly."

Jet laid her head on the window and groaned as Perry turned right on the corner of Lullwater and Dixie streets.

Now or never.

She doubled over and retched again, spitting on the floor seat. With Perry's attention momentarily diverted, she turned her back to him, flipped on the cell phone and began texting the location to Landry.

"Damn it, what the hell are you doing?" The tattooed man grabbed her right arm and Jet cried out as her shoulder muscles were pulled from their socket. The cell phone dropped and he picked it up. The Send Message had about three-quarters filled the bar when he rolled down his back window and tossed it onto a sand dune.

His partner beside him punched the tattooed man's arm. "Idiot! You should have turned it off, not thrown it out the window."

She prayed the tracer was functioning. Jet couldn't be sure the message had gone through. If it hadn't, how the hell would Landry ever find her?

He will. That certainty radiated from her gut to every

inch of her body, instantly as calming as a shot of Demerol. Landry would work tirelessly to find her. Maybe they would find her phone. Or maybe Landry was following now. Perry slowed the sedan and pulled over to the side of the road. "No more tricks, Jet," he said, pocketing the car keys. "The sooner you find what Vargas wants, the sooner you can go home."

"Liar. I'll never be free of you. There will always be new treasure or a new adventure."

He opened his mouth as if to deny it, then smiled, baring a mouthful of brilliant white teeth. "You know me too well." He leaned over and whispered in her ear, "Your secret alone could be worth a fortune."

Jet didn't doubt he'd sell her out like a damned circus act, putting the entire merfolk race at risk. Humans would hunt mermaids down to extinction, much the way of buffalos on the American plains. She'd kill herself before she let that happen.

"Hey, cut out that whispering," said one of the men behind them. "Let's get a move on."

The all exited the vehicle and she waited until the tattooed man jerked open her door. Jet stumbled out, searching for another human or a car passing by on the main road, but there was only sea and sand to witness their march from the car to the shore, where a small boat waited.

She dug her heels into the sand at the sight of the boat. If salt water splashed on her legs, she'd shape-shift in front of these buffoons. Although she could outmuscle them, and probably outrun them if she made a break for it now, she wasn't as fast or strong as a bullet.

Perry scooped her up and waded to the boat. She started to thank him, but Perry did nothing out of kindness. There must be some selfish reason he didn't want these men to see her in mermaid form. He sat her roughly in the boat.

Jet's heart quickened as she stared into the sea. *Jump!* Every instinct urged her to dive overboard. Everyone would see her fishtail, but she could outswim any human. Who would believe these guys even if they swore up and down they'd seen a mermaid?

She scrambled to the side of the boat but the tats man grabbed her shoulders and flung her to the floorboards.

"You ain't going *nowhere*," he said, punctuating the words with a vicious kick to her legs.

Jet instinctively curled into a fetal position, protecting her head and rib cage.

"Stop kicking her," Perry said. "Vargas wants to put Jet to work right away. She can't do that hurt." He knelt beside her and she regarded him cautiously. He firmly removed her hands from her face. "No one wants to mistreat you. For once, do what you're told, okay?"

She rubbed her right thigh, already swollen from the kick, and offered no resistance as the two goons placed her between them on the boat seats. Perry started the engine and they lurched forward.

They motored out only a few minutes before Perry pulled alongside a larger craft, though not nearly as impressive as she'd expected.

"This is a scout vessel," Perry explained, guessing her thoughts. "Once you locate the bomb, Vargas will bring in the big guns for excavation."

Jet wordlessly followed her captors onto the larger boat, a gun pressed against her back. Several men stood on deck watching as Perry escorted her to a diminutive man with slick dark hair and haughty eyes.

He briefly inclined his head in her direction. "We meet at last, Miss Jet Bosarge."

His accent was thick, but Jet couldn't determine his native tongue. Spanish? Greek? She said nothing.

"Perry tells me you have a unique ability to find sea treasure." At her continued silence, he went on, "He's even claimed you are a mermaid."

Jet folded her arms. "Ridiculous." Once they sent her diving, they would only see the flash of her tail fin as she swam her ass off.

"Nevertheless, I've observed your outstanding luck over the years in finding sea salvage. I've no doubt you'll find our hydrogen bomb. We'll equip you with a Geiger counter and the latest and greatest underwater metal detector. Those tools—combined with your luck or special ability—will make this venture successful."

"What makes you so sure it's here? It could be anywhere in a fifty-mile radius for all anybody knows."

A tall, thin man wearing a gray windbreaker stepped forward. "It's here," he said, pushing wire-rimmed glasses up the bridge of his nose. "The government's been looking in the wrong area all these years."

Vargas extended his hand, palm up toward the stranger. "This is Jim Tindol. His grandfather was copilot of the B-47 that jettisoned the bomb. According to his grandfather, the bomb was ejected in this area, not where the navy divers originally searched."

"Granddaddy told them to search where the Savannah River empties into the Atlantic. But they only listened to the pilot, not him."

"Why would the pilot lie?" Jet asked.

"Because he thought everyone was safer if the bomb was never recovered," Jim said. "As long as he lied about where it ejected, he figured everyone would give up the search eventually and the bomb would lie harmless forever."

Jet shook her head. "After five decades, that bomb is probably buried several feet under silt. Why did you get involved after all these years? Oh, wait, let me guess—you've been paid for this information."

"We all stand to profit from this venture," Vargas cut in smoothly. "Even you, Miss Bosarge."

"And what if I can't find it?"

"You will."

She raised her eyebrows. "How can you be so sure?"

Vargas pointed behind her. Jet swung around and saw a man-size shark cage.

"Because every day you'll be placed in that cage and lowered undersea until you find it. I'll drag you around underwater for months if that's what it takes."

Perry pointed a thumb at his chest. "My idea," he bragged.

Jet stared at the cage, rigid with horror. Caged like an animal? This was even worse than poor Dolly trapped in a small swimming pool. She found Perry standing with the others and frowned at him. This was her worst nightmare and he knew it.

Had used it against her.

In that dream, she'd been caged like a hapless manatee and put on display in a glass tank as mobs of people pressed their faces to the wall. An aquarium's newest freak show.

"Doesn't sound like much fun, does it?" Vargas's full lips curled in a humorless smile. "I reckon a few weeks of this and you'll be damn eager to show me where the bomb lies hidden."

Chapter 16

Landry's grip on the steering wheel tightened as he tried to steady the storm of fear and fury waging within. *Like April all over again.* One minute here, the next minute…

Focus. He would find her. Even now, Sheriff Angier was questioning employers and customers in the diner. Damn Perry Hammonds. If he, or anyone in Vargas's group, hurt Jet, they would pay dearly for that transgression. As a child, he'd been helpless at his sister's disappearance, but this time he could stop a tragedy.

His head snapped up at the sound of a vehicle turning in. Landry groaned inwardly as the three blondes exited.

Lily yawned and stretched. "So it's time for breakfast? I'm starving."

"Where's Jet?" Adriana Bosarge asked, squinting her cobalt-blue eyes at Jet's empty truck.

Before he could answer, Shelly spoke. "Something's wrong." Her gaze was focused on Tillman as he hurried to them.

"Have you lost my daughter?" Adriana's sharp voice cut through the morning air like a machete through butter.

Landry inwardly winced at the accusatory words. He

had enough guilt without anyone else piling it on. "She's been abducted but we know where to look and she's close by."

Jet's mother lost her ever-serene composure. Shock and grief momentarily contorted her beautiful features until she snapped her fingers. "Girls. Get in the van. Jet's gone."

"Stay here," Landry said, sliding back into the sedan. "You'll only be in our way."

All three ignored him.

He didn't have time to argue. According to the GPS, they were only .89 miles from the intersection of Lullwater and Dixie. Jet's text had been sent at 7:16 a.m. It was now 7:24 a.m. Only eight minutes had passed since she'd been abducted and placed in serious danger. He should never have agreed to let Jet come along. Screw the case against Vargas.

Tillman slid in beside him. "Someone saw a man fitting Perry's description escort Jet out a back door." Before Tillman even closed his door, Landry hit the accelerator.

Tillman craned his neck backward at the van, which was merely a few feet from their rear bumper. "Stubborn fools," he said in a resigned voice. A swelling of blue from sky and ocean flew by until the disembodied GPS voice announced they'd reached their final destination. Ahead, the road appeared to dead-end, so he pulled over in a spray of beige sand.

They both jumped out of the car and simultaneously discovered a recent set of footprints in the otherwise pristine landscape of sand. They followed until the prints stopped at the edge of a salt marsh, where they disappeared into the water. Landry shielded his eyes with his hands and gazed at the horizon. A lone boat bobbed in the waves—too far away to see who was on board.

"Hold on." Tillman rushed to the sedan and retrieved a pair of binoculars. "Try these."

Landry raised them to his eyes. She was there! The tight contraction in his chest eased a fraction as he observed someone holding out various instruments and scuba gear. He took in the sight of Vargas, puffing one of his ridiculous cigars, and several other men he couldn't identify. He returned his attention to Jet, too far away to see the expression on her face, but the slight slump of her shoulders hit him in the solar plexus, the hunched-over position a sign she was feeling overwhelmed and vulnerable.

"Give me that," snapped Adriana, yanking the binoculars away.

Irritating woman.

"What are they doing?" she asked.

Landry walked away, so Tillman answered for him. "They're showing her how to search for the bomb."

Landry whirled to face Tillman. "Notify everyone that Jet's been kidnapped."

"Why bother? There she is. Go get her," Adriana demanded.

Tillman pulled out his phone. "I'm on it."

"Wait." Shelly placed a hand on Tillman's arm. "If we handle this ourselves, it will be faster and there'll be less risk that Jet will be exposed as a mermaid."

"No!" Landry shook his head at Tillman and faced Shelly. "I don't give a damn about your secrets," Landry said. "My only concern is to get Jet away from them."

"We'll have the element of surprise," Shelly quietly insisted.

Landry rolled his eyes. "What do you think you're going to do? Swim out there and demand her release? These men have guns, for God's sake."

"So we're supposed to stand by and do nothing?" Adriana's eyes flashed. "I thought you were concerned about my daughter's safety."

He swore under his breath. Recklessness must be a family trait. Tillman paused, cell phone in hand as Landry tried to reason with Jet's family. "That's why I'm not rushing out there," he explained through gritted teeth. "I can work out a plan with the coast guard and have the FBI make an arrest."

"I think you're more interested in your career than you are in rescuing my daughter," Adriana said.

The accusation stung like falling naked into a patch of nettles.

"That's not true."

They all stared at Lily, who had remained silent while the rest of them argued, her musical voice defusing the agitation.

"Landry loves Jet," she continued. "Let's all work together."

Love?

He gazed out at the faraway boat, a small, vulnerable speck in the vast Atlantic. His heart clinched. Jet was alone out there with a team of ruthless men, desperate for treasure. *I have to save her.* Pushing aside his emotions, he thought of the best way to rescue Jet.

He could no longer deny that having a troupe of mermaids in his camp gave him a tactical advantage he'd be a fool to waste. Vargas would see any boat that advanced, but not mermaids. Talk about your "element of surprise." "Maybe y'all *can* help," he admitted. "How quick can we rent a boat?"

Jet followed Perry down the boat's narrow steps until they were alone belowdecks. In the damp, dark quarters, he thrust the dive suit at her. "Squeeze into this and then I'll show you how the air mask works."

"Really? A mermaid in a wet suit?" she asked, snatching it from his hands.

"That compression of neoprene is all that stands between you and your tail fin being exposed. Now get dressed."

"So? You already told them I'm a mermaid." Nevertheless, Jet kicked off her shoes and squeezed into the bathroom stall, which had no door for privacy.

Perry shrugged. "They don't believe me."

She narrowed her eyes at his calm demeanor. "You've been quiet since we came aboard. What's your game?"

"If this doesn't work out with Vargas, you're still my golden goose." His white smile gleamed in the dark, cramped area.

Bastard. "Turn around so I can get this damn thing on."

To her surprise, he did. The metal crackling of a zipper being undone stopped her movements. "What are you doing?"

"Changing into a wet suit, too. Vargas will send me after you if you don't follow the grid he laid out or if you trigger the alarm on the cage lock."

Vargas and his team had thought of everything. The cable wire connecting the shark cage to the crane would be maneuvered in a grid pattern designed to determine where the H-bomb lay hidden.

She leaned against the wall, shaking. Her nightmare was minutes away. *One thing at a time.*

"Explain how you think I'd bring you more money. I won't go on any more expeditions with you." She quickly shimmied out of her shorts and panties and struggled to get her legs through the wet suit.

"You're worth more to me as a circus act than as a treasure hunter."

Jet bit her lip to keep from gasping at his casual cruelty. She wouldn't let Perry see how much he'd hurt her. "Never," she managed to say in a composed voice as she got out of her T-shirt and bra and put her arms through the suit. She zipped it up and exited the bathroom, intending to ignore Perry and return upstairs.

A flash of pain sliced through the right sleeve of the suit. She looked down at Perry's fingers wrapped tightly around her right biceps. "Don't screw this up for me," he snarled. "I promised Vargas you'd find that bomb."

Jet easily shook herself free, partly because she knew it pissed Perry off that she could outmuscle him one-on-one. She walked up the creaky stairs to the blinding sunlight. All the men—Vargas, Jim Tindol, tats man and his fellow goon, and a couple of others she didn't know but assumed were aboard for technical support and machine operations—lined the boat's side. The open cage awaited.

"Find it," Vargas said unsmilingly.

The tattooed man pointed to the shark cage.

She approached slowly, mind desperately searching for an escape route. But Perry was so close at her back she felt his heat through the suit. His hand lay heavy on her shoulder, guiding her to face him. She watched, like a condemned prisoner getting electrically wired, as Perry set a bubbled hood over her face and strapped a heavy oxygen tank on her back. He curtly motioned for her to sit on the bench. Awkwardly, feeling cumbersome, she complied. Perry expertly fitted scuba fins on her feet, avoiding eye contact, as if she were some thing and not a real person.

The muscled goons each grabbed one of her arms and hoisted her up from the bench. Jet jerked her arms free and walked alone into her nightmare.

* * *

By high noon, the sun's glare off the water was like broken glass piercing Landry's eyes. The light penetrated through his brain to the back of his skull, burning like a migraine. Their vessel, an eighteen-foot Glastron bass and ski boat, lapped gently on the waves. The Bosarge women must have paid a fortune to nab it at the last minute.

Waiting was a bitch.

"My turn," Shelly said, a palm extended to Adriana.

Her aunt sighed and handed the binoculars over. "They're still showing her how to operate some tools."

Landry frowned. "Stay behind the canopy," he warned. "If they're keeping an eye out on the area with binoculars, they might see you."

Lily gathered a handful of blond hair and raised it over her neck. "It's hot under that heavy fabric. Reckon I'll go for a little swim."

"Don't go anywhere near their boat," Landry said. "If you—"

"I'm not going over there," Lily said. "Yet."

Adriana pursed her lips at her youngest daughter. "Don't you dare do anything until Jet goes underwater."

Tillman leaned down and whispered in Shelly's ear. "Keep an eye on her," Landry overheard him say.

So he didn't trust Lily, either. Smart guy. The two of them had started out rocky after Seth's premature disclosure that his brother was with the FBI. But they were so alike that an easy truce had formed between them out of respect and appreciation of the jobs they performed.

Adriana rose, graceful as a cat. He wondered briefly if the orange tabby monster had had her litter yet. "Guess I'll cool off a bit, too," Adriana said.

Landry ran his fingers through his hair and heaved a frustrated sigh, certain these women were going to do more harm than good. He squinted at Adriana. "Why couldn't you have just swum here instead of following us on land?"

"Didn't they teach you geography in high school? To swim from south Alabama to the Georgia coastline would entail swimming the entire length of Florida. We'd never have got here in time." She waved a bejeweled hand in his direction. "You gentlemen don't look while we undress."

Tillman and Landry each glued their eyes on the far-off boat until they heard the sound of three splashes.

"So you're marrying into all this—this—" Landry raised an arm into the air, at a loss for words.

"This weirdness?" Tillman supplied. "Yeah. Shelly's great. My future in-laws I'm not so sure about at times. But you get used to it. I know how much you FBI types love your protocol but you'll learn to bend a bit if you decide to hang around Bayou La Siryna. There is no contingency on the books that outlines correct mermaid protocol."

Landry gave a rueful smile and picked up the abandoned binoculars, needing to see Jet, even if he couldn't talk to her, couldn't touch her. Couldn't do anything but keep watch from afar.

She wasn't on deck. His gut clenched. Where was she? He scanned the entire deck, counting Vargas's men. Perry was also missing. "Hell," he cursed. "Jet's gone, along with Perry."

Tillman scrambled forward on the boat. "Let's drive in a little closer." He pulled a baseball cap low over his forehead. "Keep your face covered, in case they're on the lookout," he warned as he started the engine.

"What about the women? Can they find us if we change location?"

Tillman turned the key and the boat engine purred. "Can they find us?" he grinned sardonically. "You have a lot to learn about mermaids."

Landry let out his breath as Jet and Perry emerged from belowdecks, both clad in scuba gear. Fine, once in the water, Jet could swim away from Perry and her family could guide them to this boat. He would call his boss to finalize arrangements and in minutes the coast guard could capture Vargas and seize his ship for evidence. All his hired guns would turn on him soon enough under harsh interrogation. He'd seen it hundreds of times over in his career.

The wind lifted the hair on Landry's neck and adrenaline spiked through him. Finally. After hours of waiting, taking action felt great. Soon, he would have Jet in his arms.

Landry frowned. What the hell was going on? She was being led into some kind of metal contraption. A shark cage, perhaps. His spirits sank as quickly as they had lifted. Vargas had taken out a key and locked Jet inside. As he stepped back, he nodded to one of the men. A winch lifted the cage up a few feet, swung it away from the boat and then descended.

Jet was being lowered into the sea in what resembled a coffin.

Anguish stabbed him. He should have insisted she stay home in Bayou La Siryna. At the very least, he should have demanded she ride in the car to Tybee with him and Tillman, consequences be damned if Vargas found out or the FBI thought he had jeopardized the case.

Screw the agency and his career. Jet came first. A career couldn't fulfill him now that he'd had a taste of true happiness. Landry pictured what his life would have become without meeting her—and it wasn't pretty. It would be an empty existence of working long hours and joylessly shouldering of family duties solely out of a sense of responsibility. He could never go back to that again, could never settle for a life without love or magic. What kind of screwed-up universe would introduce him to a woman like Jet Bosarge and then take her away so quickly?

Landry would never wipe away that moment when Jet didn't answer his phone call or when they found her truck at the shop—empty. He'd never forget that devastation. Not in a million years.

But as much as that hurt, this moment was even worse. Worse because this time he had to stand on the sidelines and watch as she was lowered, entombed and helpless. What would happen when she hit water? Would she shape-shift to mermaid form? And if she did…her family and all merfolk would be exposed when the cage later ascended. Her kind would be hunted down and driven to entrapment like Dolly at that run-down water park.

The cage hit water and Jet disappeared. He watched while the circular eddies from the cage widened and flattened until the water was smooth as glass, leaving no trace of what lay beneath.

They were so desperate to locate the hydrogen bomb they didn't care if Jet was harmed in the mission. To Vargas, everyone was expendable. They would keep her alive only while she served a purpose.

And then?

Landry wouldn't allow his mind to consider the possibility of murder and death. He took out his rifle, prepared to shoot Vargas on deck. Her best chance for escape was undersea, especially with her family nearby.

He couldn't let that cage emerge. If Vargas and his crew saw Jet in merform, she and her entire race were in danger. They would be mercilessly hunted until extinction. And Vargas would be quick to realize that the price of a captured mermaid was more valuable than the missing

hydrogen bomb. Jet would fetch a high price for someone seeking the ultimate prize in a rare, precious-oddities
kind of collection.

Pain ripped through him, blinding and spectacular as
lightning on a Kansas prairie night, until he couldn't deny
the truth.

He loved Jet. Loved her dark beauty and deep, un-
plumbed depths. Loved the hidden softness beneath her
muscled body and even her prickly shell. Loved the woman
who sported diamond earrings while driving a battered
pickup truck.

And she might die not knowing any of that.

He remembered the first time he met her and encountered those flashing dark eyes. She'd been all brambly and
defensive, yet sparkling with such energy he'd been fascinated—but had immediately decided she wasn't his type.
Wrong. Day by day Jet had worn down his resistance and
fear to love again.

Tia's warning rang through his brain. *Your heart and
mind are closed to love and magic. You got a mighty big
test comin' up. You either pass it or you're doomed to go
through life lonely and empty-feelin'.*

He had failed the test last night when he forced Jet to reveal herself, failed in the most important part of the equa-
tion. The magic part, he'd passed. He had opened his mind
and accepted Jet's shape-shifting mermaid nature. April's
spirit had made sure he got that much right. But he hadn't
crossed over into love territory. Instead, he'd hovered, unwilling to fully commit. Was he doomed now as Tia had
warned—forever lonely and empty inside?

Landry fought to regain control of his wits; he'd need
every ounce of control over his emotions to save Jet. He
flung the binoculars onto the floorboards and signaled

Tillman to stop the boat. "I'll give Jet's family ten minutes to free her. If they haven't resurfaced by then, we'll make our way onto Vargas's boat."

No!

They lowered the shark cage toward the marsh waters. She was suffocating in the rubbery diving suit. Jet clung to the metal bars and looked up at Perry, the man she once trusted. He gazed down with detached curiosity...a stranger. He knew her deepest secret and her deepest fear and used both to send her straight to hell.

She'd forfeit all her treasure for one last glimpse of Landry. If only she had met him before Perry. If only, if only, if *only* she could go back in time and erase all her mistakes.

She was trapped like a dolphin in a tuna net. Poor Dolly. Who would save her and her unborn calf now?

The faces above disappeared in a splash. Blue sky faded to murky water. Bubbles blew out from the air mask.

Compression from the diving suit insulated her skin, preventing her from shape-shifting. Jet flailed the man-made fins on her feet. Awkward. Like a baby taking experimental steps.

The mask reduced her undersea vision, although it was still vastly greater than that of humans.

Black. She was trapped in a deep black void, powerless. No wonder the damned bomb had never been found in this inky water. Her fingers fumbled with the cage, finding the Geiger counter and metal detector attached to a bar. In the darkness, her fingers groped the cage door, struggling to trip the lock and break free.

She couldn't breathe. Jet sucked oxygen through the mouthpiece tube with rapid, shallow breaths, but the quicker she inhaled, the more her lungs ached and the less oxygen entered her bloodstream.

For the first time in her life, she wanted to give up.

Chapter 17

Today the sea held no comfort. Jet gripped the bars and closed her eyes. The neoprene compression cut her off from sensation and she imagined the result was similar to those isolation tanks she'd read about where people in them too long hallucinated and lost their grounding.

Today the sea held no camaraderie. No usual kinship with aquatic life, since she was swaddled like a human dirt dweller. No playing with the dolphins or swimming with shoals of white trout.

Today, instead, the sea was a capricious bitch and she was frightened and alone and powerless.

Black water churned and bits of sand and broken shells noiselessly popped against her scuba mask. The cage hit bottom and Jet was thrown to the ground. Huge puffs of gray sediment exploded around the bars like a mushroom cloud. It felt like being buried alive.

Jet reached her hands outside of the bars and fiddled with the locking mechanism, to no avail. It wouldn't budge. If only she had her knife, she might be able to pick it open. Normally, at sea she carried one inside the sporran belted at her waist. Always useful in case of a chance meeting with a shark. A thin steel blade was all that stood between her and freedom. Once that lock was popped, she'd tear off the wet suit and swim far, far away.

Ever so slowly the sediment drifted down like snow in a child's snow globe.

With an effort, Jet shrugged off the alienation and panic and set to work. With clumsy, enshrouded fingers, she unhooked the Geiger counter from a bar and switched it on. No sound cut through the liquid, tomblike water pressure on her ears, but rhythmic, pulsating vibrations traveled from her hands and up her arms as the instrument calculated radiation levels. The ocean held natural radiation, but Vargas had instructed how a higher concentration would result in spiked counter readings combined with a higher rate of clicking vibrations.

The cage was mechanically lifted a couple feet from the ground and Jet sensed a slow movement as the attached wire guided it along a predetermined grid.

They're jerking me around like a dog on a leash. Resentfully, Jet activated the underwater metal detector and gripped it in one hand, Geiger counter in the other. If she didn't turn on their stupid devices, they would probably jerk her back up and—beat her? She wouldn't be surprised. Greedy men would do whatever necessary to feed their inner money monster.

Jet couldn't say how long she drifted in the void, scarcely paying attention to the high-tech tools she held. If one of them indicated a promising lead, she'd promptly switch it off and tell her captors it malfunctioned. No way was she helping Perry and his gang uncover a deadly bomb.

Would they really keep sending her down day after day, hours at a time, if the instruments found nothing?

Spring and summer stretched before her, an unbroken misery chain.

Landry will find me. He knows Vargas and Perry are behind this.

Time passed—Jet couldn't say how much—and the rhythmic tumbling of the waves lulled her fears. The initial panic subsided, leaving her oddly drained and listless. Eye flutters lengthened to increasingly long eye blinks and her hands holding the instruments slightly slackened. She drifted in a womb of dark isolation in an alien undersea universe.

A sudden jarring jostled her to full alertness. Something was wrong.

Jet turned in a circle and faced a pair of luminescent eyes, mere inches from her own. Yellow ribbons from its head pillowed out in the darkness like jellyfish tendrils. Jet's heart raced double-time for a fraction of a second, until she realized this creature was friend, not foe.

"Shelly," she breathed into the mask. "You found me." Praise Poseidon, help had arrived. Shelly was the most welcome sight ever. And when Lily also swam into view, Jet thought her sister resembled an avenging angel from the old days of Atlantis when mermaids ruled the seven seas.

Shelly mouthed words she couldn't understand. Jet lifted her shoulders, dropped the counter and metal detector and raised her hands, palms out, indicating she couldn't hear. Shelly raised her arms and mimed removing the scuba mask.

Jet obligingly ripped off the headgear. As water blasted her face, her legs tightened and swelled twice their size. Before she could shrug off the air tank, the bottom half of the wet suit burst into pieces and her mermaid tail fin sea-swished in glorious freedom, a blue-and-purple glitter explosion. Jet reveled at the touch of water, tingled all over in a delightful cacophony of awakening sensation.

Shelly pulled at the cage door and frowned when it refused to yield.

"How did you get here so fast?" Jet gave her a quick hug through the bars, then laughed at Shelly's startled expression. Jet had never been the huggy type. "Never mind, we need to scram. Let me have your knife," she said quickly, suddenly desperate to get out.

Shelly opened her sporran and handed one over. Jet inserted the blade into the locking mechanism and expertly jiggled it around. Many a time before, she'd opened pirates' chests and underwater locked luggage from shipwrecks. She could do this.

Damn, nothing gave. Jet pulled off the gloves and tried again. This time she was rewarded with a distinct *ker-plop* as the lock released its hold.

A roaring, screeching vibration sent bubbles cascading upward like a miniature cyclone.

Shelly clamped her hands over her ears. "What the hell?"

The alarm. She'd forgotten all about it in her haste. They'd send Perry after her immediately.

"Go!" Jet screamed. "Get out of here. I'll be behind you shortly." She struggled to release the air tank. "Go on, I can swim faster than y'all." Not to mention, she was an awful lot stronger, too. "They'll be after me now," she added. "I can handle them. You can't." Shelly was sensitive about her TRAB status, which prevented her from staying underwater as long as a full-blooded mermaid. But now was no time for niceties to spare her feelings.

Shelly nodded. "Okay. We'll be ahead in a small boat. Tillman and Landry are on it."

Lily stayed put. "Silly Jet," she chided. "You forget I

can sing and make anyone forget their own name, much less why they dived undersea to start with."

Jet tugged at the neoprene sleeves. "Dumbass," she said with a laugh, shaking her head. "He won't be able to hear you through the scuba mask."

Lily's perfectly formed lips puckered to a surprised O shape. "Didn't think about that. If you're sure—"

"Go." Jet waved a hand, relieved when Lily swam off. A few more seconds and she'd be completely out of the damned wet suit. It felt as if she was wrestling out of a prison straitjacket. She forced her mind to slow and relax. Otherwise, she'd be a panicked kitty, too excited to think straight and make her escape. In seconds, Jet stripped down to nothing and took one last look back at her nightmare. The opened cage swayed harmlessly in the gentle undertow.

Freedom! She grinned and fist-pumped triumphantly.

Overhead, something, or someone, approached. A long, black object trailing bubbles shot downward—straight at her. Her mouth dropped open as the human in scuba gear approached. Through the mask, she saw the familiar brown eyes of her enemy rimmed in topaz; they glittered with the intensity of a hunter determined to capture his prey.

By his side, Perry carried an air-powered speargun. Her heartbeat slowed and her mind froze as he lifted the gun, centered his scope and took aim.

The first shot missed.

Shit. He'd been so close. That left him with just one more spear. He'd get her with the next one. That bitch needed to be brought in line once and for all.

Perry felt the imprint in his upper arms where Vargas's muscled men had grabbed him and unceremoniously dumped him off the side of the boat the second the alarm rang. Vargas had forced him to sit by the side of the boat, completely clad in the wet suit and at the ready in case Jet tried to escape. "Get her," Vargas had growled at him, thrusting a speargun into his hands. "Injure her if you must, but don't kill her. I need her to locate that bomb."

After that terse instruction, he'd barely had time to seal his air mask before he hit water.

Get her he would. She'd made him look like a fool in front of the man he needed to impress, at least until this venture was successfully completed. Why did Jet have to make this so difficult? What the hell was the big deal about helping him out this time? They'd worked together for years and now Jet acted as if she was too good for him. She'd actually tried to pay him off with a check and, worse, had rejected him in front of Landry Fields. As if he was some low-life, unimportant *nobody*. Perry's blood exploded like hot lava from a volcano, and a blistering heat raged through him, fueling his hunt in the dark waters.

Perry let go of the wire he'd followed into the sea. The wire had led him to the empty cage, its door ajar. Jet was a clever freak; he had to give her that. And strong as any man, stronger than he was. Perry's fingers twitched on the gun. But she wasn't stronger than a damned spear, even if she thought she was hot shit. This little baby would teach her a lesson, by God.

He forged on, swimming in the disgusting, muddy waters. He was too good for this shit. A man with his looks and smarts should be sipping high-priced bourbons on a private island with half a dozen whores attending to his every need.

Once Jet found the missing bomb, he'd be set for life and she'd be even richer. She was already filthy rich but even the wealthy always wanted more money. Money held power, provided the freedom to live life on your own terms, not beholden to a boss, social convention or, in his case, a former lover. The selfish thing—as long as Jet had money, what did she care if he had to toil all his life like some pathetic, mediocre nobody? To hell with her.

But Jet's worst sin, the unforgivable one, was that with all that money, she had let him rot in prison. She could have bought off the corrections officials in South America, but she didn't; Vargas did. So it was her own damned fault they were in this mess together.

Where was she? He had to find her down here. He shuddered to imagine what Vargas would do if he returned to the boat alone.

A sparkle of—*something*—caught his eye. Perry swam closer and an entire cluster of blue, purple, pink, green and gold appeared, shimmering and twitching like jewels against black velvet. An outline emerged as the rainbow colors morphed into a pattern. A huge tail fin. He raised his eyes, saw where fish scale merged into pale skin at the hip, saw the naked torso and rosy nipples, and continued upward to the angular jaw and dark, blazing eyes, so like his own.

Jet.

Jet Bosarge in mermaid form. He'd seen it a few times in their past, but avoided it as much as possible, uncomfortable knowing he made love to a freak fish. Perry raised the speargun again. He wouldn't kill her, otherwise Vargas would be furious. And she was worth so much more to him alive. There were treasures yet to be found and a world of people to amaze when he exposed her to the public. He could set his own price for paying customers to gawk at the mutated thing, could build an empire.

As quick as she'd appeared, Jet disappeared into the darkness. Damn it. She might escape.

Another flash of sparkles glittered; Jet was still in range.

Perry knew the spot to hurt and humble Miss High-and-Mighty. He leveled his gun at the freaky fishtail and took aim.

Landry glanced at his wristwatch, surprised to find only six minutes had passed. They'd stopped their boat about a hundred yards from Vargas's vessel. He and Tillman held fishing rods, as if they were merely out for a few bites. Their firearms were on the floorboards, hidden but loaded and at the ready when needed.

It felt as if hours had passed since Lily, Adriana and Shelly went under. Waiting here and knowing that somewhere beneath the sea's calm facade Jet was trapped and her family was down there—doing God knew what.

He glanced at Tillman, curious about his relationship with his fiancée. If Shelly and Jet were cousins, Shelly was a mermaid, as well. He'd read all about the serial killer Sheriff Angier had captured last summer, who had been caught after trying to abduct Shelly.

The sheriff's close tie to Jet's family had kept Landry from contacting him when he first arrived in the bayou. But Tillman's actions with Seth had won Landry's respect. He'd handled everything fairly. Tillman was obviously an intelligent, decent man.

But one question niggled at Landry. "Why do you keep your corrupt deputy around?" he asked.

Tillman's gray eyes narrowed. "Carl? Corrupt? What makes you say that?"

"According to Jet, Dismukes took a cut for years to keep quiet about her and Perry's more unethical treasure sales."

"Son of a bitch," Tillman spat out.

"Worse, he keeps threatening that if Jet goes back in business, he expects a share of the profits again." At the thunderstorm in his eyes, Landry felt for the guy. "What about Jet's family? Are they trustworthy?"

"Adriana Bosarge is fine when she warms up to you a bit. Now, Lily." Tillman shook his head. "Guess you have to make allowances seeing as she's a special siren."

"I thought they were all the same."

"Shelly explained that Lily's a *phonic* siren. Like in those old books where sirens entranced men with their voices and made sailors shipwreck."

Landry's palms tingled. A magical voice? "But Jet's not one of those phonic sirens," he ventured. "Right? I mean, she's drop-dead hot and has a great voice…" He stopped at Tillman's expression of amused astonishment.

"Beautiful? Jet's, er, arresting, unusual. I'll give you that."

Was the man blind? He was like Seth, unable to see what was before him. Shelly was a pretty girl—in a bland, sweet, vanilla sort of way. But Jet was a complex, surprising woman full of contrasts. Fair skin with blue-black hair, athletic and feminine, powerful and vulnerable. He couldn't get enough of her. The more she let him into her world, the more fascinated he was and the more he wanted.

A loud thump rocked the bottom of their boat. Landry jumped up, dropping the fishing pole. "What was that?"

"One of them is back," Tillman answered calmly.

"How can you tell?"

"It's a signal. At least one of them wants aboard. Let's stand together and shield them from view as they get back under the canopy, in case anyone's watching on Vargas's boat."

They moved alongside one another, examining a fishing lure Tillman held in his hand, as if they were swapping fish stories. A loud swoosh arose from the water and the boat rocked slightly. Landry had an unmistakable urge to peek. The only time he'd seen a mermaid was over two decades ago. He'd been so young, and the day so dark and long ago, that over the years he had stored the memory of that strange underwater glimpse in the attic of his mind in a locked trunk marked Do Not Open.

Thump. The boat careened side to side as a mermaid dropped onto the floorboards. Chills clawed his skin but he kept his face turned away.

"The girls found Jet." Adriana's voice was slightly breathless. "We need to go—" her words were muffled, so Landry knew she was pulling clothing over her head "—north, at least fifty yards or so."

"Is she okay?" he asked anxiously.

"I'm not sure." She tapped Tillman's shoulder. "I'm dressed. Start the boat."

Landry faced her. Jet's mother was the same handsome woman as before jumping ship, only now her long hair was dripping wet and her dress damp. Would he ever get used to this family? Landry shoved aside the wayward musing. "Tell us what's going on down there."

"Shelly and Lily are younger and faster swimmers than me. They sped ahead and by the time I saw them again, they had found Jet and were freeing her from a shark cage."

Jet was free. Landry's heart swelled with relief and he looked down into the water, expecting the blue-and-black water to shift and form a pattern, an outline of a mermaid. Jet would burst through any moment. First thing after he saw she was fine, he'd give her hell for veering off to that doughnut shop without checking in first. Stubborn woman.

Tillman accelerated the boat. "This is almost over," he growled out. Landry knew by his tense manner he'd been as worried about Shelly's welfare as he was about Jet's.

"There's bad news," Adriana warned. "Someone in a

wet suit was after Jet. I rushed back here to get y'all closer to them."

Perry Hammonds? Tension and dread slammed back into his chest and squeezed. "But Shelly and Lily are with her. Three against one are good odds. Plus, they're in their element. The diver isn't."

Tense silence greeted this remark. Hell, he didn't believe his own words. He surveyed the larger vessel and saw the men on board had finally noticed the small craft headed directly their way at top speed. Sons of bitches, all of them. Men with no morals or heart, willing to sell their own country short for a price.

Landry radioed his boss and reported their location. "Send in the coast guard or Homeland Security or whatever is closest. Vargas knows something's up and we have every reason to believe he and his men are armed and dangerous."

His boss started hammering questions, but Landry turned the radio off. He'd face his boss's ire and internal investigations when this was over. Details and explanations could wait. For now, all he cared about was saving Jet.

If he wasn't too late.

Chapter 18

He meant to kill her.

Jet whipped her tail fin and swam. Swam with all the speed and strength she'd honed from months of daily training for the Poseidon Games. She had been so close to a clean escape. She prayed Shelly and Lily were long gone and out of danger. *If anyone dies, let it be me.* All this was her fault; she'd brought this on herself and her family when she'd told Perry her secret and let him use her for his own selfish gains. Stupid, stupid, stupid.

Thrum-ripple. A spear whizzed less than three inches from her right ear. Had he aimed at her head or was it a bad shot on his part? The two-foot-long metal rod shot past and then lost velocity and fell harmlessly downward. If Perry tried to retrieve it and reload the gun, the party was over. He'd never catch up to her. She glanced back, dismayed to find Perry hadn't wasted time with the discharged spear, but swam toward her like a full-speed torpedo.

Ten feet ahead, Lily beckoned from underneath a boat, one graceful hand pointed at the aluminum hull. Almost home free! Jet surged ahead, racing. It was the only race that truly mattered. The Undines' Challenge at the Poseidon Games had been a mere dress rehearsal for this moment. The past hurt and injustices from the merfolk, her insecurity and worry about her heritage…none of it mattered.

Above water, Landry awaited. He was the world to her. In time, he'd see that she was worthy of his love. She would never, ever desert him like everyone else had in the past. All she needed was one more chance. Just one.

"Go away!" she screamed at Lily. "He's right behind me."

Instead of retreating, Lily surged toward her, eyes fixated at a point to Jet's right. Jet turned and saw another diver, armed with a speargun, had entered the fray. Vargas evidently didn't trust Perry to handle this job on his own.

Magical singing burst through every water molecule, a captivating cadence so lovely it lit the murky water like a street lantern enshrouded in fog. For a second, Lily was illuminated, the angelic wide eyes, flowing blond hair streaked with pink and lavender, Cupid's-bow lips and unblemished, alabaster skin that morphed at her hips into a glittering tail fin. The knife's blade in her right hand reflected particles of light, a beacon of justice.

The diver's eyes widened behind the mask and at last he raised the gun. His helmet had provided enough of a sound barrier that Lily's siren voice had neither immobilized nor enchanted him for long. A spear sped through the water, but Lily dodged it.

She had to help her sister. This whole mess was her fault; she'd put her family in danger. If they were harmed or killed, Jet could never forgive her foolish self. But before Jet caught up, Lily had swum up behind the diver and used the knife to saw through the diver's air hose. Bubbles exploded as the freed hose whipped and jerked like a furious eel. Her sister had the diver under control.

"Go!" Lily shouted. "Another diver's on your tail."

Jet swam upward, close to the water's surface. Small bubbling swirls from the boat's idling engine ceased. They must have spotted her and didn't want to chance the propellers getting in her way.

Another five feet and her fingertips could touch the boat. Landry's face came into view. His jaw was set in grim lines and his frosty blue eyes lasered in on her. Through rippling water, his face shifted and blurred, but always the blue of his eyes pierced through the muddy sediment like a homing beacon, calling her home.

Two feet away. Landry leaned overboard, strong arms extended, ready to pull her to safety. She could almost feel his strong, hot skin against her body, smell his clean, masculine scent as she nuzzled her nose into the curve between his neck and shoulder.

The world suddenly faded to black.

Firm pressure around the bottom of her tail fin pulled her down, away from the light. Jet twisted, propelling her arms up and away. The pressure released, but Perry emerged only an arm's distance away, exploding into her view like a sea monster from the deepest depths.

The rims of his brown irises glittered like burned topaz. Perry raised an arm, wielding a rubber-handled diving knife. It was long, hooked, lethally sharp—a fish-gutting dagger. A bluff? He'd never harmed her before but she'd never crossed him before, either. And he'd already come damned near to shooting her brains out with the speargun. For a split-second, her brain processed the danger and tried to plan an escape.

That was all the time Perry needed to lower the knife. Jet jerked back, but she knew she had reacted too late as her eyes tracked the blade's descent. She braced herself for the inevitable pain.

It never came.

A body dropped between the exposed skin of her bare shoulder and the knife's path. The weight knocked her down and backward. Lily? No.

Her mouth dropped open at the sight of light brown hair with the slight curling tips that brushed the wide nape of his neck. No, Landry shouldn't be here. The sea was her world.

The two men struggled, sinking lower as they pushed and wrestled. One bone-shattering snap later, and the knife spun out of Perry's hand. Jet watched, mesmerized, as it twirled down, innocent as a majorette's minibaton flipped skyward, glinting in the sun at a Saturday-morning football game. Falling, falling, right into Lily's outstretched hand.

Her sister, free of her attacker, had swum this way, about a dozen yards beneath them.

Jet jerked her gaze back to Landry. Despite the unnatural bend in Perry's right arm, Landry was losing the fight. His large body was slumped, sinking under a barrage of hits from Perry's one good hand.

He can't swim! Belatedly, Jet remembered Landry's shamed admission. No wonder Perry was besting him. It was an unfair fight.

Jet rushed over and thwacked her tail fin with all her might, connecting with Perry's upper back. The oxygen tank ripped away from its moorings and sank. Perry thrashed about, futilely trying to grab his fast-sinking lifeline.

She hadn't intentionally knocked off the air tank, but Perry was an excellent swimmer and they weren't deep. He could survive as long as he didn't panic and grow mentally confused. Jet spared Perry only a second; she firmly grasped his chin, making sure he made eye contact with her, and pointed upward. All the while, she kept her attention on Landry. He was the one in the greatest peril, and he was the one she loved. Landry's eyes bulged and he gulped copious amounts of water while uselessly flaying his arms and legs to stay afloat.

Jet shot past Perry and swam to him. She hooked an arm across Landry's waist, scooping him up and hurtling to the sea's surface with the speed of a dolphin. She breached the water and lifted his head out to take in oxygen. His face was gray, lips blue, eyes closed.

"Over here, quick!"

Jet wildly sought out the location of her mother's voice. Adriana waved from a small vessel. They were all there—Tillman, Shelly, Mom—but no Lily. Jet couldn't spare her sister another thought as she dragged Landry to the boat. Lily could take care of herself, always had.

Tillman grabbed underneath Landry's arms and heaved him on board while Mom and Shelly hovered over her as she climbed in. Shelly darted nervous glances over her shoulder.

"There's a nearby boat," she explained. "Can't let them see us in merform."

Vargas and his men. But Jet didn't worry about it. All her attention focused on Landry's inert body. Tillman rolled Landry onto his side and seawater spewed out his mouth. Jet sank to her knees, only vaguely aware of her mom's hands, dressing her as if she were a little child.

"There, there. I'm sure he's going to be fine," she whispered in a low, soothing tone. A cotton robe slipped against her skin. Her mom wiped clumps of wet hair from her face with a towel, then gently rubbed her scalp, drying the dripping hair.

Live. Damn it, live. Jet wrapped her arms around her waist and shivered violently. Shelly patted a knee, offering unspoken sympathy. Tillman administered CPR, alternately breathing into Landry's mouth and pumping his chest. Jet closed her eyes, unable to bear watching the trickle of brackish water run down the corners of Landry's mouth. Despite the midday sun, her chilled body shook uncontrollably.

Her mother, in a rare show of tenderness, engulfed Jet in her arms and rocked her like a baby. Jet clung to her, savoring her mom's strength. When she most needed them, her family had rallied behind her in their own special way.

"Where's Lily?" Shelly asked.

"Sh-she was fine when I saw her," Jet said between chattering teeth. "She was out of harm's w-way and Perry was—"

A large, hacking cough rent the air. Jet's eyes flew open. Landry lay propped on an elbow on one side, wheezing huge gulps of air into his lungs. Jet found it the most beautiful sound she'd ever heard, far lovelier than any siren's song. She crawled to him at once and ran her fingers down his unnaturally pale cheeks flecked with golden, morning stubble.

Landry's blue eyes opened at last, zeroing in on her. "You okay?" He frowned, looking over her body as if checking for wounds.

His voice was rough as sandpaper. The second most beautiful sound she'd ever heard in her life. The trembling and cold whooshed away in a warm wave of joyful release. "I'm fine, you fool." She sobbed and laughed at the same time. "What do you mean jumping in the ocean when you can't swim?"

"I saw Perry raise the knife and I had to stop him. I knew..." A large round of coughing racked his lungs before he continued, "I knew you'd save me."

Landry trusted her. That was a start, something she

could work with. She'd prove to him every morning that she would stay for as long as he wished.

"Where's Perry?" Tillman cut in, looking in all directions.

The only answer was a faint lapping of waves licking the boat's hull. They all leaned over the side of the boat but the smooth, dark surface yielded no answer.

"Maybe I should go look for him," Jet said reluctantly.

A chorus of "No" greeted the lukewarm offer, along with a "Hell, no" from Landry, who gripped her arm. "Lily's down there," he said. "She can save him if he needs rescuing."

If Landry noticed an odd silence, or a furtive exchange of glances between the Bosarge women, he let it pass without comment.

A bullhorn sounded from around the bend, rousing everyone to action.

"The coast guard can search for Perry," Landry said, standing up. His legs were surprisingly wobbly but nothing would stop him from finishing this case.

Help had finally arrived and Landry smiled in grim satisfaction. He would take great pleasure in arresting Vargas. Their boat was close enough now he could see the panic of the men on board as they gathered on deck and gestured wildly with their hands. Vargas must be stunned that Jet had escaped and Perry was unaccounted for. Someone had pulled up the wire cable and the shark cage hung swaying and dripping in the breeze.

Empty.

"Time for me to get out of here and check on Lily," Adriana said. "You coming with us, Shell?"

Shelly placed a hand on Tillman's forearm. "We rented

the boat in my name, so I better stick around or they'll ask questions about it later."

Landry's brows drew together. "Where are you going?"

"Swimming home, of course," Adriana answered matter-of-factly, then turned to address Shelly. "Good idea. Plus you'll have to return the rental car, as well."

"Home?" Landry repeated incredulously. "As in…swim all the way back to Bayou La Siryna?"

Adriana nodded. "Watch over Jet." She dived overboard in a perfect arch, leaving only the tiniest of splashes in her wake. Seconds later, her yellow cotton sundress bobbed on the mucky salt marsh like a happy daisy in a mud field.

"You'll get used to their ways," Tillman said drily. "Sort of."

The horn blew again, shaking Landry out of his mermaid musings. Time for that later. Now he needed to focus on his job. After years of tracking Vargas, the FBI needed a charge that would stick. They couldn't get him for illegal salvaging; he'd bet anything they had all the proper licenses and permissions in place. There was the kidnapping charge against Jet. But he'd rather leave her out of this matter, if possible. Jet and her family needed their anonymity to guard their secret race.

With all the men trapped on board, one of them was bound to talk and rat out Vargas's involvement in trying to get the bomb. But Vargas could always claim that if he found it, it was his intention all along to offer it to the United States government for a small reward.

How ironic if the only charge that stuck on Vargas turned out to be a murder or manslaughter charge on the missing Perry Hammonds. He radioed his boss. "Tell the coast guard we have a man-overboard situation."

Landry surveyed the muddy, salty water half expecting Hammonds to pop up like a monster creature from the black lagoon. Too much time had passed for a rescue, unless Lily or Adriana had taken pity on Perry and reattached his oxygen tank.

He rather hoped they hadn't.

Chapter 19

"So what happened to the bad dude?" Seth asked with wide eyes. "Did y'all ever find him?"

"Navy divers found Hammonds two days later, along with another one of Vargas's men," Landry reported with satisfaction. "Both drowned. One evidently had some equipment malfunction with his tank's air hose. Hammonds had been in a struggle and had a broken arm and a huge bruise on his upper back."

"Must have got in a fight on the ship and one of the other guys threw him overboard."

"That's the official theory on the final report." That report had tied him up for five days in Atlanta, days he'd much rather have spent with Jet.

"What about the bomb?"

Now, *that* was the million-dollar question. Homeland Security sent a letter to the FBI stating that Jim Tindol's claims were unsubstantiated, although in Landry's mind, all the government agencies involved had given up rather quickly on the search.

Officially, that was.

"Nothing found," he said. "But at least Vargas is in cus-

tody and charged with kidnapping and manslaughter. His
international crime ring will be easier to dismantle with
their boss put away."

Seth frowned. "Don't see why they had to take Jet."

Landry stole a sideways glance at his puzzled face.
Would he and Jet be able to guard her secret around one
very curious, constantly underfoot teenager?

"She and Perry used to be partners and he convinced
everyone that Jet's underwater skills could prove useful."
Underwater skills…understatement of the millennium.

"Jet's cool. I hope she's okay."

Bubbles of uncertainty skittered in his gut. During their
brief late-night calls over the past few days, there had been
some emotional undertone, some nuance in Jet's voice he
couldn't quite decipher. "Says she's all right when we talk
on the phone."

"But you don't believe it."

"Jet's the strongest woman I've ever met, but she went
through major trauma. And it doesn't help she's alone right
now."

Seth straightened. "Where are Lily and Shelly?" he
asked with way too much interest.

"Shelly's off with Tillman and Lily…" Landry strummed
his fingers on the steering wheel. "Lily went on a long trip
with her mother."

Seth leaned back in his seat, clearly disappointed.

Landry wondered, yet again, what the hell had happened at the bottom of that Tybee Island salt marsh. Had
Lily killed Perry? Or perhaps she had merely let him
drown, watching the oxygen bubbles from Perry's lips
slowly trickle to nothing while she held the oxygen tank
with that blank, serene gaze and slight upturn of her lush
lips. And what had happened to the other dead diver? Malfunctioned diver equipment, his ass.

He shifted uncomfortably in his seat. Maybe he judged Lily unfairly. Truth was, he didn't want or need to know what happened down there. Jet and Lily had been under attack while undersea—it was their world, a mermaid realm. *Not my jurisdiction,* he thought wryly. All that mattered was that they were alive and safe.

Landry whipped the BMW into a used-car lot on the outskirts of Bayou La Siryna.

"Why are we stopping here?" Seth asked. "Thought you were in a hurry to get home."

"If you're coming to stay with me for good, we need another set of wheels."

Twenty minutes later, Landry signed the papers on a slightly rusted pickup truck that was over ten years old. Outside the dealership, he tossed a set of keys to his brother. "It's all yours."

Seth gave a tentative smile. "I'll pay you back one day." He took a few steps toward the truck, then turned back to Landry. "Wait. Wrong keys."

"Truck's mine," Landry said. "If I'm going to become a local here, this truck's more practical."

"So, you're going to let *me* drive your car?"

"It's not mine anymore. I'm giving you the BMW. When we get home, sign it and the car's officially yours."

Seth stood immobile, frowning. Hardly the reaction Landry had expected.

"Why are you doing this for me?" his brother asked suspiciously. "What do you want?"

Patience. The kid hasn't had much experience with kindness. Landry put his hands on his hips. "I want you to be honest with me, attend classes next fall and stay out of trouble."

"That's it?"

"Yep."

Seth nodded, serious. "I can do that." He walked to him and extended his right hand. "Thanks, bro."

Seth didn't make the usual "half brother" reference. Landry clasped his hand. "Get out of here," he grinned. "And no speeding. I know the sheriff here, but he doesn't cut me any deals."

Seth got in the car and carefully backed up in the gravel parking lot. Landry motioned for him to let down the window. "Do me a favor. Run by Jet's shop and see if she needs help with anything. Tell her I'll be along in a bit."

Seth gave a mock salute. "Okay, then I'm going to see Jimmy. Wait until he gets a load of my wheels."

"Tell his grandma thanks for keeping an eye on the kittens." Baby Girl had delivered a litter of six while he was away at the FBI office in Atlanta. He owed her big-time.

Landry waved and headed for his new-to-him truck. Maybe the big-brother-role-model thing wouldn't be as hard as he feared. After all—

The screech of tires peeling onto blacktop brought Landry up short and he spun in time to see gray gravel spitting on the road. Over four-hundred horsepower of German engineering roared off.

On second thought, coaching Seth through another year of high school might be the most difficult job he'd ever tackled.

After years of driving a smooth, sleek sports car, the truck would take some getting used to. He felt every bump in the road on the way to Bayou La Siryna Water Park. Landry navigated through the numerous potholes, parked by the entrance, and followed a group of chattering middle-school kids and their chaperones as they skipped inside. Before he spoke to the owner, he wanted to see Dolly. He waited patiently in line to pay, listening to the kids' chatter. The dolphin was quite the draw; no wonder Andrew Morgan kept it around.

He took in the cracked pavement, sinking pool liners and faded umbrellas. The park was tidy and clean, but old and in need of repairs. Ticket paid, he followed the kids again to the saltwater pool. A man in bathing trunks and a Bayou La Siryna Water Park T-shirt was at the side of the pool with buckets of fish.

"Welcome," he bellowed. "Y'all ready to feed Dolly?"

The kids scrambled for the buckets. In the far right corner, taking up nearly a third of the pool space, a large silver blob lolled underwater. Even to his untrained eye, Landry could see the pool was too small and inadequate. No wonder Jet worried about the dolphin.

As minnows were thrown in, Dolly ambled toward the kids.

"Don't throw out all the fish at once," the trainer said. "Let's see if we can get Dolly to perform some tricks first." He waited until Dolly gobbled up the fish already thrown in, then held up a bright red hula hoop.

Dolly ignored him.

One eager red-haired boy sank to his knees and leaned out so far over the pool, a whisper of wind could knock him over. "Can we go for a dolphin ride?"

The other kids squealed and clapped.

"Oh, I don't know about that," one of the teachers said, frowning. "Could be dangerous."

The trainer rushed to reassure her. "We don't have insurance in place yet for rides, but we're working on it."

The teacher's face smoothed. "Not today, kids," she announced.

Amid a chorus of boos, Landry left. He was doing the right thing today. Before seeking Andrew's office, he went back to the park entrance and scanned the parking lot. A large van marked Aquatic Rescue Operations pulled in. An entourage of three more vans and trucks snaked in behind it.

Landry hurried to the manager's office and rapped sharply on the door before entering. A bearded, lean guy, in his mid-fifties or so, glanced up from a pile of paperwork. Landry automatically reached in his back pocket for his FBI badge, only to realize before his hand hit his pocket that it wasn't there. Old habits would take a while to break.

"I'm here to transport your dolphin to a wildlife refuge." He put an authoritative command into his voice, born of over a decade in law-enforcement training.

"Wh-what?" The man jumped to his feet. "You can't do that. Who do you think you are?"

"I'm the new deputy sheriff in Bayou La Siryna." Or at least he would be as soon as he got to Tillman's office and filled out the paperwork.

"I ain't broke no laws." Andrew looked more scared than angry, despite the bluster.

"I'm sure you haven't." Landry paused for effect. "Not knowingly."

"What do you mean?"

"I mean that there've been several complaints about the dolphin's housing." Landry glanced out the window. A crew of over a dozen muscular men exited parked vehicles and made their way to the entrance. "You've violated a host of marine-mammal protection laws."

"I—I didn't mean to," Andrew said. "I took her in after she was injured and beached. I'd never hurt her."

The man's eyes were huge. Landry read a flash of guilt in them along with a huge dose of nervousness. He lowered his voice, tinged it with understanding. "I'm sure you never meant to," he agreed. "But over the winter season,

Dolly became a tourist draw, a way of bringing in needed money at a time when you normally don't have business. Now with warmer weather arriving, you see the potential profits she can bring your park."

Andrew folded his arms. "I take good care of her."

"No. No, you don't."

"Who says I don't? Bring—"

"Did you know she was pregnant?" Landry cut in.

The man's mouth dropped open. "How would you know?"

"Didn't think you did." Landry pointed to the men approaching the entry. "These men are going to transport Dolly to a safe home in Florida." He leaned over Andrew's desk. "You're a decent man, Andrew. You want what's best for her and this is it."

Andrew hung his head and sighed deeply.

Landry straightened. "Look at it this way. Let these trained professionals rescue Dolly and not only have you done the right thing, but you'll also save yourself from huge fines and a ton of bad publicity."

Andrew nodded slowly. "Yeah, guess you're right."

Landry went to the door and motioned the crew leader inside the office. "The owner will sign off on any paperwork you need."

Outside, most of the schoolkids had already tired of the lethargic Dolly and headed for the bathrooms to change into their bathing suits for a swim. The rescue workers expertly carried over a huge nylon sling. Landry knew from his research that Dolly would be hoisted to a saltwater vat and placed in a padded fiberglass transport unit to make the nine-hour trip. The mammal would be stressed by the journey, but after today, she and her unborn calf would be healthier and happier.

They'd better be. A huge portion of his savings had been donated to the Florida Aquatic Wildlife Center to make it happen.

Three days without Landry felt like three years. Jet listlessly ran a dust rag over a shelf. The morning had been filled with easy, mindless tasks, mere final touches before The Pirate's Chest's grand opening. Yet she was tired, drained, as if her body still hadn't recovered from the arduous return home after the stress at Tybee Island.

The front doorbell chimed. Jet laid down the rag and turned. "We're not open—" She stopped speaking as the wall of fury came her way. It took a moment to recognize him in street clothes. She couldn't recall ever seeing him dressed in anything except the Englazia County sheriff's uniform.

Carl Dismukes got within three feet and stopped, waving a gnarled finger in her face. Jet blankly took in the nicked fingers from years of whittling, and other fine, white scars at the base of his fingers—scars from plastic surgery to correct a congenital disorder. Like so many other bayou residents, he was born with webbed fingers and the soft tissue between the digits had been removed. Unlike most of the other bayou residents, Carl knew the webbing came from mermaid ancestry.

"This is all your fault," he growled. "What did you tell Tillman about me?"

Jet slapped his hand away with enough force to show she was no pushover. "It was bound to come out one day. You're lucky you got away with blackmail all these years."

"Lucky?" His face reddened. "There was no *lucky* to it. I'm a hell of a lot smarter than that dumbass sheriff and his dead daddy that held the job before Tillman took over."

"Shut up, Carl. Tillman's almost family."

"Did you tell your new boyfriend about me?"

"Not about your mermaid heritage. Only that you're a corrupt, untrustworthy, backstabbing crook."

He angrily ran a hand through his silver, short-cropped hair.

Jet lifted her chin. She was finally free. "You don't have anything on me anymore. Now get out of my store."

His face reddened even more, hands fisted at his sides. Carl lowered his voice to a growl. "Better watch your back from now on, bitch." He backed away with one last sneer and left.

She let him have the last word, ready for the confrontation to end. As the chimes announced his retreat, Jet sank into a chair. The air compressed in on her and she took a deep breath to counteract the swimming lightness in her body. What the hell was wrong with her today? She wiped tears off her cheeks with a rough fist. This was stupid. Resolutely, she went to the restroom and splashed water on her face. A few more details to take care of and she'd close shop.

When she reentered the store, Seth was at the counter, eyeing the antique swords. He looked up with a grin that washed away as he studied her face. "Have you been *crying?*" he asked with such a look of horror that she laughed, her spirits lifted.

"I'm fine," she answered, waving a hand dismissively. "I've been alone at the house too much." She looked past him and spotted the BMW parked across the street. Her heart lightened and beat faster. "Where's your brother?"

"He had a couple errands to run." Seth followed her gaze. "Oh, that's my car now."

"Really?" Landry was so proud of that car.

"He bought a used truck. Said it was more practical."

After all the cracks he made about her old beater? She grinned.

"He wanted me to stop by and see if you needed me for anything."

Seth's animated face was so different from the first time she met him. Landry had told her his brother was moving in. No doubt Seth was happy with the arrangement. "No, go enjoy your car."

Relief washed across his face. Really, teenagers could be so comically transparent. "I'm going to Jimmy's now," he said. "Got a big weekend planned."

Jet stood. "I'm going to start my weekend early, too, and head home."

She grabbed her purse, locked up and got into her truck. The day was sunshiny and held a humidity that hinted at the coming summer meltdown, which lasted from June until practically Christmas.

She went past the downtown mermaid statue, its eternally perfect face staring out to sea. The smooth stone, steel and copper facade, as familiar to her as the sight of her own home, hit her with an unforeseen poignancy that had her eyes watering—again. Hell, this wasn't like her. She was happy, damn it. By tonight, she'd see Landry, be able to hold him in her arms and not just hear his deep, sexy voice on the phone. Jet put in a Lynyrd Skynyrd CD. The upbeat Southern anthem of "Sweet Home Alabama" always lifted her spirits.

Tapping her fingers on the steering wheel, Jet drove mindlessly out of town and into the rural landscape of lush live oaks draped with Spanish moss like long, dangling earrings. She unrolled her window, letting in the tang of brine that wafted in the breeze, a scent as familiar and deep-rooted as soap and baby powder. Birds and bullfrogs and crickets played background to Skynyrd's melody.

An unseen force guided her hands and she drove past Perry's old cottage rental. In the driveway, the red Mustang sat like an abandoned orphan. She'd been in touch with Perry's mother. His body had been shipped home to Pennsylvania and Mrs. Hammonds would arrive next week to take care of what little remained of Perry's last worldly possessions.

A memory tugged like an undertow, pulling her down into the past. Perry, dark hair whipping in the wind, grinning and waving at her on the dock, the first time she laid eyes on him. The promise of fun and adventure in his wide smile that had beckoned her.

She swallowed past the painful sting in her throat, emotions churning chaotically. At one time, he'd had some goodness, and that was what she'd try to remember—the laughter in his eyes on day one, not the flashing hatred in those same eyes on his last day on earth.

Jet reached home, even more exhausted from memories of Perry. She unlocked the door and entered the too-quiet house. Rebel finally roused from somewhere and ran to her, barking. He launched himself at her feet and lay on his back, exposing a hairless, extremely freckled tummy. She rubbed him while he made high-pitched moans of delight. He'd been good company while the family was gone.

The thing to do was take a little nap, get refreshed before seeing Landry tonight. The promise and anticipation of the night lifted her spirits. As lonely as the house had been with everyone away, the good news was that she and Landry would have privacy. She finally reached her bedroom, stripped down to a pair of panties and threw on an oversize T-shirt. At last, she sank into the mattress, curling into herself like a child under the cool cotton sheets. Rebel lay at the foot of the bed, immediately settling into snoring slumber. Delightful lethargy descended and she relaxed into a dream.

Water surrounded her body and she drifted—content to let the tide take her in any direction. Bits of seaweed brushed against her arms like the touch of a friend in greeting. Fish swished past, paying her no attention in their endless hunt for food. Jet wiggled her tail fin, admiring the shimmering colors against the turquoise waters. She surrendered to the sea's surge, the constant to-and-fro of the tide, the pull of the moon, the mysteries of the deep. Her belly distended and she placed one arm under her lower tummy and the other across the top in a loving, protective, gesture borne by women down the ages as they cradled...

Jet came to with a startled intake of breath. No. It couldn't be. Could it? She rubbed a hand over her flat, muscular abs. Of course it was possible. TRABs like Shelly weren't uncommon. Jet winced at even thinking the slur name for halflings. She never considered them "traitor babies" unlike so many of her kind.

"It's a dream," she said aloud. "I am *not* pregnant." Even she could hear the fear underlying the denial. She flung off the sheets and went to the window, surprised that twilight approached. She'd slept for hours. And wasn't *that* telling. She crossed her arms and rubbed them. No need for panic until she knew something for sure. She'd get dressed, run to the drugstore and....

A loud knock at the door made her jump. It had to be Landry. Rebel's ears perked and he ran downstairs, barking and growling. She glanced in the mirror, running hands through her mussed hair. She frowned at the reflection, at the fear and worry banked in her eyes. That wouldn't do. The last thing she needed was Landry pestering her to tell him what was wrong. No need to bother him until she knew for sure one way or another. Jet gave a mechanical smile at the mirror, but it only marginally improved the effect. It would have to do.

She raced downstairs and stood at the door. "Who is it?" she called out.

"It's me. Landry."

Just the sound of his voice sent eager tingles from her toes to her scalp. The past few days had been a lonely hell without him. "Stay," she ordered Rebel before flinging the door open.

His tall, lean body filled the doorframe. In one hand he carried a mass of red roses.

"For me?" she squeaked. No one had ever brought her flowers. *Ever.* Her vision blurred with dumb tears. Until this moment, she hadn't realized that such a quaint, romantic gesture could reduce her to a quivering mush of joy, that it was something she'd love.

Damn, she loved this man.

Jet took one of his arms and drew him inside. Landry bent and offered his hand to the growling Rebel.

"We've met before, ole boy," he said softly. "Remember?"

Rebel sniffed and poked his malformed face into Landry's palm. Even Reb, leery of strangers, apparently loved this guy.

She had to tell him. Jet took a deep breath. Why was this so hard to do? She couldn't ever remember telling anyone she loved them, except maybe her mom when she was little. "I—I, um…"

He waited, roses in hand.

"You know that I…" Again, the words failed to come.

His jaw clenched and his blue eyes darkened with intensity. "You love me."

She gulped and nodded. Landry had figured it out, just

as he'd been able to deduce she was a mermaid without her saying a word. "Do you—"

"Yes. Hell, yes."

Jet threw her arms around his neck. "I love you, too," she mumbled, burying her face in his broad chest.

Oh, the things she wanted to do with him and for him. She inhaled his clean, masculine scent, which intermingled with the roses. She tightened her arms around his lower back and hugged him fiercely. He kissed the top of her head, his warm breath heating her scalp, a previously undiscovered erogenous zone. One hand raked through her hair, the other pressed against her lower back.

Rebel jumped on their legs and pawed. Jet didn't let go of Landry as she pushed open the screen door with a leg. "Go outside."

Reb shot through the opening and she closed it behind him. She pressed against Landry hard enough that his back crushed the door.

He chuckled. "I take it you missed me, too," he said.

The rumble of his voice vibrated deep in his chest, and she pictured the amused smile on the face that was buried in her hair.

"Not a bit," she denied. "I didn't miss these cute curls—" her fingers played with the ends of his hair "—or these lips—" she traced his mouth with a fingertip and a chaste kiss "—or, you know, this hot body of yours." She ran her hands down his chest and gave him a once-over stare.

"Liar." He held out the flowers. "But you still get roses."

Jet accepted them and closed her eyes as she inhaled their bouquet. "Thank you. They're beautiful."

"Not half as beautiful as you." There was no trace of a smile on his face.

"Oh," she breathed. He was truly at least a little in love to think so. If she was in a beauty contest with Lily, Shelly and other mermaids, well, she couldn't even win Miss Congeniality with her acerbic personality. Now that Landry was staying permanently in Bayou La Siryna, maybe in time she could prove to him that he could count on her forever. She wouldn't disappoint him like so many others in his past. That was, if he didn't bolt at the *p* word.

"Something wrong?" he asked.

Jet shook her head, appalled he could read her emotions so easily.

"You've been through so much, it's perfectly understandable." His mouth tightened. "Perry's death must be hard to deal with."

"No. There was nothing between us for years. I do feel sorry for his mother, though. She doted on him."

"You sure?"

Landry's hesitation and vulnerability undid her. "I'm sure," she said huskily. And she would make him understand that, would love him like no one else. Jet kissed him; her tongue probed the warm slickness of his mouth. The contact sent flaming arrows down to her core and dampness pooled in her panties. She whimpered, a needy sound from the back of her throat.

His hands cupped her ass and he groaned. "You're so damn hot," he muttered.

Jet wasn't sure she could make it all the way upstairs to the bedroom. She wanted him now. She jerked away and took his hand. "This way." She dragged him into the living room and shoved a mound of sea-treasure books to the floor. She carefully placed the roses on the coffee table and lay on the soft cushions, arms reaching upward for Landry.

He slowly lowered his body on top of hers, bearing most of his weight on his elbows. Jet arched her hips against him and felt his body's hard response to her own. She kissed him eagerly, her hands at the back of his neck, urging him deeper as their tongues collided.

"I missed you," he said in a ragged breath. One hand traveled up her rib cage and cupped her breast. "Missed this." He squeezed a nipple between his thumb and index finger, making her insides clench. His mouth replaced his fingers and he suckled her, dampening the cotton fabric of her T-shirt.

More. She wanted so much more. Landry switched his attention to her other nipple and she groaned. She tugged at the waistband of his jeans.

He stood and unfastened his belt, eyes riveted on her. It was the sexiest thing she'd ever seen. With no trace of embarrassment, he pulled off his jeans and boxers at the same time, then removed his shirt.

"Your turn," he said succinctly.

There was no more need for pretense or subterfuge. He knew all her secrets. Except, she corrected herself, perhaps one teeny, tiny secret. Jet immediately thrust it from her mind. Time to sort all that out later. Right now, her body was on fire for Landry. Jet pulled the T-shirt over her head and wiggled out of the panties.

A warm, slightly callused hand stroked the gill markings on the side of her neck. "Do these bother you?" he asked matter-of-factly.

She searched his face closely, looking for any sign of distaste. "No. Do they bother you?"

"Of course not." He leaned over and brushed a gentle kiss on the scars.

Jet's stiff spine relaxed under the caress. And again, she was caught off guard at the tightness in her throat and the tears pooling in her eyes.

"Are you sure nothing's wrong?" he asked again.

She stroked the inside of his thigh, working her way up until she cupped him. "You talk too much," she whispered.

"Yessss," he hissed. "God, it feels so good."

Jet explored his long shaft with a featherlight touch. Landry placed his hands over hers and squeezed. "Harder."

His face scrunched in an agony of pleasure that turned her on as much as his caresses. The last time they'd been intimate, they'd been in the cramped car and he had pleasured her. Now it was her turn. Jet placed her mouth where her hands had been and her tongue fondled his manhood.

Landry pulled away and leaned his face down by her belly button. "I want to taste you." His hot breath fanned her stomach as he traced light kisses downward. When he reached her core, Jet shuddered with anticipation. His tongue found her wetness and she was lost. The center of her world, all that mattered, was the desperate fury for release. His finger entered her and she bucked.

"Now," she commanded. "I want you in me."

Landry grabbed his jeans and pulled out a condom. "We weren't careful the first time."

No shit. What would he say if she was pregnant?

He ripped the foil and quickly put it on. The moment he entered her, Jet's worry dissolved into a storm of need. He drove into her hard, fast, and it was even better than the first time. Landry matched her passion. Watching his face tighten with need fed her own desire until the unbearable tension released into a climax.

Jet held Landry close as his body immediately found its own release. Afterward, they lay entwined and she lazily rubbed the insole of one foot up and down one of his muscled calves. Landry lazily surveyed the living room. "Everything's so shiny in this room."

"You mean like...clean?" she asked, puzzled.

"No." He rubbed his jaw. "Must be all the mirrors."

It was true. Mirrored tiles banked a large part of the back wall and silver lay scattered everywhere—from the large antique tea-serving set to silver-handled brushes and combs. Funny, she'd never noticed before. Small wonder her family loved this room. They could sit and surreptitiously preen for hours at their lovely reflections.

Unfair? Perhaps in Shelly's case. But not for the full-blooded mermaid Bosarges, especially Lily. Not even the teeniest drop of jealousy trickled through her mind. Let them have their vanity. Jet ran a hand down Landry's hip. As long as he thought she was gorgeous, it didn't matter how she stacked up against other mermaids.

And even with their vanity and somewhat privileged airs, her family had come through for her in the end when her life was in danger. If not for Lily, she'd never have escaped that dark salt marsh alive. They loved her in their own way.

A high-pitched whining accompanied a scratching at the front door. Jet reluctantly got up and pulled the crumpled T-shirt over her head. "Guess I better let Rebel in. He won't shut up until I do."

Landry stretched out on the sofa, hands behind his head. Jet sucked in her breath. The sight of him stretched out buck-naked in her living room made her insides tighten with desire all over again.

"Aren't you getting the door?" he asked, amusement lacing his voice. He knew damned well the effect he had on her.

Jet let in Rebel, who rushed past her to his food bowl in the kitchen. The mutt was always hungry. Hell, so was she. Starving, actually. "How about I fry us some shrimp?" she asked Landry, who was up and dressing.

"We can grab a bite on the way out."

"Out where?"

"I've got a surprise for you." He buckled his belt and sat down to put on shoes. "Thought it would be fun to take a little vacation after the craziness of last week." He held up a hand, as if to forestall any objection she might have. "Only a couple of days. You'll be back in time for your store opening."

It sounded like a lot of bother. "But we could hang out here all weekend. I've got the house to myself."

"I've made the arrangements already," he argued. "C'mon. It'll be fun. I promise."

"If you have your heart set on it," she said, trying to muster some enthusiasm. She'd rather have spent the weekend in bed, just the two of them. Her family came and went at unpredictable times and now that Seth would be staying with Landry, it might be hard to have privacy. "Where are we going?"

"Florida." He glanced at his watch. "Pack light, nothing fancy. I've got a room reserved."

Jet stifled a sigh. "Give me a minute to pack." She started up the stairs and then paused. "Besides grabbing some gas-station fried chicken on the way, I need to stop at the drugstore."

Epilogue

Moonlight flickered like fairy dust on the gentle sea swells. A few small boats were tethered to a wooden pier along the small harbor.

"Why are we stopping here? It's—" Jet checked the radio on the truck's dashboard "—almost one o'clock in the freaking morning." They'd driven for hours yesterday, spent the night at a motel and hit the road again this morning, leisurely stopping in scenic coastal towns to eat or shop.

"There's an envelope in the glove box. Hand it to me." His voice sounded tight with either worry or excitement, she couldn't determine which.

She found it and handed it over. "What gives?"

"Got a little surprise for you," he said, ripping it open and pulling out a set of keys. "Let's go."

She followed him out of the truck. "We're going on a boat ride? Now?" This made no sense. They both had boats at home. No novelty there.

"Trust me." He grabbed her hand and pulled her onto the dock, surveying the boats until he found the one he wanted. "Here it is." They climbed aboard the small craft, Landry dutifully putting on a life jacket.

"I'll have to teach you to swim. It might be the only perk of having a mermaid girlfriend."

He grinned, obviously enjoying some secret surprise. She'd play along.

Landry started the engine and they shot forward. Jet closed her eyes, enjoying the rush of salty air. Only minutes later, Landry shut off the motor. "This should be the place, as far as I can tell anyway."

"Okay. What gives? Did you bring me out here to secretly kill me?" she teased. "'Cause if you did, drowning a mermaid isn't the brightest idea for a former FBI man. I expected better."

"Especially since you're stronger than I, and I can't swim," he agreed. Landry took her hands in his. "I know how much you worry about Dolly."

Jet didn't know what she had expected, but Dolly hadn't entered her mind. "And?"

"She's here."

Jet jumped up and spun in a circle, looking for Dolly to breach the water. "Really?" Seeing nothing, she faced Landry. "Explain, please."

"This is an aquatic-wildlife refuge. They take injured or mistreated sea lions and dolphins and provide a home and safe care for them."

She wanted to believe him. "But how?"

"There's over ninety thousand square feet of seawater lagoons here with low fences that separate them from the open waters of the gulf. They're protected from predators, but the fence still lets in fish and other marine life they need for food. A natural tidal wash flushes the lagoons daily. A lot more hygienic than Andrew Morgan's setup at home."

Her mouth dropped open. She'd never heard of such a place. "Will they take care of her forever?"

"That's up to Dolly. They've already examined her and found she's a bit malnourished and weak, but she should recover quickly. After her calf is born, they'll open the fence and give her the option of returning to the open sea to find a maternity pod that will accept them, or she can stay here."

"I want to see her."

Landry gestured at the sea. "Go ahead. We should be near the fence."

She hastily stripped, leaned over and kissed his mouth. "I love you," she said. It felt wonderful to say the words out loud, not hard at all. "I love you, love you, love you," she repeated for good measure.

"I know." He tapped her lightly on the ass. "Go say hello to your friend. She's probably stressed after the move."

Jet eagerly poised on the edge of the boat to dive.

"Have fun and take your time," she heard Landry say before she dived in and the water enveloped her. Legs instantly morphed to tail fin and the nictitating membrane covered her eyes. She adjusted to the low light and spied the fence, only a few yards away.

"Dolly," she called out, swimming over the fence. "It's me, Jet." She swam close to the ground. The lagoon pools were blasted out of coral and were fairly shallow, anywhere from a few feet deep to about twenty feet deep.

Water vibrated with the approach of several dolphins, clicking away in their undersea language. Jet had no idea what they were saying, but knew curiosity drove them to check out this new addition to their world. "I come in peace," she said. They wouldn't understand her words any better than she did theirs, but her calm voice would show she bore no ill will. "I'm looking for my friend. She's new here." Jet rubbed her belly. "She's pregnant, too."

One of the dolphins, missing a dorsal fin, gestured with its beak for her to follow. Could he have possibly understood? She would never bet against a dolphin's intelligence. She swam in its wake, repeatedly calling out Dolly's name.

A faint, warbling cry arose from one of the deepest lagoons and Jet swam to it.

A large gray shape came into view. She'd recognize Dolly anywhere. Jet let out a gasp of delight. "It's me, Dolly. Are you okay?" She went closer, extending a hand. Dolly perked up and pushed her beak into Jet's palm. "It's okay, baby. You're going to be fine." Jet stroked her smooth head. Minutes passed as Jet tried to convey to Dolly that all would be well.

Clickclickclickclickclickclick.

Several dolphins came their way, gently brushing against Dolly's side. The one with the missing dorsal fin blew bubble rings at Dolly's face.

"See?" said Jet. "He wants to play and be your friend."

After much coaxing, Dolly responded to the other dolphins' gestures of acceptance.

Time for her to leave. Jet slowly backed away. Although relieved to see Dolly in her natural environment, she would miss her. Jet waited until she caught Dolly's eye, then waved goodbye with a forced smile. She abruptly turned and headed toward the fence. As she breached the fence and reached the boat, Dolly came up from behind, clicking excitedly.

Jet eyed her, the fence between them. "Go back," she said. "I'll visit you again if you decide to stay."

Dolly regarded her a moment and dipped her head once before turning to rejoin her own kind.

Jet burst out of the sea, startling Landry. She slipped

aboard, fins shifting to legs. Her face heated in embarrassment. Landry had seen her naked many times, but never in merform.

"That's amazing. *You* are amazing." He shook his head, looking stunned at the transformation.

He'd get used to it.

"Thank you," she began. "I don't know how you arranged all this, but you're wonderful. No one has ever done anything like this for me before." The niggling doubts about their future were wiped away by this one act.

"Happy?" he asked.

"Extremely. You know what they say. Good things always come in threes."

"What do you mean?"

Jet held up a hand and ticked off her fingers. "First, I discovered Dolly was with calf. Two, you found a cat about to have babies. And three…" She let the night's silence settle over them.

His brows drew together. She watched as understanding dawned. "Do you mean what I think you mean?" he asked cautiously.

"Yep." She went to him and nuzzled her face in the crook of his neck. "You okay with that?"

Landry crushed her in a fierce hug, then abruptly held her at arm's length. "I didn't hurt you, did I?" He looked down at her stomach.

"I couldn't be better. Or happier," she assured him.

Landry sank to one knee. "In that case…marry me, Jet."

Bliss bubbled inside her like an underwater spring. And she'd thought the roses had been the grandest romantic gesture of all time. This was more than she'd ever dared dream. A man who loved her and a child on the way. A real family.

Jet sank to her knees and took his hands in hers, felt the

hot strength of him travel through her fingers and palms. "Yes," she said, loud and clear in the dark night.

The boat's engine revved up in three loud, quick bursts. "What the hell?" Landry looked over his shoulder at the dashboard and patted the front pocket of his jeans. "The key's here, not in the ignition," he said slowly.

Jet waved and blew a kiss into the wind. "Then I'm guessing your sister is letting us know she approves of our engagement."

Dolphins splashed nearby, as if sensing her joy. "I love you," she added. Those three words came so easily now. She'd tell Landry that every day, the rest of their lives.

Forever.

* * * * *

HARLEQUIN®

A *Romance* FOR EVERY MOOD™

JUST CAN'T GET ENOUGH?

Join our social communities
and talk to us online.

You will have access to the latest
news on upcoming titles and special
promotions, but most importantly,
you can talk to other fans about your
favorite Harlequin reads.

Harlequin.com/Community

 Facebook.com/HarlequinBooks

Twitter.com/HarlequinBooks

Pinterest.com/HarlequinBooks

To bring down a serial killer, two detectives must pose
as husband and wife. They infiltrate a community, never
expecting love to intrude on their deadly mission!

Read on for a sneak peek of

UNDERCOVER HUNTER

by *New York Times* bestselling author
Rachel Lee, coming January 2015!

Calvin Sweet knew he was taking some big chances, but
taking risks always invigorated him. Coming back to his
home in Conard County was the first of the new risks. Five
years ago he'd left for the big city because the law was closing in on him.

Returning to the site where he had hung his trophies was
a huge risk, too, although he could claim he was out for a
hike in the spring mountains. There was nothing left, anyway. The law had taken it all, and the sight filled him with
both sorrow and bitterness. Anger, too. They had no right
to take away his hard work, his triumphs, his mementos.

But they had. After five years all that was left were some
remnants of cargo netting rotting in the tree limbs and the
remains of a few sawed-off nooses.

He could close his eyes and remember, and remembering
filled him with joy and a sense of his own huge power, the
power of life and death. The power to take it all away. The
power to enlighten those whose existence was so shallow.

HRSEXP1214

They took it for granted. Calvin never did.

From earliest childhood he had been fascinated by spiders and their webs. He had spent hours watching as insect after insect fell victim to those silken strands, struggling mightily until they were stung and then wrapped up helplessly to await their fate. Each corpse on the web had been a trophy marking the spider's victory. No one ever escaped.

No one had escaped him, either.

He was chosen, just like a spider, to be exactly what he was.

Chosen. He liked that word. It fit both him and his victims. They were all chosen to perform the dance of death together, to plumb the reaches of human endurance. To sacrifice the ordinary for the extraordinary. So he quashed his growing need to act and focused his attention on another part of his life. He had a job now, one he needed to report to every evening. He was whistling now as he walked back down to his small ranch.

A spiderweb was beginning to take shape in his mind, one for his barn loft that no one would see, ever. It was enough that he could admire it and savor the gifts there. The impulse to hunt eased, and soon he was in control again. He liked control. He liked controlling himself and others, even as he fulfilled his purpose.

Like the spider, he was not hasty to act. It would have to be the right person at the right time, and the time was not yet right. First he had to build his web.

**Don't miss UNDERCOVER HUNTER
by *New York Times* bestselling author
Rachel Lee, available January 2015 wherever
Harlequin® Romantic Suspense books and
ebooks are sold.**

HRSEXP1214

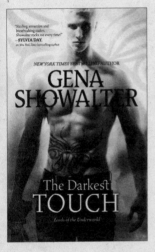